NOBLE BETRAYAL

THE JACK NOBLE SERIES™ BOOK SEVEN

L.T. RYAN

contact@ltryan.com

http://LTRyan.com

https://www.facebook.com/JackNobleBooks

CONTENTS

PART 3

EPISODE 13

PART 4

EPISODE 14

PART 5

EPISODE 15

THE JACK NOBLE SERIES

The Recruit (Short Story)
The First Deception (Prequel 1)
Noble Beginnings (Jack Noble #1)
A Deadly Distance (Jack Noble #2)
Ripple Effect (Bear Logan)
Thin Line (Jack Noble #3)
Noble Intentions (Jack Noble #4)
When Dead in Greece (Jack Noble #5)
Noble Retribution (Jack Noble #6)
Noble Betrayal (Jack Noble #7)
Never Go Home (Jack Noble #8)
Beyond Betrayal (Clarissa Abbot)
Noble Judgment (Jack Noble #9)
Never Cry Mercy (Jack Noble #10)
Deadline (Jack Noble #11)
End Game (Jack Noble #12)
Noble Ultimatum (Jack Noble #13)
Noble Legend (Jack Noble #14)

PART 1
EPISODE 11

CHAPTER 1

Jack Noble stood in the narrow aisle of the British Airways 777. He coughed into his hand to clear his throat of the taste of stale air. His joints ached, and his muscles were tight and sore. First Class had been sold out so he had to settle for a seat in coach. The perils of booking a flight at the last possible minute, he figured.

He reached up and grabbed a bag from the overhead for an elderly woman. His shoulder popped as he lowered the bag and handed it to her. She smiled and thanked him. He nodded, turned, joined the crowd pushing toward the front of the plane. For the first time ever, he didn't mind the wait and the throng of people. It gave him time. It gave him cover. He decided to go with the flow and remain a part of the crowd. It gave him a sense of certainty at a time when he was unsure of what he'd find upon reaching the gate.

So after he exited the plane and entered the wider jetway, he found himself surrounded on all sides by other travelers. He was shoulder to shoulder with the two people he'd shared the flight with. Jack thought he remembered the guy introducing himself as Kyle. He was British, bald and heavy, smelled as though he hadn't had a shower in over forty-eight hours. The woman, in contrast, was young and cute and smelled pleasant. She had introduced herself as Hannah. She was from West Virginia, returning to London where she attended college and worked as a nanny. She wore too much makeup, as

Jack believed most young women often did. The fact of it was evidenced by the smear of eye liner that stretched from the corner of her eye to her ear lobe. A casualty of the three hours she had spent curled up in her seat, asleep, and getting too close to Jack. Evidenced by the smear of eyeliner on his shoulder.

Good thing I'm not meeting a woman.

He'd spent the last seven hours squished between the man and the woman. What's a few more minutes, he figured. He only spoke to the guy long enough to know he didn't care to ever see him again. Not that he would. And the woman had been pleasant and cute enough that he wouldn't mind bumping into her again. Although he knew he wouldn't.

Who ever runs into flight buddies a second time?

The herd of passengers came to an abrupt stop like hundreds of fallen leaves adrift in the water where the stream bottlenecks. Ahead, people jostled for position as the group merged into a single file line out of necessity. At two or three wide and shoulder to shoulder, they couldn't get through the jetway's exit, or the entrance to the gate, depending on one's point of view. For Jack, the opening meant passage into a terminal at Heathrow Airport. One that he'd walked through at least a dozen times, using the same number of aliases.

Today, however, would be the first time that Jack Noble officially walked through London's international airport.

One by one, people passed through the narrow opening and the line got shorter. Jack breathed deeply, remained calm and relaxed. The young woman had settled in line in front of him. She crossed her arms and tapped her right heel into the floor several times.

"Relax," Jack said. "We'll be through in a couple minutes."

She turned her head, nodded, smiled. The line pushed forward and she followed. So did Jack.

Finally, they escaped the jetway. Jack was met by a burst of stale disinfected air pushed out from a blower above. Moments later the smell gave way to a rush of foul odor as the older man behind him reached out and placed his hand firmly on Jack's shoulder.

"It's good to be home, isn't it?" the guy who might be named Kyle said as he leaned in close to Jack's right ear.

Jack's first instinct was to deliver an elbow to the guy's solar plexus. Instead, he shrugged free of the man's grasp, turned his head to the right, nodded once without making eye contact.

The man pushed forward, bumping into Jack, and continued talking. What he said, Jack wasn't sure. He had tuned the man out while he scanned the terminal in both an effort to gather his bearings and isolate any potential threats. It wasn't hard to do. All he had to do was spot the wave of people. The line coming toward him was maybe two or three people wide. But the one flowing away was seven wide at its narrowest. The way to the exit, he presumed. So he stepped into the walkway and joined them. Assimilated into them.

Not always the easiest thing for Jack to do.

When the opportunity presented itself, Jack broke free from the group. He heard the man call to him from behind and ignored him. He wanted to get as much distance between himself and the guy. Jack knew there would be another logjam at customs. No matter how far a leaf got ahead of the cluster, it would be knocked back into the group as soon as the stream dammed up again.

Although he'd try to get through with nothing to declare, he'd be stopped. He was always stopped. He couldn't recall a time when he wasn't stopped. Even at the age of twelve, traveling with his brother Sean and his parents, he'd been stopped.

Today was special because it would be the first time in over a decade that he'd hand over a passport with the name Jack Noble on it.

The thought already caused a tightening in his stomach.

Had Frank Skinner stayed true to his word? Would the SIS director clear Jack's name from every database known to man? At least those in the known free world?

A few weeks ago, Jack Noble was a ghost. Presumed dead after a shortened stay at Black Dolphin, Russia's notorious maximum security prison. Jack had then been transported to Greece, where he took cover on the island of Crete. It took six months for Ivanov's men to find him. When they did, Frank made the call to bring Jack back to the U.S. It wasn't all for Jack's benefit, though. Frank needed a job done, and Jack obliged. Did he really have a choice? It turned out to be worth it. He had his freedom and a semi-clear conscience.

The slow moving line put him into a kind of trance. He didn't realize he'd reached the counter until the man spoke.

"Passport, sir."

Jack didn't need to look directly at the man with the thin brown mustache to know that the guy was sizing him up. They always did. Could he blame them? At six-foot-two and a touch over two hundred pounds, Jack commanded attention. Police officers and customs agents always watched him a little closer than other travelers. It wasn't that he fit a profile, per se. He had the look of a man who knows how to handle himself and might have ulterior motives. Whether he did or not didn't matter.

The customs agent whistled a basic tune while he waited for his computer to return information. The guy's partner rifled through Jack's carry on. Although Jack knew the agent wouldn't find anything, he felt nervous. What if he had mistakenly placed or left a false passport in the bag? *Impossible,* he thought. He'd never used this bag, and his false passports were scattered among a dozen safe deposit boxes in eight different countries.

"What business do you have in London, Mr. Noble?"

"Visiting my cousin," Jack said.

The agent lifted an eyebrow, beckoning Jack to continue.

Jack didn't. He knew that a simple answer was all he had to give. Saying anymore would open him up to further questioning. If the guy needed more, he'd ask.

"Very well," the agent said. He handed Jack his passport while the other agent placed Jack's bag in front of him, opened. Both men looked toward the next person in line, seemingly forgetting all about the man named Jack Noble.

Which was fine with him. He grabbed his bag, pulled the zipper shut, slung it over his shoulder. He rejoined the throng of people making their way toward the arrivals gate. Once again he found himself in close proximity to Hannah and the guy who might be named Kyle. Jack made the mistake of making eye contact with the guy. He turned away as the man lifted his hand to wave to Jack.

"Jack," the guy called out.

Jack did his best to avoid the man, weaving his way through the crowd to get further ahead. Kyle's girth would prevent him from doing the same with any kind of efficiency.

Jack reached the arrivals gate, scanned the faces in the crowd who were waiting around for loved ones or business associates or for the person they were hired to pick up.

No one waited for Jack, which was what he expected. He was in England to work with professionals. Placing themselves in the airport would link them with Jack if someone dug deep enough.

And when you bring a man in to assassinate someone, you don't want to be linked with that man.

Jack continued to weave his way through the crowd, reached a point where the herd had thinned enough that he could walk without needing to turn his torso to the side in order to squeeze past someone. Finally, he found himself standing outside. He used his hand to shield his eyes from the sun while he searched for the taxi line. He found it and found Hannah standing nearby, frustrated and upset. She had her purse opened and was digging through it, shaking her head. Jack figured she'd lost her keys or her wallet.

Kyle was standing next to her, car keys in hand, thin smile on his face. How had he managed to beat Jack outside? Regular traveler, Jack assumed. The guy knew the ins and outs of the Heathrow like he knew his own house.

Jack approached Hannah and said, "Everything OK?"

Kyle said, "It's fine, Mr. Noble. She just —"

"I asked her," Jack said.

Hannah avoided his stare. Her anger was obvious. Her ears and cheeks were bright red, eyes narrowed, nostrils flared. "I lost my wallet. All my money, my credit card, even my damn library card, it was all in there. I need to be home in, like, thirty minutes. How am I supposed to get there now?"

Kyle twirled his keys around his index finger and whistled, like Hannah was a dog. "I told you I can give you a ride."

She looked up at Jack. The tension in her face lifted, her eyes pleaded with him for help. Jack hadn't liked the guy from the moment the man flopped into the seat next to Jack. He sensed during the flight that Hannah didn't care much for him either. But the look on her face signaled something other than dislike, and Jack wondered if she was scared of the man.

"Where are you going?" Jack asked.

"Kensington," Hannah replied.

"Me too. You can tag along with me."

"Nonsense," Kyle said. "I'll give both of you a ride. I have a car parked right over—"

"Shut up, Kyle," Jack said. "I'm sick of your blabbering. You've got five seconds to get out of my face."

"What? Why? I...?" Kyle's face reddened with embarrassment and he turned around and began walking. Every few steps he'd look back at Jack, hurt.

Jack figured he should feel sorry, but he didn't. Just because he was semi-retired didn't mean he had to go soft and start treating everyone nicely.

"Ready to get that cab?" Jack said.

"Oh, you were serious?" Hannah said.

Jack looked sideways at the young woman.

"Sorry," she said. "I thought you were just being nice. You know, getting rid of him for me."

"I was. But the offer still stands. No point in you being stranded here."

She chewed on her bottom lip while the gaze of her brown eyes traveled up and down Jack's frame.

"I'm harmless," he said.

"For some reason I don't believe that. But, I don't think you'll try anything with me with a cab driver present."

Jack laughed. He liked the girl's confidence. He said, "Tell you what, Hannah. Why don't I just give you money for a cab?"

She hiked her shoulders in the air an inch and pushed her bottom lip out. "That'd work, I suppose."

He escorted her to an awaiting cab, opened the rear passenger door, waited for Hannah to slip inside. Then he reached into his pocket for his wallet. He turned his head to the left as he did so, taking in a view of the long line of taxis and people standing in line, shoulder to shoulder. Amid the wall of faces, one man stood out. He was tall, wore a dark suit, stayed a few yards away from the crowd. His eyes were locked on Jack's. A moment passed and the two men faced off, separated by fifty feet.

The man started walking toward the cab.

Jack stuck his leg inside the open vehicle and said, "Scoot over."

"What? I thought you were going to get your own?"

"Change of plans," Jack said as he lowered himself into the back seat, forcing Hannah to slide over. He slammed the door shut and looked over his right shoulder.

"What are you looking at?" Hannah asked. She turned in her seat.

"You don't have a crazy ex-boyfriend who might have been expecting you, do you?"

Hannah laughed. "No."

Jack didn't figure the man to have anything to do with Hannah, but he knew it was best to know for sure.

The man hadn't broke stride and was now within twenty feet of the cab.

"Go," Jack said.

"What do you want me to do?" the driver said. "We got to wait for our turn."

The man stopped ten feet from the cab. Jack looked over his other shoulder and saw that a black sedan had stopped in the middle of the road. The guy in the suit hopped inside.

"That'll be too late," Jack said. "Go. Now."

CHAPTER 2

THE DRIVER GRABBED THE SHIFTER LIKE HE WAS REACHING for the pull handle on a slot machine. He licked his lips, wrapped his fingers around the knobby end and dropped the transmission into first gear. The vehicle made an audible click and gave a slight jerk as it passed through neutral. The driver eased away from the curb, nosed into the next lane, aided by the fact that the sedan behind them was blocking it.

"Faster," Jack said.

"What is your problem?" the driver said, glaring at Jack in the rear view mirror.

Jack leaned forward and placed his right forearm on the shoulder of the passenger's seat. "Put your foot on the gas or I'm going to kick you out of the cab and do it myself."

"Fine," the driver shouted. He jammed the gas pedal to the floor, sending Jack lurching backward into his seat. He managed to tuck his left elbow in, away from Hannah. Still, his shoulder collided with hers, and she let out a painful squeal.

"Dammit," she said.

"Sorry." Jack stared into the rear view mirror, eyes locked on the driver who seemed too scared to look back at Jack. Perhaps the guy preferred to concentrate his efforts on the road. Jack figured it was the latter considering the man was doing roughly seventy miles per hour in an area designated for thirty.

"You want to tell me what that was all about?" Hannah said.

"No." Jack shifted in his seat, repositioned himself so that he could check behind the cab. He spotted the black sedan about ten car lengths behind.

The driver started to ease up on the gas.

"Don't slow down," Jack said.

"Why not?" the driver said.

"You see that black car back there?"

The driver's eyes shifted from the road to the rear view mirror. His gaze fell upon Jack, then traveled past him. "Yeah, I see it."

"I don't know who that is, but they're either looking for you or for me. I don't know what kind of man you are, but I can tell you this for sure. If they are after me, you want nothing to do with them. Got it? So you better do what I say when I say it. Pick up your speed. Get us as far ahead as you can, then when we are in an area you are very familiar with, I want you to get off the highway and start weaving your way through the city. Avoid traffic at all cost."

"This is London. How am I supposed to avoid traffic?"

"I don't care how you do it, man. Figure it out or we all might be dead."

"How about I stop and get out and offer you up to them."

"Are you really that stupid?"

The driver locked eyes with Jack. The taxi picked up speed, distanced itself from the black sedan. Not for long, Jack figured. But as long as the other car stayed that far behind, the cab driver should be able to lose them if he knew the city well. If not, then all Jack could hope for was that the men would be unarmed.

"Who are you?" Hannah asked him.

Jack shrugged, told her, "It's complicated."

"How so? Seems like a pretty simple question to me."

"Look, Hannah, I don't know if those guys got a good look at you or not. If they did, then the less you know about me the better."

"Why?"

"Because." Jack paused, searching for the right words. "You need plausible deniability on your side in the event someone asks you questions about me."

Hannah narrowed her eyes, shook her head, looked away. Jack caught a glimpse of the anger in her eyes reflected in the window.

He returned his attention to the vehicle tailing them. The car had closed the gap and now paced them from two car lengths.

"Pick it up," Jack said.

"I can't go any faster. One more ticket and I'll have my licensed revoked."

"That car catches up to us and you might have your life revoked."

This garnered a frightened reaction from Hannah, but Jack ignored it.

The vehicle tailing them jerked to the left and sped up. Jack cursed under his breath. Hannah slumped down in her seat until her head was below the window. Fear or street smarts? Within seconds the two cars were side by side. The other vehicle's windows were tinted. Jack couldn't tell how many people were inside the car. He knew there were at least two, so he planned for a third.

Jack reached inside his coat. There was no gun there, though. Not even a holster. He couldn't travel with a weapon. In years past, he'd have had someone meet him at the airport who would have provided him with a pistol at the very least. In some cases he was able to leave from a government installation, which allowed him to travel with a weapon hidden in the false bottom of a bag or suitcase. This time he'd have to wait until one of Dottie's people met him. He had no idea when that would occur. Certainly not in time to deal with the men following him.

For a few minutes it felt as if the two cars were standing still. Then, the black sedan pulled away and exited the highway.

"You can sit up," Jack told Hannah. "They're gone."

"Can you tell me who they were?"

"No."

"If my life's in danger I'd like to know who it might be. Why can't you tell me?"

"Because I don't know."

Hannah righted herself in her seat and said, "You can get off at the next exit."

"Stop a few blocks short of her building," Jack added.

Five minutes later the driver pulled the cab to the curb. Hannah jumped out. Jack pulled out his wallet, handed the driver three ten pound notes, exited the cab.

"What are you doing?" Hannah asked.

"Walking you home."

She crossed her arms, arched her back. "I'm starting to think I would have been better off letting creepy Kyle drive me home."

So that was his name.

"I'm thinking the same," Jack said. "But he didn't, I did. And I need to make sure you get home OK."

She studied him for a moment. "My building has a doorman. He's bigger than you. Try to come in and I'll have him kick your ass."

Jack smiled. He liked the girl's attitude. "Sounds good to me."

Jack didn't have the layout of London committed to memory, but he knew they were in close proximity to Buckingham Palace and Hyde Park. The only reason he knew this was because he saw a sign saying so before they exited the highway.

"This looks like an expensive area," he said.

"It is."

"How's a college girl afford to live in a place like this?"

She smiled. "Well, for one, I live in a tiny little apartment. It's like a master bedroom converted into an apartment. One room has everything. And the family I work for pays for it."

"Who do you work for?"

She turned her head slightly and looked at him out of the corner of her eye.

"OK, question withdrawn," Jack said. "I know where you live, though. I could just follow you."

She stopped, turned toward Jack, grabbed his arm. "That's not funny, Jack. Seriously, don't you even think about following me or popping in on the family I work for when I'm there."

Jack raised his hands in mock defense. "Don't worry. The moment you step into your building is the last time you'll ever see me."

"Is it?"

Jack nodded. "It is."

She pointed and said, "That's it right there."

"Where's the doorman?"

"I lied." She smiled. "Going to walk me the rest of the way?"

"I think you got it."

She extended her hand. "Bye, Jack."

He watched her climb up a set of concrete stairs stained by years of exposure. She pulled out her keys, entered the building without looking back. Jack lingered for several minutes. The air was mild and the breeze light. He scanned the street and surrounding houses, ensuring that no one was watching him or Hannah's building. He'd provided the world with enough collateral damage and didn't want to add Hannah to that list.

After half an hour, he decided it was OK to leave. He pulled out his cell phone, turned on the GPS, punched his hotel's name into the search field. He was staying at the Plaza, other side of Westminster Bridge. A fancy place, but his choices had been limited. The distance to the hotel was less than two miles. Jack decided to walk.

CHAPTER 3

THE MAN HANNAH KNEW AS JACK NOBLE LINGERED OUTSIDE her building for close to thirty minutes. What were his intentions? She didn't think he meant her harm. He'd seemed overly protective in the taxi line, in the car, and after they got out. But the sight of him out there freaked her out a bit. Although he seemed to be watching the street and other buildings, not hers.

She considered calling for assistance. After all, her employer had some muscle behind her, and she had always said that if Hannah found herself in a bind, just call.

Hannah didn't call, though.

Jack had been nice enough on the plane, and he had a face that seemed familiar to her. She didn't know him, but he made her feel at ease. Not an easy thing to do around *always anxious Hannah*. She laughed at her description of herself. Her father had always said she had a high motor. But she knew there was something else. Feelings that she repressed. Thoughts she hid from others. Always calm on the outside with a fake smile plastered on her face.

Jack began to walk away. Hannah moved to the other side of the room where she had a better viewing angle of the street. He'd been standing in plain view for all that time. Surely he knew it, too. There was nothing to stop him from walking half a block and waiting for her to leave her apartment.

So she was back to calling for assistance. Then his words came back to her.

Plausible deniability.

Forget everything about him, she told herself. That's what he wanted. That's what she would do. Calling would have the opposite effect. It would indicate that she did know something about him, and the look in his eyes when he said those words let her know that was not what she wanted.

Perhaps if she were older she would have treated the situation differently. But she wasn't, and she didn't.

The thoughts of Jack faded away and Hannah turned her attention to the stack of mail on the triangular wooden table next to the white door stained and chipped from decades of neglect.

The envelope on top was from her college. She slid her finger under the flap at the corner and opened it. The glue held, the envelope tore. She spread the opening, pulled out a letter printed on heavy stock ivory colored paper. It was folded in thirds, smelled like tree bark. She shook the letter open, read the contents to herself.

The letter did not contain the news she had hoped for.

Hannah fell back against the door. A few tiny chips of dried white paint fell to the floor like springtime flurries. Her eyes watered. She brought her hand to her mouth to stifle a sob.

This can't be happening.

Hannah brought her arm up and stared at the letter. The black lettering looked wet and raised. A handsome message despite the bad news it contained. Once again, she read the words that shattered her dream. The message had not changed. She'd lost her scholarship, partly due to lack of funding, and also due to her lack of attendance. She'd had no trouble acing her subjects, despite the classes she missed. The only reason she was not in attendance was because her employer needed her around a bit more than usual last semester. And while the scholarship helped, so did the funds her boss paid her. Without both, she could not afford college in London.

She slammed her free hand into the door. More paint chips fell and gathered together on the ground. A pile of snow that would never melt. She wiped the tears from her eyes, cleared her throat. "Enough feeling sorry for yourself," she said. "Nothing happens for those who stand idly by, watching life race past."

Hannah decided that she'd go see Ms. Carslisle and ask if she could take on extra duties. Being a nanny to Mia was nearly a full time job, but there were other things she could do in the house. Ms. Carlisle had taken a liking to Hannah. That had been obvious from the beginning. The woman had mentioned a few times that she'd like Hannah to be around more. What would be the harm in asking? Besides, without the scholarship money, she couldn't afford school this semester. She'd have the extra time available. Extra work would allow her to save more.

Tired, partially defeated, but hopeful, Hannah retired to her single bed in the far corner of the room. She pulled back the pale blue down comforter and crawled onto the mattress where an intoxicating sleep overcame her.

CHAPTER 4

JACK STOPPED IN FRONT OF THE SMOKE TINTED GLASS DOOR, caught sight of his reflection. Wrinkled blue striped button-up shirt partially tucked into his matching wrinkled khakis. He'd taken his jacket off during the walk to the hotel and it was draped over his forearm. His brown hair was matted on the left side, a relic from his nap during the flight.

He became aware of the fact that while he couldn't see inside, anyone in the hotel's lobby could see him. He pulled on the brass door handle, walked through the lobby, stopped in front of the check-in counter. A young man squatted on a stool in front of a computer monitor. He didn't acknowledge Jack's presence. Jack cleared his throat a few times, and the man responded by saying, "Be right with you," without looking up.

Sure you will.

He watched the man for a moment. The guy's skinny fingers danced across a dusty black keyboard. The white lettering on the black keys was all but faded. After it became apparent that *right with you* in fact meant *whenever the hell I feel like it,* Jack turned away from the counter and found an empty seat nearby. Not just any seat, though. He couldn't have his back to the hotel's entrance. That would afford someone the opportunity to get the drop on him. Likewise, he couldn't face the entrance, leaving himself exposed to anyone entering the lobby from the elevators.

And he didn't want to be facing away from the man behind the counter when the guy finally deemed Jack worthy of his attention.

So he sat down in a high-back blue fabric chair. It was rigid and uncomfortable, which was fine, as he felt drowsy from the flight and his adventure getting from the airport to the hotel. If the chair had been soft, he might have dozed off.

His position in the lobby allowed him to monitor the entrance, elevators, and desk with nothing more than a slight turn of his head. The sidewalk in front of the hotel was busy, but no one who passed alarmed him. Tourists and locals alike, none deemed immediate threats. An elderly couple entered the hotel and shuffled toward the reception area. Jack looked at the guy behind the counter. The clerk looked up for a fraction of a second, like he had when Jack entered. Again the clerk's eyes returned to his screen. But this time his arms jerked up and down in a quick motion, then he stepped to the side. He had a smile plastered across his narrow face.

"How can I help you?" the clerk addressed the elderly couple.

Jack shook his head. Did he come across as such an ignorant American that he wasn't worthy of the same attention? Whatever. No time to dwell on it.

He heard a ding, turned his head, saw brass plated elevator doors slide open.

Jack moved his head slightly, moved his eyes more, brought his right hand up and rubbed the side of his face, shielding it from whoever stepped out of the elevator and into the lobby.

The guy was tall, handsome, dark hair, two or three days' worth of stubble on his lean, broad face. He wore what appeared to be a designer suit, custom tailored. White pinstripes knifed through dark blue fabric. Most would figure the guy to be a millionaire on vacation. Not Jack. Because while most stop at the rugged good looks and custom suit, Jack's eyes moved to the shoes. And the shoes this guy wore were those of a working man. Expensive? Yes. But these shoes were designed to get the guy from point A to point B and everywhere in between no matter the circumstances. Mud and rain? No problem. Off road? No problem. Hop a few fences? Again, no problem. Kick a few heads? Now that's what they were made for.

And they had to look good, too.

Jack noted that the guy bore a resemblance to the man he saw in the taxi line at Heathrow.

The guy pulled out his cell phone, turned away from the lobby.

Jack rose, slowly so as not to draw any attention. He moved to the corner of the room and positioned himself near the machine that dispensed free coffee to hotel guests. A fake ficus provided extra cover. The man was out of his view, but he knew not for long. The only areas beyond the elevator lobby were two halls that led to additional rooms, the pool and the gym. The guy had a room already, and he was overdressed for the pool or the gym.

The man entered the lobby, cell phone in his left hand, held up to the side of his head, blocking his view of Jack. Still, Jack didn't like where he had positioned himself in relation to the man. It would have been better if he had moved toward the front doors and perhaps gone outside.

The guy stopped at the front desk, turned his back toward the lobby.

Jack saw that as his opportunity. He started toward the front of the lobby, clutching his cell phone in his right hand and holding it up to his face. When he reached the half-way point between the coffee machine and the doors, he heard the man speak, his accent British.

"Jack Noble."

He'd been expecting it, but was not ready for it. Jack turned his head to the right. The clerk shifted his stare from the man in the custom suit to Jack. The guy in the suit started to look over his shoulder. The guy didn't move. He wasn't speaking *to* Jack. He'd been asking about him.

Jack diverted his eyes forward, placed his hand on the door, heard the guy say, "Who was that?"

Jack assumed the man was referring to him. He didn't wait to hear the clerk's response. His feet hit the sidewalk and he turned right, crossed the street diagonally and pushed through the first door he came to. As he stepped inside, a burst of warm air barreled down on him. The beads of sweat on his forehead evaporated. He didn't take the time to assess his surroundings. Instead, he turned, took two steps to his right and positioned himself behind a sequined covered mannequin next to the tinted glass.

"Can I help you?" The voice was female, British, cold.

Jack shifted his gaze to the left. He saw the woman's reflection hovering in the window. She was thin and middle-aged and beyond that he didn't care. He noticed that she was standing next to a rack of evening gowns. His eyes darted left and right. The place was a designer women's clothing shop. That explained the overbearing smell of perfume.

"I said, *can I help you*?" She arched an eyebrow.

"I'll be out of your way in a moment," Jack said.

"If you aren't going to buy something, please leave," the woman said.

Jack glanced back at her to drive his earlier response home. She flinched at his glare. He spun his head around in time to see the hotel lobby door opening. The man in the suit stepped outside, looked left, then right, turned in the direction of the latter, stayed on the other side of the street. The man's eyes moved methodically, square by square.

Jack cursed under his breath. He was dealing with a professional. He took two steps back, hoped that would reduce the chance of him being seen from the outside.

"It's tinted and mirrored," the woman said. "He can't see you."

"That's gotta be a real pain for window shoppers," Jack said.

She forced a rhetorical laugh. "I don't want them. They dirty up my shop. Serious buyers only. Which you obviously are not. So as soon as your little friend is out of sight, get out of my place."

British hospitality.

"Yes, ma'am." A moment later he added, "Any chance you have a back door?"

"No." She aimed a pale thin finger toward the front door.

Jack waited until the man in the suit passed by, then he left the store. Cool spring air, a mixture of cherry blossom and exhaust, greeted him once again. The remaining dampness on his forehead grew cold. He paced the guy across the street, staying far enough back that he could get away should a chase ensue.

The man stopped in front of a place called Libby's, went inside. From where Jack stood, there looked to be a menu taped to the outside of the window next to the front door. Jack waited a minute, then crossed the street and continued toward the restaurant. He stopped when he reached the corner. The smell of wood smoke enveloped the building. Jack cupped his hands to his face and pressed against the glass.

Four people dining at a table next to the window flinched when they noticed him peering in at them. They stared up, mouths agape, eyes narrowed.

Jack shrugged, offered a half-smile, returned to scanning the room. Where had the guy gone? The place was dimly lit. It offered some sense of privacy despite the wide open layout of the place. Rows of tables with nothing separating them from one another. He spotted the man, twenty feet in front of him, seated at the bar. The guy seemed confident. He wasn't constantly checking over his shoulders or looking around the room. He laid in wait, looking helpless and limp. The same way some of the most lethal predators on the planet act.

"What the bloody hell are you doing?"

Jack jerked back, whipped his head to the left. He'd dismissed the portly man in the black pants and white button-up shirt heading toward him.

"Well?" the guy said.

"Looking for my brother," Jack said.

"Well you're scaring the piss outta my customers. So either come inside and have a drink and a bite to eat, or beat it." He tossed his thumb over his shoulder.

Jack placed his hands on the window and pressed his face to the glass. The man in the suit rose from his barstool and walked toward the back of the restaurant.

"I'm going in," Jack said. He pushed past the portly man and pulled the door open. "Where's your restroom?"

"Loo's in the back."

Jack moved cautiously through the restaurant, concerned that the guy in the suit might not be the only person in the place looking for him. The restaurant could have been a designated spot to meet should things fall through.

Glances were cast his way. None lingered. They almost immediately returned to their plates or their drinks or their lunch mates.

It took Jack less than ten seconds to cross the length of the room. He entered a dimly lit corridor, stopped in front of the men's room door, pushed it open. Warm light flooded the hall, carrying with it the floral smell of chemical air freshener.

Jack stepped in, unarmed, cautious.

The guy in the suit stood in front of a urinal, his back to Jack.

Jack stopped.

"Help you with something?" the guy said in a British accent.

Jack said nothing, took a quiet step forward.

"I'd caution you not to go any further. I'm armed."

Jack ignored the warning, took another two steps, reassured by the belief that the man would conclude the task at hand. Only then would the guy reach for his gun and turn around. In that time span, Jack could close the distance and neutralize the guy.

He was wrong.

The man in the suit whipped around in a half-circle, pistol drawn, grin on his face.

"Hello, Jack."

CHAPTER 5

JACK STOOD FOUR FEET AWAY FROM THE MAN IN THE DARK suit. His heart raced. His muscles tensed. His stomach was in his throat. The guy had his pistol out, but his aim was off and he was unbalanced. The guy's position opened up a window of opportunity for attack, albeit a small one. Jack did not hesitate. Years of training and finely tuned instincts took over. He turned to the side, lunged forward. His right arm neutralized the threat of the gun. His left fist neutralized the threat of the man.

In two seconds the fight was over.

Jack retrieved the pistol. He leaned over the man, slapped the guy across the face. When the guy didn't come to, he slapped him again.

The man groaned. His eyelids fluttered open, eyes focused on the bright lights behind Jack's head, then rolled back, replaced by bloodshot whites.

"Who are you?" Jack said.

The guy moaned, refocused his eyes, said nothing.

"Answer me," Jack demanded.

The man cleared his throat. "Slater. Leon Slater."

"What do you want with me, Leon? Why were you waiting for me in the hotel?"

Leon shook his head.

"That was you at the airport, wasn't it?"

Leon nodded.

"Why?" Jack said. "No one knows I'm in England."

"You're wrong." Leon scooted back and propped himself up on his elbows. His head lingered below the base of a stained urinal.

Jack rose, offered his hand to Leon, helped the man to his feet. "How's that?"

"You traveled over here under your own bloody name. You don't think the moment they scanned your passport every damn agency in the U.K. became aware of your presence?"

The point was a good one and gave Jack reason to pause. Of course he had been worried about it, but his name had been cleared. He wasn't wanted in the U.K. for anything. And he figured if something was going to happen, it would have been at customs, and a quick call to Frank would have fixed it.

"I'm retired," Jack said. "Hadn't really thought about it. How'd you get to the airport so fast if they'd only recently flagged me?"

"We knew your flight plans. Dottie insisted I come meet you and escort you in case someone else tried to get to you first."

"Dottie?" Jack hadn't considered that Leon was there to meet him and escort him to Dottie's place.

"Yeah," Leon said. "I work for her. Anyway, you took off in a damn hurry and you were in the cab with the girl. I figured it best to reach out to you later."

Jack walked over to the bay of sinks, ran the hot water, splashed a handful across his face. "Why'd you draw your gun on me?"

"I was offering the gun to you." Leon patted his left side, close to his underarm. "My piece is holstered right here. I knew you'd be unarmed and thought you might appreciate a weapon. Didn't you think it funny I wasn't aiming at you?"

"You could have said something other than I'm armed."

"I wanted to finish my piss. Christ, is that a crime?"

Jack inspected the handgun he'd knocked from Leon's hand, a Browning High Power 9mm. It told him a few things. Leon had been in the Special Air Service (SAS), and had probably retired some time ago as most of the guys now carried the Sig Sauer P226. He also surmised that Leon had no intention of hurting him. The Browning's safety was on.

"You're welcome, by the way," Leon said.

Jack nodded once. "How long have you been out?"

"Of what?"

"SAS."

"Who says I was SAS?"

"Who else still carries a Browning?"

"I've heard some members of various intelligence organizations do."

"Does that mean you were never SAS?"

"I didn't say that." Leon flashed a grin and Jack smiled back.

"Come on, let me buy you a drink," Jack said.

Leon wet a paper towel and wiped his face. The two men exited the restroom and took a seat at the end of the bar. Leon ordered for both of them, a lager that Jack had never heard of. When the bartender set the beer down in front of him, Jack immediately noticed that a tan frothy head filled a third of the mug. The sun's setting rays found their way through the tinted glass of the restaurant, knifed through Jack's mug, turned a burnt orange as they found a final resting spot on the antique bar top.

Jack lifted the mug containing the sun soaked lager and took a large gulp. He savored the head that was left over on his upper lip while swirling the liquid in the mug in a counterclockwise motion. Bubbles and brew mixed.

"It'll be dark soon," Leon said. "We should get going."

"What's the rush? My hotel is half a block away."

"You can't stay there now, Jack. If I could find you, anyone can."

Jack shrugged. "I can handle myself."

"Besides, Dottie wants to see you tonight."

"I'm tired. I just want to rest tonight. I haven't had a decent night's sleep in weeks."

"You can sleep on the way. We've got a bit of a drive ahead of us."

"I thought she lived in the city?" Jack said, concerned now that everything Leon had told him up to this point was a lie.

"She does. She also has a place outside of the city. Tonight, like every night the last couple months, she is outside of the city. It's a place that *he* doesn't know about. And she wants you to stay with us tonight so she can discuss terms with you tomorrow."

Jack's lingering doubts remained. He reached around his back, pretending to scratch an itch. The stiff handle of the Browning brushed his palm. Relief washed over him like the warm waters of the Mediterranean. Would a man hell bent on killing him offer him a loaded weapon? Jack thought not. So he lifted his mug, tilted it toward his open mouth, finished his beer. He patted his chest and pockets, mostly out of habit, making sure he'd left nothing behind.

"Let's get going then," he said.

Leon led the way to the door. The portly fellow nodded, faked a smile, and then looked away. Jack followed Leon outside.

"Dammit." Leon stopped, took a step back, bumped into Jack.

"What is it?"

"Get inside."

Jack did.

"Four men in front of the hotel," Leon said. "Black Bentley parked on the street."

Jack slid his head through the opening and saw the men. They were dressed in dark clothing, long sleeved t-shirts, and black or dark gray cargo pants. Heavily muscled. Probably armed. Two of them entered the hotel. One stood on the sidewalk, looking up. The fourth leaned back against the Bentley.

"Who are they?" Jack asked.

"I presume they work for someone who has an interest in why you entered our country."

"In or out?" the voice called from behind.

Jack turned and saw the portly man.

"Whatever you guys decide, you need to stop blocking my doorway."

"Shut up," Jack said.

Leon placed a hand on Jack's shoulder. "What my American friend meant was, do you have a back exit?" Leon pulled open his jacket, revealing his holstered weapon.

The man's expression was blank. He jerked his head back, motioning toward the kitchen. He said, "Through there."

Leon said, "Many thanks," and he handed the guy a folded bill.

As soon as he left the dining room, Jack retrieved the Browning. He racked it, left the safety on. Two quick taps remained in order to file a round. He hoped it wouldn't come to that, not in the middle of London.

The kitchen was loud, bright, full of stainless steel countertops and shelves. Voices went mute as stares fell upon the two armed men hurrying toward the exit. A large red-haired man with a long braided goatee stepped away from his duties at the fryer and blocked the narrow path between the kitchen equipment and the door leading outside. He looked like a modern day Viking.

"Who the frig are you guys?" Red said.

"Do you really want to find out?" Leon said, casually aiming his pistol in Red's direction.

"I want to know what you're doing in my kitchen. You're putting the food at risk." Red's head leaned back on his thick stump of a neck. His eyes were wide. Jack wondered if the guy was high or just had a death wish.

"We're only passing through. Take it up with the fat guy out front. He told us not to linger in the doorway."

"You could've gone through the front."

"No, we couldn't," Leon said.

Jack wondered what the hell was going on. If he'd been in the lead he'd have taken Red out and stepped over his unconscious body. Yet, here was Leon treating the guy like they were in the debate club. He nudged Leon forward.

"Just step aside, mate," Leon said. "You don't want us to be in here when the other guys come through."

Red narrowed his eyes and studied the two men for a moment. Then he took a step back and allowed them passage through the kitchen.

They stepped into a narrow alleyway. The sky was a deep shade of pink. Tall buildings shielded the area from the sun's final rays. The air was cool and crisp, especially after being in the hot kitchen.

"My car is two blocks from here." Leon took off in a jog.

Jack hesitated, thought about turning and sprinting off in the other direction. Four hours in town and already he'd been chased, had a gun pulled on him in a bathroom, seen a Bentley with four guys obviously looking for him, and been confronted by a pissed off cook that resembled a Viking god covered in grease and flour.

Perhaps he'd be better off returning home.

Leon's footsteps slowed to a shuffle. Jack looked up and saw the man facing him, jogging in place.

"You coming?"

Jack looked back. A block or so, then the open road. He already had a good thirty foot lead. If he sprinted he might be able to lose the guy.

"Well? We haven't got all bloody night."

Jack turned, started walking, sped up to a jog. "Let's go," he said as he neared Leon.

CHAPTER 6

THORNTON LEANED BACK IN HIS CHAIR, RESTED THE BASE OF his skull on the ridge of the chair back. He stared down his nose at the four men who cowered on the other side of the overbearing mahogany desk. He looked from one man to the next, shook his head as he made eye contact with each. He said nothing, figured the men would have been more comfortable if he was yelling at them. At least then they could accurately gauge his level of aggravation. Instead, the silence in the room told the story of his anger at their failure to bring in the man who earlier that day showed up on their screen like a Great White's dorsal fin, spotted by a lifeguard, too close to shore, circling its prey.

None of the men knew Noble as intimately as Thornton. None of them had been in Monte Carlo when he'd had an encounter with Jack, who had used a pseudonym at the time. Perhaps if they had been there, Noble would no longer be an issue. Then Thornton wouldn't have had to drop a million plus in legal fees to get him off the hook for slapping Dottie around after she'd insulted and embarrassed him.

Those are the chances you take when you bring your B team.

What did that say about his A team, though? They couldn't get the job done tonight.

Thornton placed his palms on his desk, leaned forward, rose out of his chair. He lifted his hand. His index finger shook out of anger. The men across from him straightened.

"Leave." Thornton jabbed toward the door. The four men turned, heads hung in shame, and headed toward the door. "Not you, Owen," Thornton added. Owen was the lead man. The A guy on the A team. When a job was done right, he took the majority of the praise. Tonight he'd take the brunt of his boss's anger.

Owen stopped, turned, waited. The three other guys left, one by one, through the open doorway. The last man crossed the threshold. The heavy reinforced door shut with resonance that told the men in the room they were isolated, separated, protected.

Owen lifted his head and made eye contact with Thornton, who smiled and gestured toward the chair across from his. Both men sat. Thornton pulled out a cigar, lit it, remained quiet for a minute for dramatic effect. The heavy odor of the cigar enveloped his senses and he recalled meeting Owen at a back room poker game. The man had thrown a hand that Thornton was all-in for. He'd seen Owen's cards. Pocket aces. An Ace on the flop. Thornton had a potential full house. He went all-in. Owen called. Garbage on the turn, an Ace on the river. Owen folded his cards, nodded, got up for a beer. Two days later Thornton had the man in his office and offered him a job.

Tonight was the first time he'd ever been let down by Owen.

"So tell me again, Owen. How did you fail to find Mr. Noble?"

The muscles in Owen's jaw rippled. The man appeared to be doing his best to control his temper. *A good thing,* thought Thornton. *He knows better than to challenge me.*

"He had reservations at the hotel. We went there. He wasn't there."

"You had all exits covered then?" Thornton said.

"It didn't matter—"

"It always matters."

"He never checked in."

"Yes, so you said."

"We even tried a few of his known aliases, in case he made multiple reservations."

Thornton nodded. "And you showed the picture?"

Owen closed his eyes, took a deep breath. He was the picture of calm, except for his clenched fists and rippling jaws.

"Yes," he said tersely. "We showed the picture. The girl behind the counter did not recall seeing him."

"Did you check any other establishments in the area?"

"There's a pub nearby. We went inside. The manager said he hadn't seen anyone fitting the description."

"Any place else?"

"There was a ladies clothing store across the street, but I figured he wouldn't have gone in there."

"You figured, eh? Someone in there might have seen him. Didn't you think of that?"

Owen said nothing.

"You're telling me you didn't check under every stone then?"

Owen still said nothing. His hardened look softened.

Thornton rose, stepped out from behind his desk. He paced the perimeter of the room then stopped behind Owen. He placed his hands on Owen's shoulders, squeezed reassuringly. How could his best man, his A guy on his A team, have failed him like this?

"Who is this guy?" Owen asked.

Thornton pulled his hands away. "Seven months ago. Monte Carlo."

"I see." Although Owen had not been there, Thornton had told him what had happened. "You think he's here because of you?"

"I don't know. That whore wife of mine knows him though, so I wouldn't put it past her being the reason he's here. And if that's the case, then *I* might be what he's here for."

Owen nodded slowly while tapping the tips of his index fingers together. "We should have someone watching the house."

"She's not there. Hasn't been there in weeks." Thornton rounded the desk, sat, slumped. "I'm not sure where she is right now. I was hoping you'd bring Mr. Noble in and he could tell us."

"What else do you know about this guy?"

Thornton shrugged. "Not much. He can handle himself, I know that. I'd like you to use your contacts to find out more."

"My contacts are your contacts."

"You know who I mean."

"Why can't your contacts look into it?"

Thornton smiled at his associate. "They are busy with something else."

Owen lifted an eyebrow and made a *do continue* gesture.

Thornton waved him off with a brisk flick of his wrist. "Soon, Owen. I'll tell you more soon. Get on the phone with your guy and find something out."

Owen shifted in his seat. His hands were wrapped around the arm rests. His body angled toward the door. Clearly he was ready to leave the room. "Anything else?"

"No. You can leave now."

Owen nodded, rose, left. Thornton waited a few minutes then pulled a cell phone from his jacket's inside pocket. It was not his regular cell phone. That lingered face-down on his desk. He had been aware for some time that certain local and foreign agencies liked to monitor that phone. He'd use it, but not for anything related to business, only to jerk them around. But right now he needed to make a business call, and that required the phone that no one knew about.

He cradled the phone in his hand, cool plastic against a sweaty palm. His finger grazed against a button on the side. The phone's display came to life. A tranquil pond with swimming koi fish greeted him. He navigated to the dialing screen and pressed and held down the number 5. A moment later, the phone began to ring.

"Hello?" a man answered.

"Naseer? Is that you?"

"Hello, Thornton. Is everything going according to plan?"

"That's what I'm calling to ask you."

"My plans are all set, Thornton. They hinge on our prior arrangement, though."

"And our arrangement hinges on you paying me."

Naseer laughed, his mouth too close to the receiver. Thornton pulled the phone away from his ear.

"We'll meet soon, my friend," Naseer said.

"When?"

"In a day or two."

"I need a time."

"I can't give you one."

Thornton paused. "OK."

The men stayed on the line, though no one spoke. Finally, Naseer said, "Is there something else?"

"Yeah," Thornton said. He reached for a tumbler, half-filled with scotch. "Jack Noble. You ever heard of him?"

Naseer repeated the name. "I am not familiar with him. Would you like me to make some calls?"

"Yes, please do."

"I will, and I'll bring my findings to our meeting."

CHAPTER 7

NASEER THUMBED THE END CALL LABEL ON HIS PHONE'S screen, then set the device on the table. He lifted his gaze toward the dark-haired beauty sitting across from him, smiled at her. There was only one reason a woman that attractive was with him, and he was OK with that. Being a billionaire had its advantages. Beautiful women throwing themselves at his feet was one of them. Controlling equally wealthy but weaker men was another, and that summed up his relationship with Thornton Walloway.

Thornton had a need to fit in with *real* powerful men. Men with money weren't good enough. Hell, the guy could get that kind of fraternity at his country club. No, Thornton wanted to be a part of something. The kind of something that would make other men fall to their knees and openly weep. Thornton wanted the same kind of power that Naseer enjoyed. And as long as Naseer let Thornton believe that the man would achieve that same power and standing within his group, Naseer had Thornton by the balls.

The woman set her fork down and leaned forward. She asked, "Is everything OK with your friend?"

Naseer nodded as he sipped from his wine glass. He was curious why she asked. She had seemed to know better than to try and discuss his dealings.

"What was that about a Jack somebody?"

Naseer lifted an eyebrow and smiled curiously. Twice now?

"Why do you ask?" he said.

"No reason," she said. "Just sounded out of place. I've met most of your friends and don't recall any Jack's. Don't recall any normal names."

"Yes, well," Naseer slowly rotated his neck. "First of all, you haven't met a tenth of my friends. Second of all, he is not one of *my* associates. I do not know who Jack Noble is, nor do I care. He's probably just some British creep that pissed off another British creep who expects me to do him a favor."

The woman placed her elbow on the table, made a fist and rested her chin atop it. She smiled and blinked slowly. "You, my dear Naseer, are a British creep."

"And you are an American bitch," he said playfully as he leaned back in his chair and swirled the wine in his glass. "You know, I've killed men for less than that."

"Good thing I'm not a man." She turned in her seat, facing him directly.

He pushed back from the table, let his knees fall open. "It's good that you are not."

She slid out of her chair, crawled toward him, climbed onto his lap. "No man would do this, would they?" She straddled him and kissed his neck while her fingertips danced across his bare chest. She scratched him with her nails, lightly at first and increasingly harder as her nails traveled down his tight abdomen.

"I'm sure there are some," Naseer said. "But I'd have to kill them."

She nibbled on his earlobe, kissed his cheek, his jawline. Her lips inched closer to his. She arched her back, pressing her breasts into his chest. She dipped her head, licked his lips.

A knock on the door prematurely ended the moment.

"Naseer, we need to talk," a man said from behind the door.

"Always with the damn disruptions," Naseer said.

The woman slipped off his lap and returned to her seat.

"You won't be leaving again, will you?"

She shook her head.

"You were only here a few days the last time." He frowned at her. "No more sick aunts or uncles or whatever taking you away to the U.S. for a couple weeks?"

"I'm all yours for the foreseeable future."

"And don't forget it."

CLARISSA REMAINED SEATED AT THE TABLE UNTIL SHE HEARD the click that indicated the solid door had shut. The lingering smell of Naseer's cologne faded. Confident she'd be alone for a few minutes, she let her emotions out to play. She breathed in and out, heavily, warily. Her shaking hands wiped tears from her cheeks. She forced herself to her feet, staggered across the room and threw herself into the restroom and flipped on the light. A tear stained reflection in an oval mirror greeted her. Dyed dark hair hung in strands across her face. She tucked it behind her ears. She reached for a tissue and used it to wipe her tears away, being careful not to spread running mascara.

For a moment, she stared into the mirror, then said, "What are you doing that these guys are so interested in you, Jack?"

She knew what kind of man Naseer was. She knew the kind of men Naseer associated with. Like him, they were psychopaths, cold and cruel. They were hell bent on reshaping the world in their image through whatever means necessary. Her purpose in London was not only to gather information on Naseer, but also his expansive network.

Adding Jack to the equation would only complicate her mission.

She considered calling Sinclair and having herself removed from the situation. Given the circumstances, it was probably the best option. She decided against doing so. She had to find out why Jack was in London, and why someone asked Naseer to look into him. She thought it best not to make Sinclair aware of Jack's presence until she knew why he was there. She had a contact she could use who might know why and would keep her query private.

The trickiest part would be finding Jack and alerting him without making him aware of her presence. If there was one person who could ruin her cover she'd built with Naseer and his group, Jack was the guy. That would set them back months, and in those months, anything could happen.

The thought sent a shiver down her spine. *God help the world if Naseer unleashes his vengeance,* she thought.

She closed her eyes, inhaled, exhaled, opened her eyes.

"Get it together, girl," she told her reflection. "Stay focused. Naseer first, then Jack."

She cupped her hand, filled it with water, splashed it on her face. She grabbed a light green towel, used it to dab her eyes and cheeks. She opened the door, bracing herself for an inquisition from Naseer in the event he overheard her talking to herself or noticed the faint tear tracks on her cheeks.

But the room was empty.

Clarissa rushed past the table and exited the dining room. The dining room sat between two halls. Naseer had exited to the west. Clarissa used the door on the east.

The winding hallway led past an oversized living area equipped with three sixty inch flat panel televisions. The men routinely watched soccer and squash and criquet in there. Clarissa avoided the room as often as possible. Tonight the room was empty. She figured that they were all meeting. Whatever Naseer had been called out for was important. She hoped she'd find out more later, but up to this point, Naseer had been reluctant to share information with her. All of the intelligence she'd gathered had been through other methods.

She continued down the hall until she reached her room. She performed a quick scan looking for bugs. It had become routine for her to do so. She didn't find any. Hadn't up to that point. Either Naseer trusted her and didn't plant them in her room, or he planted them where she couldn't find them. Clarissa had to assume the latter. She grabbed her bag from the closet, set it on the bed, and then flipped it over. The bag contained a false bottom which had come in handy on several occasions. In this case, it contained a cell phone and scrambling device. Not even Sinclair knew she had this phone.

She connected the micro USB male connector of the scrambler into her phone and waited for both devices to power on. The phone's contact list was empty and the call history was not saved. Should the device ever be confiscated, they'd get nothing out of it. She dialed a number from memory, one that Jack had given her years ago should something happen to him or should she find herself in trouble and unable to reach him.

On the third ring, a man answered. "Who is this?"

"Brandon?" Clarissa asked.

"Depends," he said.

"It's Clarissa. Jack's friend."

"What do you want?"

"I need to know if you know anything about Jack's whereabouts."

"Who is this again?"

"Clarissa."

"Colonel Abbot's daughter?"

"Yeah."

A pause. Then, "I think if Jack wanted you to know that, you'd already know."

"I'm concerned about him, Brandon."

"You are or the CIA is?"

"*You* would know if they were. Don't try to tell me otherwise. You're more connected than anyone."

"You got a point," he said. His breath filled the earpiece and she imagined that he held the phone between his cheek and his shoulder, hands free. "You said you're concerned. Why?"

"I can't say."

"How come?"

"What I'm doing is classified."

"What if I already know what you're doing?"

"Then I shouldn't have to say anything."

Brandon chuckled, leaving Clarissa feeling a little more at ease.

"OK, Clarissa," Brandon said. "You didn't hear this from me, but Jack is in London. He got an offer from a former employer to do one last job for them. He's there to take out a man named Walloway comma Thornton."

Clarissa nearly dropped the phone. She knew the name, had heard it mentioned in passing by Naseer. She reached behind herself and sat down. The bed bowed in the middle under her lithe frame.

"Any idea why?" she said.

"Nope, and that's where my involvement ends. Goodbye."

"Wait."

The line was silent, but still connected.

"What?" Brandon said.

"Don't tell Jack I was looking for him, OK?"

"Why not?"

"He wanted me to leave with him, and I kind of declined. I don't want him thinking I'm trying to find him. Or, you know, pining for him or something."

Brandon laughed. "That's what all this was about? You got me giving up the man's secrets because you're regretting leaving?"

"No, that's not it at all, I just—"

"Whatever, lady. Listen, none of this gets out, you got it. Remember, my friends are more powerful than your friends."

The line disconnected. Clarissa felt like throwing her phone at the wall. How could she be so stupid? Why couldn't she just leave things alone?

Because of Jack, that's why. And now she had to figure out where she could find Thornton Walloway. And make sure Jack wasn't walking into a trap.

CHAPTER 8

BRIGHT LIGHT SPILLED THROUGH THE CRACKS IN THE vertical venetian blinds. Thin fingers of lights danced across Jack's face. He squeezed his eyelids tight, rolled away from the source of the light. He hadn't bothered to turn on the light to look at the room the night before. Fatigue had won out. He had dropped his bag and collapsed onto the oversized bed. Asleep before his head had hit the pillow. He caught his first glimpse of the room. It was white, bright. An antique armoire stood at the foot of the bed, a chest of drawers to the left. Tall double hung windows to the right. His eyes adjusted and he rolled toward the window, split the blinds in two and looked out over the backyard. The sun hovered inches above a cluster of trees.

He swung his legs over the side of the bed, reached down and grabbed his shirt and khakis from the day before. He put them on, got up and stopped in front of the mirror, attempted to iron out the wrinkles with his hand. His hair was still matted on one side. He ran his hands across the top and sides of his head, but it didn't make a difference. And it didn't matter. He was among old friends here.

The dark aroma of freshly brewed coffee greeted him when he opened the door. He glanced at his watch. Eight a.m. He ignored his body telling him it was really only three. As far as he knew, there was no other way to adjust to the time difference. His feet left the comfort of a shag rug and landed on the cool hardwood floor that led to the staircase. He descended quickly, each step down resulting in a snap or a pop, either from the wood or his stiff joints. At the base of the stairs he heard the sounds of the kitchen, pots clanging, light chatter, plates and silverware being set on a table. He followed the noise that inevitably led him to his destination.

Leon spotted him first. The guy smiled and nodded and turned his broad shoulders and faced Jack. Next to Leon stood Dottie. She looked twenty years younger than her age. She always had. If he'd told anyone that she had reached the other side of sixty, they wouldn't believe him. And she'd neuter him for saying so. Women like Dottie were a rare breed, but Jack was more accustomed to them than most people were.

"Good morning, Jack," she said, smiling, a mug dangling from an outstretched arm. "Coffee?"

Jack took the mug full of steaming black liquid and lifted it to his face. The steam singed the inner rims of his nostrils. He sipped from the edge of the cup. The coffee warmed his mouth, throat, chest, belly.

"Glad you're not tea people," he said.

Dottie gave him a merciful grin while shaking her head. "You'll never understand our humor, Jack."

"That's OK with me."

Jack looked past the man and woman in front of him and stared out through the extra wide and extra tall bay window. The ground floor view of what he saw through his bedroom windows. The lush green scenery combined with the smell and taste of the coffee could lull him into a false sense of security. He wondered if every day of retirement would start with this exact feeling.

His eyes lazily scanned the area behind the house. Neatly manicured grounds boasted a tasteful selection of flowers and shrubs. There was a children's play set in the far corner, probably a relic left behind by the previous owner. At least it added credibility should someone come snooping around. Mature trees ringed the property, offering extra privacy and protection from curious eyes. They kept Dottie and her people out of sight. They also kept intruders hidden until the last minute.

"It's safe here," she said.

Jack shrugged.

"I see you looking," she said. "No need to worry. I've got security everywhere."

"Bet I could spot them."

"No, you wouldn't," Leon said.

"I spotted you, didn't I?"

Dottie lifted an eyebrow, a curious look on her face. Jack figured that Leon hadn't told her how the two men had met. She'd sent her best, and Jack had bested him.

Leon smiled, shook his head. "You said you could spot them. Not that you had. Watching your eyes, you passed over at least three of my men."

"There," Jack said with a nodding gesture. "And there," another dip of the head. "And there," a final toss of his jaw to the left.

"Interesting," Leon said.

"Anyway," Jack said. "Do you want to shoot the breeze for a while, or do you want to tell me what I'm doing in England?"

"That's why I always liked working with you, Jack," Dottie said. "No pussy footing around. Always right to the point."

"And you dance around it," he said.

"You know me well," she said.

"Too well," he said, wondering how long the tango would go on before she got down to business.

"Should I leave?" Leon said, grinning.

"No," Dottie and Jack said at the same time.

The three shared a smile, sipped from their ceramic mugs, moved to the other side of the kitchen. They each took a seat at the round oak table, each one a point in a triangle. Jack's stomach roared with hunger, but he declined to ask for food. Dottie appeared to be ready to talk, and he didn't want to give her a reason to procrastinate any longer.

"You had the misfortune of meeting my estranged husband in Monte Carlo," she said.

Jack nodded, said nothing.

"He wasn't always like that, Jack. Honest, he wasn't." She took a moment. "I thought that when I left the agency I was through with men like that. You know, all ego, all about them, no matter the expense."

Jack nodded again. Still said nothing.

"I met him around the time you last did a job for me. I was attending some Lord's party. I forget who. It was a fancy event, lots of powerful people there. *Quid pro quo*. My former Deputy Director at the agency invited me. He now holds my old position as Director. I always enjoyed those kinds of things when I was in charge, so naturally I accepted. And it was there that I met Thornton Walloway."

"You must have been instantly charmed," Jack said, his words laced with sarcasm.

Dottie waved him off. "He wasn't like that when I met him. And don't forget, I was younger and more than capable of taking care of myself. So, yes, maybe he came off a bit rough. It didn't bother me. After years of working with some of the deadliest men in Britain," she paused, smiled, looked between Leon and Jack, "in the world, for that matter. Well, I couldn't be with a guy who retired at night in front of the TV, falling asleep in an oversized recliner, his hands resting atop his beer belly while I fetched him another pint."

Jack smiled. "I wouldn't have expected you to."

"What can I say? I'll always be a gal ready for action."

Jack's smile lingered, then faded. "So what happened?"

"What happened?" she repeated the question, perhaps trying to find an answer. "Thornton made his money in glass. You believe that? A billion dollars from glass?"

Jack didn't believe it. Didn't say as much though.

"But that was only half the story. He invested his money with certain people. Some of them the same people I fought to put away, you see. Some of them the type of people I hired you to take care of, Jack. I didn't know this at the time, though. I thought all of his wealth was from glass."

Jack nodded. Had nothing to add yet, so he said nothing.

"Things were good for the first four years. Then, a couple years ago, they changed. *He* changed. Thornton became abusive, verbally and physically. He became secretive. I thought maybe he was having an affair. His anger a reflection of the guilt he felt. If I asked a question, I got hit. Simple as that."

"Why'd you stick around?"

Dottie looked away. Jack followed her stare. Her gaze traveled beyond the window, past the garden, settled on some imaginary point that Jack couldn't see.

"I don't know," she finally said.

"You don't?" Jack said.

Dottie turned her head ninety degrees, locked eyes with Jack. "Maybe I do, but I don't want to say."

Jack lifted his hands in an *I surrender* gesture. If she didn't want to tell him anymore, that was her prerogative. He wouldn't push. Some things were better left for therapy.

"So as you can see, after the month I spent in a hospital in Monte Carlo, I retreated to this place. He doesn't know where it is. I never told him. I bought it years ago. I knew if things went wrong, either with Thornton or one of his associates, I'd need a place to hide. This place works well. I have a security force in place that he doesn't own. He's got money, but I brought my own dowry to the party. All this is mine, Jack. He paid for none of it."

"What else?" Jack said, ready for her to get to the point.

Dottie nodded, shifted her eyes to her right for a second, a signal for Leon to leave the room.

Plausible deniability.

"I'll be back in a few." Leon rose, nodded at Jack, then slipped past the table and out of the kitchen.

Jack placed one arm on the table, leaned forward. "So what is it you want me to do, Dottie?"

A smile formed and quickly rescinded. Her expression eroded, leaving behind a face twisted with pain and fear and anger. "End him."

"Why me? Why not Leon, or one of your other guys here, or one of your old agents?"

"Because you are the best. And he's scared of you, Jack. The moment he sees you, he's going to panic, and that will buy you a few extra seconds. Those few seconds are all you'll need to finish the job."

Jack leaned back, inched to his left, placed his left arm across the back of the chair, held the half-full mug in his right hand. He swirled the coffee in a counter clockwise motion, causing the lighter brown residue on top to form a spinning island in the center. He thought that he'd like to be on an island this morning. Someplace tropical and nowhere near mainland Europe. He owed Dottie in more ways than one. She'd helped him get started. Got him back on his feet when his world had crumbled around him. She introduced him to people who had helped him to become a wealthy man. But above all, she'd always been a friend, and now she was in need. And he couldn't turn her down.

He took a drink from his mug and then set it on the table. "I'll do it."

Dottie rose and walked around the table, past Jack.

"I need to know some things first," he said.

"Of course." Dottie went on to give Jack Thornton's home and office address and the security codes required for access. She told him the restaurants and bars and strip clubs that he frequented. She gave him the names of Thornton's most trusted men. She mentioned the names of his women, of which there were many. When she was finished, she said, "Anything else you might need?"

"I'll need access to weapons. An M40 for the hit, if I can do it ranged. Two pistols, preferably 9mm. I'll need an HK MP7, S model, with a suppressor and at least three spare magazines, in case I go to war with his men." Jack picked up the mug and took one final pull on the lukewarm liquid. After he swallowed, his mouth was littered with coffee grounds like silt trapped in a net. "Also, I want a lethal pen."

"A lethal pen?"

"Looks like a pen, equipped with a needle and a reservoir filled with poison. When you place the end of the pen to someone and then click the tip, the needle protrudes and penetrates and a moment later the fluid is forced out of the reservoir and into the victim."

"Interesting."

"If it comes down to me doing this in a crowded bar or strip club or on the street, I don't want to be spotted with a gun drawn. Everyone has a camera phone these days. Last thing I need is my face on the TV again. I've got nobody to help me out anymore if things go south."

"I'm behind you, Jack."

"But you can't afford to be associated with a known assassin, Dottie. It won't take them long to put the pieces of the puzzle together. I know that a lot of the work I did for you was not sanctioned. You don't need that stuff coming to light now."

She nodded, forced a smile, said nothing.

"So can you get the weapons?"

"Leon has access to some. I'll make some calls for the rest. By tonight I should have everything you need."

"Got a car?" Jack asked.

"Out front. It's ready for you."

"Thornton doesn't know about it?"

"Just bought it yesterday, cash, my money. Registered under a false name. He knows nothing and will find out nothing about it."

Jack pushed back in his chair, got up and refilled his mug. He placed the cup on the counter and hunted for a travel mug. He found one in the cupboard and transferred the coffee and topped it off.

"Keys are in the ignition. There's some cash, an ATM card, and an untraceable cell phone in the glove box."

"Thanks. I'll be back this evening."

"No, don't come back. Get a hotel. It's best that you not return in case you are spotted and followed."

Jack agreed she had a point. "Give me a number to reach you and one for Leon then."

"Already programmed into the phone. I'm speed dial number two, he's number three. Four and five are for emergencies."

"What about one?"

"I never program one, Jack. Too hard for me to reach with my thumb."

Jack reached out to Dottie, pulled her close in an embrace. Her perfume overpowered the strong smell of coffee, bringing back several of the memories that he had repressed for so long.

"You be careful, Jack. If you don't think it's going to happen, call me. I can get Leon or someone else out there to help."

Jack shook his head. "Alone, Dottie. This one needs to be done alone."

He wasn't sure if he meant it, or if it was some kind of false bravado. Maybe he could use the help. Maybe it would only hinder the mission. He didn't know, yet he'd already sealed his fate. It'd be tough to go back on his statement.

He pulled away and left the kitchen. Dottie remained behind. Leon met him by the front door, handed him a second Browning.

Jack tucked the pistol in his waistband. His pants tugged downward under the weight of the two handguns. "Got anything lighter?"

"It'll have to do for now. I'll have better weapons by tonight. Call me at five and we'll arrange a place to meet."

Jack exited the house without replying. He saw a lone car, a red Fiat, parked in the center of circular driveway. He tilted his head to the side, wondering how he was supposed to fit inside. Did she have something against Land Rovers? Even something mid-sized would have worked for him.

Reluctantly, Jack slipped in behind the steering wheel. He found it to be roomier than it looked. He turned the key in the ignition and shifted the transmission into first gear. He eased off the clutch as he depressed the accelerator and the car rolled down the driveway.

CHAPTER 9

HANNAH HEARD THE HIGH PITCHED WHINE OF A SMALL engine combined with the sound of tires kicking up loose gravel. She hurried to make sure that she hadn't missed Ms. Carlisle. The last thing she wanted to do was hang around outside the house waiting for her boss to return home. She emerged from behind the hedges in time to see the rear of a red Fiat pulling away from the front of the house. The car was unfamiliar. Hannah took a deep breath, felt confident that she hadn't wasted her time coming to the house unannounced.

She stepped across the trenched gravel, kicking loose stones back into place as she passed. She stood before the tall wooden entrance door. She took a deep breath in preparation of the groveling she expected to have to do. An aged brass knocker stained from years of rain and snow and ice hung from the mouth of an equally aged brass lion fixed to the middle of the door. She lifted the heavy brass ring and let it fall. It creaked as it dropped and then hit the door with a solid thud.

The door cracked open, an eye peered through. It opened a bit further. The man greeted Hannah with a smile.

"We weren't expecting you," he said.

"I know, Leon. I really need to talk to Ms. Carlisle, though."

"Is everything OK?"

Hannah shrugged and held out her arms, palms up, thumbs out.

"Well, come on inside, then. Ms. Carlisle is upstairs getting ready for the day. She'll be down in a few minutes."

"Hey, who was in the car that just pulled away?" she asked.

Leon turned and walked away without replying. Hannah followed him inside. Instead of turning left and following him toward the living room, Hannah continued straight into the kitchen. The smell of fresh cut melon and strawberries and coffee enveloped her. She glanced toward the counter, saw three mugs next to the sink. Upon closer inspection, they had all been used recently. Each had a thin layer of black sludge at the bottom. One was stained around the top with red lipstick, the same shade that Ms. Carlisle wore. Her gaze drifted across the granite countertop. The coffeemaker was on and the twelve-cup pot less than half full, indicating that at least one person had refilled their mug. If Ms. Carlisle was only now getting ready for the day, then who had been drinking coffee? Did this mean that Erin and Mia were home from vacation already? Or had Ms. Carlisle and Leon been sitting with whoever left in the red car? Surely Ms. Carlisle would have already prepared herself if a guest had been by.

"Hannah, what a treat."

She jumped at the sound of the voice. She hadn't heard anyone enter the kitchen.

"Would you mind pouring me a cup too?" Ms. Carlisle asked.

"Sure, ma'am. Which mug were you using?" Hannah waited for her response without turning around.

"Those are from last night, dear. Grab fresh mugs from the cabinet."

The mugs could be explained away, but not the half-filled pot of coffee. Hannah dismissed it, filled two mugs, brought them both to the table where cream and sugar were already waiting. She touched the pewter cream dish. It was cold, as was the cream inside of it. She looked up and smiled at Ms. Carlisle. Why had the woman lied to her? What was she hiding?

"What are you doing by today?" Ms. Carlisle asked. "I didn't expect you for at least a week."

Hannah chewed on the inside of her cheek for a moment while she pushed aside the coffee mug mystery and focused on her real problems.

"Hannah? Is everything all right?"

"They took away my scholarship, ma'am. I won't be able to afford school."

"Well, I'm sure I can help you out with that."

"I don't want a handout, ma'am. If I have to take this term off, that's fine, I'll do it. What I'd like to know is if I can put in some extra hours. I'm willing to do things outside of being a nanny for Mia. I can work here, or at one of the other houses. I'm willing to do anything you need."

Ms. Carlisle rose and walked toward the window. "I don't know if that is possible, Hannah. At least not right now. I've—" She paused, turned to face Hannah. "We've got to leave for a while. Probably, that is. I don't know for sure yet. But I might be gone for a month, maybe two. Mia won't be around, and the houses won't need tending by anyone other than the staff already at hand."

"Please, ma'am," Hannah said. "I'll have to go home, and you know I can't spend that much time around my father. He can't handle it and he'll—"

"OK, Hannah," Ms. Carlisle placed a comforting hand on Hannah's shoulder. "You won't be attending school this term?"

"That's correct. Without the scholarship I can't afford it. I'd hoped that I could work extra for you and save the money and have my scholarship reinstated next semester."

"What if you accompany us? You could be Mia's travel nanny. Since you'd effectively be working at least double the hours, I'd increase your pay by two and a half times your current rate. How's that sound?"

Hannah rose and threw her arms around the older woman. She inhaled the subdued aroma of her sweet perfume, noting that it wasn't as strong as it should be if she had recently put it on.

"I'll take that as a yes," Ms. Carlisle said.

Hannah pulled back. The lump in her throat prevented her from talking. She nodded at the tear-blurred image of her boss and then leaned in and hugged her some more.

"All right, that's enough." Ms. Carlisle wrestled herself from Hannah's grasp. "Why don't you spend the next few days helping out the maids? You can start in here with the kitchen."

“Yes ma’am.” Hannah turned and walked to the sink. She grabbed the three mugs, placed them under the faucet. She soaped a rag then wiped the coffee sludge and lipstick and fingerprints from them.

CHAPTER 10

JACK SAT IN THE FIAT ACROSS THE STREET FROM THE BUILDING that bore the address Dottie had given him. Thornton's office. It was a three-story gray brick building that occupied half the block. Three rows of evenly spaced mirrored floor-to-ceiling windows wrapped the exterior. Behind one of those windows was Thornton's office. Jack wondered if the man was in there. Who else was in there? Did Thornton keep a security force with him all the time, even at his corporate office? Did the man's employees know what else Thornton was into? Hell, were some of them into it as well?

Jack had a number of questions eating away at him. Sitting outside the building and waiting left him with little else to do other than question the situation. It had been obvious to Jack when he'd laid eyes on Thornton in Monte Carlo that the guy was bad news. Still, it was shocking to find out that the man was as heavily involved in criminal activities as Dottie had said. He had no reason to doubt her, but he still couldn't get rid of the nagging in the back of his mind telling him that she'd made some of it up just to harden Jack toward the man.

It didn't matter, though. He remembered how Thornton tried to kill him. He'd saw what Thornton had done to Dottie. If he'd seen it before the police arrived and detained Thornton, Jack would have killed the guy on the spot. But he hadn't, and he didn't. And now he was in London to do what should have been done over six months ago.

He figured his image was burned into Thornton's memory. But would the guy notice him in bright daylight? The casino bar had been dimly lit. The docks where they'd had their confrontation were dark, with only an orange overhead light or two. Maybe Thornton held a distorted image of Jack Noble, one that barely resembled reality.

The thought gave Jack the courage to enter the building and finish the job right then and there. But he didn't. He knew that he couldn't take that kind of chance so soon. There were too many potentially innocent people inside, for one. And there was the possibility that Thornton knew exactly who Jack was and, given the advent of security cameras and systems, Thornton would know Jack was in the building the moment he stepped foot on the property.

And so Jack's mind wandered. He began to think about the implications of doing the job, which led to him once again questioning why him. He knew that Dottie trusted him. Always had. They'd worked together in the past on both sanctioned and unsanctioned jobs. He'd never let her down, and she'd never let him down. But in nearly all those instances, Jack had the element of surprise working in his favor. His target didn't know his face. Except for two hits when he was contracted to take out rogue agents. But those were sanctioned, and he had the freedom to do whatever he deemed necessary without fear of the government or police or anybody, except the rogue agents themselves, of course.

Now here he was, outside the offices of his target. A target that knew his face and knew his name. Hell, Thornton might even know Jack was outside.

What if Dottie had set him up? What if she was working with someone like Frank and together they had arranged for Jack's life to end? He had thought it odd that the call from whom he presumed had been Leon had come shortly after he told Frank that he was done with the agency and the business. All he wanted was his freedom, to retire. Perhaps Frank had a different idea.

Suddenly, every face he saw became a threat. Not a possible threat, but a real bona fide threat. Every man, every woman. Young, old, in between.

Because in the world of espionage, it's not the one you expect to kill you who does. It happens when you let your guard down around the innocent looking person who seems incapable of taking a life.

Jack slapped his cheeks, open-handed then backhanded. Left, then right. He shook his head and dispelled the paralyzing thoughts contained within. This was not the time to allow himself to be overcome with fear and panicked thoughts. If Dottie had set him up then he'd treat it like every other time he'd been set up.

Self-preservation, first and foremost.

Then revenge.

So the only thing for Jack to do was wait and watch. Watch the elderly couple pass by his car. Wait while the funeral procession of someone not very well liked passed by in a matter of seconds. He waited and watched as half the building emptied onto the sidewalks at lunchtime. And again when they returned. Through it all, there was no sign of Thornton Walloway.

So Jack waited even longer.

He paid particular attention to the people who entered and exited the building at irregular times. He'd make a quick assessment, then if he felt they fit his profile, he'd snap a picture with the cell phone Dottie had left in the car. There were only a few who deserved such attention. But he considered the fact that he didn't know Thornton's criminal partners, and he figured it wouldn't hurt to have the pictures.

Through the scanning and profiling, one thing filtered through Jack's head without being properly processed. A car had been parked behind him the entire day. Not too close. Not too far away. It had arrived shortly after he did. He never saw anyone get out. That didn't mean nobody had. But if they had, he'd missed it. Which seemed unlikely considering that he'd noticed every dog that stopped to piss on the fire hydrant visible in the bottom right corner of his rear view mirror.

The sun reflected off the vehicle's windshield, making it impossible for Jack to see if someone was inside. He contemplated getting out and walking over to the car. Decided against it. Not here, not in front of Thornton's office building.

Then Jack got the break he'd been waiting for.

He shifted his focus from the car positioned behind him to the building. His gaze drifted from the first to the third floor, back down, and settled on the shadowy hole where vehicles had disappeared into and emerged from throughout the day. His focus once again started to drift, but before the entrance to the parking level had left his field of view, a black Bentley emerged.

And it looked to be the same one from the night before, outside the hotel.

The Bentley turned left out of the garage, drove forward, stopped at the corner twenty yards behind Jack. It made another left and approached his position from the rear.

Jack looked away. The windows of the Bentley were tinted on all four sides. Staring at the car would only get him noticed. The Bentley passed. Jack turned the key in the Fiat's ignition. He punched the clutch, eased his foot onto the gas, pulled away from the curb. Shifted from first to second. He glanced up at his rear-view mirror and saw the car that had been parked behind him all day pull away from the curb too.

Jack paced the Bentley, staying about thirty yards behind. He took note of the names of each street he passed, committed them to memory. The layout of London, and most major European cities for that matter, did not mesh logically with his brain. They spread out from one central point with no grid to make getting from point A to point B as simple as requiring only the cardinal directions to navigate.

So he did his best to create a map in his mind. If it came down to it, he knew he could switch on the cell phone's GPS. Although past experiences made him leery of doing so. He'd been tracked through GPS once before and preferred not to relive the experience.

The Bentley's brake lights lit up like a pair of seductive eyes, and then the sleek black vehicle pulled off to a stop in front of a custom tailor's shop named *Federico's*. The driver's door opened. A man stepped out. He looked a lot like one of the men Jack had seen in front of the hotel. The guy left his door open, took two steps toward the rear of the car, and opened the back door. The driver looked north, south, east, west. He lifted his sunglasses and his eyes swept side to side in huge arcs. He said something, then the man in the back of the Bentley stepped out.

The passenger was older. His silver goatee was cropped as close to his face as his hair was to his head. His dark suit told anyone within eyeshot that money would never be a hindrance. Without a doubt, this was the man Jack had encountered in Monte Carlo. The man who'd tried to kill Jack. This was the man who'd beaten Dottie within an inch of her life.

Thornton Walloway.

Jack rolled by slowly. He used his left hand to shield his face from view. Kept his sunglasses down to hide his eyes. The seconds it took to pass felt like minutes. He pulled against the opposite curb and let the Fiat idle. Using his side and rear view mirrors, he watched Thornton step inside the tailor's shop. The tinted glass door shut. The driver disappeared inside the Bentley. Headlights cut into the dreary mist that hovered over the street. The black luxury vehicle pulled away from the curb, passed Jack, turned left at the intersection.

"Dumb luck," Jack muttered.

He could end it right there. Best case, he'd walk in and place a bullet in the center of Thornton's forehead. There was the possibility of accidental casualties, but Jack could live with that. Worst case, he'd have to kill a few people in the store and then take on the driver, who probably doubled as Thornton's bodyguard. Either way, he liked his odds.

He pulled out both Brownings. The pistols were well taken care of, recently oiled. He reseated each magazine and put a round in each chamber. He had two shots before anyone could react. For a man like Jack, that was plenty.

He leaned over, opened the glove box, rifled through it looking for something to cover his face. He found a blue rag of a t-shirt, stained with oil. He held it up to his head. A perfect fit. He tugged on the emergency brake and pulled the keys from the ignition. Gas fumes filled the cramped interior. He rolled down the driver's side window a couple inches, then opened the door and exited onto the sidewalk. He scanned the street, north to south. Quiet aside from a few pedestrians. His preparation ended there.

In most scenarios, time was an ally. Not today. Not here. Jack decided he couldn't even take the time to walk down the sidewalk opposite the shop, then cross the street and loop back. By that point, the driver might be on the street again. And the driver might know what Jack looked like. The driver could position himself between Jack and the Fiat, and that would complicate matters greatly.

Jack knifed through the damp air, headed across the street diagonally on a line toward Federico's. He planned to turn his head the opposite way when he hit the sidewalk, preventing anyone inside from seeing his face. At best, they'd have body type to go on. And while Jack was somewhat of a physical specimen, he wasn't impressive enough to be one of a kind.

But it didn't go according to plan. He didn't reach the other side of the street. Instead, the car that had been tailing him screeched to a stop in front of him. The driver's side window rolled down. A man with buzzed blond hair and almost white eyebrows aimed a gun at Jack.

"Get in the car, Jack."

Jack hesitated, took a step back. He realized that the vehicle was government issued.

"Don't try to run. I'll gun you down."

Jack's hands went to the handles of his pistols.

"Don't even think about drawing on me."

Jack looked down both ends of the street. To his left, the tailor's shop, and half a dozen vehicles climbing toward him. To his right, the driver of the Bentley.

"Hurry, Jack, before you get shot."

The Bentley's driver stared in Jack's direction. He reached into his coat pocket. Was he going for a handgun? Or a cell phone? Was it better to face that man, or the blond guy inside the cheaper government sedan?

The Bentley's driver pulled a pistol.

"Now!" the driver of the government sedan said.

Jack stepped to his right, grabbed the rear door handle, dove into the vehicle as it peeled away.

CHAPTER 11

"WHAT ARE YOU DOING, JACK?"

Clarissa hunched behind the wheel of her small car, full of disbelief at what she had just witnessed. It was bad enough that Jack appeared to be ready to attempt a hit inside a store in a busy area. But to get inside a vehicle owned by British Intelligence? What the hell was he thinking?

As she eased down the street, she realized that Jack had only had two options after the car pulled up. Get in or get shot by either the driver or the man who stood on the sidewalk between the shop and the corner. She recognized him, having seen him before at Naseer's place. The guy gave her the creeps. She'd do her best to look away when she passed. A guy like him would not likely believe in coincidences. He'd put two and two together, tell his boss. His boss would get on the phone to Naseer, then all hell would break loose. The last thing Clarissa needed was Naseer questioning her about her whereabouts and intentions. She'd be pulled from the assignment the moment she sent a status update. If she lived that long.

As Clarissa approached the intersection before the tailor's shop, she had a decision to make. Turn and drive up two blocks, then merge back onto the road, and risk losing Jack. Or continue on and pray that the man didn't see her. She was already losing ground to the sedan, so turning at the intersection looked to be the less attractive option. She pressed the gas pedal. The little car shook and picked up speed.

The guy now stood closer to the entrance to the tailor's. His head moved inches. His eyes did the heavy work, scanning the street, the buildings. He looked relaxed, but aware. He'd been spooked by Jack, but in the end, the government car might have aided Jack. Perhaps the guy figured it was a regular shakedown. She knew he was trained to spot anomalies and to take action immediately. And that was something Clarissa could use to her advantage.

So she made herself look like everyone else on the road. She brought her left hand up to her head, cell phone cradled in her palm, pressed to her cheek. Her right hand waved wildly in front of her, animating her fake conversation. At the last second, she whipped her head to the right like she saw something super cute in a store window. The effort served to further conceal herself from view. After she passed, Clarissa checked her side mirror. The guy stared off in the opposite direction. If he'd noticed her, he hid his reaction well. Likely, he'd seen a woman in a car and filed her away as a non-threat.

She reached the next intersection and slowed to a stop. A line of three cars approached from the left. Five from the right. She glanced up toward her rear view mirror. The guy approached her direction. Her eyes lowered an inch. The government sedan distanced itself further. If she didn't make it across the intersection soon, she'd lose them.

"Come on, come on, come on." She tapped the heel of her free foot and bounced her knees.

Knuckles rapped against her passenger side window.

Clarissa gasped, jumped, looked over.

The guy peered back at her over the top of the sunglasses now perched atop his nose. He motioned with his hand for her to roll down the window.

She reached with her right hand and pressed a button. The window glided down.

"You're Naseer's lady, right?"

Clarissa said nothing.

"What're you doing in this part of town?"

"I don't answer to you."

He smiled, placed his forearms across the window ledge. "What say you come have a drink with me?"

She said nothing.

"No? Perhaps I should dial up Naseer and tell him you're out and about clear across town from him."

"And while you're at it, why don't you mention to him that you just hit on me."

The guy's smile faded. He lifted his head a few inches, worked his lips side to side. He muttered something under his breath that sounded derogatory.

"What's that?" Clarissa said.

He shook his head, said nothing.

"Yeah, that's what I thought. Get your grubby hands out of my vehicle." She pressed the gas and pulled away before he had a chance to fully disengage from the car. His arm or elbow or hand collided with the door frame with a thud and maybe a crack. She glanced up at her rear view mirror and saw him bent over, cradling his right arm.

Her elation faded when she realized that she'd lost sight of the government vehicle.

And Jack.

CHAPTER 12

"I'VE BEEN WATCHING YOU SINCE YOU ARRIVED," THE GUY told Jack. "We couldn't believe your name flagged. Thought it had to be a mistake, or maybe some other Jack Noble traveling from the U.S. to London. I mean, why would Jack Noble travel under his own name? Really, why would you?"

Jack massaged his temples with his thumbs. He took a deep breath, sucking in the stale air that carried the faint odor of pine needles. His fear had been realized.

"Why should I tell you?"

"I'm Security Service. MI5, mate. I already know a lot about you. Former Marine with CIA ties. At one time you worked for an agency that shares an acronym with our MI6. You left long ago, but still contracted with them for non-sanctioned hits, both foreign and domestic. You were working with them as recently as a week ago. A Russian General was assassinated in a theater just north of Moscow. You were there. Ask me how I know that?"

Jack said nothing, focused on the road ahead.

"Look, mate, I'll find out what you're doing here one way or another. You can tell me here. Or you can tell me in a cell, if that's what you prefer."

Jack turned away, looked out the side window, sighed.

"Or if you really don't like yourself, I can find people that you do like and start questioning them. How 'bouts I start with my old boss? Reckon she'll be more cooperative."

Jack whipped his head around, studied the guy for a moment. Would he really go after Dottie? He decided to buy some time and try to figure out what the guy really wanted. "Got ID?"

The guy produced a badge and ID card. Both had the name Mason Sutton printed on them. He worked for British Intelligence, Security Service, MI5. The address on the badge said Thames House. Jack knew that was across the river from Vauxhall Cross, MI6 headquarters. Jack had spent time there in the past when working for Dottie on sanctioned hits. He recalled what the badges looked like then. If Mason had faked his credentials, he'd done a pretty good job. His badge looked the same as the ones Jack saw in his head. He figured the design hadn't changed much in the past ten years. Didn't have a reason to. British Intelligence didn't succumb to a version two-point-oh.

At this point, Jack's options were limited. Give Mason what he wanted or fall between the bureaucratic cracks and become indefinitely incarcerated.

"What do you want to know?"

"Like I said, why'd you travel under your real name?"

"Quit jerking me around."

Mason smiled, leaned in, placed a hand on Jack's forearm. Said, "Humor me."

"I'm retired," Jack told him. "My name's good. I'm free and clear in the U.S. and all friendly nations. I'm not wanted in connection with any crimes. I'm not wanted for questioning in regards to any crimes. I can travel without restrictions. Why would my name flag in your system? Maybe you're looking for another Jack Noble. Ever think of that?"

Mason let go of Jack's arm, began laughing. "Oh, Jackie boy, you are something else. You know that, right?"

Jack didn't reply.

"You are who we think you are, mate. Yeah, you're right, you're not wanted for anything. Now. But you better be certain that when your name pops up, governments are going to worry about what you're doing in their country. Hell, Carnival Cruise Lines would worry if you showed up on their itinerary. A guy like you doesn't travel for pleasure. And don't you bother feeding me a cockeyed story. I'm not a stupid customs agent pushing through the day until it's time to punch the clock."

"I told you, I'm retired."

"Yeah, so you said." Mason steered with his knees while he lit a cigarette. He took a deep drag, exhaled in Jack's direction. "Men like you don't retire, Jack. Not until someone puts a bullet through your thick skull."

"Is that what you're here to do?"

Mason shrugged, puffed out his cheeks and forced air through loosely sealed lips, creating a flapping sound. "Give me a reason, and yeah, I'll terminate you."

"Have I given you a reason?"

"Not yet."

"Then what do you want from me? You didn't stop me in the middle of the street and drive me out of town to ask me why I got on a plane using my real name. And I don't know of any popular shops that a cross dresser like yourself might visit. So, what is it?"

Mason smiled, nodded, said, "Right, I'll get to the point, mate. What'd you want with Thornton Walloway?"

"Who?"

"It is not in your best interest to—how did you say it—jerk me around, Jack. As of this moment, I'm your friend. Got that? Friend. You don't want me as an enemy." Mason paused. His eyes flitted between Jack's. He continued. "You've been outside his office building all day long. As soon as his car hit the street, you took off after it. His Bentley stops, you drive half a block then pull over. He gets out, goes inside a clothing store, then you get out of your little car and cross the street looking like you were hell bent on introducing him to his forsaken fate. I've got your number, Jack. I could build a case for conspiracy to commit murder right there. So what say you let me in on what's going on?"

"Seven months ago I messed up. Did something I knew I shouldn't have. I wasn't given the whole story and could plead ignorance, but the fact is I knew what was going on. I figured that what I'd procured would never end up in hands of someone with the ability to execute. And I did it for the money, plain and simple. I'd been thinking about getting out of the business, setting off into the sea, retiring. That job would have allowed me to do so. But then I had a life altering experience, minutes before I was supposed to make the drop. Everything changed."

"What was it?"

Jack studied the man for a moment before deciding against telling him about the Mandy and Clarissa situations. No reason to give the guy extra ammunition. "Let's just say it was something I'd never dealt with before."

"OK."

"So anyway, this chain of events leads me to France, Italy for a brief time, then to Russia. I had a pit stop in a lovely place called Black Dolphin, narrowly avoided a shallow grave, and found myself relaxing in Greece for a few months. I got roped into helping out the SIS, you were right about that. But I had to do it. It was, for all intents and purposes, my mess to clean up. And I did. I ended it. Lost a few friends in the process."

Mason narrowed his eyes, rubbed his chin, said, "You took out that old coot, Ivanov, didn't you?"

Jack hiked his shoulders in the air an inch, looked away. He did both on purpose. Two simple gestures that both affirmed Mason's thoughts, and said *I didn't do a damn thing*.

"So, great, you're a hero. You saved the world. You cleaned up your mess. How does that get you to London? What does it have to do with Walloway?"

Jack stared ahead. He hadn't been paying attention to the route they had taken and wasn't sure where he was. The cityscape had turned into a quickly diminishing suburban setting. A densely forested area was ahead. He shifted in his seat, looked between Mason and the road.

He said, "I had a chance encounter with him in Monte Carlo."

"What were you doing in Monte Carlo?"

"Killing time." Jack paused for further questioning. When there was none, he continued. "I ran into Dottie there. It had been more than a few years since we last worked together. I bought her a drink. Walloway comes up and makes a scene. Total hothead. I ran into him again that night, him and his guys."

"You kill any of them?"

Jack said nothing.

"Right, OK. So what else?"

"Who says there's more?"

"I get that you and he have a history. But it doesn't jive that you'd risk everything to come over here just based on that. You said yourself, you're done, retired."

"He lit into Dottie that night. She spent a month in the hospital. He bought off the courts down there and got off scot-free. That is, minus the time he spent in jail."

"Ah, so she reached out to you and asked you to take him out." Mason turned his head and made eye contact with Jack and added, "Don't reply to that."

Jack didn't. He kept his mouth shut, his eyes open. The car started to slow. Up ahead he saw a clearing on the right that led to a gravel road or driveway. The vehicle continued to decelerate, then turned onto the path. Neither man said anything as the car dipped and bounced and swayed left to right and back again. Finally, the sedan rolled to a stop and Mason put it in park.

"Here's the deal, Jack—"

"I'm armed, Mason. You might shoot me first, you might not. But before you do anything, take into consideration the fact that I have two Browning HP pistols on me, and I can get to them before you can react."

Through his laughter, Mason said, "You think I brought you out here to kill you?"

Mason's upturned, squinted eyes and full-on belly laugh set Jack at ease.

"Just being cautious," Jack said.

Mason took a moment to compose himself, exhaled with a high pitched *whew*. "I'm here because I wanted to find out your intentions toward Walloway and to tell you that we want you to take him out. We'll pay you two-hundred thousand euros over whatever Dottie is paying you."

Dottie wasn't paying him anything. Jack had taken the job for personal reasons. That would not prevent him from taking money from the British government, though.

"So why'd you stop me back there. I had him. He was alone in that store with one, maybe two employees."

"We know when we want it done. There's going to be a meeting."

"MI5," Jack said. "You're counter-terrorism, right?"

Mason nodded, a singular and decisive movement.

"So that means...?"

Another singular and decisive nod of Mason's head confirmed that Thornton Walloway was involved with some bad men.

"And this meeting, there'll be others there you want taken out?"

"Not necessarily," Mason said. "We want them scared. We want them to know that we know about them. "

"So that's why you need me. Walloway is the only target. The hit won't be from a distance, though, so the shooter has to get close. Close enough that he might be spotted. And you can't have one of your operators being seen at the hit. But being close is going to put me in a precarious position. Others might die."

Again, a single nod. No words spoken.

Jack understood. They had enough on Walloway to justify it, but not the others. If Jack had to kill them, so be it.

The heavy odor of wood smoke had filled the car. Jack's gaze drifted, darting around the surrounding forest. Odd shadows spiked his awareness. He still didn't know if he could trust Mason. Why did they have to come out here to discuss this? How close was the nearest person or house? He'd noticed several driveways after they passed the last neighborhood. Someone was probably close enough that any gunfire would be heard. Would it be unusual, though? Did people in England hunt? Of course they did. But did they hunt here, in these woods?

"Open the glove box," Mason said, breaking the silence that had lingered the way wood smoke hovered in the leafy canopy covering them.

Jack slid his hand along the pitted dash until he found the latch. The glove box door dropped open. Inside was a Beretta M9, Jack's preferred handgun. He pulled the weapon out, inspected it.

"There's a silencer and spare magazine in there, too," Mason said.

Jack reached in and placed his hand on the silencer. He threaded it on the end of the barrel. He pulled the spare magazine out, then closed the glove box.

"OK," Mason said. "Now get out."

"What?"

"You heard me. Out. I'll be in touch soon."

"I have no idea where I am. Got no car."

"A man is going to be along with your car shortly. They left just after we did."

How many had there been following him? Jack placed his hand on the door handle, hesitated.

"Go on, Jack. Do you really think I'd leave you here to be ambushed after giving you a weapon?"

The sound of tires crunching and spitting out gravel roared from behind. Jack craned his neck and saw the Fiat approaching.

Mason held out his arms. "Happy?"

Jack nodded, opened the door, stepped out.

Mason's car roared to life and pulled away and stopped fifty feet from the road. The Fiat pulled up next to Jack. A man hopped out, pushed past Jack and ran to Mason's car. The guy got in and took the seat Jack had occupied. The sedan started forward, hurling gravel in its wake.

Jack found himself alone with the Fiat in the middle of nowhere.

CHAPTER 13

NASEER DRUMMED THE FINGERS OF HIS LEFT HAND IN A rhythmic pattern along the edge of his desk. One, two, three, four, pause. Over and over again, his fingertips repeated the beat.

Thornton was fifteen minutes late for their meeting. Naseer had little patience for tardiness, but today he did not allow it to upset him. He did not wait patiently or impatiently. He was neither calm nor anxious. He just was.

And he continued to be.

His feet rested on the corner of the antique desk that had cost him several thousand dollars. The desk had a history, but Naseer didn't know it. He paid little attention to the man who rattled off names of people who had some prominence in history. The desk had the look that Naseer wanted. Visitors often commented on it, too. That was what really mattered to Naseer. That and the fact that the big, bold piece of furniture immediately put him in a position of power, something he found helpful, most of the time.

Not that he needed help in that area.

In addition to his money, of which he had plenty, he had forces that would carry out any command he ordered, and with nothing more than a phone call. Anywhere in the world, anytime he wanted.

Walloway brought something new to the table. He had the money to match Naseer's wealth. He also had contacts that Naseer couldn't touch. Important people in industry and the government. For that, he'd put up with the man longer than the guy's personality and attitude warranted. Lately, he'd grown tired of Walloway's demands and incessant narcissism.

The still image on the security monitor on his desk came to life. One of his men walked down the hall toward Naseer's office. The guy stopped in front of the office door. Naseer waited for the knock on the door, then he pressed the button that controlled the lock and said, "Enter."

Samir walked into the office, cast aside formalities. "He's here. Him and one of his guys."

"Which one? Bodyguard?"

"Maybe."

"How is he?"

"He's a prick, as usual. Seems hopped up a bit."

"How so?"

"Going on about how he shouldn't have to wait."

Naseer placed his hand over the computer mouse and guided the pointer to a thumbnail image below the footage of the hallway. He clicked the small square and the feed switched to the lobby. He saw Walloway standing, back against the wall, right arm over his left, left leg crossed over his right. His cheeks looked red. His eyes were narrow. Naseer thought the man looked like an angry little troll.

"Naseer? Should I bring him back?"

"Yes. Only him though, not his mate."

"Very well." Samir took a step back, turned, closed the door behind him as he left Naseer's office.

Naseer switched the main screen footage back to the hallway outside his office and he unchecked the box that muted the sound. If Walloway decided to fuss and throw a fit on the way, he'd know.

Feeling the need to ensure his own protection, Naseer slid open the top left desk drawer. It squeaked as the bent slides scraped against one another. He pulled out a titanium case, opened it, retrieved his Heckler & Koch MARK 23. He secured the suppressor and tested the laser sights. If he had to use it, it would be both silent and accurate.

Naseer owned several expensive firearms. Behind him, mounted on a shelf, was a Pfeifer-Zeliska .600 Nitro Express Magnum. He'd fired it once and it had nearly knocked him off his feet. The gun was made for hunting elephants. It had cost him close to twenty-thousand dollars. A pittance for a man of his stature. Locked up in a safe was a silver plated P-38 made by Walther that he'd paid over one million dollars for at auction. He'd never fired that one.

He didn't need an expensive weapon when it came to his personal defense. He required power and carnage. The MARK 23 was more than capable of providing both.

Walloway and Samir appeared on the monitor. Through hidden desk speakers, Naseer heard Walloway's hard soled shoes reverberate off the hardwood floor. He shifted the MARK 23 to his left hand, grabbed the mouse and clicked the mute box. He figured it would be best to conceal his weapon, so he slid the middle desk drawer out a half-foot and placed the handgun inside. Easy enough for him to retrieve, if necessary.

There was a sharp rap at the door. Large knuckles struck three times in rapid succession.

Naseer reached under his desk, pressed a button. A click from across the room signaled that the door had been unlocked. The knob turned, the door swung open. Samir stepped inside. He extended his arm and ushered Walloway into the office. Walloway walked toward Naseer's desk, stopped, extended his hand.

Naseer declined to take the man's hand. Instead he pointed at a chair and said, "Sit."

Walloway fell back into the chair, crossed his right leg over his left. "What's this all about?"

"They are ready to meet with you," Naseer said.

"Who?"

"My people."

"If they are your people, why the hell do *I* have to meet with them?"

Naseer sat back, smiled. He rhythmically tapped his fingers on the ledge of the open drawer that held his handgun. The weathered wood there felt like sandpaper. Thornton Walloway had become more of a pain than he was worth. Naseer had the money to fund this entire operation. But he needed a patsy. He planned for Walloway to be that guy. The man had money, a need to fit in, and a lack of common sense. However, Naseer began to doubt he could deal with the man much longer.

"I say that only in a sense of the word, Thornton. These are people I have done business with in the past. They have reached out to me. They are willing to do business with you. You want to work with me, and therefore, with them. Only thing is, they want to meet you first."

"Yeah, whatever. When?"

"Tomorrow morning at eight."

"You had me come out here to tell me to meet again tomorrow morning?"

Naseer smiled, said nothing. Everything was a power play.

Walloway's cheeks turned red. "I'm beginning to wonder what you even bring to the damn table, Naseer. It's my money being used. My contacts that are going to get the right people to look the other way. My guys that are going to be doing the heavy lifting."

"If you want out, the door's right there." Naseer extended his arm, pointed at the door. "We'll get by with or without you."

Walloway's entire face reddened. He forced air in and out of his wide nostrils. A wheezing sound emanated from his throat. He sat still, hands gripping the padded leather chair arms.

"OK, then. I'll call later with the location of the meeting."

"One more thing," Thornton said.

"What's that?"

"Jack Noble. You turn anything up on that?"

Naseer nodded.

"Well?" Thornton said, arms out, palms planted on the desk, their heat forming a ring of condensation around his hand.

"He's here to kill you."

PART 2
EPISODE 12

CHAPTER 14

JACK DROVE FOR AN HOUR BEFORE HE FINALLY MADE THE decision to turn on the GPS. The navigation system confirmed that he had been traveling in the right direction. He was only a few miles from Dottie's house. He didn't plan on returning there, but he wanted a hotel close enough that he could get to her in a few minutes if necessary.

The time Jack had spent lost did him some good. Things had happened so fast that he hadn't had time to formulate his own plan. He had expected he'd have time to perform some reconnaissance and map out the hit ahead of time. While not one to step out of the way of opportunity when it presented itself, attempting to take advantage of the situation outside the tailor's shop had been out of character. There were too many things that could have gone wrong. At the time he'd been pissed at Mason for interfering. Now he knew the man had done him a favor. If Jack had pulled off the hit, he might now be sitting on a metal bench, shackled and confined in a nine by nine cell.

So Jack decided that the best option was to wait for the moment when preparation and opportunity met. Random chances had to be ignored from now on.

He began to feel the need for a partner now that a third party had become involved. He was concerned that MI5 had been added to the mix. He couldn't discount that MI6 might be involved as well since they were the agency that monitored worldwide events and likely notified MI5 to his presence.

Who could he get to help? His closest trusted option, Pierre, was laid up in a hospital in France. Although Jack planned to visit the man after he completed his work in London, he knew that the Frenchman would be of no use to him in this situation.

Jack reached inside his coat and retrieved his cell phone from an interior pocket. He dialed a familiar number, placed the phone to the side of his head, listened to it ring. He glanced up from the road and noticed at the last possible moment that the traffic light had turned red. He slammed on the brakes, reached for the steering wheel with both hands, dropped the phone. The car screeched to a stop halfway into the intersection. Horns blared, old men stared. One waved an obscenity at him. Jack waved back, then lowered his hand down between his knees and felt along the floor for the cell phone. It didn't take long to find it. He looked at the display and saw the cell was still connected, so he pushed the speaker icon. Still ringing. Jack kept the line connected and it kept ringing, never diverting to voicemail.

Finally, he hung up and redialed. Perhaps he'd hit an inadvertent number last time.

The line connected, rang. No answer. No voice mail.

"Come on, Bear," Jack said. "What's going on?"

He knew what was going on, though. He had dialed Bear's forwarding number. In the past, it had always rang to whatever phone the big man had on him. It was obvious that Bear had removed the forwarding. Now it rang into emptiness, drifting away like a wayward asteroid that had recently passed by Earth and been sling-shotted around in orbit, hurled back out toward deep space.

He couldn't blame Bear. The man had found peace in his life, had Mandy to live for. Her life had been at risk twice because of Jack. It was in Bear's best interest to stay away from him.

Still, Jack figured that perhaps there'd been a mistake with the forwarding number. So he did something he'd never done before. He dialed Bear's personal number direct.

The line didn't ring though. Instead, there were a series of tones and then the voice of a woman who'd probably been dead for twenty years came on the line and told him that she was sorry because the number he was trying to reach had been disconnected. And, unfortunately, there was no more information available that she could provide.

Now this didn't mean that Jack couldn't reach Bear if he wanted to. He still had connections that could find anyone, anywhere. But it was obvious that his friend had moved on and wanted to maintain his distance and obscurity.

It was for the best, probably.

Jack decided that in a few months he'd find Bear. At the very least, he wanted to make sure his old partner received his cut of their earnings.

That left him with no one to turn to, except for maybe Leon. Dottie trusted him, which meant that Jack should be able to as well. Her opinion had held weight with him in the past. This time was different, though. He couldn't place his finger on why though, and he couldn't shake the feeling.

The other option was asking Mason for help, whether from the man himself, or one of his agents. But that'd be a dead end. Jack knew it. They were willing to pay him to do the job so they could distance themselves. He figured it wouldn't hurt to ask, though. Maybe it would result in Mason recommending someone from outside his organization.

So Jack had three choices. Work alone, work with Leon, or work with an unknown agent. Each presented positive and negative aspects. Leon had Special Forces experience and that could not be discounted in a situation like this. It didn't mean he was a perfect partner, though. Jack had been around many guys who fit the same profile, and rarely did his and their methods mesh. Anyone Mason knew would have a background similar to Jack's, which meant they might be able to follow his methods without too much instruction. The problem was he didn't know if Mason was trustworthy, and anyone he provided might be there to spy and give a firsthand account back to MI5. *Boom, roasted* was the thought that came to Jack's mind.

Working alone was the only option that made sense. If something went wrong, Jack would be the only one responsible and he'd only be accountable for himself. Better that way, he figured.

He spotted a hotel a block ahead, on the right. He slowed down, pulled into the lot, parked behind the hotel. Twenty minutes later he was in his room, on his back, close to asleep. The cell phone rang, the one Dottie had given him. He answered it without first checking the number.

"It's Leon," the man said. "I have the things you requested. Where are you?"

Jack told Leon the name of the hotel and Leon said he'd be there in a half hour.

CHAPTER 15

CLARISSA AVERTED HER EYES IN TIME TO AVOID THE STARE OF the older man dressed in the designer suit. She entered the house. He exited. She felt him leering at her, even after she passed. She felt certain if she turned her head, she'd see him looking back at her.

"Hello, doll," he said.

She smiled, nodded, didn't look back.

"I said hello."

"And I heard you."

He said something else, but she'd already passed through the foyer and turned down the hall that led to Naseer's office. He had called her a few moments before and told her he wanted to see her. Fortunately, she was close to home. She did not want to have to answer to where she'd been all day.

The hall lights were dimmer than normal. The hallway felt muted, warm. She took a few deep breaths before reaching his office, then stopped shy of the door. She straightened her shirt and slacks. She felt silly doing so. She knew that Naseer watched the hallway on his computer monitor.

Clarissa heard the door unlock. She reached for the knob and pushed the door open and stepped inside. Naseer didn't look up as she entered his office. He nodded once while his stare remained glued to his monitor.

"Who was the old guy?" she asked.

"Just an old guy," he replied.

"Was that the British creep?"

"I thought I was the British creep."

"You are, and I'm guessing he's your twin?"

Naseer laughed and his gaze broke free from the monitor.

"I think his suit alone cost more than my entire wardrobe," she said.

"You do wear some rags."

"Yeah, but I make those rags look good."

"That you do."

"So, what did you want to see me about?"

Naseer glanced back at his screen, clicked his mouse a few times while jerking it side to side, then returned his focus to Clarissa. "I have a meeting in the morning."

"With that old guy?"

"Why are you so interested in him?"

Clarissa shrugged. "No reason. He just seems…different."

"He is different. Anyway, he is of no consequence. The reason I am telling you about my meeting is that I am likely not going to return for a few days. They may need me elsewhere, just for a little while."

"OK."

"You may want to consider traveling for a few days. Perhaps take the train to Paris and replace those rags you are wearing." He reached down and pulled open his middle desk drawer. He smiled, reached inside, pulled out a wallet and placed it on the desk. "There's about fifty thousand in euros and traveler's checks in there. That should cover your expenses."

Clarissa took the wallet and stuffed it in her purse without inspecting it. She suspected it contained a bug or a tracking device.

"Why can't I stay here?"

"It might not be safe."

"It'll be safe when you get back?"

"Safer than when I'm not here."

"Are you worried about external forces? Or internal presences?"

"Sometimes I think you are too sharp to be with me."

"You're probably right."

Naseer leaned forward. "Go on, leave me. Book your ticket as soon as you get back to your room. I want you to leave first thing in the morning."

"Yes, sir." Clarissa rose, left the room. She felt him watching her on his monitor as she made her way through the halls to her room. He had every square inch of the place covered. That probably included her room. Would he watch her all night? She figured he had better things to do, but she wouldn't take any chances with the wallet until she'd left the house.

So she opened a drawer and placed the wallet in the back, under a stack of shirts. That would make it difficult for a bug to pick up anything she said.

Ten minutes later she had booked her train ticket to Paris. Whether or not she was going was another story. She needed to check in with Sinclair and update him. He might have something she could do tomorrow. Calling him from the house scared her, though. Naseer was a paranoid man. And rich. Very rich. The combination of the two meant he had nearly every inch of the place under surveillance. She'd combed her room and found nothing, but that didn't mean there wasn't something there. Even the bathroom had to be considered risky.

She decided to take a walk. She stuffed her cell phone down her pants and left her room and navigated through the house, taking a route that limited her exposure and reduced her chances of running into Naseer. She passed Samir near the foyer and said hello. Aside from returning her greeting, he ignored her.

She stepped outside into the cool evening air. The sweet scent of cherry trees in bloom enveloped her. They lined the quarter-mile long driveway and littered the property. Pink blossoms, dark and pale, floated through the air like bloodstained snowflakes. Clarissa dragged her feet along the ground, creating trails. The bare space quickly filled in as fresh blossoms landed.

Mindful of lingering too long, Clarissa started down the driveway. The further away from the house, the better. She reached the end of the drive-way. There she turned right and walked another block. Aside from one passing car, the street was deserted. She pulled out the cell and placed her call.

Sinclair answered.

"I need to know what you know about Jack Noble being over here," she said.

"Funny," Sinclair said. "I was going to say the same thing to you. How did you find out about that?"

"Naseer was on the phone and mentioned his name."

"What does Naseer want with him?"

"Nothing. It was whoever he was talking to. The guy wanted Naseer to dig up any information he could find on Jack."

"OK, then. Well, shortly after you last saw Jack, he received a call asking him to do someone a favor."

"He's here to kill someone."

"Presumably."

Clarissa knew there was nothing to presume. People didn't have Jack travel four thousand miles for nothing. She couldn't tell if Sinclair knew the details and chose to withhold the information from her. She sure didn't plan to offer up the information that Brandon had divulged to her the night before.

"And I'd recommend you stay away from him, Clarissa. No good can come from getting mixed up with him over there. You'll blow your cover, and we'll have to start over. Correction, I'll have to start all over. You'll find yourself in Alaska for three months."

"Yeah, yeah. Nothing's getting blown, don't worry."

"What else can you tell me?"

A heavy gust of wind blew by, carrying with it a wave of cherry blossoms. Strands of her hair covered her face. She tucked them behind her ears while waiting for the breeze to die down.

"Big meeting tomorrow. Something is going down. He wants me to go to Paris for a few days."

"Interesting."

"You know anything about it?"

"No. Do you?"

"Not really. Ran into some older British guy when I returned today. I believe he's involved in some way."

"Got a name?'

She decided to feed one piece of information to Sinclair in hopes that it would get the man to reciprocate. "Walloway. I remember hearing the name Walloway."

There was silence on the other end, and Clarissa figured Sinclair had punched the name into his computer and now waited on the results.

"That ring any bells with you?" she asked.

"Thornton Walloway," Sinclair said. "He's a billionaire, made a lot of money from a glass company. We believe he has terrorist ties, but nothing has ever been proven. He's stayed pretty clean, although there was an incident last year in Monte Carlo."

"What happened?"

"Um," Sinclair clicked his tongue against the roof of his mouth three times. "Domestic issue."

Clarissa said nothing.

"Well, if he's involved with Naseer, or anyone else for that matter, he is quite discreet about it. Anyway, I need you close to that meeting."

"I don't know how. He gave me a wallet with a lot of cash. I'm guessing the wallet's bugged. Probably stuck a tracking device in there."

"Tell you what, Clarissa. If I can find out where this meeting is, I'll have someone meet you at the train station. You give them the wallet and then you go to the meeting."

She didn't like the sound of that. "If he spots me near there then this whole thing is over."

"You're right, you're right. Dammit, we've got to get eyes on this meeting."

"Let me reach out to Jack. He can help."

"Not a chance. He's not right for this kind of work anymore, Clarissa. You involve him, you are going to get him killed. Might get yourself killed, too."

"Just a thought, that's all."

"OK."

"OK, so I'm getting on a train for Paris in the morning?"

"Yes, but call me before you board, in case something changes."

Clarissa said OK and goodbye and hung up. She didn't like it, but she knew she had little say in the matter. They'd worked hard to get her into this position, and ruining her cover was not an option.

She walked up the blossom stained driveway, returned to the house, to her room, hid the cell phone in the false bottom of her bag. Then she went to the dining room for dinner. She found the room empty, which suited her fine.

Halfway through her meal, Samir entered.

"Naseer wanted me to make sure you are all set for tomorrow. You have your ticket for Paris?"

Clarissa nodded.

"What time?"

She swallowed her food and managed to say, "The train leaves at eight a.m."

"Check with me before you leave. I may be accompanying you."

Clarissa smiled and nodded, portraying the image of calm to Samir. On the inside, panic took over. Her heart raced, her palms dampened, her lungs tightened. Why would he travel with her? Had Naseer found her cell phone and bugged it? Did he have parabolic microphones in use? She might have been in range of them while speaking with Sinclair. Could that be the reason he skipped dinner tonight? If that was the case, and this is how they planned on taking care of the matter, she felt confident she'd have the upper hand against Samir. Nothing about him intimidated her.

"OK," she said.

Clarissa waited until Samir left the room. She finished her dinner and retired to her quarters for the night.

CHAPTER 16

JACK AWOKE TO A KNOCK AT HIS DOOR. IT HADN'T STARTLED him or caused him to jolt upright. He simply opened his eyes. His hand slid out from under his head and down his side until it found the handle of the Beretta. He waited for another knock if for no other reason than to verify there was someone at his door. Why expend energy if he didn't need to?

He heard the second knock, looked at his watch. Thirty minutes had passed since he spoke with Leon.

Right on time.

He swung his legs over the bed and took his time getting up. Another sharp knock. He reached for the door knob with his left hand. Lifted the Beretta to chest level. An awkward set up for sure. The door opened from left to right. He jarred it a crack. Leon stood on the landing carrying a black duffel bag and a cardboard cup holder containing two paper cups filled with coffee. Steam escaping through the thin sliver in the lids. Jack took a step back to his right and opened the door.

A minute later the men sat across from each other at the small round table on the opposite side of the room next to the wide window. A slice of yellow light from a street lamp split the table in half. Jack on one side, Leon on the other.

"Everything you need is in that bag," Leon said.

"Show me," Jack said. He reached over and pulled the blinds open. The windows were mirrored on the outside, so he had no concern over being watched.

Leon rose, took two steps to his right toward the bed and unzipped the bag. He pulled out an M40 sniper rifle, held it out for Jack to inspect.

Jack waved him off with a flick of his left hand.

Leon placed the rifle on the bed, reached back into the bag and retrieved an HK MP7 with a suppressor affixed to the barrel. Once again, he held the weapon out. This time Jack reached out and took the submachine gun from Leon. He set it down on the table, to his right.

"What else?" Jack said.

Leon smiled, reached in the bag a third time. He pulled out a Beretta M9.

"How'd you know?" Jack asked.

"I've got my ways." He placed the 9mm on the table and sat down. "No lethal pens or any nonsense like that. You'll have to do this like a man."

Jack rolled his eyes. The SAS prick had no idea how to handle a job the way Jack did. "Already figured I wouldn't be able to pull off a covert job like that."

Leon nodded, turned toward the window. Jack watched the guy's eyes reflected in the window. They darted left and right. The man wore a concerned look on his face.

"What?" Jack asked.

"Nothing," Leon replied.

"You sure? Doesn't look like nothing."

Leon's eyes shifted to the right, stopped when they met the reflection of Jack's in the window. "You should let me partner with you."

Jack's stomach tightened. He had already discounted Leon as a potential partner. He had no idea of the man's skill set other than that he used to be SAS. And used to be's didn't mean anything to Jack. Leon wouldn't have done Jack a lot of good even when the guy was active duty special forces. Then again, given the circumstances he would likely be facing, having a man with Leon's knowledge there might be helpful. There was no way to know if the skill set remained though.

"What d'ya say, Jack?"

"What's your motive?"

"Pardon?"

"Your motive," Jack repeated. "Why do you want to do this?"

The guy shifted in his seat, brought his head around slowly. He interlaced the fingers of his right hand with his left. There was silence between the men for a minute. Their eyes were locked. Neither blinked.

"I want to see his life end. You don't know the things that man has done, Jack. You just don't. Dottie doesn't know the half of it. Before I was her bodyguard, I was his. I went everywhere with him. Saw the things he did. He's a real bastard, Jack."

"Then you are definitely out."

"Why?"

"It's too personal."

"It's personal for you too."

"But I know how to control myself."

"You think I don't know how to control myself? I'm SAS, man."

"No, I don't think you can. And you *were* SAS."

"I've worked privately ever since."

"You're a glorified personal assistant."

Leon's cheeks turned red, a thin film of sweat coated his forehead. He clenched his fists and slammed them on the table.

"See," Jack said. "You can't control your temper. What happens if we get into position and you see Thornton and you decide that you want to do more than just put a bullet in between his eyes? That rage starts building. You move in. You blow our cover. Next thing you know, you're dead. Or worse, we both are. Or even worse than that, captured. See, a guy like you is gonna want to make a point. You want to show Thornton that you're the boss, not him. You want to come down on him and make him pay with pain for the things he's done."

Leon said nothing.

"I could care less about all that stuff. I just want him dead, and then I want to move on with my life. I knew coming out here was a damn mistake. But bringing you along would compound that mistake by a thousand. So stay home. Stay with Dottie. Do your damn job so I can do mine."

Leon lowered his head. He brought his hand to his face and rubbed his cheek. "You're right, Jack. I want revenge."

"Then let me take care of Thornton. Alone."

A moment passed, the men said nothing. The silence stretched on for five long minutes. Finally, Leon rose and walked to the door.

"Make him suffer," he said.

Jack nodded, said nothing. He waited for Leon to leave the room, then he engaged the security lock and returned to bed. As he reached for the TV remote, his cell phone vibrated on the nightstand.

"What now?"

He grabbed the phone, didn't recognize the number.

"Hello?"

"Jack, it's Mason."

"What?"

"Nice to talk to you too, mate."

"Piss off, Mason. What do you want?"

"There's a meeting tomorrow morning. All the principal parties will be there. It's in an old warehouse, abandoned. We need to get you in there tonight."

Jack took a deep breath, exhaled. "OK, tell me where."

"I'll send a guy out to get you."

Jack didn't like that idea, but he had little choice in the matter. "OK, I'm at the—"

"I know where you are. He'll be there at two a.m."

"Great." Jack pulled the phone away from his head.

"And Jack..."

He didn't bother to listen. He pressed the red end call button and tossed the phone to the foot of the bed.

CHAPTER 17

A MUSCULAR MAN WITH A SHAVED HEAD ARRIVED AT TWO A.M. He did not introduce himself. Simply asked if Jack was ready. He had been ready since quarter after one, so naturally he replied yes. They left in the man's car, a vehicle so small their shoulders touched. He mentioned that the vehicle was more economical since it ran on battery power.

Five minutes into the drive the guy said, "Hungry?"

Jack said, "Nah."

The guy said, "OK, we'll stop."

They pulled behind a twenty-four hour Italian restaurant in Soho. Despite the hour, the place was packed. The guy ordered meatball marinara. Jack ordered coffee and two slices of cheesecake. He figured pasta would be just as heavy in his stomach, so why not get his favorite dessert instead. They were in the restaurant for thirty-five minutes, during which time neither man spoke. Jack glanced at the guy occasionally, only to find the man staring right at him. It made him a little uncomfortable.

At three in the morning the guy drove past the warehouse.

"That's it," he said.

Jack turned his head, focused on the warehouse as they drove by. "Big place."

The guy nodded. "That it is, my friend."

The car rolled to a stop two blocks away. The guy got out and started walking toward the warehouse. Jack waited a second, then joined him.

Wide-spaced street lamps cast hazy orange pools of light. The wet street glistened. Their muted footsteps echoed off the buildings that made up the industrial corridor. A dull mechanical roar persisted.

They stopped in front of the warehouse's main entrance. The guy reached into his pocket and produced a key. He inserted it into the lock, winked at Jack, turned the key.

"How'd you get a key to the place?"

"After we heard where the meeting was to be, we sent a guy."

Fair enough, Jack figured.

The man pulled the door open, stepped inside. Jack followed. Heavy, musty air enveloped him. Every step they took resulted in dust kicking up two feet into the air. Jack thought he could feel the mold spores entering his respiratory system, anchoring themselves to the lining of his lungs. If the place was still in use, the men and women that worked there probably had one hell of a lawsuit to file in the future.

Jack stopped in the middle of the room. Something scurried across the floor, a few feet away. He shifted his duffel bag from his right hand to his left. Wrapped his arm around his back and took hold of his Beretta.

"Just rats, mate." The guy closed the door, switched on a flashlight equipped with a red filter. The diffused light was less likely to be noticed from the outside should someone be watching the dilapidated old building.

Jack followed the light, committed the room to memory.

"Figure they'll be gathering over there." The guy panned the light to his right, Jack's left, the north end. The space was bare. Beyond it a bunch of trash and wooden pallets.

"Why?" Jack said.

"Why not?"

"It's out in the open."

"No one gonna be in here, mate."

"Why not the office?"

The guy shone his light along the floor and brought it up at the south end of the room. Aimed it at the office. "Take a look."

Jack walked toward the office. The door had been boarded shut. The glass pane covering the front was cracked, but still intact. Unless these guys wanted to spend precious minutes deconstructing the barrier, they'd meet on the warehouse floor.

The man raised his arm, pointed a bloody beam of light to the corner of the ceiling. "Up there."

"What about it?"

"That's where you should set up."

Jack wasn't keen on being told by the guy where he should wait and later carry out his job. "What about the other corner?"

"Well, for one, you won't have the same kind of cover. Look up there."

Jack did. He saw a solid metal box, maybe six by nine feet, about six feet tall, a slit that looked to be six or seven inches high spanning the width of the front.

"Now," the guy said as he swung his arm toward the other corner. "Look up there."

Jack saw a platform wrapped with steel railings. A good spot to shoot from, but no cover. He'd be spotted the moment they entered the warehouse. Up in the box he had protection. And if something happened, and they decided to investigate, he could pick them off one by one.

"See my point?"

Jack nodded, aware that the man might not see the gesture in the dark. He thought about asking about the other end of the room, but figured he'd have to investigate on his own after the guy left.

"What you got in that bag, mate?"

"Rifle, spare pistol, sandwich."

"Mind if I take a look?"

"Yeah, I do mind."

The guy shrugged. "Whatever. Here." He held out a spare flashlight.

Jack grabbed the solid handle, felt the weight of it in his hand. If necessary, he could use it as a weapon. Of course, things would have to be pretty dire to do so. He switched it on, focused the beam toward the corner of the room, started toward the ladder.

"Wait," the guy said.

"What?"

The guy reached into his pocket, pulled out a small cell phone. "Press and hold five and it'll connect you with us."

"Will you answer?"

"No."

"OK. Who?"

"Someone."

"When should I use it?"

"When the job's done."

"What if things go bad?"

"Use it."

"Will they send reinforcements?"

"No," the guy paused a moment, smiled. The red glow of his light cast devilish shadows across his face. "It'll just let them know they need a plan B and they have to collect your body."

Jack turned again, headed toward the corner of the room. He heard the guy stop at the door. Said, "Hey, Baldy."

"Yeah?" the guy said, his shoulder pressed against the door, hand on the knob, flashlight reflecting off the floor.

"This turns out to be a setup, let Mason know I'm coming for him first."

The guy said nothing. He pushed through the door and disappeared into the night.

Jack waited until he heard the door close, then he walked every inch of the ground floor. He checked behind every piece of left behind machinery, moved every weathered pallet. He shone his light inside the boarded up office. He wasn't looking for anything in particular.

He returned to the ladder near the warehouse office, located in a small corridor between the office and the outer wall of the building. It led up to a thin catwalk consisting of wooden planks placed over irregularly spaced metal cross beams. The planks were gray and splintered. Every few steps he took, the wood bowed and creaked. He slung the duffel bag across his chest and grabbed hold of the railing with his left hand. It would buy him a few seconds in the event the wood below his feet gave way. There was no right railing, so the sudden drop would be painful. Perhaps enough to separate his left shoulder or bend his wrist until it snapped.

But it didn't come to that. The old wood held and Jack reached the metal enclosure. It was the only thing in the place that looked like it had been constructed in the past twenty years. He rapped on it with the barrel of his gun. The resulting sound indicated that the enclosure was thick, solid. A good place to hide out, he figured. Only thing was he didn't like the idea of being confined inside after he fired.

One problem, though. The enclosure was secured with a thick chain and padlock.

Jack pulled on the chain. It threaded through two eye bolts. The padlock connected the ends of the chain together. Very little slack. He could pull the enclosure door open, but only about four inches. Nowhere near enough for him to squeeze through. He knew he could attempt to shoot through the lock. But even with a suppressor, the sound might be heard by anyone passing by. In an industrial area like this, people worked all hours of the day and night. If one person heard the sound and called the cops, the setup would be ruined.

He saw a gap between the enclosure and the ceiling. He grabbed the ledge, pulled his head up until he could see over the top. The roof of the enclosure looked like it had been cut from a chain link fence, and below that were several crisscrossed thin steel beams. There was no way inside. He could set up on top, on the fence, but that would leave his head exposed when he took aim.

He dropped to the catwalk, shone his light across the room and scanned the perimeter of the upper level of the building. The catwalk extended another few feet to his left, then continued down the left wall. On the opposite end of the room he saw a ledge that extended out maybe eight feet. There were a few large barrels, and what looked to be two canvas tarps. He figured he might be able to take cover there.

Jack grabbed his duffel bag, slung it over his shoulder and started down the catwalk. He reached the middle of the room, heard the door below being pulled open. The door cracked open, allowing a sliver of light to penetrate inside. It started off thin by the door, expanded to maybe three feet wide at its zenith. Jack pressed back against the wall. He clicked off his flashlight, which he'd previously tucked against his stomach to hide the beam. He heard voices, but couldn't make out what they were saying. No one entered. They hung around the entrance while talking. Then the door closed, but not all the way. It remained open a crack. Still no one had entered.

Who was out there? A couple drunk guys, lost? Some guy just off work, looking for a place to get high? A whore turning a trick?

Jack kept his back to the wall and sidestepped the rest of the way to the other end. The boards creaked and bowed and bent. They felt like they were going to snap, but they never did. If someone had come inside, they would have heard the racket, no doubt about that. Perhaps they could hear it from outside the warehouse.

Jack reached the platform, took two minutes to stand in the shadows and listen. When he felt sure no one was outside, he went to work. He dragged the two barrels to the edge, separated them by four feet. He draped one of the canvas tarps over the side of the barrel to the left, pulled the tarp as far over as he could toward the outer wall. He bunched the other tarp up in between the two barrels. That's where he planned to take cover. He hoped the stretched tarp would draw glances away from his position.

He crawled under the musty tarp, laid his M40 to his right, his MP7 to his left, kept his hand around his M9.

And Jack waited. A minute stretched to ten. Ten stretched to thirty. Passersby blocked the sliver of light produced by a street lamp that spilled across the warehouse floor. The smell of cigarette smoke wafted in. He felt a slight crave for nicotine, pushed it aside. The rhythm and cadence of the voices were similar, but the tone always sounded different. Never the same people. Were they people on their way to or from work? Or was a large group of people hanging out in front of the building?

Still, no one entered.

Two hours had passed and faint traces of light, warm and bright, not artificial and contrived, filtered in through painted over windows and cracks in the exterior, ceiling and the slightly open door. A single window ten feet up hadn't been covered by paint or boards, just a bit of grime. Through it Jack saw the crest of the shimmering sun, like liquid silver behind thick clouds. Its rays dulled by the gray sky. He watched for a moment, breathed deeply, relaxed.

And then, someone entered.

CHAPTER 18

CLARISSA WALKED TOWARD THE PLATFORM, SURROUNDED BY at least two hundred other travelers. She checked the time on the large clock that hung at the north end of St. Pancras International station. Seven-fifty a.m. She looked up, mesmerized by the intricate latticed steel beams. Though stuck in the middle of a mob of people, she felt happily alone. No one here knew her. No one had any idea of her past. They knew none of what she did for a living. She was simply Clarissa, an American tourist traveling from London to Paris.

Alone.

A fact that had not gone unnoticed by some male travelers, and possibly a few females.

She ignored them, though. Kept her eyes focused ahead.

The crowd thinned slightly as people veered to the left or right to get their tickets or a paper or grab a cup of coffee or a Danish.

Clarissa carried on, forward. So did a portion of the crowd. Together, they made their way to the platform and stopped in waves. She found herself about a quarter of a way from the front of the line. She stood motionless for a few moments. Forced air blew warmed recycled air down. She checked her watch. Seven-fifty-eight.

She heard a low hum in the distance, possibly the train. Maybe the sounds of people talking.

The hum grew louder. She leaned forward, looked up and down the track. The train appeared, yellow and white. It pulled into the station, brakes squealing sharply. A blast of hot air blew past her, lifted her hair into the air. She inhaled deeply. It reminded her of the subway in New York.

The train came to rest. Air brakes settled, steel and fiberglass popped and groaned. It sounded like an old man flopping into his worn out recliner.

Doors slid open, stale air eased out. Clarissa stood at the front of her line and was the first to enter the cabin. She assessed the seating area and made her way to the end, took a seat that placed her in the corner, allowing her views of everyone inside as well as anyone who entered from the doors on either end.

Fifteen minutes later, they were in motion. She leaned back, tried to relax. Not an easy thing to do.

Twenty minutes after that, they approached the tunnel. She recalled watching a show that detailed the construction of the tube that ran beneath the English Channel. The Channel Tunnel. Some referred to it as the Chunnel. From what she remembered, it'd take thirty minutes or so to pass through.

Five minutes after the train entered the Channel Tunnel, she spotted the man as he stepped through the far door. He locked eyes with her, walked toward her. He had dark hair, shoulder length. Long stubble lined his jaw, framed his chin and his mouth. A quick smile formed on his lips. He stopped three feet in front of Clarissa, looked to her left, then right, then sat down next to her.

"Clarissa," he said.

She said nothing.

He leaned in closer, staring at her the entire time.

"What do you want?" she said.

He smiled, shrugged. "Nothing really."

"Then move along, sport."

"Don't be like that, Clarissa."

"How do you know me?"

"I just do, Clarissa."

"Don't use that name here."

"Why not?"

"Who do you work for?"

"You know the people."

"CIA?"

He shrugged. "Maybe."

"Are you with Naseer?"

"No."

"Tell me."

"Why should I?"

She reached into her pocket, wrapped her hand around the .22 caliber pistol she had placed in there. She lifted her hand, gestured toward him. "Who are you?"

His smile retreated. "You wouldn't."

"I would."

His eyes narrowed. She figured he was sizing her up.

"Name's Spiers. I'm in a group similar to yours. Mainland Europe, mostly. Some North Africa. You could say the job I do is more like what your Randy does."

Randy is there to clean up the messes they made.

Clarissa gripped the handle of her pistol tighter, threaded her index finger between the trigger and trigger guard.

"I got a call last night about a potential problem. They sent me your name, picture, general information. Told me to get to London and get on this train. So I did."

"What are your orders?"

"Aside from meeting you here and escorting you to Paris, I don't know."

"What do they want with me there?"

"Like I said, I don't know."

She shifted in her seat, straightened her aim.

He glanced between her face and her gun, then back again. "Don't worry. If I was here to take you out, they would have told me right away so I could make the necessary preparations."

She glanced around the train. Saw nothing but blank stares and nowhere to run.

"You'll only make it harder on yourself if you run."

The look on his face told her he meant the words he spoke. She leaned back in her seat, settled in for the rest of the ride. She knew there was no getting rid of him. They emerged from the tunnel, and Clarissa shifted her focus from Spiers to the scenery outside the train.

His cell phone rang. Both of them stared at it. He answered it and held it up to his head. The only words he spoke were *yeah* and *no*. He stared at her for the duration of the call.

He hung up, lowered his gaze to the floor. He brought his right hand to his forehead and rubbed his eyes. He shook his head back and forth.

"What is it?" Clarissa asked.

"Bad news."

"What kind?"

"The worst kind."

"Involving me?"

"Yeah."

"What?"

He looked up, still shaking his head. "I have to keep you in Paris with me for a week."

CHAPTER 19

THE DOOR CREAKED OPEN, RUSTED PINS ON RUSTED HINGES. Four men, Middle Eastern, walked into the warehouse in single file formation. Jack recognized none of them. They huddled together in the middle of the room, smoking and talking in hushed tones. They spoke in a foreign tongue, one that was not familiar to Jack.

Minutes later, another Middle Eastern man walked in. He had a commanding presence. The men in the room fell silent, separated a bit from one another. All turned toward the new guy. He spoke, but again, foreign words that were meaningless to Jack.

One of the guys headed toward the opposite end of the room. He slipped around the side of the office, climbed up the ladder.

Jack reached for his MP7, pulled it forward a few inches. He had thirty rounds in the magazine and the weapon was set to three shot semi-automatic bursts. He'd aim for the man he presumed to be the leader. Maybe one of the other guys would step up, take a bullet. Jack doubted that, but either way, first shot would take someone out. How would the men react? His gaze shifted from man to man. They had the look of battle hardened warriors. Perhaps not conventional warfare. But what was that, really? It changed over time, and if nations wanted to survive, they adapted.

Jack wondered how fast another man would react after that first shot? How quickly would they figure out where the shot had come from? How many more men could he take out during that time? One? Two? All four of them?

The man at the south end of the room who had climbed the ladder now stepped onto the catwalk that crossed over the office, headed for the metal enclosure.

Why? Did Mason rat him out? It seemed odd that the first thing they did was head for the box. Not the office. The inconspicuous metal cage in the corner.

Jack waited for the guy's next move. If he stopped at the cage, then he was just being cautious. If he continued down the catwalk, then Jack would presume they had inside info and knew he'd been planted there. And if that was the case, then all bets were off. He'd start with the leader and work his way out from there.

But he didn't see where the guy would go next because the guy never made it to the cage. He hunched down in the middle of the catwalk, directly across from Jack. And he did so because the front door opened and three more guys entered. The first two were carbon copies, short, stout, white. Most likely ex-special forces. The third guy was fit, but older. And Jack recognized him.

Thornton Walloway, welcome to the show.

The first group of men formed a line, with the leader in second position from Jack's point of view. The guy held out his hand. Thornton stepped forward and shook it. Across from Jack, the man on the catwalk stayed low.

No one looked up. Not Thornton and his men, because presumably they wanted to keep their eyes on the other guys. And the other guys didn't want to give the Brits a reason to look up, so they kept their eyes fixed and level.

The stand-off benefited Jack. But the guy across the room didn't. Now Jack had to monitor the floor and the six men there, and he had to keep an eye on the guy laying low on the catwalk. What was his purpose? Was he going to investigate the metal cage? Or was he going to take position in it? Was he up there to provide extra security? Or to take out the other group of men?

Jack's gut feeling was that the guy hadn't gone up there for Jack. It was for security purposes.

With the man across the way, Jack knew that pulling off the hit with his M40 rifle was no longer an option. He had to slide back to get into position. Not a problem if all the men were on the ground floor. The ledge of the overhang blocked most of his movements. But the guy across from him had a perfect view.

So Jack moved slowly, and he pulled his MP7 closer and retrieved his Beretta M9 pistol. The former inches to his left. The latter remained held tight in his hand.

Then the leader of the Middle Eastern guys began talking loud enough for Jack to hear.

"Did you secure the materials?"

"Not yet," Thornton said.

"Why not?"

"It's not like I'm walking into a drugstore and picking up some cough syrup, Naseer."

Jack went to work on the name Naseer. He had no recollection of it, though.

"This is radioactive material," Thornton continued. "It takes some time."

Naseer placed his hands on his hips, straightened his back, rotated his head left then right. "I chose to work with you because you said you could make things happen."

"And I have. You needed muscle, I got it for you. You needed ins with politicians, MI5, I got them on the hook for you."

MI5? Mason?

"But you failed to deliver what I need for an RDD."

RDD? Jack replayed the word over a couple times. He knew it. Radioactive dispersal device. A dirty bomb. The guys were terrorists, and Thornton was right there in the middle of it.

"It's coming," Thornton said. "I just need another few weeks."

"I'm running out of time," Naseer said. "I have other sources, you know. They are outside the country, so a new set of problems presents itself. But with the contacts you've given me, I can get it here in under two weeks. You know what that means, right? You'll no longer be required."

"Then I'll deliver in a week."

No one spoke for a minute. Jack noticed the man across the way lift his torso, resting on his elbows. He wondered if the guy had taken notice of him, or if Naseer's silence was a cue for something. He pulled a scope from his pocket and aimed it at the guy. Saw him looking down. Saw his hands empty.

Saw a chance to put his rifle into a better position. The way this job was shaking out, shooting his way out would be Jack's only option.

So he reached behind, pulled the gun forward, scooted his body further into the canvas tarp. His left hand cradled the M40's barrel. His right index finger rested on the trigger, squeezed out the eighth-of-an-inch of slack. Naseer would be first, then Thornton.

Screw Mason. He'd kill them all.

Jack heard for himself that MI5 was in Thornton's pocket, and they now supported Naseer. Maybe not the entire group, but someone inside it.

Thornton must have heard of the plot to end his life. He contacted Mason, who followed Jack. The guy said he wanted Thornton taken out, yet he intervened when Jack was about to pull off the hit in the middle of the city. The guy sent Jack on a suicide mission. Why had Mason cared if Jack got caught or not? He didn't. And he sure as hell didn't care about putting Jack into a no-win situation in the warehouse.

Jack had expected three guys, hoped for two, planned for four. There were seven in the warehouse, not including himself.

Bad odds for anyone.

He had expected to be able to shoot from the safety provided by the metal cage.

It had been locked.

Did Mason know? Had he scouted the place ahead of time? Had Mason and Thornton picked it for that very reason?

But that didn't explain the man on the catwalk above the office. He had a purpose. What, though?

"A week is not good enough," Naseer said. "You've got four days."

Thornton turned, huddled with his two men. After a minute, he turned, said, "Piss off, Naseer. You'll get it in a week."

Naseer took a deep breath, exhaled loudly. He nodded twice, exaggerated movements. Thornton smiled, pleased with his small victory. The guy was a billionaire and not used to being told no, or that his option wasn't the best.

Then, it hit Jack. He knew the name Naseer. Had read a write up about him a few years ago. Naseer was a billionaire, too. Old money from what he recalled. A powerful man. He had the resources to buy anyone with a price tag. Getting materials into the country should not have been a problem for the guy. What did he want with Thornton?

Naseer smiled.

Thornton smiled.

The men behind Thornton smiled.

Jack looked across the way, scope to his eye, and saw a grin on the face of the guy on the catwalk.

Had someone opened up a bottle of nitrous oxide, or was Jack missing something?

He adjusted his stare and saw one of the men behind Thornton reach inside his coat, pull out a gun. The guy took a quick step forward, placed the barrel of the gun to the back of Thornton's head, pulled the trigger.

Two of the Middle Eastern men flinched to their left, bringing their right arms up to cover their face. Naseer's movements were opposite. He flinched right, shielded with his left. A leftie, Jack figured.

All that remained in the spot where Thornton had stood was a pink cloud of mist. It hovered in the air before settling on Thornton's lifeless body and the surrounding floor.

Naseer straightened, resumed his stance, looked down. Disgust spread across his face.

"Dammit, my shoes are ruined."

He doesn't care about the dead man, Jack thought, *only his precious shoes.*

"Well done, Owen," Naseer said, nodding to his right. "I didn't think you'd do it."

The man on the catwalk rose, headed toward the ladder.

"I gave you my word," the man named Owen said. "You didn't need that guy up there."

Naseer shrugged. "I've seen men crap on their word before. Until proven, a man's word means a little less than nothing."

"It means everything with me, Naseer."

"Did you ever give your word to him?" Naseer gestured toward the dead man on the floor.

Owen dropped his head, lowered his stare toward Thornton's lifeless body.

"That's what I thought," Naseer said. "Regardless, you've demonstrated your loyalty to me."

Owen nodded. So did the guy next to him.

"Now, the money?" Naseer said.

"I've begun the transfers," the guy next to Owen said. "We should have twenty-five percent transferred by noon. The rest will take a few weeks."

"Why a few weeks?" Naseer said.

"We don't want it to look too suspicious," the guy said.

"But within two weeks they'll know he's dead."

"Transfer it all," Owen said.

"We can't do that," the guy said.

"Do you know the codes, Owen?" Naseer said.

"Yeah."

Naseer nodded.

Owen spun and shot the other guy in the forehead. The man stood there for what seemed like two seconds too long. His wide lifeless eyes locked onto Owen. The horrified expression frozen on his face. He fell to his knees, then collapsed forward. The pool of blood that leaked from his forehead merged with that of Thornton's.

"I knew I was right about you," Naseer said.

"What'll we do about the bodies?" the guy from the catwalk said as he crossed the floor toward the group in the middle.

Naseer looked around, his stare stopping close to Jack. "Those tarps up there."

An icy chill traveled down the length of Jack's sweat covered back. He had nowhere to go. His only option would be to fight. He pushed the M40 aside in favor of the MP7. Thirty rounds in three-burst shots. Ten chances at five guys who were likely all armed.

The guy who had been on the catwalk walked toward the office, veered to the left, climbed the ladder. He walked toward the metal cage.

"Yafi," Naseer said.

The man on the catwalk stopped, placed his left hand on the metal cage, cupped his right hand over his mouth. "What?"

"Forget the tarps. It's too risky to take the bodies. We're going to burn the place down."

So Yafi turned and crossed the top of the office and climbed back down the ladder. He met the other men in the middle of the room. He and another guy moved the bodies beneath the overhang. Jack heard what sounded like crates and pallets being tossed around.

Old dry wood. A makeshift funeral pyre, he figured.

Then Owen left, followed by Naseer and the rest of the men. The door slammed shut. A clattering sound followed. Chains drug through welded-on door handles. A heavy clicking sound reverberated through the warehouse.

Jack realized he'd been locked inside the warehouse. He strapped the MP7 across his chest, tucked the M9 pistol in his waistband, held the M40 rifle in his left hand. There were two ways off the platform. The catwalk and a fast drop. He chose the drop. Quicker was better. He turned and let his legs slide off. He placed the rifle on the edge and lowered himself. Eight feet of emptiness remained between his feet and the floor. He reached over the top and grabbed the rifle, then dropped to the ground with bent knees. He rolled to his right, came to a stop and rested on his back. Pain lingered in his left knee and both ankles. His lower back felt like a weight bore down on it. He sat up, turned his head. Behind him were the bodies hastily covered in flammable materials.

He waited for the smoke and the flames. The warehouse remained dim and dusty and quiet. He took a chance and forced one of the windows open. The window was practically glued shut by years of dust and grime. After a minute of struggle, it gave way an inch. The sounds of industry at work flooded in. He rose up, peeked through, saw no one. He tried the door, which, as he suspected, bent but did not give. Chains rattled as he pushed. The men must have planned to return later to set the place ablaze.

It made sense. The best option was late at night. It'd be dark and semi-deserted. The fire would have time to spread and do the damage they needed it to do.

Jack returned to the window, took one last look around the warehouse and stared at the pile of kindling atop two lifeless bodies. Jack noticed Thornton's Breitling Chronomat. Stainless steel case and band, blue dial, black sub-dials. A good looking timepiece. It easily cost eight thousand dollars. Jack pulled it off the dead man's wrist and stuffed it in his pocket. He'd let Dottie decide what to do with it. Then he found each man's wallet, removed their identification and money and credit cards. He tossed the empty wallets on the bodies and replaced the wood he had moved.

"Good riddance," he said as he turned away.

He hid the M40 in the corner behind an undisturbed pallet, then he forced the window open a few feet and climbed through. The soles of his shoes hit the street with a heavy thud. He looked left, turned right, began walking.

CHAPTER 20

THREE HOURS LATER JACK STOOD IN THE MIDDLE OF THE ROAD two blocks north of Dottie's house. He stepped to the front of the cab, handed the driver four ten pound notes and thanked him for the ride.

By this point, there were a few things Jack had accepted as fact.

Mason had known why Jack was in town. If the guy had a part in what Jack had just witnessed, then he might be waiting for him at Dottie's. The guy might have even tied up any loose ends there. In fact, Dottie had told Jack not to return to the house. She wanted him to stay at a hotel. She'd feared for their safety from the beginning. Why take such a risk? Thornton had already placed himself on a bad path, one that led to his death without any intervention.

The house stood on the east side of the street. Jack walked on the west. He passed by, not too fast and not too slow. He glanced over every few steps. The semi-circle driveway appeared to be empty, but high hedges blocked part of it. The house appeared empty too, at least from what he could see. The drapes were drawn, the windows closed. After he passed the property, he crossed the street and turned left, then left again, placing him on the street that ran parallel behind the house. He recalled that the lot behind Dottie's had been vacant. Nothing but trees. The dense woods offered plenty of cover. Every step Jack took, he veered to his left a little until he found his elbow rubbing against a tree. He took one quick look to his left, then vanished into the wooded area.

The woods were thick, but the ground manicured and free from roots and shrubs. The air smelled sweet, naturally so from trees and flowers in bloom. He jogged a couple hundred feet and came to a stop ten feet from the edge of the woods. He pulled the scope from his pocket and put it up to his right eye. The windows were shut, but the blinds and drapes were open. The bedrooms appeared empty. The living room, too. He checked each kitchen window, expecting to see Dottie and Leon at the table or by the coffee maker. But they weren't there.

No one was.

Please tell me they got out in time.

He took a few steps forward, hid behind a thick oak, closed his eyes and listened. Heard a lawn mower off in the distance. Children playing. A dog barking. Wind chimes blown into motion by the light warm breeze that brushed Jack's face with air carrying the fragrance of cherry blossoms. Nothing out of the ordinary. And that was good enough for Jack.

He crossed the lawn and climbed the stairs to the door that opened up across from the kitchen table. He turned the knob, surprised to find it unlocked.

"Hello?" he called through the two inch opening. A risk, for sure. Mason or one of his men could be inside. He figured it better to draw the wolf out from its den rather than to walk right into it.

There was no response.

He pushed the door open and stepped into the kitchen. It smelled of disinfectant with a hint of lemon. The coffee pot was empty, the maker disassembled, a stack of brown filters neatly set to the side.

"Hello?" he called again.

And again, no response.

Then he saw something that he was certain hadn't been there before. A teddy bear atop the kitchen table. Brown and ragged and dressed in a pair of blue overalls. Dottie didn't have kids of her own, so it didn't belong to a grandchild. He didn't take Leon to be a father, not with the dedication he showed to Dottie. Maybe he'd been wrong. Maybe it belonged to one of the maids' kids.

He continued through the house with a plan to check each room. He didn't get past the base of the stairs, though. A car pulled into the driveway and stopped by the front door. The windows were covered, so he couldn't tell who was out there. He shut his eyes, listened, heard a man speaking, then a woman. Dottie and Leon, he supposed.

There was the sound of a key turning a lock, then the cracking of an old door that sticks in the frame, warped after decades expanding and contracting.

Dottie walked in first.

"Jack?" she said. "What are you doing here?"

"I wanted to tell you in person."

Dottie's gaze dropped an inch or two, she turned her head. Jack thought he saw the beginnings of a tear or two.

Leon walked in behind her.

"What are you doing here, Jack?"

"Beginning to feel unwanted," Jack said.

"You shouldn't have come here," Dottie said, her voice shaky. "What if someone followed you?"

"Between Leon and myself, are you really worried about a couple guys showing up here?"

She shook her head. "Not really."

Jack heard two more voices, both female, one recognizable. Dottie took a step back, reached behind and closed the door. Jack looked over her shoulder, wondered who was out there.

"So tell me, how did it go down?" Dottie said, strong and in control. She leaned back against the door. Leon stood by her side, grabbed her hand. She gripped his so hard her knuckles turned white.

"I didn't have to do anything."

"What?"

"His own guy shot him from behind then offed the third guy in their group."

"Who?" Leon said. "What did he look like?"

"I can do better than that. I know his name."

No one spoke for a few seconds.

"Owen," Jack said.

Leon said, "Why?"

"They were meeting in a warehouse with Naseer, Yafi, and a couple others. Thornton was trying to prove he had the biggest balls in the room. Didn't work out so well for him. Best I can tell, Owen and Naseer were working together before this happened. It wasn't a spur of the moment thing. It was premeditated."

"Was it quick?" Dottie asked.

Jack nodded, added, "Painless. Dead before he hit the ground. Never saw it coming."

Dottie's expression didn't change.

"Did you want it otherwise?" Jack said.

She didn't reply.

"Same thing for the other guy, although he saw it coming. Thornton was in the back of the head, the other guy was between the eyes."

Leon shook his head. Dottie wiped a tear from her cheek, the only one that fell.

"One more thing," Jack said.

"Yes?" Dottie said.

"Mason Sutton. You know him?"

"What about him?" Dottie said.

But Jack didn't reply. He didn't speak because the door opened and a memory walked in.

And she looked more beautiful than Jack remembered.

"Jack," she said.

"Erin," Jack said.

"Shit," Dottie said.

"Dottie," Leon said. "Come with me."

Dottie looked between Jack and Erin, shook her head, said, "Shit," again. Then, she allowed Leon to pull her toward the kitchen.

"What are you doing here?" Erin said.

Jack took a step forward. He wanted to smell her, touch her, make sure she was real. Her hair was darker than the dirty blond it had been seven years ago. Her eyes were still green, lips still full. She looked better than she did back then, more mature, in a good way.

"I..." The words wouldn't form.

"Auntie Dottie called you up, did she?"

Jack nodded.

"Not about me, I hope."

Jack shook his head, unable to break the stare.

"You look like you've seen a ghost, Jack." A smile, quick and playful, danced on her face.

"I never thought I'd see you again. Not after the way things ended."

"The way things ended. You mean you telling me 'Sorry babe, I gotta run'?"

"I never said that. I'd never call you babe."

She laughed and the tension between them melted, the equivalent of an inch off an iceberg.

"How long will you be in town?" she asked.

"I don't..." Jack paused, rubbed his chin. "Not long, I don't think at least."

"Oh well, probably for the best. We're getting ready to take off for a few days."

"Where are you—"

The door opened and both Erin and Jack turned their heads toward the sound.

"This is—"

"Hannah," Jack finished Erin's sentence. The girl that had occupied the seat next to him for six hours on a plane, then later a cab, was unmistakable. The fact that she showed up in the house had him wondering if her story on the flight had been a cover.

"Jack? What are you doing here?"

"You two know each other?" Erin said.

"Yeah," Jack said. "We sat next to each other on the flight over."

"What a small world," Hannah said. "How do you know Erin?"

Jack smiled and looked toward Erin, who blushed. He said, "Long story. I'm actually here on a visit to Dottie, who I'm guessing is your employer?"

"Yeah, sure is." Hannah smiled wide. "And I should probably go see if she needs me to do anything before we leave."

As she left, the door opened once again. A young girl stepped inside.

She wore a yellow and white checkered sun dress with blue buttons and a fake carnation sewn in just below the right shoulder. The outfit complimented her blond hair and blue eyes. Jack figured she was five. And shy. She avoided looking at Jack directly and took cover behind Erin. Her small arms threaded around Erin's right thigh.

"Mummy," the girl said. "Who is this?"

"You're a mother?" Jack said.

Erin smiled, shrugged, lifted her eyebrows.

"So, you're married then?" He dropped his gaze to her waist, looking for her left ring finger.

"No," she said.

"Mia."

Jack turned and saw Dottie standing at the kitchen door.

She said, "Come in here, Mia. Let your mother talk with her friend."

They waited while the little girl skipped toward the kitchen. Before she reached Dottie, she looked back and smiled at Jack. Then just as quickly, turned around and bolted past her great-aunt.

"So, that's my daughter, Mia."

"She's adorable."

"Yes, she is."

"What is she, five?"

"She's quite the character."

"I bet. Probably acts just like you. Looks like you. You probably know that."

"Mostly."

"She doesn't have your eyes."

"She has her father's eyes."

"Who was her father?"

"She likes the park, playing football, soccer that is. Natural athlete, like her father. She's faster than all the boys, even the ones two or three years older. She plays soccer against kids three years older than her. You believe that?"

Jack smiled, said nothing.

"She's not five. She's six. Six and a half, actually."

Jack said nothing. His smile faded. He took a step back.

"I didn't know," Erin said. "When we had that stupid argument, I barely remember what was said anymore. I guess something along the lines of not being able to be with a man who did the things you did. Jack, I was scared, that's all. I had no idea it would send you away. And I didn't know then. I didn't know about her. If I had, things would have been different."

"This...I...What?" His heart beat inside his chest faster than he ever recalled. He'd faced down armed men, been captured, tortured, beaten. Nothing had ever frightened and excited him as much as this moment. Chills raced down his spine. The flesh of his arms and thighs prickled. Tears swallowed up his eyes.

"She was born seven months after you left."

"She's...?"

"Yes, Mia is your daughter, Jack."

CHAPTER 21

"BEAR?"

Bear looked up from the book in his lap and smiled at Mandy. "Yeah?"

"How much longer are we gonna stay here?"

He shared the girl's frustration at being cooped up in the small motel room. When they'd left D.C., he had every intention of heading north. But a gut instinct told him drive south and go someplace he'd never been. Four hours into the trip, he made a random right turn. Now, they were an hour east of Memphis, Tennessee. He had no idea how long they'd stay, or where they'd go next. He didn't want to touch any of his bank accounts. Not yet. Not until he was sure they were in the clear. And that, he knew, could take some time.

Bear knew where he wanted to go, though. Paris. Back to Kat's.

"Please tell me?" Mandy mocked a pout.

"I don't know," Bear said. "As long as it takes."

"As long as what takes?"

He wanted to answer truthfully. But he couldn't open himself up to anyone like that, least of all an eleven year old girl.

"It," he said. "Didn't you hear me? Got wax in your ears?"

"Whatever." Mandy turned her back to him and resumed playing on the Game Boy he'd purchased for her in Charlottesville.

He flipped his book open, found the right page, but disruption interfered in the form of shouts outside his door.

"What the hell is that?" he said, rising from his chair. He glanced at his watch. Not even eight in the morning yet. He stepped between the two queen beds, slid open the nightstand drawer, retrieved his pistol. He tucked the handgun into the waistband of his khaki cargo shorts then adjusted his Hawaiian shirt so it covered the handle while still allowing him quick access.

"What's the matter?" Mandy said. "Who is that?"

"I want you to walk behind me. But when you get to the bathroom, go inside and shut and lock the door."

"Bear, you're scaring me."

He knelt, dipped his head, made eye contact at her level. "It's probably nothing, sweetie. Just being extra careful. OK?"

"OK," she said.

He knew she had put on her brave face for him. Sometimes he wondered if being around her helped the girl. He feared that the situations he put her in would do more to mess her up later in life. Maybe she'd be better off at a boarding school in France or Switzerland or wherever people send their kids when they have too much money and not enough patience.

Bear started toward the door, Mandy in tow. She clutched his left hand. He felt her breath, hot and quick, against his forearm. He glanced to his right, at the mirror, and saw her reaching for his shirt tail with one hand. There was a slight tug downward when she grabbed hold of it. He stopped in front of the bathroom, looked over his shoulder.

"All right, go in," he whispered.

She nodded, said nothing. Her small frame slipped out from behind him and disappeared into the bathroom. Most kids would have flung the door closed, oblivious to their surroundings. But not Mandy. Bear had taught her well. She carefully closed the door and turned the handle so that the latch didn't make a sound.

Good girl, thought Bear.

He crossed the remaining five feet in a couple steps, turned sideways at the waist. The voices outside rose. He cupped his hand to the door and placed his ear to his hand.

"I'm tired of your crap, Stevie," one man said. "I want my friggin' money, and I want it now."

"I don't have it," Stevie said. "I need another week, Don."

"That's what you said two weeks ago," Don said. "Yet here I am, still three large short."

The words and cadence were the same as he would hear in New York. The accents were full of southern twang, the words drawn out. This amused Bear. He found himself smiling despite the uncertainty of the situation.

He slid his foot to the left. His large frame followed. He positioned his right eye in front of the peephole. Normally, he would not have done this. The moment his face crossed in front of the small hole, it would darken on the outside, alerting anyone there to his presence. However, he felt sure that the men on the other side of the door were nothing more than common hood rats.

And Bear was a professional exterminator when it came to that kind of vermin.

One man stood tall, loose, relaxed. He leaned his elbow and forearm against the weathered wooden railing, crossed his left leg over his right. He gestured a lot with his right hand as he spoke. His hair was dark, slicked back. He wore imitation designer sunglasses. After years in New York, Bear could spot them from twenty feet away. This guy was Don.

The other guy, Stevie, stood four feet away, just out of Don's reach. He alternated from the balls of his feet to his heels, like he was ready to take off in a sprint. His hair was short, thinning, brown. His face was thin, the skin covering it pocked and scarred. He squinted against the bright sunlight. Bear figured that since the guy couldn't afford to pay his buddy back, Stevie must have figured it best to not wear his imitation designer sunglasses around Don.

Bear noticed one more thing. Stevie had had a bulge above the rear of his left hip. His left index and middle fingers twitched non-stop.

Bear cursed under his breath.

He flicked the security lock. It swung from right to left with a tiny squeak. He cracked the door open. The chatter on the other side stopped. Both men turned their heads toward him. He placed his mouth close to the gap. Turned his head to the side in an attempt to keep it out of sight.

"You guys mind taking your argument somewhere else?" he said.

"Screw you," Don said. "Close your goddamn door before I smash your face with it."

Bear shut the door. Took a step back. Clenched his fists.

The door muffled the sound of Don's laughter. The guy managed to stop long enough to say, "That guy's more of a pussy than you are, Stevie."

Bear walked toward the back of the room. He bounced around and shook his hands, like a fighter preparing for a match. But in this case, Bear was trying to calm down. He promised himself that he'd change. He needed to leave his old ways behind. He knew that. Straight was the only way forward. Petty incidents like this would only serve to get him into trouble.

But he couldn't shake the guy's smug voice from his head.

"Screw that punk."

He bolted for the door, whipped it open.

Both men turned, wide eyed. Bear dwarfed them.

"I told you to take it somewhere else."

Don shook his head and reverted back to form. "You must really want me to smash your head against the door."

Bear stepped forward. He stood inches from the man, towered over the guy. "Listen runt, I can do more than smash your face in. I can give you two solid weeks of pain so intense you'll wish I'd simply pulled a trigger and ended your pathetic little life."

Don didn't back down. He shoved Bear in the chest.

The big man didn't budge. He cocked his right arm back, poised to strike.

"Bear?"

Mandy.

Bear unclenched his fists, held his hands out in front of him. He took a step back, shook his head at Don, and continued backward into the hotel room.

The fear on Don's face faded. A smile replaced the grimace he wore moments ago. He said, "Damn pussy."

It took everything he had for Bear to close the door.

"What happened?" Mandy said.

"What are you doing outside of the bathroom?" Bear said. He clasped his shaking hands together.

"I heard you stomping by, and the door whip open, and yelling. I was scared."

He closed his eyes, took a deep breath, exhaled slowly. He knew Mandy had been frightened throughout the ordeal. As scared as she looked at that moment, he knew it had to be three times worse while hiding behind the door.

"OK," Bear said. "Look, it's going to be OK. Just a couple guys having an argument out there. They'll be gone in a—"

BOOM!

Bear yelled and pushed Mandy into the bathroom and pulled the door closed. A second shot rang out. Bear pulled his pistol. He lunged toward the door and pulled it open instead of checking through the peephole first.

Stevie stood over Don's wriggling body. He aimed the gun at Don's head.

"You just couldn't wait, could ya? You had to go and threaten my sister. Well, now you're a dead man, Don."

Don stammered, pleaded for his life. He didn't appear to be able to use his arms or legs. He had no chance of escaping. Stevie stepped forward stood over the man's chest. He leaned over, grabbed the back of Don's head with his left hand, placed the barrel of his pistol on the guy's forehead.

Don tried to lift his arms, couldn't. He had no control over his limbs. Electrical impulses caused his body to convulse. Bear figured one of the bullets severed the guy's spine.

Stevie pulled the trigger a third time. Blood and brain and skull exploded and hovered in the air like a mushroom cloud. Bear felt it coat the exposed skin of his hands and arms and legs.

"Gotta be kidding me," Bear said.

Stevie turned the gun on him. It shook in the guy's hands.

"You don't want to do this," Bear said.

The faint sound of sirens grew louder. Stevie swiveled his head around, looked up and down the walkway, over the railing at the parking lot, out at the road.

"Just run, man," Bear said.

Stevie dropped his pistol and took off running. He made it halfway down the stairs, then hopped over the railing. He collapsed on the ground, stayed there for a minute, then got up. The sirens grew louder, but Bear couldn't see the police cruisers yet. Stevie jumped into a 1980s Firebird or Trans Am. The vehicle roared to life. It darted forward, then whipped around in a semi-circle, kicking up dust and smoke and bits of gravel as it peeled out of the parking lot.

Bear stood in the doorway, arms stretched above his head, fingers gripping the trim above the door. Two cop cars pulled into the parking lot. They cut their sirens, left their strobe lights on. Red and blue lights bounced off of every surface.

"Up there," a short, stout cop said. "Don't move."

"You're wasting time," Bear said.

"Shut up," the cop said.

"This guy is toast," Bear said. "The other guy took off. Headed east. Black Firebird or Trans Am."

The short cop nodded to the other, the guy who had one foot in his patrol car and used the door to shield himself. The guy tucked his gun in his holster and slid back into his cruiser and pulled out of the parking lot.

The short cop turned his attention back to Bear. "I want you to step out of the room and place your hands on the railing."

"I shouldn't do that," Bear said.

"Do it now."

"I'm going to ruin your crime scene if I do."

The cop looked confused, unsure. "All right. Don't you move. I'm coming up there."

Bear had tucked his pistol behind his back. The cops were sure to search him at some point, and he knew that they would not let him out of their sights.

"Bear?"

He shifted his body to the right. "Mandy, I need you to come over here, but stay out of sight."

The girl approached without uttering a word. Bear lowered one hand and pulled his shirt up a couple inches. "Grab the gun, Mandy. Then I want you to take it and put it in your bag."

She took the pistol and stepped back. "Shouldn't I tuck it in my shorts, like you did? They won't search me. Will they?"

"Just hide it in your bag, sweetie. You won't get in trouble that way."

The short cop must have called for backup. Another cruiser sped into the parking lot and slammed on its brakes. The vehicle skidded about fifteen feet, kicking up gravel before coming to a stop. A few minutes later, a third patrol car pulled up. Two of the patrol cars blocked the entrances. Bear wondered why a detective hadn't showed up yet. Maybe the town was too small.

One cop stood in the parking lot while the two others approached from either end. Their hard soled footsteps alternated as they made their way up the stairs. The short cop cursed when he hit the landing and saw the bloody scene. The other leaned over the railing and threw up.

Bear figured they didn't have too many murders in this part of Tennessee.

"Just stay right where you are," the short cop said.

Bear nodded. "I'm not going anywhere as long as you guys stay cool. I saw everything that happened. I can tell you exactly what you need to know."

He did his best to shield the room from their prying eyes. It wasn't difficult for his six-six frame to block the doorway. He knew eventually they'd get inside, though, and they'd pull Mandy aside and question her. They might even get her to tell them about the gun. And all the other secrets her brain contained.

It didn't come to that, though. Bear heard the rear window slide open. Heard the sound of a bag hit the ground. Heard Mandy whisper, "There's a fire escape. I'll be hiding in the woods."

CHAPTER 22

"DOES SHE KNOW ABOUT ME?" JACK SAID.

The sun shone through a stained glass window. Splinters of red, yellow and blue light fell across Erin in disorganized patterns.

Erin shook her head, looked down at the table. "She thinks her father passed away before she turned one."

"You showed her pictures of him?"

"Yeah, I guess. I showed her pictures of some random guy. Grabbed it off the internet. A guy from Australia. Figured no chance of her ever meeting him."

"Clever."

Erin smiled, dipped her head. "I thought it for the best, Jack. I didn't think you'd ever show up again. And if you did, I planned to hide her from you."

"Didn't work so well, did it?"

"I had no idea you were here. Believe me, if I knew, we would have been clear across the country. I can't believe Aunt Dottie didn't warn me."

Me too.

"Maybe she wanted me to find out." He offered a slight smile.

"Don't kid yourself, Jack. She knows that Mia's better off not knowing you. Any of us would be."

His smile faded. The emotional impact of her words hurt more than any wound he had ever suffered. But on some level, he knew Erin's words held the truth. The people who surrounded Jack ended up dead, and not in a pleasant manner. He knew anyone he cared about was better off far away from him.

"I'm sorry," Erin said. "I have to protect her."

"I understand. It comes with the territory. Can I at least sit down with her for a bit?"

"I don't think that's such a good idea, Jack."

"Come on, you can be there too. I just want to talk to her for a few. I won't say anything about being..."

Erin shook her head, looked away. Her mouth twisted to the left. Jack knew that she was biting her cheek. A sign that she considered allowing him to talk to Mia.

"What do you say?" he said. "I just want to find out a little about her. Right now, I see this cute little girl and if I don't know more than that, I won't remember her the way I should."

Erin said nothing.

"I just want to know what she's like."

"OK." Erin rose, turned and started toward the kitchen without saying another word.

Jack followed. He entered the kitchen and saw Mia sitting at the table, eating a sandwich. He headed the opposite direction and grabbed a mug and filled it with coffee. He found it amusing that he could face any man in the world without trepidation, yet the reality of sitting across a table from his daughter frightened him.

Dottie got up and left the room. The look on her face told Jack that she did not approve. Leon remained seated, a curious smile on his face.

"Mia," Erin said. "My friend Jack used to be a spy."

"Really?"

Jack glanced over his shoulder and saw the girl's eyes widen.

"She's fascinated with spies," Erin said.

Jack walked over to the table, sat down.

"You were really a spy?" Mia said. Her gaze filled with wonder and suspicion.

Jack smiled. "Yup, sure was."

"Did you ever spy on a famous person?"

"You know I can't tell you if I did." He tilted his head forward, winked, lowered his voice. "It's all classified."

The girl sighed.

"What else are you interested in?" Jack said.

Mia told him about playing soccer and dolls, drawing and reading. She had friends, both real and imaginary. She went on for close to an hour. Somewhere in the middle of it, Leon had got up and left the room, leaving Jack alone with Mia and Erin.

"How do you know my mum?" Mia asked.

"We're old friends," Erin said.

"I asked him," the little girl said.

"Right. Of course you did," Erin said.

"We met when I was working as a spy," Jack said.

"Really?"

"Yeah, really."

"Were you spying on my mum?"

Jack laughed. "No. And of course, your mom didn't know at the time. She was quite the proper lady and wouldn't have had anything to do with me if she knew my secret."

"Were you boyfriend and girlfriend?"

Jack and Erin looked at each other.

"That's complicated," Erin said.

"Why?" Mia said.

Explaining that would confuse the girl.

"No," Jack said. "We were just friends. Good friends."

"So why have I never met you before?" Mia said.

"You know the spy business." Jack hunched over and met the girl's stare at an equal level. "Never know where it's going to take you. I haven't been in London in seven years."

Erin choked on her coffee. She cleared her throat, said, "I think it's been closer to eight or nine, Jack. Hasn't it?"

"Ah, you're right." Jack couldn't believe he had slipped up like that. "Life of a spy, I suppose. The years blend together."

The little girl giggled. The room went quiet, stayed that way for a minute.

"Did you know my father?" Mia asked.

"I met him after Jack left," Erin said.

Mia looked to Jack, who shook his head and said, "Never met him, sweetie." The words pained him as his own eyes stared back at him.

Dottie entered the room. "What do you say we go into the city today, Mia?"

Mia nodded. "I'd like that, Auntie."

Dottie turned toward Jack and Erin. "That'll give you two some time to catch up. That is, unless you are planning on leaving today, Jack."

"Not going anywhere for a while," Jack said.

Dottie met his words with a disapproving stare.

The kitchen fell silent again. Jack heard a vacuum cleaner doing its job somewhere in the house. He figured he'd never live in a place large enough to require outside help to keep it clean. Although, the thought of a maid to take care of his properties while he was away appealed to him.

Then he heard footsteps approach with intention. Fast, deliberate. They carried news. He straightened up in his chair.

Leon entered. His face looked pale. This was not the news they had been expecting.

"What's wrong, Leon?" Dottie said.

"There's been an attack," Leon said.

"What kind of attack?" Jack said.

"A terrorist attack."

"Where?"

"In the city, near Buckingham Palace."

CHAPTER 23

"HOW'D YOU FIND OUT?" JACK SAID.

"It's on the telly," Leon said.

"Show me."

Leon darted out of the kitchen. Jack rose and caught up with the man. They stepped into the study, a square wood paneled room about fifteen feet on each side. The furniture was heavy and masculine. Built-in bookcases matched. He doubted Dottie spent much time in the room. Everything in it had probably been left behind by the previous owner.

Leon grabbed the remote and unmuted the television. A frantic female reporter looked over her shoulder at the building that had been hit. Flames jutted through blown out windows. Smoke poured out and rose into the air. Dazed people stumbled around on the hazy street and sidewalk. Bodies lay on the ground. Some of them were dismembered.

"Unbelievable," said Leon.

The audio feed had cut out. Instead of the reporter's voice, all they heard was static and grinding feedback. A banner scrolled along the bottom of the screen. It read, "Suspected Terrorist Attack Near Westminster Bridge."

The image shook, then steadied. The audio returned. Voices screamed. Jack heard someone yell, "Another one!" The reporter and cameraman dropped to the ground. Another explosion ripped through the city block.

"There's been another explosion. It happened right—"

The audio cut out again.

The camera rotated from sideways to upright and focused on the shattered remains of the front of a restaurant. A large man a with red beard stood in front of it. His bloodstained apron hung in front of his round stomach. Untied, it flapped in the wind. Blood gushed from a wound on his head.

"That guy looks familiar," Leon said.

Jack nodded. He recognized the man. The cook from the back of the restaurant. And the building that had been bombed was the hotel where he had reservations.

Red looked up to his left, flinched, turned and ran.

The audio cut back on.

"Run," the reporter yelled.

The image bounced and shook and jerked as the cameraman followed close behind the reporter. Most of the image on the screen was of her head and back. Black curls bounced with every stride she took. After a few seconds, the cameraman spun around. The camera focused on the hotel. Another explosion ripped through it. A fireball exploded through the ground floor windows. The door shot twenty feet into the air and landed on top of a woman who had been knocked to the ground by the blast wave.

The building began to shake, then it collapsed. A huge cloud of dust and dirt and bits of concrete erupted upward and outward. It raced toward the camera. The cloud enveloped the reporting team in a matter of seconds.

"My dear Lord," Leon said.

Jack said nothing. He stared at the foggy image on the screen. The audio remained on. He heard sounds of the collapsed building settling and people screaming. Some for help, some out of fear, some in an attempt to be heard before they died.

How many people had been inside that building? How many people were still alive and trapped under the rubble?

The dust cloud began to thin. The frazzled reporter stared at them from the other side of the screen. She knelt in the middle of the road.

Blood covered her left cheek. Her eyes blinked slowly. Her mouth opened and closed, but nothing came out. She looked like a fish that someone had tossed on the ground beside them.

Red approached from behind her.

"There were seven of them," he said.

The cameraman angled his equipment toward Red.

Red continued. "I saw them come up from behind the hotel. Two of them came running toward me, armed with submachine guns."

The reporter appeared to become aware of the red haired man and the fact that he said something newsworthy. She slipped into news mode and back into center frame.

She said, "Can you describe them?"

"Nah," Red said. "They had masks. But they came in the restaurant, shot half the people in there."

"Including you."

He shook his head.

She pointed at the wound on his scalp. "You're bleeding profusely. Looks like you were nicked."

He wiped his palm across the top of his head, stared at his hand for a few moments. He looked up, said, "They killed the owner." His outstretched arm pointed at a mound of clothed flesh on the ground behind him. The camera focused on the body. "I dragged him out in case the building collapsed. His family deserves an open casket."

"That's the guy from the restaurant too," Leon said. "The manager who gave you a hard time."

Jack grabbed the remote, muted the TV.

"The guys that killed Thornton," he said.

"What about them?" Leon said.

"That's who did this."

"Why?"

"They talked about an RDD."

"This was simple explosives and firearms, though."

Jack nodded. "I get that."

"So why do you think it was them?"

"Because this wasn't a terrorist attack," Jack said.

"You're not making sense, Jack," Leon said.

"He's right," Dottie said from the behind.

Jack turned and saw her standing in the doorway. Dark tear tracks lined her cheeks. He said, "They had a target."

"Who?" Leon said.

"Jack," Dottie said.

Leon turned his head and stared at Jack. Said nothing.

Jack shook his head, dropped the remote. "It was me they were after, Leon. Someone set me up, and I have a good idea who it was."

"Who?" Leon said.

"I'll make some calls," Dottie said.

Jack nodded. He walked over to the window, glanced outside. His view of the street was obstructed by the high hedges in the middle of the yard and the tall fence surrounding the property. All that could be seen was the gap left for the driveway.

"What kind of monitoring system do you have here?" Jack said.

"A good one." Leon said.

"You have the back covered? Angles that cover the street?"

"Yeah, we do," Leon said. "Now you want to clue me in on what the bloody hell is going on?"

Jack pushed past the man, said nothing.

"I have contacts too, you know."

Jack stopped, turned around. "Then get on the phone and find out what they know about that bombing. Just act like you're concerned about your safety. Don't mention my name. Not yet. We'll see what intel they have first."

"Got it." Leon pulled his cell phone out and placed a call.

Jack walked to the kitchen. Mia smiled at him. Erin looked up, a worried expression covering her face. Hannah had joined them at the table and shared in Erin's worry.

"I don't think this was a terrorist attack," Jack said.

Erin looked at Mia. "Hannah, why don't you take Mia out back for a few?"

"No," Jack said. "The other room. Not outside."

"Why not?" Mia said.

"Come on, Mia." Hannah led the girl out of the room despite Mia's protests.

Jack and Erin remained quiet for a minute.

"What's going on, Jack?"

"I'm positive that explosion was an attempt on my life."

"By who?"

Jack shook his head. There was a delicate balance at work here. He couldn't tell her too much.

Erin said, "You don't know? Or you don't want to tell me?"

Jack said, "Both."

"Do you think that they believe they were successful?"

"Without a positive ID on a body? No."

"Do you think they can trace you back to here?"

Jack lied. "No." He didn't think she believed him.

"Jesus, Jack. What did you do? What did you come here for?"

Jack saw something out of the corner of his eye. He pulled his pistol out and moved toward the window. His stare darted around the backyard, scanned the woods. The scene was tranquil. The yard and woods appeared empty.

"Jack?" Erin said, her voice a little less venomous.

"I came here for a job, Erin. My last job."

"So that's why they tried to kill you? Revenge for whatever you did to complete the job?"

Jack shook his head. "I never completed it. These guys had it taken care of for me."

"Then why come after you?"

"That's what I'm trying to figure out."

"You think it's because they know that you know they did it?"

He shrugged. "Not exactly. They wanted me to know they did it. I think they planned on having me killed at the same time."

"How come they didn't?"

"It's complicated."

"So, something you did in the past then? Maybe you did something to one of them, perhaps?"

"Possibly. One thing I know for sure, you and Mia need to get out of town now."

"I'm not going anywhere unless you give me some information here."

Jack shook his head. "Still stubborn, aren't you? What do you want to know?"

"Who did this? Who wants you dead?"

Jack returned to the table. He stood two feet away, looked down. He waited a minute, then said, "Terrorists."

She inched back in her chair.

"And British Intelligence."

"Oh my God. You think they are working together?"

"As ridiculous as it sounds, it's the only thing that makes sense."

CHAPTER 24

It didn't take long for police to dismiss Bear as a suspect. The desk clerk told the cops that every square inch of public space had cameras on it. The short cop went inside the office. Twenty minutes later he returned and told Bear to stay put in his room, they'd get a statement from him later. They still wanted to know why the argument occurred outside his room.

Bear had no idea, though. Random dudes. He told them that upfront.

His large frame had done a good job of protecting the apartment from the carnage. So as soon as he handed over his blood and brain covered clothes, they allowed him to close the door. No sooner did the door click shut did Bear head toward the open window.

He stuck his arms and head through the opening. He waved his arms while scanning trees for movement. Mandy emerged from the woods. He waved her toward him. She took two steps, stopped. Reached into her bag and pulled out the gun. She held it away from her body like it was a stink bug. She shrugged, scrunched up her face.

Bear jabbed his finger toward the area behind her. She nodded then disappeared behind the trees again. When she came back into view her hands were empty.

The fact that he had just asked an eleven year old to hide a weapon caused his stomach to turn.

She ran across the open field. Her slender frame bounded gracefully through the waist high grasses. She jumped up and grabbed hold of the bottom rung of the fire escape. Her momentum carried her forward, then backward. She jerked her right shoulder back, reached for the next rung. It took about fifteen seconds for her to make the climb. Bear realized that she had dropped about six feet in order to reach the platform she now stood on.

"Wait there," he told her. He pulled the sheets off the bed and dropped one out the window. "Grab hold."

She wrapped the sheet around her right wrist and grabbed it with both hands. Bear began to pull. Mandy used her feet to scale the wall. He could have pulled her straight up, but Bear didn't bother to tell her that. Anything to build a little confidence, he figured.

A few seconds later he hoisted her over the windowsill and set her down on the table. She slid her legs over the edge and dropped to the floor where she let out a loud exhale.

"I'm sorry about that, Mandy."

She shrugged.

The awful feeling crept up again. This life appeared to seem so normal to the girl. It was only months ago that she lost her mother. Now he half-expected her to ask him for a beer.

"How were the woods?"

"Not bad. There was a nice breeze. Lots of squirrels and birds. It was kind of relaxing. Better than sitting in here."

"You didn't miss your Gamer Boy?"

Mandy laughed. "Game Boy, Bear."

Bear nodded, said nothing.

"How were the cops?" she said.

"Short."

She giggled. "Everyone's short next to you."

"Not Andre the Giant."

"Who?"

"No one. The cops were OK. The guy that runs this place caught everything on camera. They know we weren't involved."

Mandy became sullen. She retreated back in her chair.

"What?" Bear said.

"Did a man die?"

Bear hiked his shoulders an inch or two in the air. "Not sure. They took him away in an ambulance."

Mandy chewed on her bottom lip. Her stare remained locked on Bear's.

"I'm sure he'll be OK, Mandy."

She nodded. "OK."

He couldn't tell her the truth. No point in doing so. It'd only upset her. He felt confident that he'd be paying for therapy for the rest of her life. Once they settled down, of course.

"So, when can we leave?" she asked.

Bear wondered that himself. The longer they stayed in the motel room, the greater the chance of something happening. Whether it be the cops figuring out who he was, or someone else showing up with the intentions of silencing Bear. He wanted to get out of there more than Mandy.

"Tired of being cooped up in here with me?" he said.

She nodded. "And a bit creeped out, too."

"I'm sure. So am I. But the cops told me to hang around for a bit in case they needed to ask me anymore questions. I played as dumb as I could, but they saw the video. Saw me standing there when the guy went psycho on his friend."

"Are we going to stay?"

He shrugged, tapped the tabletop with his thick fingertips. *One-two-three-four.* "Maybe, maybe not. I'll decide that when I see they've left."

"Did you give them your name?"

"What else would I have given them?"

"Bear, I know you have, like, ten fake IDs."

"How do you know that?"

She shrugged, tried to change back to the original subject. "I just want to leave. Maybe we can try to go to Florida again. You have a friend there, right?"

Bear watched her for a minute. Decided to let the fake ID comment slide. There'd be plenty of time to question how she came to know that. Although, he wondered how she knew the term in the first place.

"Can I turn on the TV?" she said.

Bear nodded, and Mandy got up and grabbed the TV remote. She switched the television on. He noticed the exaggerated movement of her arm every time she changed the station. A moment later she groaned.

"What?" he said.

"Every station is showing the same thing," she said.

"What are they showing?"

"Look."

Bear rose and moved to a spot where he had a view of the screen. He flinched at the images he saw. A smoky street. Bodies on the ground. Panicked people running in every direction. A building on fire. The reporter's terrified expression. Then, the building crumbled.

"Jesus H. Christ," Bear said.

Mandy gave him a puzzled look. "What is that, Bear?"

"An expression."

"Not that. What are we looking at on TV?"

"Looks like a terrorist attack."

They remained silent for five minutes while the images streamed on the screen in front of them. The reporter's voice was nothing more than background noise. Bear didn't need her to tell him what he was looking at. He'd experienced it first hand before.

Bear's cell began to ring. He answered without thinking.

"Bear, this is Brandon."

"Brandon?" He paused for a moment. "How did you get this number?"

"I can get anything I want. You know this."

Bear said nothing.

"Anyway, turn on your TV."

"It's on."

"You watching this, Big Man?"

"I am."

"You know where that is?"

"Ticker says it's London."

"You know who's in London?"

Bear thought for a minute. He did know. "Jack."

Mandy looked at him. He forced a small smile. She didn't look convinced.

"That's right. And that's his hotel."

"You gotta be kidding me. Oh, Christ." His gut clenched. His eyes watered over.

"You know why he was there?"

Bear cleared his throat. Took an extra second or two to compose himself. "Not exactly."

"Yeah, well, I do. And it shouldn't have resulted in this."

"Can you tell me anything?"

The line went silent for a minute. Bear wondered if Brandon was debating how much he could divulge over the phone.

Brandon said, "Not yet, man. I'm working on it though. I gotta figure out who all is involved in this."

"Do you know how to reach Jack?"

"No. How would I?"

Brandon should have left it at no.

Bear said, "You knew how to reach me and I'm one of the hardest people on the planet to get a number for."

Silence. Then Brandon's breathing. "Yeah, you're right."

Bear asked the question he wasn't sure he was ready to learn the answer to. "Do we know if Jack was in that hotel?"

"As far as I know he never checked in. I checked his name, which the moron was stupid enough to fly under."

"You're friggin' kidding me."

"No, I'm not. I also checked his aliases, at least the ones I know of. No reservations or walk-ins under those. He had a reservation under his name, though."

"I need his number," Bear said. "I need to reach him."

"I'll call you or text you his number later."

"No, now."

"I have to find some things out first, Bear."

"Brandon."

Brandon didn't answer. The line was dead.

"Dammit," Bear said as he tossed his phone on the bed.

Mandy approached from behind, hopped up on the bed so she could place her hand on his shoulder. She didn't say anything. Didn't need to. Bear's reaction was enough to tell her that something wasn't right.

"I'm sorry," he said. "I'm going to London."

She nodded. "What about me?"

"I can't take you with me."

"Why not?"

"Too dangerous."

"It's more dangerous for me to be somewhere without you."

"Mandy..." Bear paused. She had a point. Anytime she was left alone or he got comfortable, bad things happened.

"If they went after Jack, they might know about me and come after me. You can't leave me, Bear."

"All right," he said. "You're going with me."

He knew the girl didn't have a passport, so he'd have to reach out to a few acquaintances who owed him a favor. It'd probably be a good idea for him to fly under a new identity as well. Perhaps he could get a package deal put together. Father and daughter. He glanced at their reflections in the mirror. Him, tall and massive. Her, short and lithe.

Yeah, he thought. *Father and daughter. It'd look legit.*

"Start packing your things," he said.

It took them less than ten minutes to pack and wipe the room down. Mandy took to the process pretty quick. After seven months with Bear she had gotten plenty of practice. Never leave a trace behind, he told her on more than one occasion.

"What about your gun?" Mandy asked.

Bear walked to the back of the room, split the blinds with his thumb and forefinger. The area behind the motel looked deserted, but he felt hesitant to retrieve the weapon now.

"You think you can find it in the dark?" he said.

Mandy shrugged. "I don't know if I could find it in the light."

He knew she was bluffing. She didn't want to go back there alone again. "All right, let's stash our gear in the car and we'll both go back there."

Bear scooped up most of their belongings. Mandy draped her backpack over her left shoulder. Her tattered teddy bear, a relic from a past life, clutched tight in her hand. Bear opened the door. The area outside the room was still covered in blood and roped off with yellow police tape. Bear lifted Mandy, angled himself out the door, and set her down clear of the carnage. Then he turned and hugged the wall and took a large step to his right.

Halfway down the stairs he pulled out his keys and held down the trunk lift button on the key fob. The black Cadillac's trunk lid popped up. He threw their bags inside. Mandy tossed her backpack on the front passenger seat.

They walked to the north end of the building, away from the office. From what the cops had told him, the owner had placed most of the motel under surveillance. He figured that the video footage would end near the woods, not in it. The easy solution was to walk a hundred yards north of the building and enter the woods there.

Once behind the tree line, Mandy led the way. It didn't take her long to locate the place where she hid the gun. No twists, turns or backtracking. She knew exactly where she had hid it. Bear reached behind himself and tucked it in his waistband. He lifted his shirt and pulled it down over the handle.

"All right, kid. Let's get out of here."

They jogged back the way they came, a hundred yards past the building, turned right, headed for the road. Then they walked south, on a cracked and uneven sidewalk.

"Shit," Bear said.

"Crap," Mandy said.

Two police cars blocked in the Cadillac.

CHAPTER 25

ERIN AND JACK SAT AT THE KITCHEN TABLE, OPPOSITE ENDS. Neither spoke. They alternated between looking at each other and staring out the window. He assumed she was trying to absorb what he'd said. The meaning had heavy implications. Rogue British Intelligence agents were working with a terrorist group. Jack assumed so at least. But why? What did they hope to accomplish? On the surface, the answer was an easy one. The terrorists had money and the agents had intelligence and access to channels that could get things accomplished quickly. There had to be more though. And why would Jack have any bearing on what they were doing? They could have saved some time and allowed Jack to carry out the hit on Thornton. Instead he watched. Something didn't add up.

And then there was this new dynamic he had to deal with.

He leaned forward and, in a low voice, said, "Who else knows?"

Erin turned her head and met his stare. "What?"

"Mia," he said. "Me being her father."

"Aunt Dottie."

"Who else?"

"That's it."

"You think she ever told Leon, or maybe her ex-husband?"

Erin shrugged. "I suppose she might have, but I don't see why. We can ask her."

Jack thought it over for a moment. "No. Not now."

A minute of silence passed. Erin said, "Why do you ask?"

"It's nothing," Jack said. "Just thinking out loud."

Erin straightened, grabbed the edge of the table with both hands. "Do you think she's in danger?"

"Anyone close to me is in danger," Jack said point blank. He paused, then added, "I think you two should leave now."

"As soon as Aunt Dottie is ready."

"No, go without her."

"That makes no sense, Jack. We're safest with her and Leon, not alone."

"But alone you two can disappear. There's no baggage holding you down. You two are mother and daughter. Dottie and Leon are former spies and SAS. You'll be scrutinized everywhere you go with them. You might feel safe, but you won't be safe."

"And then what? Can you tell me that? What am I supposed to do? Where should I go?"

Jack had no answer. Being targeted by a bomb had rattled him. It wasn't the first time someone tried to carry out a hit on him. But no one had gone to such dramatic lengths before. Perhaps his biggest concern was that he'd never checked into the hotel. Anyone with access to somebody with the right credentials could have verified that. They did, though. He was sure of that. The implications were frightening. He feared that they'd go after any place he might be, and anyone he might know.

What, or who, would be next?

He felt the slight vibration of footsteps. The faint sound they produced grew louder. Jack and Erin leaned back in their chairs, looked away from each other. Dottie stopped in the entryway. She cleared her throat. When no one said anything, she entered the kitchen and sat down at the table in between Jack and Erin. She said nothing, stared out the window. Her face was pale, solemn.

"What is it?" Erin asked.

"The agent who picked you up, Jack."

"Mason," Jack said.

Dottie nodded, said, "Yes, him. Well, I just found out that they've had him under surveillance for the past six months."

"Who?"

"Who do you think?"

The news did not come as a shock to Jack. "Any idea why?"

Dottie nodded slowly. "They believed him to be associated with known terrorist organizations."

"What kind of evidence do they have?" Jack said.

"Nothing solid. That's why they've been watching him."

"And the results of the surveillance?"

Dottie shook her head. "Nothing yet. He covers his tracks well."

"We're sure there's tracks, though?"

She nodded, looked away, said nothing.

"How much does this guy know about you, Dottie?"

"Me? Nothing. He was coming in while I was on my way out. Our paths never crossed. Even the people I know don't know him personally. He has a reputation of getting the job done. They say he always seems a step ahead."

"Well, now we know why that is," Jack said.

Dottie nodded.

Jack said, "What else?"

Dottie said, "You tell me."

"He showed up shortly after I started my stakeout. Followed me when I left. He knew the reason for my visit to London. He mentioned your name, specifically. He made what some might consider a threat toward you."

Erin looked at Jack, then Dottie. "Why would he?"

"It's nothing, Erin," Dottie said. She turned to Jack. "I'm sure he's seen my files and put two and two together."

"Only in this case that equals five. I don't see how he would deduce that."

Dottie held out her hands. "Like you said, now we know why."

Jack nodded then glanced at Erin. "Erin and Mia need to go away."

"We're leaving in an hour," Dottie said.

"No," Jack said. "Without you, and without Leon. They go alone. Hannah goes with them."

"Why Hannah?"

"She's part of your life. Anyone who is associated with you needs to go away for a while."

Dottie said nothing.

"You and Leon have to go away too. But someplace away from them."

Dottie rose. Her look turned defiant. She aimed a finger in his direction.

"I'm not letting them out of my sight," Dottie said.

"If they're in your sights then they could be in his sights," Jack said.

"I don't like this, Jack. Erin and Mia should be with me and Leon so that Leon can protect them."

"That's precisely why they need to be somewhere else. Don't you see that, Dottie?"

Dottie said nothing.

"They aren't the target. If you bring them along, they turn into collateral damage should something happen. And Leon will do his job better if he's only concerned about your safety. I don't care how good he is."

"I'm the best," Leon said from the doorway.

"Well, whatever," Jack said. "Those three will be better off someplace like Tenerife than hiding out in the English countryside or wherever you had planned."

Dottie stepped away from the table. She glared at Jack, nodded, said, "Leon, make arrangements for the girls. Tenerife is too far. I don't want them more than a few hours away, Jack."

"Excuse me," Erin said. "I am a grown woman capable of making my own decisions."

"Not now you're not," Dottie said. "OK, Jack. They go one place, me and Leon another."

"Where then?" Jack said.

Leon said, "Brussels. They can take the train. It'll be less conspicuous than flying. I can accompany them." He glanced at Erin as he said this.

Jack said, "No. You need to stay with Dottie. I have a contact in France who can meet them in Brussels."

"Who?" Dottie said.

Jack shook his head. "Let me worry about that."

"If you think I'm going to let one of your associates—"

"Look Dottie, my guys are solid and will do whatever I need them to. You know the code. If you don't want to use them, I can disappear and leave you to deal with this mess on your own."

Dottie crossed the kitchen. Her feet shuffled along the tile. She stopped in front of the coffee maker. "What about you, Jack? What are you going to do?"

"I'm going to stay right here. Got a feeling someone's going to pay a visit to the house soon. I'll be here when they do. And I'll get to the bottom of this and end it."

The foursome stayed silent for a few minutes. Jack knew better than to speak first if he wanted to close the deal. When it came down to it, he planned to do whatever he had to in order to end this whether or not Dottie complied with his request.

Finally, Dottie nodded, looked at Erin and said, "Get your things together. Mia's too. You leave from here and go straight to the train station. Tell Hannah that we'll cover any expenses she incurs. She won't be able to go by her apartment, so she can purchase an adequate wardrobe in Brussels."

Jack felt relieved and more concerned at the same time. This group that he could watch over now would soon be split up and in two different places. He would have to rely on others to keep them safe. He could only hope the nagging feeling in his gut that told him Dottie held something back was nothing more than a false alarm. He thought there were gaps in her words. Was it to hide something from him, or to keep Erin out of the loop? The less Erin knew, the better. She had heard too much as it was.

Erin left the room. She placed a hand on Jack's shoulder and squeezed as she passed him. The gesture reminded him of the relationship they shared seven years ago. He heard her call for Mia and Hannah after she slipped through the door. He wondered if he'd ever see her again.

"They probably know about her, you know," Dottie said.

"Erin?"

"And you. Your past together."

"I figured. Part of the reason why I wanted you separated."

"You don't worry about them being alone?"

"Not with the guy I'm going to send out to meet them."

Dottie shook her head. "I'm not comfortable with this."

"I wouldn't expect you to be. But you have to trust me, Dottie. I've trusted you up to this point." He decided to take a chance and lean on her. "A lot of this doesn't add up. Someone else might be inclined to believe that you had a hand in all of this. That you orchestrated it all."

"Jack, I'd never—"

"That's what everyone says right before they pull the trigger, before they plunge the blade in the back."

"You can trust me, Jack. You know that. After all these years?"

"I trust myself, that's about it."

"Is that why you want them somewhere else? You think once I get them out of your sight, I'm going to do something?"

Jack leaned back, crossed his arms. Dottie's words did not seem forced. Her shock appeared genuine. "No. I mean, maybe in the back of my head. But it's mostly because I have a feeling you are going to be followed. Someone is a step ahead of us. When the time comes, I know that you and Leon can handle yourselves. But you don't need the extra baggage of two women and a little girl."

Dottie said, "She still talks about you, you know."

Jack leaned forward. "How so?"

Dottie looked toward Leon, who excused himself and left the room.

She said, "Erin never stopped loving you."

Jack said, "She's a fool then."

"I still feel bad, Jack. I shouldn't have interfered. I wish I'd never told her your secret."

"She would have found out eventually. Probably better it happened when it did. A few more months and I might not have given up so easily."

"I wanted to tell you, but she forbade it. That's why..." Dottie turned her head and stared out the window.

"That's why you never contracted with me again. I get it. Don't feel bad."

Dottie cleared her throat, wiped a tear from her eyelid. "You've done well for yourself, Jack."

"I turned into a monster, Dottie. I did just about anything if the pay was high enough."

"And it allowed you to retire before the age of forty."

"Retire." Jack laughed. "And look at me now. I'm in England to carry out a hit."

"For an old friend, though."

"Yeah. Part of the Jack Noble Redemption Tour. Now featuring a daughter to make up lost time with."

Dottie smiled. "Right. Well, then, I suppose I should get my things ready and let you make your phone call."

Jack waited until Dottie left the kitchen. He pulled out his phone and searched for the fake name he associated with the man he wanted to have meet Erin, Mia and Hannah in Brussels. It had been a few years since he last spoke with the man. But the guy owed Jack a favor and would have no choice but to say yes.

The man answered on the fourth ring.

"Jacob, it's Noble."

"Well, well," Jacob said. "Prodigal son and all that. What do you want?"

"I'm cashing in that favor you owe me."

There was a short pause. Jack figured the man stood up or angled his body to make the call private.

"When do you need me?" Jacob said.

"In about two hours," Jack said.

"Impossible."

"How's that? You guys sit around all day long doing nothing."

"Except when we're working, which I'm doing right now."

"Cleaning?"

"Escorting."

"With your looks? Espionage has to pay a lot more."

Jacob laughed. "You'd be surprised, my friend."

"Look, Jacob, I've made more enemies than friends in the past five or six years. The only other contact I have over there is laid up in a hospital in a coma. I need you, buddy."

Jacob sighed. He spoke, but his words were indecipherable, as if he had covered the mouthpiece with his hand. Definitely not alone. The man cleared his throat, then said, "OK, I'll do it. Where do you need me to go?"

"Brussels."

"When do I need to be there?"

"Two hours from now."

"It's going to take me three."

Jack knew he'd say this. "That works. They'll be arriving in four."

"Son of a bitch," Jacob said.

"Same to you. I'll text you the rest of the information before their train arrives."

CHAPTER 26

SPIERS TUCKED HIS CELL PHONE IN HIS POCKET. HE GLANCED up at Clarissa. "Change of plans, sweetheart. We're not staying in Paris."

A twinge of panic surfaced. Clarissa feared that her initial instinct had been correct. She had to be removed. "I have to be there. What if Naseer has someone waiting for me at the station? What if he sends someone to check up on me?"

"He won't."

"You don't know that."

"Yes, I do. I wouldn't have made contact, wouldn't be here if we thought he was going to have someone meet you or check up on you. Naseer's got some big damn problems on his plate. You're nothing but a piece of ass to him. He's got no idea who you really are. Correct me if I'm wrong."

Clarissa nodded. Speirs's logic made sense. If Sinclair were there, he'd say the same thing to her.

She said, "Boss is OK with this detour?"

Spiers shrugged. The gesture did not comfort Clarissa. He said, "What Sinclair don't know won't hurt him. As long as you tell him that we had a nice stay in Paris, we'll be OK."

"And if I don't?"

Spiers smiled for a moment. Then his face turned serious. She saw anger in his eyes. "I'll tell him that you were lying. I overheard a conversation that confirmed you'd been turned by Naseer." He made a gun out of his thumb and index finger, aimed it at her. "And then I'll let him know that I had to do what I do best."

His words were met with rage. Clarissa threw her right arm forward, grabbed his crotch and squeezed. Spiers mistakenly tried to scoot away. His eyes widened. His mouth dropped open, but only the hoarse sound of breath escaping emerged. A few passengers looked in their direction.

"Don't you ever threaten me again. You got that? I didn't scrape myself out of the gutter so that some dickhead like you could try to scare me."

She released his balls from her grasp. He shifted to the edge of his seat. His knuckles turned white as he clutched his knees. He took a deep, shaky breath in, held it, closed his eyes.

"Look at me," she said.

He opened his eyes, angled his head toward her.

"I'm not scared of you, Spiers. You better think twice before you give me an ultimatum. You've got a fifty percent chance, at best, if you try to take me out."

He took a few more breaths, eased back into the seat.

"Level with me," she said. "Why aren't we going to Paris?"

Spiers said, "I owe someone a favor. I can't turn them down, not after what they did for me. Three innocents are in trouble. He's not in a position to watch over them so we're going to protect them for a couple days. We'll pick them up in Brussels and take them outside the city for a bit. I got a place we can stay where no one will bother us. No one has to know about this, Clarissa."

Clarissa shook her head. "I don't like it."

"Two women, one little girl. There's some serious trouble for them if they are found."

The words pulled at her emotional fabric. She'd faced her own share of trouble. She'd needed people to protect her in the past. If they hadn't, well, who knows how she would have ended up.

Clarissa said, "If things get out of hand, we call it in and you take the blame."

"We won't be doing that. If things get out of hand, we'll take care of it."

Despite her earlier threats, Spiers had the upper hand. If he got the drop on her, he'd make her disappear and no one would ever find the body. There'd be no body to find. Then Spiers could feed Sinclair any made up story he wanted. She didn't show up, she made trouble, he caught her on the phone with Naseer. It didn't matter. In her line of work, everyone suspected everybody else of being a turncoat. While it rarely happened, it didn't hurt to be vigilant.

So she decided to go along with his plan. If he'd deceived her, she'd take care of him before he had a chance to get at her.

"So we're in agreement?" Spiers said.

Clarissa nodded. Then she closed her eyes and leaned back.

Thirty minutes passed. They said nothing. The gentle rocking of the train had lulled Clarissa into a false sense of calm. Beyond the train tracks, a storm raged. And no matter which way she went, she'd be right on the edge of the eye wall.

Her thoughts turned to Jack. She feared that Naseer had made the connection between Clarissa and Jack. She'd find out when they exited the train. Jack had to have something to do with this, though. Coincidences were for believers of fairy tales as far as she was concerned.

Thinking about Jack left her stomach in knots. A physical pain so intense she became nauseous. For that reason, she thought less and less about him each day. But it was just like Jack to force himself back into her life after she'd made the decision to leave him behind for a second time. They weren't compatible. At least, that's what she told herself to get through the pain of shattering her own dream.

Spiers began whistling something slow and depressing. Although she recognized it, the name of the tune escaped her.

"Who are you doing the favor for?" she said.

"An old friend," he said.

"One of the three women we're meeting?"

He shook his head in response.

"Where are they coming from?"

He hiked his shoulders a couple inches in the air, looked away.

"Why are you not telling me?"

"Because I don't have to." He glanced back at her. "And because I don't want to."

"Whatever." She had at least three hours to get it out of him.

They arrived in Paris about an hour later. An hour filled with silence. Spiers exited first, checked for anyone suspicious. With so many faces coming and going, it was difficult to tell the wheat from the chaff, the good from the bad. Profiling helped, but had its weak points too. He looked back and nodded at Clarissa. She rose, walked toward the exit. At the edge of the platform the air smelled of exhaust and trash. Spiers started walking and she followed. They wove their way through the thick crowd. Clarissa scanned every face they passed. Took note of those who stood still, leaned against the walls, appeared to be looking for someone.

They reached the ticketing window. A long line left them like sitting ducks for close to fifteen minutes.

They reached the counter and Spiers purchased two tickets for the next train to Brussels.

Clarissa kept her back to the counter and studied the crowd while Spiers completed the transaction. Two men caught her eye. They were dark skinned and dressed well. Their jackets bulged by their left hips, a telltale sign they were armed. They spoke to one another, but she could tell that their conversation was pointless. A cover. They didn't look at each other, like two people would do when talking. Their eyes shifted left and right, never resting, always scanning. They divided the area in half. The man on the left took his side, while his partner watched the other side of the room.

Clarissa leaned to her right and nudged Spiers in the side.

"What?"

She whispered, "Two guys, blue suits, dark skin. They're looking for something."

Spiers turned slowly and leaned back against the ticketing counter. He worked like a pro. His eyes passed over the two men and didn't stop for even a beat. He turned back around and said, "French government agents. Definitely looking for someone. Hopefully it's not you."

Clarissa threaded her arm through Spiers's.

“Don’t get any ideas,” she said. “Just trying to make it look natural.”

Spiers reached out, grabbed their tickets. He turned toward her. “Get on the other side of me. I’ll keep you close to the wall, out of sight. But I think they would have already made a move if you were their target.”

“Unless they want to see where I’m going,” she said.

“Only one way to find out.”

They walked away from the ticketing counter. After a few minutes, they came to an intersection.

“Turn left there,” Spiers told her.

Despite her instincts telling her not to, Clarissa glanced over her shoulder. She saw the two men at the same counter they had used. Clarissa knew then that the men were government agents. They had to have used their credentials to get to the counter, because the line stretched back at least twenty people long.

One of the men turned his head in her direction. Their eyes locked. She nearly stumbled when Spiers turned left, pulling her with him. She whipped her head around, regained her balance at the last possible moment.

“They’re at the ticket counter,” she said. “One looked right at us, at me. He made eye contact.”

Spiers picked up his pace. Clarissa almost had to jog to keep up. He glanced at her. “If they’re going to do something, it’ll be now. You got it?”

“We should split up,” she said.

“No. I can’t let you out of my sights yet.”

Clarissa tried to pull away, but his grip on her tightened. Should she make a scene? That would draw attention for sure. But it might draw the attention of the wrong people. For now, the two of them had to work together.

Her instinct was to run, get a car, get out of town.

“What should we do?” she said.

“Only thing we can do. Get on the train.” He pointed ahead. The train nestled up next to the platform like a fiberglass and steel serpent stretched out on the ground. “They won’t do anything inside there.”

“They could arrest us.”

Spiers looked at her, then over his shoulder. “These aren’t the kind of agents that arrest people, Clarissa. Now come on, we best get on that train."

She couldn't ignore the feeling eating away at her. "This is a bad idea, Spiers."

He ignored her. His hand clamped down around her wrist and jerked her forward. Heads turned and eyes focused on them. A few people whispered to one another. A big guy in a baseball cap and t-shirt with cut-off sleeves started toward them. Clarissa spotted the tattoo on his upper left arm. A shield with a sword through the middle of it. A snake wrapped around the sword. Growing up with a father who commanded Special Forces soldiers, she'd seen plenty of similar tattoos.

Spiers stopped, angled his body toward the guy, shook his head. The big guy froze for a moment, then stepped back.

They weaved through the crowd. Spiers made effective use of his shoulder when people refused to move out of the way. Clarissa kept pace with Spiers and he eased up on her wrist. They reached the train. The first three cars were full.

"Let's go to the back," Spiers said.

Clarissa wasn't sure where they'd be safest, if they could be safe at all. At least in the last car the men would be forced to face them head on. If one approached from the back, he had no tactical fall back option other than suicide.

The crowd thinned the further away from the front they got. They quickened their pace to a jog. Spiers had let go of her wrist by this point. Clarissa was all-in and he must have been able to tell. They reached the final car. Clarissa boarded first. Speirs followed right behind her. Too close behind. He placed his hand on her behind. She looked back at him, fire in her eyes.

He threw his hands up in the air and said, "Sorry! Just trying to get us on board."

She continued up the steps, stopped and turned. Spiers hadn't climbed up yet. He stood half in, half out, like pictures she'd seen of trains in India, so crowded that some people rode hundreds of miles clinging to the handlebars at the edge of the cars. Spiers stared over his right shoulder.

"Do you see them?" she said.

He flung himself forward and up the stairs. Stopped in front of her. Said, "Maybe they weren't after you."

Clarissa turned, took a deep breath, shook her hands. The car was about one-third full. The rear seats were empty. She walked to the back and sat down with her back against the side wall. The vinyl seat felt cool on her flushed skin. Soon enough she'd stick to the material if they didn't turn on the air conditioning.

Spiers collapsed on the seat next to her. His head fell backward. His Adam's apple bounced up and down a couple times.

Two figures outside the train caught her eye. Two men, dark suits, dark skin, bulges on their hips.

"They're out there," she said.

"Dammit," he said.

The men stopped. One pointed inside the train car.

"Here." Spiers tossed her his cell phone. "When my associate calls, you find out where to meet the women and you take care of them. OK?"

Clarissa heard his words, nodded. She kept her eyes focused on the two men outside the train.

"Wait, what?" she said.

"You heard me," he said.

"They're not here for me. They want you."

He nodded, said nothing.

The agents approached the car. One forced the door open. They climbed the stairs. Clarissa slumped in her seat. Spiers moved across to the bench that faced Clarissa, sat down with his back to the men.

The train's air brakes hissed. The door closed again. The journey was about to start. She looked across at Spiers. He lifted his chin from his chest and met her gaze.

One of the men looked right at Clarissa. He said something to his partner, too low for Clarissa to hear. She closed her eyes, balled her hands into tight fists. Unarmed, she wouldn't have much choice if they asked her to get up. She could fight, but they'd end it with a bullet. She could only assume that Spiers handing her his cell phone meant that they weren't after her. He was their target. Why, though? Was his work in France unsanctioned? The political backlash could be huge if so.

"Vous là-bas, ne se déplacent pas."

Clarissa translated the words. *You there, don't move.*

Every muscle in her body tightened.

"I didn't do it! Let me go!"

She opened her eyes. The agents dragged a petite dark-haired woman out of her seat. The lady thrashed around at first, then her body went slack. The tips of her toes grazed the floor, her worn out soles were the last thing Clarissa saw before the woman disappeared from sight.

Spiers exhaled loudly.

Clarissa looked at him and mouthed the words, "What the hell?"

He shrugged, wiped the sweat from his forehead with his left hand. She noticed that he held his pistol in his right hand. Spiers had no intention of going with the men. That's why he handed her the phone. He planned to take them out and must have figured that one of the agents might land a shot in the process.

Spiers rose, crossed the aisle and retook his seat next to Clarissa.

"Gets the heart going, don't it," he said.

She nodded. Her heart had finally calmed down to a cool one hundred beats a minute and she was able to breathe somewhat normally again. Sometimes she doubted that she was cut out for the spy game.

"I know. Me, too," Spiers said as if he read her mind. He glanced at her trembling hands. He held out his right hand, now sans weapon. It shook uncontrollably. "Adrenaline. That's all."

The doors shut tight. The brakes hissed again. The train rolled forward.

"Two and half hours till Brussels," he said.

PART 3
EPISODE 13

CHAPTER 27

THE CADILLAC ROLLED TO A STOP NEXT TO THE POLICE station. The building was small, square, made from brick. Bear glanced at the black lettering above the double glass door. He didn't bother to read it. What did it matter? They were at a stoplight in a small town two hours away from the motel, and had nine more hours to drive.

Back at the motel, they hung back until the cops left. One of them had made the trip up to the crime scene. The cop snapped a couple of pictures, then went back down to the parking lot. After twenty minutes of waiting, the cops took off, and Bear and Mandy hurried to the Caddy and found the highway and headed east. The only drawback was that the police had his name. There was little they could do with that, though.

The light turned green. Bear dropped his heavy foot on the accelerator. Mandy made a soft whimpering sound. Bear glanced over. The cracked window allowed enough air in to lift her blond hair up and whip it against the cream colored leather seat. The girl breathed slowly, deeply. Her exhales were sometimes audible amid the wind rush and jazz playing over the radio. Bear had been amazed that he found a station that played something other than country music.

They passed an exit sign for I-75 south. It said one hundred miles to Atlanta. He thought about taking the exit and flying out of Hartsfield-Owen. He knew he could get a direct flight to London from there. The only problem was he didn't have any solid contacts in the Atlanta area. At least none that could produce two false identities in a matter of minutes instead of days.

So they drove. The sun traveled from high in the sky to deep in the west. Mandy woke up as the final rays of deep pinkish-red reflected off the rear-view mirror.

"Where are we?" she asked.

"Close to Virginia," Bear said.

"Are we going back to D.C.?"

"Maybe."

Bear hadn't decided whether they'd fly directly out of D.C. or catch a flight to New York or Boston and fly from there. He often wondered if Boston was a safer airport for him to use. He'd spent very little time there, despite its close proximity to New York.

His cell phone vibrated on the dash. He grabbed it, checked the caller ID. The number was not familiar. Bear answered anyway.

"Bear, this is Brandon. I have some information for you."

"Give me a minute." Bear set the phone in his lap. He angled the Cadillac toward the fast approaching exit. Immediately following the exit was a gas station. He pulled in and parked close to the convenience store.

"I'm hungry," Mandy said.

Bear handed her a twenty and told her to get him a Coke Zero.

"OK," Bear said. "Talk."

"Seven months ago Jack got into a tangle in Monte Carlo with a billionaire named Thornton Walloway."

"OK." Bear recalled Jack mentioning it.

"Thornton Walloway is dead. Two days ago he was alive. They found him buried under a pile of wood and garbage in an abandoned warehouse in London."

"They think Jack did it?"

"I'm looking at it like the man had a beef with Jack. He's alive before Jack gets to London. He's dead a day or two later. But the consensus is that Jack didn't do it. They tell me that they think he was being targeted as well. For some reason, he didn't show up to the site of the hit. Another guy did. They found him next to Walloway's body."

"So you think the other guy was supposed to be the shooter? Who was he? And if Jack didn't pull the trigger, who did?"

"Working on that. No ID found on the guy. Neither of them, actually. Just empty wallets. Thornton was easy for them to spot. He's kind of well known, mostly for being a prick. But this other guy is a bit of an enigma. And it doesn't help that half his face is missing."

Bear scanned the empty parking lot, said nothing.

"Where are you now?"

"Outside of Johnson City, Tennessee."

"Perfect. I got a partner in Greensboro, North Carolina. Full service stop, man. He can hook you up with IDs, passports, cash, credit cards. Hell, if you got a hankering for Twinkies, he's got cases of them in his garage. Only damn place you can find them anymore. He'll take care of your car, and we can get you on a flight out of Raleigh."

Bear thought about it while drumming the tips of his thick fingers on the hood of the Caddy.

"Which international terminal do you prefer, Atlanta or D.C.?" Brandon said.

"Atlanta. Less of a headache."

Brandon laughed. "If you say so, man."

Bear said nothing.

"OK, listen up. You're gonna hop on 26 East, then 40 East. He's a mile off the interstate. Should take you about three hours. I'll call in two and three-quarters with directions."

"Why not give them to me now?"

"You know better than to ask that, Bear."

He did. Giving too many details at this point put both parties at risk if someone monitored the line.

"All right, Brandon. We'll start heading..." Bear stopped, looked at the phone's display. Brandon had already hung up. He cursed as he tucked the phone away.

"Always with the language."

He turned and saw Mandy standing there, half his size and holding out a sweating bottle of Coke Zero. He twisted the cap and took a long pull from the bottle, enjoyed the burning sensation of the carbonated beverage flowing down his throat.

He gassed up the Caddy, then hit the road. They took 26 East, which really took them five degrees east of straight south, then merged onto 40 East in Asheville, North Carolina. Despite the dark, Bear knew they were in beautiful country.

The Blue Ridge Mountains had been one of his favorite areas as a kid. Every summer he and his father would take a fishing and hunting trip there. They'd hike for a week in, then a week out. He learned a lot during that time. How to hunt. How to field dress a deer. How to survive in the wilderness. He also discovered that despite his father's silent and rugged exterior, the man had a gentle soul. Bear wondered for a minute what his life would have been like if his father hadn't been killed when Bear was sixteen years old. Maybe he wouldn't have dropped out of school. Maybe he would have played football in the SEC. Maybe he wouldn't have joined the Marines.

"What are you smiling at?"

He glanced over at Mandy.

Maybe I wouldn't have met her. Nothing in my life is worth fixing if that'd be the result.

CHAPTER 28

JACK WAITED FOR TWO HOURS. THE GROANS AND CREAKS OF settling wood often interrupted the silence in the house. He learned to tune the noises out. He watched the camera feeds. A few cars passed by out front. Rabbits and squirrels scurried in and out of the woods. The wind blew the swings in the backyard back and forth, the seat turning and the chains twisting from time to time.

No one came. Perhaps he'd been wrong. Maybe they had figured Jack was onto them and he and Dottie and Leon would be prepared. Dottie had resources. She could enlist enough former agents and former SAS to make a decent security team. They had to know that.

So Jack reached out to an old contact who told him Mason Sutton's home address. Jack considered returning to the hotel a few miles away. The Fiat was parked there. Having a car would make the trip easier. In the end, the risk outweighed the reward of driving around in the cramped vehicle. They'd found the first hotel in London and all he'd had was a reservation there. Jack didn't doubt they knew of the hotel he actually stayed in.

He left the house, walked a mile, found a main road and caught the bus into London. The bus entered an area heavy with foot traffic. Jack got off there, hailed a cab. The taxi took him to Sutherland Road, north of the M4 highway. From there, Jack walked two blocks east, then two blocks south.

He turned east again on Gordon Road. He passed by an area that was residential on one side of the street, industrial on the other. A large warehouse took up half the block. Puffs of steam rose from its roof.

His shadow stretched out along the sidewalk in front of him. Behind him, the sun hovered low in the western sky. The orange tint made the homes in the area look older than he assumed they were.

Twenty minutes after starting his trek on Gordon, Jack stood across the street from Mason's house. The homes in the area looked like they cost a pretty penny, or pound, Jack figured. He knew that, like U.S. intelligence jobs, MI5 paid well. But well enough to afford a home like the one he was looking at? Jack doubted it.

More proof the man was on the payroll of a billionaire.

There was no point in being clandestine. Jack wanted to attack, drive fear into the man. He crossed the street, took the steps leading to the front door two at a time. He knocked with his left, grabbed the handle of his pistol with his right. If Mason made an aggressive move, Jack would be ready to strike. Thirty seconds passed with no answer. He knocked again. A minute went by, still no answer. He reached out and grabbed the door handle. Unlocked. He turned the knob and pushed the door open.

"Hello?" he called out.

No response.

"Mason? You here?" He didn't bother to disguise his voice. His British accent was awful. He knew it. Any American accent he used would be pointless. Mason would know it was him.

Again, no response.

Jack used his foot to push the door open. It glided smoothly without a sound. Well-oiled or fairly new, he guessed. The heavy odor of potpourri wafted through the open doorway. Jack stepped inside and used the heel of the same foot to kick the door closed. Then he called out once again and received no response.

He stood in a ten by ten foyer. In front of him, a set of stairs led up to the second floor. Next to the stairs, a hall. To his left, a wall. To his right, the dining room. Jack turned right. The dining room led to a large kitchen with slate floors, granite counter tops and updated appliances. Everything was clean, sleek and modern. Clearly missing any feminine touch. The sink was placed against the back wall. Above it, a window. Jack leaned over the faucet and looked out at the backyard. There were no trees or bushes or flowers, only green grass. Unnaturally so, thought Jack. He wondered if it was fake.

Before exiting the kitchen, he noticed a set of chef knives, ranging in length from eight to twelve inches. They looked fancy. Jack had seen knives like that sell for as much as five hundred dollars each.

He continued through the living room. More modern furniture, leather chairs and metal tables, and a flat panel mounted to the wall. All wires were hidden. He expected nothing less.

He returned to the front of the house and started up the stairs. Halfway up, he heard voices outside the front door. Jack froze. He reached for his handgun and then let his hand fall to his side. His leg shielded his weapon.

Outside the house, a man and a woman shared a laugh. High and low. Deep and light. They mixed together to form the sound of a couple in love.

The home lacks a feminine touch.

One of them knocked on the door.

Jack exhaled. Couldn't be Mason. What man would knock on his own front door? That didn't mean Jack could relax, though. One of them might be Mason's partner or maybe even another agent. Cops hung out with cops, soldiers with soldiers, firemen with other firemen. It worked the same way for spies.

Jack ascended the stairs backward, one step at a time. He stopped near the top. He knew he'd be out of view should they try the door handle like he had.

They didn't though. Their chatter faded.

Jack considered returning downstairs to lock the door. He decided against it, though. Mason was the kind of man who would know whether or not he locked his door when he left in the morning. Returning home to find it otherwise would set off alarms in the guy's head. Jack needed the element of surprise should Mason show up.

The upstairs consisted of a large open area near the stairs, and a closed door at the far end. The open area had a beat up leather couch and a computer desk. Neither new, neither modern. A hardback book missing its dust jacket was perched on the middle of the couch. Jack went to the desk. He opened the drawers, noted that they were filled with files labeled with simple words like snow and dog and misfits. *Code,* Jack thought.

He left the files alone and went to the other end and stopped outside the closed door. He tapped on it. The door sounded solid. He pressed at the top, middle, bottom and sides. It didn't bend or bow. He searched the wall for any false panels. Mason could have set a trap. He could control it from a device hidden inside the wall behind a false panel. Jack's search revealed nothing. He opened the door, braced for anything.

All he found was more of the same. Clean, sleek, modern. The bed was made, the top of the dresser bare. A single nightstand stood between the bed and the window. The drapes were pulled to the side. The blinds were drawn shut but made of some kind of material that let the light in.

Jack checked under the bed. Found nothing there. He opened the door to the en suite bathroom. It was minimal and unoccupied, as he expected. He investigated the walk-in closet, found two rows of clothing on either side. On the right, suits and white button up shirts and ties. On the left, casual clothing. Ten pairs of shoes ranging from beach to casual to dress lined the floor.

He exited the closet and went to the dresser. They were full of neatly arranged clothing, but nothing else.

The answer, if there was one, was in the files. Jack doubted he'd find anything of use, though. Mason didn't seem to be the kind of man who'd bring his work home. But this wasn't work. This went far beyond work. Still, Jack had no problem getting inside the house. He knew that British Intelligence would have even less of a problem. If they believed the man to be involved in something suspicious and detrimental to Great Britain's security, they'd infiltrate and get the evidence they needed.

So Jack returned to the computer desk. He pulled out the files and went through them, one at a time. It turned out that the simple words weren't code at all. Snow apparently referred to Mason's ex-wife, Gloria. Snow had been her maiden name. The file labeled dog contained veterinary records for Mason's dog, Barnaby. The last receipt indicated that Barnaby had been put to sleep three months prior due to hip dysplasia.

The misfits file was filled with random receipts from restaurants, bars and stores. And so it went. Every folder he looked through had a purpose. He found nothing nefarious or evil. Nothing that implicated Mason or himself.

Jack went back downstairs, grabbed a beer from the refrigerator and took a seat at the dining room table. His position allowed him to see the front entrance as well as the back door. And there he'd wait for Mason to return home.

CHAPTER 29

ALEX PARKIN WATCHED THE IMAGES OF THE BOMBING ON THE television for the hundredth time. Each viewing caused him to feel sicker than the last. Inside, he bled and burned with every soul who perished. And he'd say as much in his address to the people of Great Britain. That was his duty as the Prime Minister.

"Sir?"

Alex set his pen down on the legal pad on his desk, pushed back in his chair and looked up at the man wearing a blue pinstriped suit. Jon Hayes brushed back his thinning hair then placed both hands on the Prime Minister's desk and leaned forward.

"Sir, I need to speak with you."

"Then speak," Alex said.

Jon looked over both shoulders. "There's too many people in here, and I need to be frank with you."

Alex leaned to his left, looked past Jon. Select members of his cabinet sat near one another. They all stared at the flat panel televisions mounted to the walls. Every one of them, lost in thought. None had offered much advice to Alex up to that point. As far as he was concerned, there was little point to them being in the room.

"Everyone out," Alex said.

Heads turned toward him, stares of disbelief. He gestured toward the door with his head. They rose and staggered into the hall.

"Better?" he said.

"Yes, sir. Thank you."

"For Christ's sake Jon, we're alone now. We go too far back for this sir talk."

The men had a history. They'd served in the SAS together. Alex was an officer, Jon his top NCO. Their difference in rank meant nothing. They'd become best friends and still were to this day. Alex dragged Jon along for his meteoric rise through the political ranks. Unheard of, some had said, for him to become Prime Minister at the age of forty-five with only six years of public service. But his party had spoken, and so did the same public that he had served. And now he faced what he feared was the first in a series of attacks on London.

Jon said, "I'm getting conflicting reports, Alex."

This was the first he'd heard of any reports at all. "What are you hearing?"

"Some are saying this is most certainly an attack by a group led by a man named Naseer Shehata. Recognize that name?"

Alex nodded. "What about the conflicting report?"

"That this was carried out, at least in part, with the help of someone in MI5 or MI6."

Alex rose, slammed his palm against the desk. "Who would have authorized this?"

"It's not like that," Jon said.

"Then how is it?"

"We've got a rogue agent."

Alex didn't want to believe that anyone sworn to protecting Great Britain could be a part of such a nefarious act. "That's just as bad. Maybe worse. Any other theories floating around?"

"No." Jon paused. "Well, one more."

"What is it?"

"It's not really a third theory, more of a blend of the first two."

"Meaning?"

"Someone from MI5 or MI6 is working with terrorists."

"Why?"

"Any multitude of reasons I'd imagine."

"Such as?"

Jon held out his hands. "Take a guess."

"I don't have the patience for guesses. Why that hotel?"

"I've got a guy who is checking records, matching names, and so forth. It's tedious, he says, but he should have a yay or nay to us by six this afternoon."

Alex glanced at his watch. He wasn't sure he could wait two hours for the news. "Yay or nay on what?"

"If there was a specific target at the hotel."

"How will he know?"

"There's a limited number of names that run in these circles, Alex. If one pops up, it's not a coincidence."

"What if the hotel was a decoy?"

"You're thinking of the restaurant?"

"Yes, that cook, on the telly, the one with the red beard—"

"I remember him."

"—he mentioned men in masks with guns. They came in and shot up the restaurant."

Jon crossed his arms, rubbed his jawline. "What if that was the decoy?"

"What if every last bit of it was a decoy, Jon?"

"Get us to focus all our efforts on that one area and carry out a bigger attack."

"That's what I fear most."

Alex walked to the bank of windows on the outer wall. He looked out over Downing Street. Spring was in full bloom and he'd hardly noticed. Cherry blossoms, maybe an inch deep, covered the sidewalk. He shook his head at the reporters who never seemed to leave the front of Number 10.

Reporters, he thought. *Tabloid rubbish.*

Jon joined him by the windows. He placed a hand on the Prime Minister's shoulder. "It's just a test, Alex."

"I hope to God you are right. You know, I always knew this was a possibility. But I never expected it to hit so close to home." He pointed toward the plume of smoke that rose into the air and hovered over the site of the bombing. A surreal reminder of the attack carried out just a few hours before. "What if there is another attack while we're chasing down this possible rogue agent?"

Jon nodded and remained quiet. After a minute, he said, "We've got the best of our intelligence agents looking at this from every angle, Alex. We'll get them before they get to us."

There was something in Jon's words that dragged up one of Alex's deepest fears. He'd be the next target.

CHAPTER 30

MASON WAITED AT HIS DESK UNTIL THE LAST PERSON LEFT THE office. The short-walled cubes made espionage at work difficult even for a trained spy. If someone saw him pulling files from his desk and then leaving, they might stop and question him. Better to leave nothing to chance, Mason figured.

He pulled his bottom right drawer open, gathered a stack of files from his desk, dropped them inside. Before sliding the drawer closed, he grabbed a green folder. At the top of the folder the word "Jack" had been written in permanent marker. Mason inspected the folder. The strands of hair he had taped on the top and bottom of the folder were intact. While not foolproof, it gave him an indication that no one had accessed the file. He opened the folder, breaking the hairs in the process. At first glance everything appeared to be as he left it. He scanned through the papers contained within the folder. Nothing seemed out of order.

Mason rose and took a step back from his desk. He dropped the folder into his briefcase. A full day at the office never left him feeling well. He arched his back, stretched, kicked his chair away and turned. He had a clear path from his desk to the exit door. Before he reached it, his boss entered.

"Need a word with you, Mason," Cameron Mills said.

Mason nodded and followed Mills. They stepped inside his boss's glass-walled corner office. Five floors up, it had a view of the river and of Legoland, the intelligence community's nickname for MI6's building. From a distance, the green and off-white building looked like a castle made from the children's play toys.

Mills sat down, gestured for Mason to do the same.

Mason settled into his seat and said, "What's going on, boss?"

"Any word on Noble?"

Mason avoided looking at his briefcase. "Nothing yet, sir. I'd hoped he would reach out, but he hasn't."

"Do we think he's connected with the bombings today?"

"Why would we?"

"He had reservations at that hotel."

Mason nodded. He hadn't revealed that information to his boss.

"I'm afraid the link ends there," Mason said. "Besides, why would he blow up the place he'd been staying?"

"Maybe to fake his own death?"

"Unnecessary, sir. He's clean as a whistle now. The only reason he showed up on our radar was because of an old travel warning we had in place arising from an incident in 2006. In fact, a brief came through today advising to remove him from our list."

"A man like him should never be removed from our lists."

"I agree, sir. But it is what it is."

Mills nodded, coughed. The order would have come from above him, so he had little recourse.

"Anything else, sir?" Mason said.

"Not for now. Tomorrow I want you to go to the site of the bombing, then to the hospital to interview witnesses."

"The hospital?"

"Anyone that saw what happened is either dead or in a hospital bed, Mason."

Mason considered this kind of work to be below him and his skill set. But orders were orders.

"Yes, sir." Mason rose, grabbed his briefcase and started toward the chrome-rimmed glass door.

"Mason."

Mason stopped, turned. “Yes?”

“This is no coincidence.”

“What’s that?”

“The bombing, a billionaire being murdered, and Jack Noble being in town. We need to find him.” Mills paused, removed his glasses. He chewed on the frame for a second. “Understand?”

Mason nodded, said nothing. He stood in the open doorway for a minute, then headed toward the elevator. The empty elevator whisked him to the ground level floor. He ignored the security officers positioned there. He placed his gun and holster and briefcase on the conveyor belt. The items passed through the x-ray machine. Mason retrieved them and headed for the door.

The ride home was longer than the short distance should have taken. Traffic in London had that effect on travel. He had no choice, as did none of the seven million residents who worked normal hours. Not that Mason’s job could be classified as such, but some days that’s how it shook out. Despite the traffic, Mason enjoyed his ride home. It provided the one time of day when he did not think about the job. At first he had to force himself to keep his eyes and mind focused on nothing but the road and cars in front of him. Now it came naturally. Nothing mattered. Not the job, not national security. Not his past or his future.

An hour later, Mason pulled to the curb in front of his house. He got out of his car and walked toward the front door. He climbed the seven stairs, stopped on the landing. He reached for the door. A warm breeze blew past, carrying with it the smells of the White Swan, the local pub two blocks away. The smell of beer and the grill mixed together caused his mouth to water. Home could wait. What he wanted was a drink.

So Mason turned around and walked down the stairs and made a right at the sidewalk. Ten minutes later he sat at the bar, a pint in his right hand.

Mason contemplated his recent decisions. What had seemed like a good idea now backfired. The Jack Noble situation had gotten out of hand. He should have reported the man’s presence as soon as Jack landed in London instead of taking matters in his own hands. Thornton was a pain and had to be dealt with. That had been a foregone conclusion. Without

Mason's interference, Jack would have handled it. But Mason needed Jack for more than just the hit, so he couldn't allow him to carry out the hit inside a store on a busy road. The result would have been a choice between imprisonment or fleeing for Jack. The warehouse meeting had been a mistake, though. He admitted that.

The problem now was that he'd gone too deep. Making a confession at this point would end his career and ensure that he spent the rest of his life in a cage. The Jack Noble situation had to be handled. He had to end it.

The bartender dropped a plate in front of Mason. The pork pie sent clouds of steam towards his face. His mouth flooded at the aroma. He finished his beer, signaled for a second, and then began eating his meal.

A slender female hand came to a rest next to his beer. A white mark where a ring once wrapped the third finger. The perfume that mixed with the smell of his food was a not too distant memory to Mason. He turned and saw the one woman he had no desire to see at that time.

"Hello, Gloria."

She smiled. "Mason, nice to see you."

"What are you doing so close to my place?"

"I was thinking about coming by. Saw you get out of your car and then come down here, so I followed you."

"Well, you shouldn't have."

"Mason, I'm sorry for what happened. How many times do I have to apologize?"

"Doesn't matter. You can apologize until I'm dead and withered away, it won't change anything. I'm never taking you back."

"Can I at least buy you a drink?"

Mason shook his head. He stuffed an overloaded forkful of pork pie into his mouth. He kept his lips parted as he chewed. Gloria watched him in the mirror. Her lip curled upward and turned away.

"I guess I should go, then," she said a few moments later.

"Yeah, you should."

Gloria pushed away from the bar and headed toward the door. He watched her in the mirror and then spun on his stool in time to see her leave.

"Way to be strong, mate." The bartender set down a third pint and gave Mason a wink and a nod.

Thirty minutes later, Mason left the bar and headed home, slightly buzzed after four pints of beer. The air had cooled and the sky had darkened. The street lamps cast shaded pools of light along the sidewalk. Shadows from tree branches looked like gnarled fingers on the ground.

He reached his home, took the seven steps to the landing. He cursed himself as he reached for the door. He now regretted the fact that he had left it unlocked. What if Gloria had come back to his house instead of her own?

Mason wasn't entirely surprised when he saw Gloria sitting at the dining room table. What did surprise him was that Jack Noble sat right next to her.

CHAPTER 31

JACK WATCHED THE MAN AS HE STEPPED INTO THE FOYER. Mason's eyes had been focused on the floor, so he flung the door closed before realizing Jack was there. The guy's expression changed from annoyed to surprised to scared, though he quickly downshifted back to surprised. Guys like Jack and Mason knew better than letting an opponent see their fear.

Mason dropped his bag and reached for his handgun.

"Don't move, Mason," Jack said. He aimed his Beretta at Mason's stomach.

"No," Gloria said. She jumped up from her seat.

"Sit down, Gloria," Jack said. "I got a feeling that he doesn't much care if I shoot you, but I know you don't want me to kill him. So sit your butt in that chair and shut up."

Gloria lowered herself into her seat. The wood groaned in response. She placed her hands flat on the table. Her eyes remained locked on her ex-husband.

"Mason," Jack said. "I want you to lift your hands in the air."

Mason did as told.

Jack said, "Now with your left hand I want you to show me where your gun is."

Mason hiked up his jacket.

"Good, now with your thumb and little finger I want you to take it out of the holster, set it on the ground in front of the stairs and step away. Keep your front to me the whole time or I'll sever your spine with a bullet."

Mason pulled the pistol from its holster as instructed. The weapon looked awkward in the unusual grip. He shuffled toward the stairs, placed the gun on the first step.

"On the ground," Jack said.

It didn't seem like much, but the step was approximately eight inches off the ground. That's eight inches less Mason would have had to stoop to retrieve his pistol.

Mason grimaced, grabbed the handle by his thumb and little finger and then placed it on the ground. He straightened and shuffled a foot forward, both hands in the air.

Jack said, "Now come have a seat at the table."

"You've any idea what you're doing, Noble?"

Jack glared at Mason. The guy had used his name so that Gloria heard it. That could cause problems later.

"I know exactly what I'm doing," Jack said.

"I'm not necessary here," Gloria said. "Mason, tell him I shouldn't be here."

"Any ideas on how to get her to shut up?" Jack said.

"Good luck with that, mate," Mason said.

Gloria leaned back in her chair, fired a look at Mason. Jack knew that no words had to be spoken. He'd been on the receiving end of a stare like that a time or two.

"So, what happened, Mason?" Jack said.

Mason shook his head, shrugged, said nothing.

"Don't play stupid with me."

"What do you want to know?"

"I want to know why you set me up. Why did I go into a warehouse to finish a job, only to be in a situation where I should have died?"

Mason straightened up in his chair, said nothing. The guy's eyes switched focus from Jack to the pistol in Jack's hand.

"I could have taken him out the day before, but you stopped me. Why?

What do you care about what happens to me? You wanted him dead. Should it matter where or how?"

"I thought..."

Jack waited a moment, then said, "You thought?"

Mason shook his head, tight and terse.

"So then I'm brought to a warehouse," Jack continued. "Told where to set up and where to shoot from. It's the place I would have chosen myself. Only thing is, it's locked and I can't get in there. A couple hours later, there's a guy standing on the catwalk, a few feet from that same spot I was supposed to be. If I didn't know any better, I'd think that guy had been told that someone would be up there, and the moment he spotted the guy, he should shoot. Fortunately, I was nowhere near that spot. But I was exposed. I still don't know how I wasn't spotted. It's as if they knew I was in there and decided not to bother with me."

Mason said nothing.

"And in the end, Walloway's own guy did him."

"Really?" Mason said.

Jack nodded.

"Who's Walloway?" Gloria said.

"Not now, Gloria," Mason said.

The woman rolled her eyes, crossed her arms and leaned back again. Jack imagined she had a few hostile words lined up for Mason if she ever got the chance to be alone with him again.

"What then, mate?" Mason said.

"Two guys came in with Thornton. One guy killed Thornton. The second guy didn't seem to care, but he balked on something regarding the money. The guy that shot Thornton shot the second guy too. Naseer seemed like he knew it was coming. Like they had it all arranged."

Mason nodded.

Jack said, "And I think you knew that all along."

"No, you got it all wrong, mate."

"You wanted me to be there. I was the backup plan. And depending on how things went, they might have taken care of me along with Walloway. You didn't care about that. Probably figured after what I'd witnessed, I'd run. Right?"

Mason leaned over the table.

"Both hands where I can see them." Jack lifted his pistol.

Mason leaned back, showed his hands. "I had no idea, Jack."

"And then, we had the bombings this morning."

"Mason, you didn't," Gloria said.

"Shut up, Gloria," Mason said.

"You knew where I made my hotel reservations," Jack said. "You're probably the only person that did. You tipped Walloway off that first day. He sent a crew, but the hotel had no record of me. But that could've changed. Maybe I checked in later. So you had them go back and blow the place up. You're responsible for a hundred deaths. And for what? The chance that you might have killed me?"

"What?" Mason appeared shocked.

Jack stood, shoved the table toward Mason, kicked his chair against the wall.

"Well guess what, Mason?" He took aim at the man's forehead. "You got to me. At least twice you tried to have me killed. There'll be no third chance."

Gloria covered her face. The sounds of her sobs slipped through her fingers. Mason leaned back in his chair, held his arms out to the side, elbows bent, fingers pointed to the ceiling.

Mason said, "Jack, you gotta believe me, mate. I had nothing to do with all that. I was acting on intelligence that I'd received. We had no idea the warehouse was going to be a bunk spot and definitely no idea that things would go down the way they did. Think about what you said. Don't you think if I wanted you dead, they would have done it there? If I was working with them, I wouldn't have sent them in without telling them about you being there. I have no idea why the hatch to the roof was locked. You should have had access and been able to make the shot from that window up there."

"What hatch and window? Who else knew I was there?"

Mason furrowed his brow, squinted. "What do you mean what hatch? My partner was the only other person that knew you were there. He's the guy that took you there."

"Muscles, bald-headed, doesn't talk much."

"What? No, my partner is the guy that dropped the Fiat off in the woods. He's the antithesis of what you just described. Lord knows he doesn't shut up when we're out."

At that moment, Jack believed Mason had told him the truth.

"When's the last time you talked to your partner?" Jack said.

"Last night," Mason said.

"Before or after he picked me up?"

"What?"

"Before or after, Mason?"

"Before."

"And you haven't talked to him since?"

"Right."

"Is it normal that you wouldn't hear from him all day?"

"Yeah, he was going fishing today. I wouldn't—" Mason's hands fell to his side. He closed his eyes, shook his head. "He betrayed me. He's the only other person that knew about you, Jack. When you showed up on the radar, we didn't report it. I knew what was going on, why you were here. Walloway's been untouchable for so damn long. Money buys anything, you know. I saw your arrival as a sign we could finally take care of him."

Jack nodded, said nothing. He pieced the puzzle together along with Mason.

"I can't believe this," Mason said. "Joe's gone and bloody stabbed me in the back."

"It looks that way," Jack said. "But we don't know that for sure. Maybe they got to him. Maybe they were trying to get to you, too. They just found him first."

A minute of silence passed, then Mason said, "I've got to tell Mills."

"Who?"

"My boss."

"No," Jack said.

"Why not?"

"I know that someone in MI5 or MI6 is involved. Whether they got the information from Joe or you through spying, I don't know. We have to figure out who it was without tipping our hand. Hell, it could be more than one person. We have to keep this close to the vest, for now. Too risky to bring anyone else in on it."

"I promise I won't tell anyone," Gloria said.

Jack looked at her, then back at Mason. "Sorry about this, *mate,* but you're stuck with her for a while."

Mason said nothing.

"Here's how this will work," Jack said. "I've got parcels on the move. International fare. Once I get verification that they're safe, we make our first move."

"What will that be?"

"I need you to find out where Naseer is right now."

"How?"

"You're the spy. Figure it out."

"OK. Then what?"

"I'll let you know when I do."

CHAPTER 32

CLARISSA FELT THE TRAIN SLOW. SHE OPENED HER EYES. THE train stretched along a curved track. The station lay ahead. She tugged on the cord dangling in front of her chest. White earbuds fell to her lap. The quick beat of electronica gave way to grinding brakes, steel on steel, and the low murmur of anticipation. The natural daylight that poured through the windows was replaced with fluorescent yellow as the train entered a short tunnel before pulling into the station.

Spiers didn't seem to notice. He leaned his head against the wall, eyes closed, mouth open.

She nudged him. He didn't stir, so she kicked his shin with the pointed toe of her boot. He grimaced, then opened his eyes. He yawned. Stagnant breath headed in Clarissa's direction. She fanned her hand in front of her face, but it didn't make a difference. The odor had already invaded her space.

"Why'd you kick me?" he said.

"You would rather I have left you here?" she said.

He waved her off, rose, grabbed hold of the metal railing that ran overhead. The train came to an abrupt stop. Clarissa jerked forward, then back. Spiers did too. He came close to falling on top of her. She had her doubts that the move was unintentional.

The doors slid open with a hiss. Cool air, fresh only in the sense that it was new, rushed inside and mixed with the warm stale air they'd been trapped in for the past two hours.

Spiers said, "You get off first. Scan the area. If everything looks good, put your right hand behind your back and hold out two fingers. If you are concerned, same hand, make a fist. Got it?"

"Two fingers good, fist bad. Got it."

She rose, grabbed her bag and walked toward the exit. A hundred pairs of disinterested eyes greeted her. She knew that it only took one pair being interested for her day to take a serious turn for the worse. They might lurk somewhere in the crowd. Clarissa slipped into profiling mode. Discount the kids, their parents, the elderly. Forget about anyone too heavy and out of shape to keep up with her. They might be a threat, but not one she'd take seriously. By the time she went through her checklist, there were five people to be concerned about. They all stared at her as she stepped down from the train and onto the platform. She knew she could cross them off as well. No one intent on harming her or taking her into custody would have dared to make eye contact.

She reached her hand behind her back and extended her middle and index fingers. Then she started away from the train. The thick crowd stood shoulder to shoulder. Instead of trying to fight her way through, she turned to the left and walked in front of the throng of people. She and Spiers had sat in the rear car, so naturally they were at the end of the terminal. She didn't have to walk far before she came upon a spot where a clean exit was possible.

Spiers caught up with her five minutes later.

"See anything?" he said.

"No. You?" she said.

"Nada."

"What now?"

"Guess we wait."

"Seriously?"

"I'm going to make a call and find out what's going on here."

He reached into his pocket and pulled out his cell. Clarissa stood a foot away, eyes on his. He stared back.

"What?" she said.

"A little privacy?" he said.

She rolled her eyes, walked fifteen feet away and took a seat on a mesh metal bench. A familiar smell, that of hot dogs, wafted past her. Her stomach groaned in response. She ignored the pangs of hunger, leaned her head back against the wall, studied the crowd. Nothing seemed out of the ordinary. She saw nobody who didn't belong there. When it came down to it, she was the biggest threat in the room. Next to Spiers, of course.

He stuffed his phone back in his pocket and approached her, shaking his head. He stopped in front of the bench. Said, "No answer."

She looked up at him. "What now?"

"He sent a text, like he said he would."

Clarissa said nothing.

"We're looking for two women and a little girl. Thirty-three, twenty-one, six-and-a-half. Dirty blond, brown, blond. Green, brown, blue. Well dressed, traveling light."

Clarissa appreciated his succinct style. "When do they arrive?"

"Ninety minutes."

"I don't like being exposed for that long."

Spiers glanced to his left, then his right. "Neither do I."

"Want to get some lunch?"

"We'll need a ticket to get back in here."

She reached into her pocket, pulled out a wad of euros. "I think we can handle that."

"Then let's go."

It turned out they didn't have to go far. Clarissa followed the smell of the hot dogs and it led them to a small restaurant in the terminal. It hadn't been hot dogs that sent her taste buds into overdrive and caused her to salivate. It was blood sausage, which, despite the name, she found fairly tasty. Spiers ate a beef dish that she didn't catch the name of. They shared double fried Belgian Fries, served in a paper cone held upright by a metal stand.

For fifteen minutes, they remained silent while they ate. They lingered in the restaurant for another forty-five minutes. Spiers tried to order a couple beers. Clarissa didn't let him. She told him once they were safe with the women and the girl, he could have a beer. But only one, no more.

She didn't know the man and didn't trust him. Not yet, at least. He had managed to last four hours without attempting to hurt her, though. That carried a lot of weight in Clarissa's book. Better to not ruin it by him getting drunk.

They left the restaurant and located an arrivals board. Spiers pulled out his phone and pulled up the text message again. He pointed toward the train's arrival information. Clarissa took note of it and ten minutes later they sat on a bench in front of the stretch of track where the train would pull in.

"Wish we had a picture," he said.

"Description should be good enough," she said.

Spiers rubbed his eyes, yawned.

"That nap you took wasn't enough?"

He shrugged, said nothing.

Clarissa felt a shift in the air, as if it were being drawn away. The squeal of the brakes precluded the train pulling into the station. A blast of hot air followed. She felt her hair lift into the air and then settle across her shoulders. Apparently, it had reached further than that. Spiers made a spitting sound and pulled strands of her hair off of his face where it had become intertwined with his long stubble.

"That's why you should shave," Clarissa said.

Spiers said nothing. He rose from his seat and stepped toward the train. There were fewer people here. When she got off their train, there had been at least one hundred people waiting. Clarissa guessed this was the train's last stop. For a while, at least.

"You take that end, I'll take this one," Spiers said.

Clarissa nodded, started off to her right. She turned, said, "What if it's a set up?"

"Not a chance. Not with this guy. If he were out to get me, he'd face me like a man."

Clarissa figured that if someone was looking for Spiers, they would only be looking for him. They wouldn't recognize her or know that she accompanied the man. So she headed further down the track with little fear of being spotted.

The doors slid open and people began to exit the train. She stopped three-quarters of the way down the length of the train. She scanned the faces that emerged. None matched the description Spiers had given her. Through the windows, she could see that there weren't many people left on board. She wondered if Spiers had better luck at the other end of the track. She looked to her left, tried to spot him. The crowd that filed toward the hall prevented her from seeing more than twenty feet away.

She returned her gaze to the train. If she hadn't waited another five seconds, she would have missed them.

The younger woman with brown hair stepped off first. She turned around when she reached the platform and then reached up for the little girl. The child's blond hair had been pulled back into a pony tail. Her blue eyes stood out. They seemed familiar. The last to exit looked to be the girl's mother. They were alike in every way, except for their eyes.

Clarissa weaved her way through the crowd. Her height and the two inch lift of the boots gave her an advantage, and she managed to keep track of the women as they approached.

The brunette was the first to make eye contact with Clarissa. She saw the woman stop, turn toward the other lady and say something. The other woman's gaze drifted left to right and stopped when she found Clarissa.

Clarissa approached the group. She smiled, left her hands exposed, fingers extended.

The little girl hid behind her mother. The woman reached out and pushed the brunette behind her as well.

Clarissa held her hands in the air. When she was close enough, she said, "I'm here to help."

"You're Jack's associate?" the woman said.

Clarissa nodded, unsure what to say. She had no idea the name of the man who'd asked Spiers to help.

"How do you know him?" the woman said.

"I'm traveling with the man who does. His name is Spiers. Your Jack reached out to him for help." Clarissa looked to her left and saw Spiers approaching. She waved to him. The two women followed her stare. "That's him."

Spiers stopped five feet from the group. "Ladies, we're here to protect you. I gave Jack my word that we'd do everything in our power to help and protect you. Between the two of us, we have more than enough experience to keep you safe."

The woman nodded, pulled the brunette forward and lifted her child onto her hip. Spiers took their luggage. He turned and began walking toward the tail end of the crowd.

Clarissa caught up to him. She said, "Jack who?"

Spiers looked at her, said nothing.

"Tell me."

"Why do you want to know?"

"Because I do."

Spiers hesitated, looked over his shoulder at the women, then back at Clarissa.

He said, "Noble."

CHAPTER 33

BEAR DROVE PAST THE TWO-STORY COLONIAL HOUSE WITH RED shutters and a matching front door. It looked well-maintained. The lawn neatly manicured. Newly installed siding. It was as Brandon had described it.

He parked on the opposite side of the street, half a block away, along a stretch that butted up to a vacant lot. The car glided to a stop on the recently paved street. The smell of tar penetrated the vehicle. He and Mandy remained in the car for fifteen minutes, then they got out, walked further down the street, crossed the road, and finally made their way to the house.

When they reached the driveway, Bear saw a man with shoulder length brown hair tucked behind his ears waiting on the other side of the storm door. The guy had a trimmed beard and a crooked nose. He wore plaid cargo shorts and no shirt. As they got closer, Bear noticed stray hairs on the guy's chest.

The man opened the door. "Thought you were never gonna come up."

Bear nodded, said nothing.

"What's your name?" the guy said to Mandy.

Mandy looked up at Bear, unsure. He shook his head, then looked at the guy. Brandon hadn't given Bear the man's name, and he assumed that went both ways.

"Whatever our contact told you is enough. No more questions, just give us what we need and take us where we're going."

The guy mocked a retreat and smiled. "Just trying to be cordial, my large friend."

Bear stepped inside. He drove his shoulder into the guy as he passed. Said, "I'm not your friend."

It wasn't personal. Bear didn't trust anyone. Even those closest to him had gotten him into his fair share of trouble. He often wondered what his life would have been like if he'd retreated to the woods and lived like a hermit. A bear in the woods. He could even imagine the sign saying so, carved in wood, hanging from his mailbox.

Mandy clutched his hand. She brushed up against his side as she walked. Stray strands of her hair tickled his wrist.

"Go on into the kitchen," the guy said. "I've got some pancakes made, although they're probably cold by now."

"We just ate," Bear said.

"I'm hungry," Mandy said.

Bear looked at the girl, rolled his eyes. He had to remind himself that she was still a kid in many ways.

"What?" she said.

"Nothing. Go ahead, eat." Normally, he wouldn't allow it. But since Brandon knew they were there, Bear figured the chances of this guy doing something were slim to none. Plus, it gave him a little space to complete the transaction.

"Go ahead, sweetheart," the guy said. "Eat as much as you want. There's some O.J. in the fridge, too."

Mandy pulled out a chair and sat down at the round oak table. She wasted no time, grabbed a fork and plunged it into the deflated stack of pancakes.

Bear watched her for a minute, then turned to the guy. "Let's get down to business."

"We leave for the airport in an hour." The guy walked over to the kitchen island and picked up a blue folder. He opened it, nodded and added, "These are your passports and some background info."

Bear took the passports, flipped them open. The one with his picture said his name was John James Bova, from Mission, Kansas. Mandy's new alias was Brittany Alexis. He glanced in her direction. *Blond and uppity,* he thought. *She'd make a great Brittany.*

"Why're we traveling?" he said.

"Vacation," the guy said.

"What do I do?"

"Car salesman."

Bear laughed. "Seriously?"

"No," the guy said. "You work for the phone company stringing cable."

Bear shrugged. "Good enough."

"And the girl." The guy looked at Mandy, smiled. "Well, she's just a girl." The guy swung his back around. His smile faded. He looked concerned. "Of course, you could leave her here with me."

Bear noticed a slight twitch in the guy's upper lip and dilation of the pupils.

Stinking pervert.

He restrained himself from striking the man, but did not discount the possibility of returning at a later date to deal with him.

"Just a thought," the guy said.

"She's staying with me." Bear repositioned himself to stand between Mandy and the guy. "Anything else?"

"Unfortunately, you're flying out of Raleigh, so I can't arm you. But, I can give you the name of a guy in London who can get you anything you need."

"That's OK. I've got my own contacts." He had no interest in being tied to the guy in any way.

"Suit yourself." The man turned, started toward the hallway. "I'll be back in half an hour."

"Where are you going?"

"To take a nap."

Bear waited for the man to disappear from view, then he walked over to the counter. A wood block sat on the counter, next to the stove top. Four knives rested in the block. Bear reached for the one with the largest handle. He went over to the table, sat down, rested the knife along his thigh.

Mandy smiled at him. A small chunk of chewed pancake fell to the table. She brought her hand to her mouth and giggled.

Bear shook his head and chuckled. This resulted in the girl laughing and sending most of the food in her mouth spraying out across the table.

"Can't take you nowhere, can I?" Bear said.

Mandy continued laughing, uncontrollably. He joined in. They laughed for more than three minutes. And as the tears streamed down his face, Bear realized that it was the simple moments such as this one that proved he was where he was meant to be and with who he was meant to be with.

CHAPTER 34

CLARISSA HADN'T BEEN ENTIRELY SURPRISED WHEN SPIERS told her that Jack Noble had been the man who had asked for help. She kept her expression neutral and gave no indication to Spiers that she knew Jack. Nothing about the way he responded told her that Spiers had been aware of Clarissa's on-again, off-again relationship with Jack. She had nodded her acknowledgment and carried on with a *business as usual* attitude.

They walked through the station, Spiers in front, the women and girl in the middle, and Clarissa in back. She took note of every face that approached. She would have been vigilant no matter what, but now the assignment carried extra weight.

They exited the building. The bright sun negated the bite of the crisp breeze. She glanced around and saw a park about a block away. Several benches lined the sidewalk. She led the women there while Spiers placed a series of calls and arranged for a car. He had an associate close by who agreed to meet them four blocks from the station.

A short walk later, they arrived at the agreed upon spot. They did not have to wait long. The man pulled the car to the curb, got out, nodded and walked away. Simple and efficient. Spiers took the driver's side, Clarissa sat in front next to him, and the two women and little girl sat in the back.

This was Clarissa's first visit to Brussels. She hoped it wouldn't be for long. Paris beckoned, although not for the right reasons. They never were for Clarissa.

They passed through the city so fast that she barely had time to register any landmarks. The city gave way to residential areas, which in turn gave way to the countryside. The women in the back spoke occasionally. The little girl asked several questions. Spiers said nothing, neither did Clarissa. For most of the drive, she stared out the window watching the sun complete its arc through the sky, her thoughts stuck on the man she tried to leave behind in D.C. In all, the ride took forty-five minutes and ended after they passed through a small village consisting of an intersection with a few homes and shops. A spire with a cross affixed to the top stood off in the distance. After they passed through the village, Clarissa saw the modest church. She assumed by the scaffolding along the right side that the town was making improvements or repairs.

"That's it," Spiers said, breaking a ten minute stretch of nothing but wind rush and road noise.

Clarissa looked ahead as Spiers turned onto a bumpy dirty driveway. The little house stood about a quarter-mile off the road. It looked centuries old, made from brown and gray stone. A red brick chimney rose from the roof, likely added sometime after the home had been built. There were two darkened windows in front, about ten feet on either side of the front door.

"Who's place is this?" she said.

"A friend's," he said.

"Are they home?"

"Does it look like it?"

"It looks abandoned."

"It is."

Spiers continued past the end of the driveway and parked the vehicle behind the house.

"We should check it out first," Clarissa said.

He rolled his eyes, said nothing.

"Take no chances, Spiers."

"OK, OK." He turned sideways in his seat. "Ladies, if you'll excuse us, we're going to make sure the place is safe for you to enter."

Clarissa stepped out of the car. With the sun no longer visible, the air felt cold. The exposed flesh on her arms prickled. She wished she hadn't forgotten her coat on the train. She waited for Spiers by the side of the house, out of the wind.

"Nice bit of drama back there," she said when he appeared.

He shrugged. "Someone's gotta keep them feeling at ease. Should be you, but it appears you're the one with a real penchant for drama."

She looked over in time to catch him grinning. "Whatever. Let's just clear the house and get them inside."

"OK, I'll go in. You wait by the door."

"We both go in."

"Just me, Clarissa. I don't need an earful from Sinclair if something happens to you."

"What if something happens to you?"

"It won't as long as I don't have to worry about you."

"Yeah, well," she fumbled as she thought of an appropriate come back. Nothing came to mind, so she settled with, "Whatever."

She watched as he slipped around the corner. Ten seconds later she followed, stopping by the front door. She scanned the fields surrounding the house, the road. Her gaze drifted toward the small village a half-mile away. A few windows were lit, the rest dark. She doubted the kitchen would be stocked with fresh food and wondered how long the store remained open.

"It's clear," Spiers said, emerging from the darkened doorway. "Happy?"

"Yes."

"Good. Go get those women. I'll wait here."

She jogged around the side of the house, tapped on the rear window of the car. All three occupants inside turned their heads. She smiled. Only the little girl smiled back. The women filed out of the car and followed Clarissa around to the front. Spiers abandoned his post at the door when he saw them.

Clarissa found a half-stocked pantry and empty fridge. Spiers told her that the store would likely be closed, so if she wanted to get anything else, she'd have to wait until the morning. So she grabbed some canned soup, fired up the gas stove, and cooked enough soup to get them through the night. She hadn't realized how hungry she was until the soup began to boil and filled the kitchen with the smell of tomatoes.

Spiers declined dinner, instead telling Clarissa that he'd rest now and take the overnight watch so she could get a full night's rest. She didn't mind. It would provide her the opportunity to probe the women and find out their relationship to Jack.

Clarissa and the women gathered around the small square table and ate in silence. Mia slurped her soup, which drew a harsh look from her mother. The little girl smiled and made sure to open wide for each subsequent spoonful.

Clarissa broke the silence. "So why are you ladies on the run?"

Erin set down her spoon. She looked shocked that the question had been asked. She wiped her mouth, cleared her throat, said, "We're not sure, entirely. It has something to do with the bombings in London today."

Clarissa had heard about the attack, but knew little about what had occurred.

"Were you afraid of additional attacks?" Clarissa said.

"Not me," Erin said. "Jack. And not more attacks, more so attacks against us. See, Jack," she paused, looked up and bit her bottom lip. "I don't know how much I should tell you."

"It's OK, you can tell me. I work for the U.S. government."

"Are you a spy?" Mia asked.

"She's fascinated with spies," Hannah said.

Clarissa smiled at the girl. "I sure am."

"Really?"

"Yes, really. And I'd love to tell you all about it, but first I need to hear what your mommy has to say."

"OK," Mia said.

"The bombs that went off were at the hotel that Jack had reservations at," Erin said.

"Do you know why he's in London?" Clarissa said.

Erin sat silent for a few moments. "Yes, well, I thought I did. I'm not sure, though. I'm sorry, I really can't say without knowing definitively."

"It's OK. So Jack wasn't in the building when it exploded?"

"Oh, Heaven's no. He was with us."

"Where?"

"At Aunt Dottie's house."

Clarissa tried to place the name. It didn't register, but something else did. Mia's eyes. She knew them the moment she saw the girl, and now she knew from where. Mia was Jack's daughter. She was sure of it.

"Where's the girl's father?" Clarissa asked.

Erin shifted in her seat. "I'm sorry, I don't see how that has anything to do with this."

Clarissa glanced at the girl and saw that she had cast her stare down toward the table. "I'm sorry. I didn't mean—"

"You really should think before you say such things." Erin rose. "Come with me, Mia."

The little girl didn't get up right away. Erin picked her up and carried her into the other room. Clarissa felt bad for a moment, but there were questions that she needed answered. She'd try again after Mia fell asleep.

"She's kinda protective," Hannah said.

"All mothers are," Clarissa said.

"All?"

"Most."

"I never knew mine."

"I barely knew mine."

Hannah nodded. "She's never told me who the father is, but I think it might be Jack."

"How well do you know him?"

Hannah smiled. She placed her right forearm on the table and leaned forward. "It's a funny story. I met him on the plane ride over here. I had been home for break. And, I guess you'd call it a coincidence—"

"There's no such thing as a coincidence, Hannah. The sooner you realize that, the better off you'll be."

"Yeah, I'm sure. Anyway, we sat next to each other on the plane. He helped get me a ride to my flat afterward. Then I saw him at Ms. Carlisle's house, out of the blue. At first I was scared he was there for me. But why? Like I'm the kind of person that someone would follow. So, anyway, when

I seen him and Mia together, it was obvious. Everyone says she looks like her mother, and she does, for the most part. But those eyes, the shape of those eyes, without a doubt, father and daughter."

Clarissa forced a smile. The news unsettled her stomach. She eased back in her chair, crossed her arms over her chest.

"So, what's the story with Jack and Erin?" Clarissa said.

"What about them?"

"Are they a couple, an item, whatever you kids call it now?"

"As far as I can tell, they aren't. I mean, there must have been something between them at one time. But now? I didn't see any sparks or hints of anything going on."

Clarissa nodded, said nothing.

"Of course, it's not like he was around all that much. At least not while I was there. So, who knows?"

"Yeah," Clarissa said. "Who knows. So what is Ms. Carlisle like?"

"I dunno, not much to say, I guess. She's taken good care of me since I started school in London."

"What do you know about her past?"

"Not much."

"Come on, you must have heard something."

Hannah looked over her shoulder in the direction that Erin had gone. "She used to work in British Intelligence. That's part of the reason why Mia is so interested in spies."

Clarissa nodded. She knew who the woman was. At one time, Jack had worked with Dottie. It all made sense. During one of his assignments in England he'd met Erin. They'd had a relationship, and Mia was the result. Her cheeks burned hot. She had no cause to be angry, though. After all, this was during a time period before the two of them had become romantic. But that didn't stop the feelings of betrayal that surfaced. How could Jack not have told her he had a daughter?

She looked up when she heard someone clear their throat. Erin stood in the doorway. She glared at Clarissa.

"Hannah," Erin said. "Leave us."

Hannah opened her eyes wide and forced a smile at Clarissa, then she rose and slipped past Erin.

"Let me say that I'm very sorry I spoke out of turn," Clarissa said.

"You should be. I try so hard to protect that little girl. She believes her father died when she was a baby. She has a picture and clutches to it like it's the only thing keeping him in her thoughts."

"It probably is."

"What would you know?"

"I know what it's like to lose a father."

"Most everyone does, at some point."

Clarissa watched the woman's angry expression fade. "Will you ever tell her the truth?"

"What truth?"

"About her father."

"She has all the truth she needs."

"Erin, I need to level with you."

"About what?"

Clarissa took a deep breath. She placed her hands on the table to steady herself. The information she was about to divulge could change the dynamic in the house and compromise her mission. "I know Jack Noble. I've known him for years. After my father passed, he kind of looked after me. From afar, mostly."

"Clarissa. Of course." Erin gazed over Clarissa's shoulder. "You're the girl he used to go on about then."

"Suppose so. Kind of an uncommon name these days."

"So you can tell?"

"That he's the father? Yes."

"Jack figured it out, too. I'm still pissed off at Dottie for not telling me he was around. It's like she wanted him to know. It was never her damn choice to make. It was supposed to be mine and I never wanted him to find out."

"Why?"

Erin said nothing.

"Jack's a good guy, you know. He can provide for her. In time, be there for her."

"No, he can't. Trouble follows him everywhere."

"I understand what you're feeling. He takes a lot of risks."

Erin nodded, said nothing.

"But at the same time, they both deserve to know about each other. At least have a chance of knowing each other."

"Who are you to say that? She's my daughter. Not yours. Not his. Mine."

They both turned their heads toward the doorway at the sound of a sniffle. Mia stepped out of the shadows. Tear tracks stained her cheeks.

"Oh, my little darling," Erin said. She rose and went to her daughter, embraced her tight.

"Jack is my father?" the girl said through choked sobs.

Erin said nothing. She wrapped her hand through the girl's hair and pulled her closer.

Clarissa rose, walked past mother and daughter. "I should leave you two alone."

CHAPTER 35

THE ROOM WENT DARK AS THE LAST RAYS OF SUNLIGHT FELL behind the houses across the street. Jack rose and gestured toward the kitchen.

"Let's go in there for now," he said. "Getting too dark in here."

"He's got lights," Gloria said.

"Yeah, and if you flip them on the sniper on the roof across the street will have an easy shot."

Mason turned toward the window. "Where is he?"

"I'm speaking hypothetically," Jack said.

"Can I get my gun?" Mason said.

Jack still felt unsure about what Mason's role was in everything that had happened. His being there had been more than coincidental. Jack didn't know why, though. If he was to make any use of the man, he'd have to at least give off the vibe that he trusted him.

"Get it. Holster it. Don't dare pull it."

Mason nodded, picked up his pistol, stuffed it in his holster. He placed two fingers on Gloria's elbow and led her into the kitchen. She reached out and flipped the light switch on. Jack found the move curious. To him, it had been evident that the home had always been Mason's and Mason's alone. The documents upstairs proved that he'd moved in after the divorce. But the way Gloria flipped the switch without having to look told him that she'd spent more time in the house than Mason's attitude toward her indicated.

"Want a beer, Jack?" Mason said.

He'd only had one, and that had been a couple hours earlier. "Sure, why not."

"I can fix some dinner," Gloria said.

Jack nodded and she went to the fridge and pulled out a package of steaks. Jack wondered why Mason had a whole package defrosted.

"I cook in bulk," Mason said.

Jack hiked his shoulders in the air an inch. Said nothing.

"We're both spies. We think alike. Just want you to know that no one's going to be knocking on the door. No spy convention dinner party here tonight."

"Outside of us, at least."

Gloria brushed past Jack as she walked to the other side of the kitchen. She slid the knife block out of the way, then stood on the tips of her toes and reached for the top shelf. Her blouse lifted a few inches. A colorful tattoo decorated her lower back. Jack only saw half and couldn't determine what it was. From what he saw, it appeared to be a butterfly. At that moment, he saw why Mason still allowed Gloria to hang around despite the man's hatred for his ex.

She set three plates on the counter, reached up again, set down a serving dish. She shuffled to the side, pulled open a drawer with her right hand, reached inside for silverware.

Then she made the wrong move with her left hand.

Jack pulled his gun and aimed it at Mason.

"What the bloody hell, mate?" Mason said. A plume of beer rose into the air as Mason's arm jutted upward. It splashed on the floor, created a couple small puddles.

"Turn around real slow, Gloria," Jack said. "I mean it. Slow. Too fast and your ex will have two holes in his stomach."

Gloria lifted her hands above her shoulders. The long knife blade reflected a beam of light. She turned around, her face frozen in fear, mouth open, eyes wide.

"What were you planning to do with that?" Jack said.

"S-S-Separate the steaks. They're kind of frozen in the middle still."

Still. Had she been here when they'd been pulled from the fridge?

Jack studied her for a minute. Her hands trembled, eyes watered. She wasn't a killer, not even close. He'd never met anyone who could act that afraid without actually being that afraid. He lowered his gun, looked from Gloria to Mason and back again, began laughing. Mason joined him.

"I'm sorry," Jack said.

Gloria dropped the knife on the counter and grabbed the steaks and brought them to the sink. "I'll just let them sit in the water for a bit." Her voice shook and rose to a high pitch. Jack imagined her throat closed in upon itself as she tried to keep from sobbing.

Jack turned toward Mason. "No hard feelings."

Mason shrugged. "I left you in the middle of the woods with no directions. If you can look past that, I can look past this."

Idle talk prevailed for the better part of half an hour. They waited for one of Mason's contacts to call. They were in the dark. The news couldn't provide them with solid information, so they were reliant on outside sources. And none of those sources were forthcoming at that time.

Gloria had just begun cooking the steaks when Mason's cell vibrated. The phone skated along the counter top. Mason grabbed it and held it out. "Speaker?"

Jack looked at Gloria, shook his head. He'd have to rely on Mason to provide him with accurate details.

Mason answered the call and slipped into the living room. Jack and Gloria stared at each other while the steaks simmered in a frying pan, coated in a mixture of butter and olive oil. He avoided listening to the one sided conversation so that his brain wouldn't fill in the blanks with inaccurate information.

Gloria opened her mouth to speak. Jack shook his head and brought his right index finger to his lips.

Mason reentered the kitchen, shook his head.

"What'd they say?" Jack said.

"Not much, unfortunately," Mason said.

"Do they know where Naseer is?"

"No. They lost track of him early this morning. Before he went to the warehouse. Apparently, he slipped out some time late last night. Their best guess, at least. They trailed everyone who left the house, but nothing came of it. One woman who'd only recently been spotted at the house went to the train station. She bought a ticket to Paris. Guys at the other end lost sight of her in the station. Something about a couple of French agents following her through the terminal. They didn't want to raise any red flags, so they hung back. Lost her. A couple other guys left the house and went about routine activities, chores and the like. But no sign of Naseer and his main man, Samir."

"So he had this planned. Probably wasn't even at the house last night."

"That or he has another way of leaving the house that we haven't figured out."

"Or whoever is reporting back to you is our rogue agent."

Mason shook his head. "Doubtful."

"Possible."

"Not probable."

Jack nodded. No point in pushing that argument until they had something substantial. "He's under twenty-four hour surveillance, right?"

"Naseer?"

"Yeah."

"Right. We've always got a team positioned near the house. I can't go into any more detail on that, though."

"Think he knows?"

"About the surveillance?"

"Yeah."

"I'm sure he knows."

Jack nodded. "With the people that your guys saw leaving, how many were left unaccounted for?"

"Half dozen, give or take one or two."

"Some could have been inside."

"Others outside with him."

"The bombing could have been remote."

Mason walked across the room. "But the shooters had to be there."

"Could have been men in the organization, but from outside his compound."

"Most likely guys from out of the country."

"That or you have an entire team of corrupt agents in MI5."

"Or across the way at Legoland."

Jack had considered this. "You think that's a possibility?"

"I've been around long enough to know that anything's a possibility."

"And money has a way of getting people to forget their ideals and convictions."

"Steaks are ready," Gloria said.

Both men turned to toward her and said nothing.

"Just letting you know," she said.

Jack and Mason ate and then returned to discussing the situation.

"Here's the problem, mate. I don't know who I can and can't trust."

"I know the feeling."

"Right, well, for all I know, the guy I just spoke with, and no, don't ask me his name, is corrupt and on Naseer's payroll."

"And he fed you a line."

"Right."

"But you said, not probable."

Mason shrugged. "I just don't know, mate. The more we talk, the less sure I become."

"Talk to everyone you can then. Someone's bound to make you feel sure."

Mason paused for a moment then responded. "You don't think that won't draw some unwanted eyes?"

"It might. In fact, I'm hoping it does."

Mason lifted a curious eyebrow, said nothing.

"Build a better mousetrap."

"Plus, the more people I talk to, the greater the chance of talking to the wrong person."

"And a greater chance of talking to the right person."

Mason pointed toward Gloria. "What about her?"

"Stuck with her for now."

"It's putting her in danger."

"I think she'll be in more danger if she's alone."

"How so?"

"Someone is after me, Mason. That someone might be able to put you in that car with me. Now, if they can, then we both know that person will be pretty much able to find out whatever they want about your life. Meaning they'll find out about her. They'll go after her if they can't get to you. I know it's not a good long term idea for her to stick with you, but until we have a better alternative, she goes everywhere you do, which, for the time being, will be here and nowhere else."

Jack left the kitchen, headed toward the front door.

"What about you, Jack?"

Jack stopped, his hand on the doorknob. "Every mousetrap's gotta have bait."

CHAPTER 36

No one knew of the house, not even Naseer. He had received a call late yesterday. They'd told him that the bombings would be carried out and that it was best for him to disappear for a few days. He had the home swept for bugs the moment they arrived. He didn't trust anyone. Couldn't trust anyone.

He and Samir stood side by side at the edge of the wooden deck at the rear of the house. Naseer reached for his drink, which he'd set atop the deck railing. The cold sweat on the glass coated his palm. The moon was full and it illuminated the property. He saw clear to the edge of the woods. His gaze darted left and right, scanned the area in sections. Paranoia, he believed, was what kept him alive. Despite being over two hundred kilometers from London, he would not let his guard down.

Leaving his own house undetected had been easier than he thought. His contact had seen to it that one of the agents watching his property was on the payroll. The guy had been the one responsible for the front of the house. All Naseer had to do was place a phone call and the agent turned his back.

Naseer and his men spent the night at a hotel, then arrived at the warehouse early that morning. From there, they traveled to the hideout.

"What do you think of Owen?" Naseer said.

"He killed for you," Samir said. "Doesn't that say enough?"

"I paid him to do that. Plus, Walloway was one of the biggest jerks I've ever met. I'm sure Owen agrees with that. And think about it like this, he spent a lot of time with the old bastard. I bet he was happy to pull the damn trigger."

"But he killed his partner, too. Simply because the man stood up to you. While he might have hated the old guy, he and his partner had likely gone through a lot together. When it came down to it, he didn't hesitate to kill him. That has to tell you something."

"So you agree with bringing him along?"

"Yes, I think he'll be a valuable asset. He killed for you. Maybe he'll die for you as well."

Naseer nodded. Dying for him was the unspoken requirement. He paid well for it. His people understood this. But Owen wasn't one of his people. The man was an outsider. When the time came, would he place himself in the thick of the hail of a thousand arrows if told to do so?

"What of the women?" Samir said.

Naseer opened his mouth to answer when Samir hunched over and pointed toward the woods. He reached for his sidearm and dissected the area with his aim.

Naseer ducked when he saw Samir draw his weapon. He no longer had a view of the property. "What is it?"

Samir paused for a minute. The sounds of the night amplified. He chuckled, holstered his weapon. "Nothing to worry about. A dog or something."

Naseer peered over the railing as he rose. The grounds were still. He took a deep breath, grabbed the railing to steady his shaking hands. "What did you ask?"

"The women?" Samir said.

Naseer took a few deep breaths, steadied his shaking hand. "Paris. Then they diverted to Brussels. Our contact has men that are chasing down a lead. Hopefully we'll know something by morning."

"What of that other thing?"

Naseer glanced over his shoulder, back to Samir. "The pieces are in motion, but there's still plenty to work out."

"Think we can pull it off?"

"I believe so. As long as we continue to create distractions, they'll be diverting their attention away from the target."

Samir nodded, said nothing.

"The trick will be getting someone close enough to pull it off."

"Owen?"

"Doubtful. He's already associated with Walloway. They'd spot him."

"None of us, then."

Naseer smiled, shook his head. "Of course not. We fit the profile and would be monitored before we even realized we were spotted."

"Then who?"

"I've got someone working on that."

CHAPTER 37

JACK CLOSED MASON'S FRONT DOOR BEHIND HIMSELF AND jogged down the seven steps to the sidewalk. The sky was clear, the air cool. Fortunate, he thought, since he had no place to stay. The wind blew from the west, carried the smell of the factory he had passed earlier that day. He looked down the street, left then right. About half the homes had their lights out. He turned left and put one foot in front of the other, headed east.

He passed a few people along the way. People out walking their dogs. Couples taking a stroll together. A few late night joggers. Some smiled, others avoided his stare, one crossed to the other side of the street to avoid him. That didn't bother Jack. In fact, he preferred it.

After a short walk he stopped in front of a pub. There was no sign that said the place was open. Wasn't one indicating it was closed either. So he stepped inside. The room was dimly lit and alive with chatter. Blues played in the background. He had planned on asking the bartender to call him a cab. Instead he ordered a pint of Hobgoblin. In the dark room, the ale looked black. The frothy tan head stood out in the glass. He savored the drink, then ordered another and asked the bartender to call for that cab.

For the first time all day, he didn't think about the bombings or Thornton Walloway or what Mason's role might be in the mess. His thoughts didn't turn to his longtime friend and partner who he had left behind. Didn't focus on the woman who slipped away a few days ago in D.C. He thought about that angelic face he had met at Dottie's. At times, the fact that he had a daughter felt real to Jack. But there were moments where it felt surreal and he had trouble believing the truth. He tried to avoid feeling betrayed by Erin. She had her reasons for keeping this a secret. He understood, and in some ways he agreed with her choice.

Jack Noble, family man was not a phrase that would be uttered by any who know him.

"What's your troubles, son?"

Jack lifted his gaze from the half-settled head of his beer. The guy on the other side of the bar had about thirty years on him. His gray hair was limited to the sides of his head. He kept a neatly trimmed patch of scruff on his chin and above his upper lip.

Jack offered the bartender a half-smile and shook his head.

"Everybody needs someone to talk to," the man said.

"Not me," Jack said.

"Girl troubles?"

"In more ways than one."

"Baby momma got you down?"

"What?" Jack laughed.

The guy grinned. "I watch MTV in my spare time. Got grandkids in the U.S., want to stay hip to their lingo."

At ease, Jack said, "I met my daughter for the first time today. Found out about her a little bit after I met her."

"How old?"

"Six."

"Congratulations." He turned and poured another beer and set it down in front of Jack. "On the house."

Jack lifted his glass and finished his second beer, then slid the fresh glass toward himself.

"So why's this got you down? She reject you?"

Jack shook his head. "She doesn't know. Guess it's complicated. I'm questioning some things. Why didn't the mother tell me? Do I even deserve to know or be a part of the kid's life? Would she be better off if I never showed up?"

"So, how'd it work? You tracked down the mom, showed up, and saw she had a kid?"

Jack took a pull from his mug. He wiped the foam away from his upper lip. "Something like that."

"We all do things we shouldn't have, son. But the only thing to truly regret is not making amends with those we love."

"You speak from experience?"

The bartender nodded, said nothing.

"So what happened?"

The man shrugged. "It's not worth talking about."

"Everybody needs someone to talk to," Jack said.

The man smiled then looked to his left. "Your cab's here, son."

Jack glanced toward the front of the pub and saw the taxi. He reached into his pocket, dropped a twenty pound note on the bar top. He left the establishment without another word spoken between him and the old man.

Jack slid into the backseat of the cab. "Take me to a hotel that doesn't require ID."

The driver studied Jack in the rear view mirror.

"I'm not a criminal," Jack said.

"Then why no ID?" the cabbie said.

"Just trying to throw my crazy ex-wife off my trail."

"Ah." The cabbie gave Jack a knowing nod and a wink and then put the taxi into gear.

They drove for twenty silent minutes.

The cabbie slowed down in front of a rundown building. "It's a bit dodgy over here, but you look like the kind of fellow who can take care of himself."

Jack handed the man a twenty and exited the cab. He assessed his surroundings. He was in the rough part of town. No one appeared to be an immediate threat, although some unwanted glances were cast his way. He made eye contact with everyone in view. Criminals preferred to prey on the unsuspecting and unprepared.

He crossed the sidewalk and entered the lobby and approached the middle aged woman behind the counter. He held one finger in the air and said, "One night. Just me. Cash."

She pulled the half burned cigarette out of her mouth and said, "One night is eighty pounds, if you're paying cash."

Jack looked around the place. The wallpaper peeled away from the wall in long strands. The floor looked like it hadn't been cleaned in months. Smelled that way, too. Roach traps were visible, as were mouse traps. Droppings along the baseboards confirmed the hotel had a rodent problem.

"You're kidding, right?" he said.

"Want to pay less, drop a credit card on the counter."

Jack reached into his pocket and pulled out a wad of cash. His had limited options. And since he was in a not-so-great area, sleeping outside held less appeal than it had a half hour ago. The woman handed him keys in exchange for money. Directions to the room were not provided. The room number was 814.

Top floor accommodations, Jack thought, *maybe even the penthouse.*

He started toward the hallway, stopped, turned. "Can I get a wakeup call?"

She pulled the cigarette from her mouth again and dropped it. "This ain't the flippin Ritz, boy."

"Of course it's not. What was I thinking?"

Jack turned and found the elevator lobby. Calling it a lobby was being generous. He saw a single elevator. The door was stuck open. Two-by-fours and yellow tape covered the gaping hole. Curious, he poked his head into the opening. The dark shaft revealed no secrets. He couldn't help but wonder what might be at the bottom. The shaft had to be at least a century old. It was as if he stood before an exhumed casket, full of a hundred years of hopes and dreams and horrors.

He found the stairs and quickly ascended them to the eighth floor. The temperature rose the higher he climbed. At the top, he pushed through the stairwell door. The hall was dark, with only one in every five or so lights on. The bulbs must have been 15 watt. They cast small pools of light on the hallway floor, but illuminated little else.

He pulled out his cell phone and brought up a blank web page. The white light given off allowed him to use his phone like a flashlight. This was one of the ways that technology was useful to Jack. He found his room halfway down the hall. He paused outside the door for a moment. No sound came from the room. He tried the handle before inserting the key. The door was unlocked. As he cracked the door, a smell like rotten bananas wrapped in sweaty socks hit him. He kicked the door open with his foot and took a step to the side. After a moment he reached inside and felt along the wall until he found the light switch.

"Christ almighty," he said as the room brightened. The bed was unmade, the sheets strewn about the floor. The dresser drawers hung open. The smell seemed to get worse the longer he stood there. He walked inside, his gun drawn. The sound of flies buzzing intensified with every step he took. He expected to find a body on the other side of the bed. It didn't smell of death, but the corpse could be fresh. He craned his neck as he neared the bed, peeked over the edge. The flies whipped around in a frenzy. He stopped when he saw the source of the smell.

Someone had left four trays of rotten food on the floor.

Jack backed out of the room, left the door open, headed for the stairs.

When he reached the bottom of the stairwell, he kicked the door open. The lobby's overhead light flickered. He made a line toward the check-in counter.

"Hey," he said.

The woman didn't look up.

"What the hell's your deal giving me that room?"

Her head slowly lifted. Her gaze met his. She studied him for a minute, then said, "What about it?"

"What do you mean what about it? It's filthy. The whole floor is. Whole damn place, for that matter."

She rose and placed her hands on the counter and leaned forward. Her eyes narrowed as she looked him up and down. "I'm sorry, I thought you were someone else."

Jack shook his head. All he wanted was four or five solid hours of sleep. "Just give me a new room. A clean one."

She took a step back and slid open a drawer. "Here you go, 204. Cleaned it myself this morning."

"Great."

Jack grabbed the key and headed for the stairs. He stopped at the entrance to the stairwell. Again, he contemplated sleeping outside. In the end, he took the stairs to the second floor and found his room. It smelled, but not as bad as the previous room. The bed had been made. The dresser only had a fine layer of dust on it. He wondered about the space between the furniture and the wall. Checking would only serve to anger him further, and that would be counterproductive. What he needed now was sleep.

He patted the bed. A plume of dust rose into the air. He glanced around for something to place over the sheets. The towels in the bathroom appeared to be the cleanest items in the room, so he grabbed four and placed them on the bed and then laid down on them. He crossed his right ankle over his left and his arms across his chest and faded off to sleep with the image of Mia in his mind's eye.

CHAPTER 38

CLARISSA CREPT THROUGH THE HOUSE TOWARD THE FRONT door. Spiers slept on the couch near the far wall. She stopped in front of the window and pulled back the curtains. A silver haze of fog hovered over the ground. Muted sunlight penetrated, the dew covered grass shimmered. She opened the door and stepped out into the damp air. Though she couldn't see the village, she could see far enough ahead to get there. All she had to do was place one foot in front of the other and keep moving forward.

Story of my life.

She hoped the store would be open. Though it was only six a.m., in a place like this, people started their day early. And if the fridge inside the house was any indication of how those people lived, they'd need food from the store early and often.

Spiers had left the keys to the car on the counter, but she opted not to use it. A walk through the crisp morning air would do her some good. Things had been happening at a breakneck pace. She needed some time to chill and collect her thoughts.

Her sleep had been disrupted throughout the night by a single question. What if her mission had been ruined? By this point, Naseer would have the method of her murder chosen if he knew that she hadn't stayed in Paris. Months of planning destroyed by a single choice. Of course, not her planning. And not her choice. Things were coming to a head with Naseer and his men, and if they carried out a major attack, one that she could have prevented but failed to because of this decision, she'd have trouble living with herself.

By the time she reached the village, the fog had lifted. She looked back toward the house. The path she had taken remained veiled in liquid smoke.

The store was open. Clarissa entered and smiled at the elderly man behind the counter. A woman that Clarissa assumed was his wife tended the coffee pot. She looked over her shoulder and smiled at Clarissa.

"It'll be ready in five minutes," the woman said in French.

Clarissa smiled, nodded. She located the refrigerated section. There she grabbed two pints of milk and a dozen-and-a-half eggs. She set the items on the counter and waited for the coffee to brew.

Outside, a silver sedan stopped in front of the store. She couldn't tell if it was a Mercedes or a Lexus. For all she knew, it could have been an Audi. The windows were tinted black. The passenger door opened, then pulled closed and the car took off.

The old man stared at the spot where the vehicle had stood a moment before. Clarissa wondered if the man felt disheartened by the car leaving, the customer who didn't enter his store, and the sale that didn't happen.

The steady stream of coffee pouring into the pot slowed to a trickle. She grabbed an insulated paper cup and filled it three-quarters of the way. She topped it off with thick cream and sugar, then covered the cup with a lid.

The old man tallied her items. He tried to make small talk, but Clarissa only smiled and looked away. She grabbed the paper bag he had placed her items in, and then she left the store.

Outside, the sun shone brighter and burned away the remaining fog. She could see as far as the driveway. The house remained hidden.

And through that last patch of fog, Clarissa saw two balls of red light. They flashed and then disappeared.

Brake lights.

She quickened her pace.

A minute later a shot was fired.

She dropped the paper bag containing the milk and eggs, and tossed her coffee to the side, and she started to run toward the house.

A second shot rang out. She heard screams, at least one adult and Mia.

Still she could not see the house. It worked in her favor. She'd be able to get close without being seen.

The field next to the house was full of waist high grasses. She cut through the field. Crouched low when the house finally came into view. The screams had stopped almost as quickly as they had begun. Why, she wondered. What were they doing to the survivors inside?

A man exited the house and went to the silver sedan. He was tall, blond, and dressed in dark cargo pants and a dark long sleeve shirt. He opened the passenger door, reached inside, came back out with a lit cigarette. The guy had his back to Clarissa. He placed his pistol on the hood of the car. She decided that she had to act. There was at least one more person inside, maybe more. The car could carry five. How many actually had been in it when it arrived depended on what the men intended on doing with the people inside the house.

Clarissa made her way through the last of the high grass. She picked up a fallen branch, three feet long, three inches in diameter.

The smell of burning tobacco wafted past her.

The guy leaned forward against the car, forehead pressed against the roof, arms at his side.

Must have been a long trip, she thought.

Clarissa slipped off her shoes. Dew coated the bottoms and sides of her toes. She exploded into a sprint. The balls of her feet hit the ground for a fraction of a second at a time. She barely made a sound. By the time the guy realized someone was heading his way, it was too late.

The man lifted his head, started to turn to his left. His eyes widened when he saw Clarissa. He brought his left hand up in a defensive position, but it didn't help.

Clarissa had both hands on the branch. She brought it up and across her left shoulder, like she was holding a bat. She leapt, twisted at the hips, swung the bat. Her coordinated movements provided ample torque, turning the branch from a hunk of wood into a deadly weapon. It smashed into the guy's arm and his face with more force than a major league baseball player's swing. His forearm and jaw snapped with sickening cracks. The skin on his chin split. Blood poured from the gash, and from his ear and his eye. He collapsed to the ground, unconscious.

Clarissa grabbed the pistol off the hood of the car. She brought the handgun to her face. The warm barrel smelled of cordite. She aimed the weapon at his head and went through the man's pockets. Found them to be empty.

The guy moaned. His eyes fluttered open. Clarissa picked up the branch, tucked the pistol in her waistband. The guy moaned louder as Clarissa brought the branch up. She twisted at the waist, the branch followed a half-second later and connected on the side of the guy's head, a little further up than the last time. A sheet of blood flowed from the side of his head, over his hair, down his neck. He fell to his side. The dirt around his head quickly turned to dark crimson mud.

"You better hope to God those women haven't been touched or else you're gonna wake up with worse problems than a headache."

She ran to the side of the house, crouched, stayed low as she approached the door. It lingered open a few inches. She dropped the stick. Mia's soft cries filtered through the doorway. One male voice spoke low. Clarissa couldn't make out what he said, although she could tell he was British.

She paused for a moment, waited for signs of another person inside. All she heard was the voice, Mia's cries and nothing else.

She reached out and nudged the door with the barrel of the gun. It glided open. Rusted hinges groaned. The man's voice continued, uninterrupted. She still couldn't decipher what he said, but the fact he kept talking told her that he hadn't noticed the door. Or maybe he figured it had been his partner, in which case he'd remain casual. At least as casual as one could be in this situation.

With the gun stretched out in front of her and cradled in both hands, Clarissa slipped inside. Spiers lie on the floor halfway between the couch and where she stood. She scanned the room, then went to him. He laid on his stomach, the right side of his face pressed against the floor. He clenched a fire place poker in his right hand. A pool of blood surrounded his head. The tilted floor caused it to spread away from his body. His eyes were wide open, unblinking. She knelt before him, placed a hand on his neck, felt no pulse.

Clarissa stepped over Spiers's body. To the right were the bedrooms, the left the kitchen. The man's voice and Mia's sniffles came from the left. She moved silently toward them.

As she approached the opening, she saw the backs of the women. They held hands behind the chairs they sat in. Even Mia. They weren't bound. Perhaps that was why the man went to the car, for rope. Clarissa's ears burned. Her breath and pulse quickened. She gripped the pistol tighter in response and clenched her chest and stomach muscles. After five seconds, she released. Her body responded by relaxing.

She took another step.

"So from this point on," she heard the man say, "you speak no more. We drive to the coast. A boat will be waiting to take us to England. We'll meet another car there, then you'll be taken to see our boss. And during that whole time, you keep your mouth shut."

Mia sobbed.

"Especially you, you little—"

Clarissa moved forward, quickly and decisively. She trained her aim on the man's head. His eyes grew wide when he saw her. He raised his pistol, but the position of his body left him off balance.

Clarissa didn't have time to tell him to freeze or stop or drop his weapon. She pulled the trigger. Time slowed and the next several actions happened in freeze frame. Her shot was true and it hit the man in the center of the forehead. At the same time she fired, so had he. His gun had been aimed in the direction of the women. They screamed. It sounded like shouts underwater to Clarissa. The man fell to his knees. Clarissa fired again, this time hitting him in the chest. He dropped his handgun, fell backward.

Time resumed. She rushed toward the guy and verified that he was dead. Behind her, Mia continued to cry. Expected, she figured, since the kid was six years old. But Erin screamed again. She sounded like she was in pain. Hannah yelled for Clarissa.

Clarissa turned, saw blood on their hands, the floor and Erin's right leg. She said, "Clean towels."

No one moved.

"Hannah, go get me some clean towels. And find me a belt."

Hannah rose and rushed out of the kitchen. Clarissa went to Erin's side. She found where the bullet had entered, just above Erin's right knee. Blood flowed from the wound. Clarissa feared that the woman's femoral artery had been hit. She placed her index and middle fingers inside the hole in Erin's pants and pulled. The fabric ripped half a foot in either direction. She inspected the wound. The bullet had gone through and through, but not evenly. Her concern that the femoral artery had been damaged grew.

"Mia," she said. "I want you to look through the drawers and see if you can find some scissors."

The little girl said nothing. Her cries had stopped.

Clarissa looked over. The girl looked catatonic. Her eyes wide, focused on her mother's wound. Clarissa placed herself between mother and daughter. She lowered her head until their eyes met. Mia broke free from the spell.

"Scissors," Mia said.

Clarissa nodded. "That's right. And don't you worry, she's going to be OK."

"Promise?"

"Promise."

As soon as the girl turned, so did Clarissa. At the same time, Hannah returned with a handful of white towels and four belts.

"I didn't know what size you needed," Erin said, offering the belts to Clarissa.

"That's fine. You did good. Now I want you to go to the sink and wet a couple of those towels and bring them back over here."

Hannah dropped the belts and a couple towels and headed to the corner of the room. Before Hanna started the faucet, Clarissa heard a car engine roar to life.

"Hurry with those towels," she said.

The faucet cut off. Hannah brought the towels, then moved to the side and grabbed Erin's hand.

"Any luck with those scissors?" Clarissa said.

"Found them," Mia said.

"Hannah, go get those, then keep Mia behind me. Don't let her look at her mom."

"OK."

Hannah retrieved the scissors, handed them to Clarissa.

Clarissa used the scissors to cut the leg of Erin's pants around mid-thigh. She wiped blood away from around the wound. Then she grabbed an inch-wide belt, wrapped it around Erin's leg, and cinched it tight. The blood flow slowed to a trickle.

"Wait here," Clarissa said.

"Where are you going?" Hannah said.

Clarissa did not respond. She grabbed her handgun and left the kitchen. She passed Spiers's body, stopped at the front door. She no longer heard the car's engine. Either the man had left, or he had turned the vehicle off and now waited for her outside. He likely watched the front of the house, waiting for the opportunity to kill her.

Clarissa closed her eyes, brought her hand to her forehead. The warm barrel of the pistol almost singed the skin there. She took a deep breath, reached out and opened the door a crack. Cool air blew inside. The sweat that coated her exposed skin turned cold. She peered through the crack, but the angle prevented her from seeing the spot where the silver car had been. The one thing she could tell was that if the man remained outside, he wasn't out in the open.

Clarissa took one more deep breath, then pulled the door open and crouched down. She eased her torso through the open doorway. The pistol moved with her eyes.

The car was gone. The man had left.

She fell back and rested against the door frame for a moment.

"We should go."

Clarissa looked to her left and saw Hannah standing there. She nodded, said, "Grab the keys and pull the car around."

Hannah did as told. Mia started after her, but Clarissa stopped her from leaving the house.

"Wait for the car."

Clarissa then went to the kitchen. Along the way, she grabbed a chair with caster wheels. She lifted Erin, set her in the chair, wheeled her to the front door. The car appeared a moment later, and with Hannah's help, she got Erin into the front seat. She ran back to the open doorway, took one last look at Spiers's lifeless body. She made a promise to have someone return for him. Everybody had someone to go home to.

She jumped in the car and raced down the driveway, then turned toward town. The car screeched to a stop on the sidewalk in front of the store. It was the only place that Clarissa knew would have people inside. She bolted out of the car and jerked the door to the store open.

"Is there a doctor in this town?" she said.

"Yes, of course," the old man said.

"Where?"

"Why?" the old woman said.

"Just tell me where he is?"

"She," the old man said.

"OK. Where?"

"Right here," the old woman said. "I practiced medicine for over forty years. Now, what's wrong with you?"

Clarissa said nothing. She grabbed the old woman by her arm and pulled her through the store. Hannah had already opened Erin's door. She scooted toward the rear of the car when she saw Clarissa and the old woman emerge from the store.

A small crowd had gathered. The old woman addressed some of them by name, asked them for help. Two men stepped forward. They pulled Erin from the car, interlocked their arms beneath her, and carried her inside.

In the back of the store, on a stainless steel table, the old woman inspected Erin's leg.

"She's very lucky," the woman said.

Clarissa waited for her to continue.

"The bullet tore through her flesh, nicked the bone, but did no further damage. I'll ease the tourniquet and clean and stitch this up. In a few days she should be OK to leave."

"I don't have a few days," Clarissa said.

"Well, she can't—"

"Fix her. Fast. We have to go."

The old woman's lips drew tight. She nodded and began to work. The old man brought back a bottle of pills and a flask of whiskey. The flask was chrome and had two tulips engraved on one side. Erin took two pills and three shots of whiskey with no protest.

The old woman finished in under half an hour. Erin emerged from the back room. She walked with the help of crutches.

"How are you feeling?" Clarissa said.

"Like I've been shot," Erin said.

"I can relate."

The old man went out front and ushered the small crowd away. He helped Clarissa and Hannah ease Erin into the front seat.

"Dear," the old woman said from under the store's awning.

Clarissa turned to face. "Yeah?"

"I had to call the police. It's obvious a crime was committed."

"What did you tell them?"

"You have a thirty minute head start."

Clarissa shook her head, got inside the car. She eased the transmission into gear. They left the town, headed west toward the coast.

CHAPTER 39

LEON STARED AT HIS CELL FOR A MOMENT BEFORE SETTING IT on the counter. The time indicator flashed forty-five seconds. The call felt like it had lasted an hour. He imagined the twisted feeling in his stomach would remain at least that long. His worst fear when he let the women leave had been realized. They'd been attacked and he couldn't do a damn thing about it.

"Dottie," he called out.

She appeared a moment later, her full length robe wrapped tight around her. It trailed along the ground behind her as she walked. "What is it?"

Leon lifted his gaze from the floor. "Someone found them."

Dottie reached for the counter to steady herself. "How? Where?"

"Outside of Brussels. Don't know how. Two men, English, killed the bodyguard Jack had arranged to protect them."

"Are they OK?"

"Erin got shot in the leg."

"Oh my God."

"The wound isn't serious, Dottie. She's already seen a doctor."

"Where are they now? Do those men have them?"

Leon shook his head. "Fortunately, there was a woman traveling with the bodyguard. She had been out when the break-in occurred. She returned, killed one man, the other got away."

Dottie released her grip around the counter, sat down. "What do we know about these people?"

"The attackers? Nothing."

"No, the ones who were tasked with keeping my nieces and Hannah safe."

"Nothing at all. That's why I didn't want to do it this way."

Dottie said nothing. She stared blankly at the wall.

"I think it's time we called Jack to find out more."

"Where are they now?"

"I told them to head to Ostend."

"The ferry?"

"Yes, to Ramsgate."

"Do you think that's safe?"

"Safer than the airport."

Dottie nodded. "Who will meet them there?"

"I will."

"You can't leave me here. If someone found them, they can find us."

Leon turned his head, stared out the window, scanned the front of the property. "Then you'll need to come with me."

"OK. When do we need to leave?"

"It'll take two hours for us to get there. They'll arrive in six. We should leave no later than three hours from now."

"Are you sure they aren't being followed?"

"I'm not sure of anything right now, Dottie."

Neither spoke for a few minutes. Dottie rose, poured a cup of coffee for herself, refilled Leon's mug.

"They should have been with us," he said.

"Those men might have come to us," she said.

"And I could have dealt with them."

"The same way Jack's man did?"

Leon said nothing.

"I have no doubt that the man Jack reached out to was as capable as you, if not more so. And he knew someone was coming. He had to have known."

"I fear that Jack had some involvement in this, Dottie."

"Never. I've known him for ten years. Jack Noble is the most loyal man I've ever worked with."

Leon looked away. "Then you should hire him to be your bodyguard."

Dottie reached for his arm. He pulled away at her touch. "I didn't mean it like that, Leon. I trust you, and only you, with my life."

Leon left the kitchen. He exited through the back door. The small cottage had been in his family for over two hundred years. Situated on England's southern coast, it offered him a place to get away from the stress that came with his line of work. He hadn't used the house in five years, though. Not since the day he started working for Dottie. He'd heard people complain about working a full time job. They had no idea what it meant to be committed to their work.

He walked to the edge of the beach. The wind whipped past and sent tiny particles of sand and sea spray toward him.

Dottie's words had been hurtful, but that wasn't what he focused on. He thought only of Erin. From the moment he'd first laid eyes on her, he'd loved her. It took close to six months for him to get her to speak to him. And as Mia grew, he befriended the child. The relationship with her gained him further access to Erin. He was sure any day now their friendship would blossom into a romance. Her smiles lasted longer, as did the glances they shared.

Of course, the arrival of Jack Noble had thrown a wrench into his plans. He'd heard the rumors, confirmed them the moment he laid eyes on Jack. No denying the child's eyes were his.

And now that bastard had placed Erin in danger. Wounded. She could have died. Leon cursed himself for allowing the women to leave his protection. No man would have harmed Erin had he been around.

"Leon," Dottie's voice struggled to find him through the wind.

He pretended not to hear her, walked onto the packed sand where foam danced along the beach ahead of the waves.

"Leon," she said again.

He looked over his shoulder. She stood ten meters away.

"What?" he said.

"I'm sorry."

He said nothing.

"I know..." She paused, looked up at the sky, then walked toward him. "I know of your feelings for Erin."

He forced a confused expression. "I don't know what you're talking about."

"I know you better than you know yourself," she said. "You've loved her for a long time."

Leon looked away. His gaze scanned the sea, lifted to the hazy gray horizon.

"I'm worried for her too, Leon. We can't do anything until she's on shore, though. So you have to put it behind you. We don't know if we're next."

Leon nodded. In an instant, his mind shifted and focused. "OK." He turned and walked past Dottie, toward the house. "We should probably leave now."

They made their way inside. Dottie showered and dressed. He fixed breakfast and placed the food in plastic containers so they could bring it with them. When Dottie returned, they tossed their bags in the car and left the cottage, headed east toward Ramsgate.

CHAPTER 40

THE THIN DRAPES DID LITTLE TO BLOCK THE EARLY MORNING sun. Jack woke up and glanced at his phone. He performed time zone calculations in his head. Six-thirty a.m. He'd managed to sleep an hour longer than he expected. According to his running tally, that still left him a year behind on the recommended eight hours a night.

He rolled out of bed and headed to the bathroom. The mildew covered shower did not appeal to him. He figured he'd end up dirtier if he used it. So he splashed some water on his face, then left his room.

The same woman sat behind the counter in the lobby. He walked toward her, cleared his throat about ten feet away. She didn't look up.

"Can you call me a cab?"

She didn't reply.

He looked between her and the phone that remained a foot to the left of her.

"Can I use the phone?"

Again, no reply.

"Just wait till I leave you a Google review, lady."

Jack left the hotel. The area looked dodgier in the daylight. Homeless hung out in the front stoops of the buildings. A man dealt drugs on a nearby corner. A group of younger men stood on the other side of the street. They chased away the men that passed, made obscene gestures at women.

Jack looked up and down the street. He wasn't sure which way to go, but he knew he couldn't linger for long. Stares fell upon him. A couple of bums headed toward him. He noticed that he'd caught the attention of at least one of the men across the street. It all added up to an impending confrontation. And that was something Jack needed to avoid.

So he began walking. He headed away from the approaching bums, and held eye contact with the guy across the road long enough to let the man know Jack would not be an easy target.

Another block further, Jack spotted a bus stop. A few people waited on a bench. He looked back. The group of men walked in the same direction, at roughly the same pace. They remained on the other side of the street. Their loud talk and exaggerated actions told Jack all he needed to know. They preyed as a pack. Individually, they were nothing. But together they might be trouble.

He had a choice to make. Wait for the bus and risk a confrontation with the guys, or keep on walking.

He stopped at the bus stop. "How long until the bus arrives?"

"About five minutes or so," an elderly lady said. She patted her white curls into place and smiled.

Jack nodded. He looked back toward the group. They'd stopped, too. He decided as long as they stayed in place, he'd wait for the bus. Another minute later, the men turned and walked away. It had been nothing, after all. At that moment, he appreciated the extra hour of sleep. He knew he'd need it today.

The red bus pulled up a couple minutes later. Jack waited for the other passengers to board. He stepped onto the first step of the platform, said, "I'm trying to get to the tourist area."

"This bus don't go there," the driver said.

"Are you going somewhere that will allow me to get there?"

"Might take you all day."

Jack figured he was maybe ten miles from the center of the city. He could walk there in three hours, so the thought of public transportation taking all day didn't ring true.

"Any other suggestions?" he said.

"Get on, son. I stop by the underground a few miles down the road."

Jack nodded, stepped up and took a seat behind the driver. He used the rear view mirror to study the passengers. Everyone on board looked like they were low-wage working class or poorer. Half were elderly. Probably not as old as they looked. Aged prematurely by a life that kicked them to the ground and put a knee in their lower back, refusing to let them up.

The bus rolled to a stop and the driver pointed to the underground entrance. Jack tucked a ten pound note in his palm and shook the driver's hand. If the man appreciated the gesture, he failed to let Jack know.

Jack hopped from the bus to the sidewalk. The area teemed with activity. A mix of people. In that short two miles he'd gone from the ghetto to that in between zone where classes mix. He stopped in front of a map and determined the series of trains he needed to catch in order to reach the city center. He had to switch trains once. The straight forward route allowed Jack to use the time to clear his head.

Forty-five minutes later, he emerged two blocks from the site of the bombing.

The hotel he'd had reservations at no longer rose into the sky. It lay in shambles, its guts spilled out into the street. A smoky haze lingered. A smell he'd only experienced one time in his life enveloped him.

Yellow police tape cordoned off the area. Onlookers were kept a block away on all sides. Tape would not keep Jack from entering, though. The bomb had been intended for him, after all. He had to investigate the scene. Perhaps the attackers had left something behind that only he'd recognize.

It wouldn't be easy getting closer, though. Several police officers guarded the scene. They were positioned every fifty feet or so along the road, behind the barrier of yellow tape. Jack walked the perimeter but could not locate a spot to slip through.

And the help arrived in the most unusual form.

A group of reporters and cameramen rushed past him. They spoke excitedly through ragged breath. Jack looked toward the end of the road. He saw a gray Rolls Royce pull up and stop in front of the police tape. Several officers abandoned their posts and went to the Rolls. They formed a barrier between the vehicle and the throng of reporters. Voices rose. Cameras flashed. Cops shouted. A horn blared.

Jack walked another twenty feet, stopped, scanned the area. Security from that point on had been abandoned. They'd all rushed to the aide of the Rolls. Jack crouched and slipped underneath the tape. He glanced around, saw that he'd gone unnoticed. He made his way behind the row of buildings that led to the crumbled hotel. The empty alley provided him with a clear path. He didn't rush. Instead, he chose to act like he belonged there.

And in his mind, he did.

He faced his first test as he neared the restaurant where he initially encountered Leon. Forensic techs were working behind the building. He spotted a woman collecting shell casings. The woman looked up at Jack. She studied him for a moment. He prepared himself for her to question him, or worse, alert others to his presence. He was armed and roamed a crime scene unchaperoned. At the least, he'd spend half a day in a police station if caught.

He nodded at the woman. She nodded back and returned to her job. Jack watched as she placed numbered cards on the ground to mark the spots where she'd found evidence.

He'd wanted to enter the restaurant, but decided against it while the team worked. So he continued past them, then came to a stop behind the spot where the hotel had stood. The hill of rubble blocked him from anyone on the other side of the building. Not that it mattered. He was in the heart of it now. The people here were busy working, not protecting the scene of the attack.

Jack spotted a blue police issued windbreaker hanging from a post. He glanced around, then pulled the jacket from its perch and put it on. If anything, it would attract fewer questioning eyes in his direction. He decided that if questioned, he'd state that the U.S. agency SIS had sent him to assist MI5. It'd take the authorities several hours to track down Frank Skinner, acting director of the SIS, by which point Jack would have made contact and Frank would have everything in place.

So Jack rounded the remains of the building. He made his way through the scattered concrete slabs that lay in the street. It was difficult to avoid the dried pools of blood. A clump of matted hair that stuck to a jagged section of the building's facade caught his eye. Linens and clothes littered the road. Papers rode the wind. A fine powder-like layer of dust coated everything.

He spotted a patch of brown, knelt down and moved a pile of debris aside. He reached in and pulled out a teddy bear. The stuffed toy was intact, if not a bit dirty. He rose, patted the stuffed bear. A gray plume rose into the air in front of him. He continued on his way, teddy bear in hand.

"You there," a female voice called from his left.

Jack ignored the voice, kept moving forward.

"I said, you there. Wait up."

Jack stopped. He went over his story in his head again.

"What did you find over there?"

Jack turned toward the woman. Her brown hair was pulled back tight in a ponytail. She lifted her glasses and rested them on her head. She had gray eyes with bursts of green and brown. He figured she stood about five-six. The wind caused her baggy jacket to hug her torso, revealing her slender build.

"Well?" she said.

He held out the bear. "I'm hoping there's a child looking for this."

"You're American."

"You're kidding."

She cocked her head, smiled. "What are you doing here?"

"I'm with a counter-terrorism organization. We've often worked hand in hand with MI5 and MI6. They sent me over immediately."

"Why do you have a police jacket on?"

"Didn't come prepared. An officer had a spare, let me borrow it."

"What was his name?"

"I should get going." He turned and started toward the front of the building.

She followed. "What's your name?"

"Jack."

"Jack what?"

"Jack is all I can tell you. The rest is classified."

"And you'd have to kill me to tell me, right?"

"Only in the U.S., ma'am."

"Then there shouldn't be a problem telling me in London. We won't be breaking any treaties that I'm aware of."

"It's better that you don't know, Ms.?"

"Sasha."

"Sasha what?"

"That's classified, and if I told you, I would have to kill you."

Jack smiled. "Fair enough."

"I'll take that teddy bear, Jack. They've got a little collection shrine type thing going on over there."

Jack stopped, faced Sasha. He extended the bear toward her. She reached for it. He didn't immediately let go.

"Find me before you leave," she said.

"Why?" he said.

"I'd like to exchange notes."

With that, she turned and jogged away. Jack watched her for a minute, then continued toward the front of the building. When he approached the corner, he noticed an uptick in the chatter level. He kept moving forward. A large group of agents stood on the street in front of the hotel. All but one of them ignored him.

Jack noticed the guy standing off to the side. The man's stare fell upon Jack and didn't waver. Jack stopped, knelt, pretended to investigate something on the ground. He kept the agent in his peripheral vision. When the man started walking his way, Jack rose and turned away.

"Jack Noble," the man said.

Jack looked over his shoulder. The man extended his hand above his shoulder as he got nearer. He waved, called out for Jack again.

Jack turned to face the guy.

"Jon Hayes," the man said. "We worked together, maybe ten years ago when I was in the SAS and you were—"

"A Marine working with the CIA."

Jon nodded. "What brings you here?"

Jack looked toward the group of people in front of the building. "You with them?"

"Only one."

"Who?"

"The only important one."

"Which is?"

"The Prime Minister."

Jack squinted and scanned the group of agents until he saw another face he recognized. "Wait a minute. Your Alex Parkin is Prime Minister Alex Parkin."

Jon smiled. "Come on, old friend. Let's go have a chat."

PART 4
EPISODE 14

CHAPTER 41

Alex pushed through the tangle of agents, cops and reporters. He moved toward the rubble. A sea of voices called for him, full of questions he had no answer for. Everything he had been prepared to say to them had slipped his mind. All he could think of were the hundreds who had perished in the attack. The children who'd lost a parent. The parents who'd lost a child. Friends and neighbors, gone. He oversaw a nation that feared they'd lost their might.

Alex spotted Jon talking to a man. The guy looked familiar, but he couldn't place him. Alex turned around, placed his hand on his copper's shoulder, and said, "Keep them back."

As he approached, Jon nodded and gestured for Alex to join them.

He walked toward the men, his gaze alternated between Jon and the man, and the destruction that surrounded them. It seemed surreal. He wondered why this had happened. No one credible had yet stepped forth and claimed responsibility for the attack. Would they find clues at the bottom of the rubble? Would they unearth important information inside the restaurant?

As Alex neared, the familiar looking man stepped forward, extended his hand and said, "Prime Minister, good to see you again."

Alex nodded, shot Jon a look.

Jon said, "This is Jack Noble, Alex. We ran a few missions with him some ten years ago."

Alex thought back. So much had happened since then that a lot of the details had faded into some recess in his mind.

"You were partners with the big guy, right? What was his name? Moose?"

"Bear," Jack said with a smile.

"Ah, that's right, Bear. What is he up to these days? How have you been? What are you doing here?"

Jack glanced around. "I have information that might help you get to the bottom of this attack."

Alex glanced at Jon and lifted an eyebrow. Jon shrugged as if this were news to him, too.

"Do go on, Jack," Alex said.

"Can't. Not here, out in the open."

"Why not?"

"It's not safe."

Alex held out his hands and looked back over his shoulder. "All those men serve me. I assure you, it is safe here."

"And the reporters, too?" Jack said. "They have your best interest at heart?"

Alex said nothing.

"What about those agents over there?" Jack said, gesturing toward a group that had gathered on the other side of the street and watched the meeting with interest. "How do you know one of them isn't involved in this?"

"That's enough, Jack," Jon said.

"I share your concerns," Alex said. "But if you have information, I need to hear it. Jon needs to hear it. For the love of God, everyone that can help needs to hear it."

Jack nodded, said nothing.

"Let's go to the car," Jon said.

"And travel through that mess," Jack said, his eyes on the reporters.

"They've already snapped your picture. You can expect to be in the papers."

The guy grimaced, something that Alex understood well. He'd never gotten used to the idea of the paparazzi always in his face. Even legitimate reporters stayed too close these days.

"Well, have you any ideas?" Alex said.

Jack glanced around, his eyes settled on a spot over Alex's shoulder.

"How about in there?" Jack said.

Alex turned, saw a shop with its door open. A woman appeared with a garage broom in hand. She pushed a large pile of dust and debris out of the store. It erupted into a cloud as it slid over the curb.

"Think it's safe in there?" Alex said.

"I was in there the other day. It's safe."

Alex and Jon looked at each other.

"Which day?" Jon said.

"Did you see the attack happen?" Alex said.

"No," Jack said. "It was before that."

"Let's go," Alex said.

"Prime Minister," a woman called out.

Alex stopped, turned, saw Sasha Kirby headed his way. The woman had been a fast riser within the ranks of MI6. She'd earned Alex's and Jon's trust along the way, and now personally advised Alex on matters of national security. He'd yet to speak with her since the attacks.

She came over, nodded at each man.

"Agent Kirby, this is Jack Noble." Alex extended his hand toward Jack.

"Nice to meet you, Mr. Noble," she said.

"Likewise, Ms. Kirby."

The two shared a smile.

"Right," Alex said. "Well, Agent Kirby, Mr. Noble has information about the attack. We were about to go talk in private. I'd like you to join us. He might have some information that will help your investigation."

She nodded and they started toward the shop. Jack and Jon led the way. Agent Kirby walked next to Alex. No one spoke. Jon wagged a finger at the reporters who came toward them, and at the cameramen who raised their devices over their heads like submarine periscopes. There would be no prying eyes or ears invited to this discussion.

CHAPTER 42

THE PAPER THIN BARRIER THAT BLOCKED OFF THE ATTACK SITE would do little to stop Bear from crossing. The police ten feet away with HK MP5s draped over their chests were a different story. He approached the yellow police tape with Mandy hanging on to the back of his shirt. The sight of the collapsed hotel made his heart sink. If Jack had been inside, there was no way he was still alive. Bear had to accept that now and be prepared in case he never found his friend.

They'd come straight from the airport. He hadn't arranged accommodations and had no idea where they'd go next. The black taxi expertly navigated traffic filled roads and let them off a couple blocks away. They'd walk the rest. Crossing the street had been an adventure. Some drivers had no respect for a pedestrian in the street, it seemed. He'd witnessed traffic in most major cities in the U.S., but the drivers in London, and many European cities for that matter, took aggressive driving to a whole new level.

"It smells funny," Mandy said.

He squeezed her hand, looked down at her, nodded. He'd noticed the odor before he stepped out of the cab. He imagined that most of the apartments and offices in the surrounding area were steeped in it. He presumed that the locals had probably started to become used to the mixture of lingering dust and smoke by now. The odor at least. The physical effects were a different story. Those with a predisposition likely struggled with dry eyes, itchy throats, burning lungs.

Behind the tape were tight faces, questioning eyes, men and women wearing blue windbreakers.

Bear approached the tape, veered toward a female agent who stood about five feet behind the line. He caught her attention. The woman looked at him, then down at Mandy. She gave the girl a smile.

"I'm trying to find information on someone."

The woman pointed. "There is a table over there. Those people can help you."

Bear shook his head. "No, this is different. I need to get past this line."

The woman took a step back, pulled her pistol.

Mandy grabbed hold of Bear's shirt and scooted behind him.

Bear lifted his hands. "It's not like that."

"I need you to back away, sir."

The crowd surrounding them shifted back. All eyes fell upon Bear. He'd also attracted the attention of several other agents and police officers. They approached from both sides, guns drawn.

"I said back away," the woman's voice rose.

"I'm not going anywhere," Bear said.

"Sir," a man shouted. "You need to turn around and leave or else we'll be forced to detain you."

"You want to detain me?" Bear shouted back. He'd lost his patience, and perhaps his sanity. "Fine, you do that. Maybe then I'll end up in front of someone with half a brain who'll help me out instead of trying to send me away."

Three male officers ducked under the tape and came toward him, weapons extended. Two holstered their weapons and reached for Bear's arms. He stepped forward to create some distance between them and Mandy, but the girl held onto his shirt and stayed close.

The officers grabbed his arm. He resisted, shouted. They shouted back. The third officer threatened to shoot.

"Bear." The shout came from behind the yellow line.

Bear shifted his focus from the cops to the groups of people surrounding the attack site. He didn't see anyone he recognized. Again, someone shouted his name.

"Who's calling your name, Bear?" Mandy said.

The cops eased off as Bear let them have control of his arms. He continued to scan the faces behind the line. The warm breeze carried his name to him a third time. It echoed off the buildings. He saw arms waving and a face he'd recognize anywhere.

"I'll be...," he said. "It's Jack, sweetie."

CHAPTER 43

JACK STARTED TOWARD BEAR AT A QUICK PACE. "TELL THOSE men to let go of him," he said to Jon.

Jon rushed to Jack's side. They jogged toward the gathering near the perimeter. "Is that Logan?"

"Yeah."

"You there, officers," Jon shouted. "Let that man go. He's with us."

Jack and Jon slowed to a walk as the officers escorted Bear and Mandy past the police line. A minute later the two friends embraced.

"Christ, Jack, I thought you were dead."

Jack pulled back, looked at Bear. "You know me better than that. Takes more than blowing up a building to take me down." He took a step back, smiled at Mandy. "How is it possible you've grown so much in just a few days?"

She said nothing, stepped forward with her arms wide. Jack scooped her up and hugged her. Although Bear had been the one to assume responsibility for the child, Jack would never forget the impact she'd had on his life. Without her, the Jack Noble redemption tour would have never begun.

"Jack," Jon said. "We need to get back to the Prime Minister."

Bear pointed toward Alex. "I'll be damned. Parkin is Prime Minister Parkin?"

Jon nodded.

"Man, he got old looking."

"Politics can do that to you," Jon said.

"So can women," Jack said.

"And drinking," Jon said.

"And kids," Bear said as he nudged Mandy.

"Hey," Mandy said. She elbowed Bear in the stomach. He pretended to buckle forward.

They walked toward the Prime Minister. A couple of agents followed a dozen feet behind.

"What are you doing here?" Jack asked Bear.

"Got a call, was told you might be in trouble. Started getting those feelings, man. You know, that something was wrong. We got some help and came over."

"Anyone I know?"

"Of course."

"Why'd you bring the kid?"

"What else could I do? She's my responsibility now, Jack. If she's not with me, she's not safe."

"If she's around me, she's not safe."

"I balance that out. Don't forget that."

"You always have," Jack said.

They stopped and Jon dismissed the agents that had accompanied them. Alex walked toward them.

"Now this guy I remember." Alex extended a hand to Bear.

"How you doing, Alex?" Bear said.

"Stressed."

"You look it."

"Goes with the territory."

"So I've heard."

Jon introduced Bear and Mandy to Sasha, then said, "Let's get to that shop now so we can talk."

The woman emerged from the store again. The bristles of her broom pushed a large pile of debris onto the sidewalk. She shuffled toward the street, stopped when she noticed the group approaching. Her gaze traveled from person to person and stopped on Jack.

"What are you doing here?" she said. "You show up, a day later the damn block explodes, and now you're back? I should call those cops over here."

"The cops answer to me, lady," Jon said.

"Ma'am," Alex said as he placed a hand on Jon's shoulder. "We need to use your shop for a meeting."

"Piss off," she said as she turned and headed toward the door.

Jon stepped forward. "Do you know who you're telling to piss off?"

She stopped, turned. "Yeah, I know who he is. But I didn't vote for him, so he can piss off."

Jon turned red, started toward the woman. Alex reached out again and grabbed him.

"Ma'am," Alex said. "Either you let us use it or the police will force you to. It's as simple as that."

She dropped her broom. A cloud of dust kicked up when the handle hit the ground. She headed into the store and said, "Fine, use it."

They went inside. Bear told Mandy to stay near the front door and let them know if someone approached. The girl smiled and accepted the position of lookout.

"She's come a long way," Jack said.

Bear nodded and smiled. "Sure has. Figure with the way her life has gone, might as well teach her everything I can."

"What are you going to do after this?" Jack said.

Jon interrupted. "Jack, you said you had information for us. Let's hear it."

Jack took a deep breath, exhaled, said, "I came to London for a reason. As you may or may not be aware, after I left the Marines I went to work for the U.S. agency, SIS. After that I partnered up with Bear and we became freelance contractors. You up to speed on that?"

Jon looked at Alex and nodded. Men in his position were likely to know of Jack and others like him.

Jack continued. "I'd decided to retire, but a friend called and needed help. I figured one last job and that was it. It was personal anyway. I'd had a run-in with the guy some time ago. It resulted in him taking out some frustration on his old lady."

"I think I know where this is going," Jon said. "Jack, you don't have to say anymore on that." Jon glanced at Sasha. "It's probably better that you don't."

Jack nodded. "OK, well, I'll speed this up. I had reservations at the hotel."

"That hotel?" Alex said, pointing across the street.

"Yes, that hotel."

"Under what name?"

"Mine."

Silence for a moment.

"You think you were targeted?" Sasha said.

Jack shrugged. "That or it was one hell of a coincidence. The first day I was in town, I went to the hotel. A sequence of events prevented me from checking in. I went to the restaurant next door. Saw a car pull up. Some guys got out like they were looking for someone. Looked like the kind of guys who'd be sent to find someone like me."

"Sasha, get your team to look into this," Jon said.

She nodded, started to leave.

"Don't go anywhere yet, Sasha," Jon said.

She stopped, glanced at Jack.

Jack held her gaze for a moment, then said, "So then I went to stay with an old friend. Next day I had a run in with a guy named Mason Sutton. You know him?"

Jon and Alex and Sasha glanced at one another, nodded at Jack.

"Is there a story there?" Jack said.

"Sutton is kind of a," Sasha paused, looked toward the ceiling. "I guess you could say he's a loose cannon. He does things his own way. Doesn't always take things up the chain of command like he should."

"Why's he still around?" Jack said.

"Because he's that effective," Sasha said.

"Maybe there's a reason for that," Alex said.

Jack said, "Yeah, well, I don't know whether to trust him or not. So far he seems to be on my side. He could have hurt me more than once and he didn't."

"He could be setting you up for something," Jon said.

Jack shrugged. "He already had me in position for that. If he were going to do it, it would have been then."

"The warehouse?" Sasha said.

"How'd you know?"

Sasha said nothing.

Alex's cell phone rang. He pulled it out. "Personal line. Give me a moment." He walked toward the rear of the store.

Jon said, "Jack, can you think of any reason why these guys would want you dead?"

"I can think of plenty of reasons, but none of them make sense. It doesn't mesh. If I was the target, and these guys carried this out, then someone else put them up to it. I never checked in here. So someone used them, tricked them into believing there was something else behind this."

"What if they didn't know that you hadn't checked in though?" Jon said.

"I don't buy that. If anything, someone was trying to get my attention. Why? I don't know."

Jon nodded, said nothing.

"Who's come forward to claim responsibility?" Jack said.

"No one credible," Sasha said.

"It's gotta be payback for something," Bear said.

"Yeah, but what?" Jack said.

No one had an answer.

Alex returned. His face looked pale, drained. Sweat covered his brow.

"What is it?" Jon said.

"They just told me that I'm next in line."

"Who? For what?"

"Them." Alex licked his lips, coughed. "They told me they're going to assassinate me."

CHAPTER 44

THE WEIGHT OF THE WORDS HOVERED OVER THE GROUP, DREW the air from their lungs.

"Who was it, Alex?" Jon said.

Alex stared ahead, his gaze fixed on the crumbled remains of the hotel. His lips were parted a half-inch. He didn't speak.

"Alex?" Jon said. "Who was on the phone?"

Alex shook his head. "A man."

"What did he sound like?"

"A man."

"Alex."

"Jon."

The men faced off, anger in their eyes. Perhaps not for each other, but anger nonetheless.

"Listen, Jon, he sounded like a man. A normal every day English man. It could have been any one of fifty million people."

Sasha stepped between Jon and Alex. She faced the Prime Minister. "Sir, what number did the call come from?"

Alex reached into his pocket, pulled out his phone. He tapped at the screen. He and Sasha both shook their heads.

"No number," Sasha said.

"Maybe they can trace it?" Alex said.

"Doesn't work that way," Bear said. "If no number was displayed, that means the receiving switch didn't get any information."

No one spoke for a minute.

The woman who owned the store came back inside. "Are you folks going to be taking up my store much longer? I have to get this place cleaned up, you know."

"Oh, shut the bloody hell up," Alex said.

The woman stopped dead. "Well, that certainly won't win my vote in the next election." She turned and exited through the open doorway.

Silence, then laughter.

After a moment, Sasha said, "We have to treat this seriously. The men that did this are more than capable of pulling off another attack. They might not come directly for you, sir. Instead, they might choose to attack a place where you'll be. Maybe even where you might be. Or multiple places at once. It's not just your life at risk. It could be hundreds, maybe thousands of innocent people that die. You signed up for this full well knowing the possibilities. They didn't."

Alex nodded. "We'll get everyone—"

A cell phone rang. All eyes turned to Alex. He reached in his pocket, pulled out his phone. It was silent.

"That's me," Jack said as he pulled his phone out. He stepped a few feet away and answered. "Dottie, we've got a crazy situation over here."

"So do we, Jack," she said.

"What's going on there?"

"That man you sent to protect Erin and Mia."

"Yeah?"

"He's dead."

"Dead? How?"

"Murdered."

"Oh, Christ. What about the girls?"

"Erin was shot in the leg."

"Is she all right?"

"She's going to be fine."

"And Mia? Hannah?"

"Scared, but OK."

"What happened?"

"We don't have all the details yet, but what I know is this. They took up outside of Brussels. Your man had a woman with him. She went out early in the morning. The house was attacked shortly after she left. When she returned, found one of the men outside. She crept up on him, knocked him unconscious. Inside the house, she found your guy dead. She killed the second attacker. Erin took a bullet in the shootout."

"Who's the woman?"

"I don't know her name, Jack. Supposedly we'll meet her shortly."

"Where are they now?"

Dottie said nothing.

"Dottie?"

"I don't know if this line is being monitored, Jack. Best I don't say. Anyway, what is the problem there?"

"I'm with the Prime Minister now. We're at the site of the attack."

"How's he taking everything? We go back a ways, you know."

"He was OK."

"Was?"

"He just got a call."

"What kind of call?"

"One where someone threatened to kill him."

Silence for a beat. "Jack, put me on speaker."

"Why?"

"Because, I want to talk to both of you."

Jack held the phone out and switched it to speaker. He walked back to the group. "Alex, I've got Dottie Carlisle on the phone. She wants to talk to both of us."

"Hello, Prime Minister."

"Dottie, you know you can call me Alex."

"Yes, well, Alex. Jack told me that you just received a rather disturbing call."

"Correct."

"Listen to me, Alex. If I was heading things up, I would see to it that Jack Noble does not leave your side."

"We've got things in place," Jon said.

"Who's that?"

"That was Jon Hayes, my—"

"I know who he is. Jon, this is not meant to be an insult to you. Frankly, you can't have too many good men around in a situation like this. You know that. You have to believe me. I trust Jack. Leon trusts Jack. You two have to trust him. He provides a different kind of perspective. He sees things differently. He understands how this works on both ends. He will be valuable both in protecting you and in strategizing when it comes to finding these terrorists. If you don't keep him around, you'll only have yourselves to blame when one or both of you ends up dead."

No one spoke for a minute.

Jack said, "What if I decline? I've got things to figure out here too."

"Jack, we're tied together on this," Alex said. "They came after you. They're after me now."

"And if we're together we make their life that much easier," Jack said.

"They'll never know," Dottie said.

"Fifty reporters follow this guy around all day long," Jack said.

"We can move around in secret if need be," Jon said.

"If you can manage to get through the front door undetected," Jack said.

"Are we in agreement, gentlemen?" Dottie said.

Jack and Alex stared at each other. Everyone else stared at them.

Alex extended his hand toward Jack. "Yes."

Jack shifted the phone from his right to his left and took the Prime Minister's hand in his own. "OK. But Bear stays with us, too."

"Excellent. Jack, I'll call you with details on that other thing in a few hours. Keep your cell switched on."

She hung up. Jack stuffed the phone in his pocket.

"She would have made one fine Prime Minister," Alex said.

"No argument there," Jon said.

"What now?" Jack said.

"I want to look at the damage some more," Alex said.

"The reporters got their shots," Jon said.

"You bloody well know this goes beyond public relations."

Before they could leave the shop, the woman appeared at the door again. She breathed heavily and struggled to talk.

"What is it, you old hen?" Alex said.

"Gas... leak," she said.

The group looked at each other with confused expressions.

The woman took a deep breath, yelled, "Did you hear me?"

An agent shoved her aside and said, "Get out now! We just discovered a gas leak a half block away. The hotel is still smoldering. It's only a matter of minutes before there's an explosion."

CHAPTER 45

THE CALM SEA SPLIT IN TWO. THE LARGE FERRY CUT THROUGH the channel like a giant lumbering blue whale. Salt water spray rode the wind. It fell upon Clarissa's face in sheets of a thousand particles. She let the water dry on her skin. The smell reminded her of summers spent on North Carolina's outer banks where her family had a beach house. The area had been spared the megaliths built by investors in the '80s and '90s. Peaceful times. Calmer times.

Mia's head rested against her arm. The gentle swaying of the ferry had put the girl to sleep moments after they departed. Hannah and Erin sat close by, but inside, protected from the elements by walls and windows.

They'd left the car behind. It wasn't registered in any of their names and it would have drawn unwanted attention to them. The quarter-mile they had to walk had been difficult for Erin. The woman had pushed hard and made it, though. Clarissa glanced back at her, saw her resting her head against the window, eyes closed.

At the rate land approached, Clarissa estimated another ten minutes before they docked. Speculation, of course. She had no real way of knowing.

Laughter from a few seats down woke Mia. The little girl sat up straight, stretched her arms and legs. "Are we there?"

Clarissa shook her head. "Not yet, honey." She extended her arm toward shore. "We're close though."

Mia reached out, grabbed the railing, leaned forward. "It looks pretty. Like a painting."

"Yes, it does."

Five minutes later they were close enough for Clarissa to make out the individual cherry trees that lined the bank. Most trees had half their blooms remaining. Others had considerably fewer. She wondered if the shore would be lined with the fallen blooms, or had they floated into the channel and drifted off to sea?

The ship's loud horn blared. Erin and Hannah met Clarissa and Mia outside. They joined the pedestrian crowd and moved toward the front of the boat. The group molded and conformed to the confines of the bow like an amoeba.

Leon greeted them at the end of the pier. Mia ran to him, hugged him. Hannah hugged him as well. He tried to offer his hand to Erin, but she shook her head, continued on with her crutches.

Leon watched her go, then he turned to Clarissa. "You must be the mystery woman?"

"That's me. Clarissa Abbott."

"Thank you for saving our girls."

"It's what I'm trained to do."

"Well, we're indebted to you. Come on, follow me. It's going to be a cramped ride, but we had better get going."

The older woman had remained in the car. She nodded at Clarissa, but did not introduce herself. It left Clarissa feeling uncomfortable.

She took a seat in the back of the vehicle, behind the woman. The doors shut and Leon started the car.

Clarissa had a vague idea of where they were. When Leon picked up the M2 in Faversham, she knew they were headed to London. A series of exits and merges led them to the M25 and soon they were on the southwest side of the city.

They exited the highway and traveled through a few residential areas before turning onto a driveway and stopping in front of a house. The car hid from the street behind high hedges. Clarissa waited a minute, then exited. The older woman stood before her.

"You are about to enter my house, Clarissa. So help me, if you harm a hair on any of my girls, I'll kill you myself."

"If I were going to do that, I would have done it in Belgium. You'd think the fact that I got them this far would earn a little trust."

"I don't trust anyone." The woman's eyes batted between Clarissa's. She stood there for a moment, said nothing else. She turned and went to the front door.

"Wait, Dottie," Leon said. He rushed to her side. "Let me check it out first."

Dottie stepped to the side and he entered. A minute later he appeared in the open doorway and said it was safe to enter. Clarissa followed Dottie inside. The woman turned to the left and disappeared into her study. She shut the doors behind her.

Clarissa felt a hand on her elbow.

"We've got a room for you upstairs," Leon said.

She followed him up the stairs and into a spare bedroom. It was small, which was fine with her. She didn't need much more than a bed anyway.

"You can stay as long as you need to," he said. "If you're hungry, follow me to the kitchen."

They left the room and went back down the stairs. Before she had entered the kitchen, she noticed that someone had already started a pot of coffee. The rich aroma comforted her for a moment. For the first time, she realized that she had a headache due to caffeine withdrawal. It amused her, the things she had learned to ignore.

Hannah smiled at Clarissa as she entered the kitchen. "Care for a cup?"

"Please." Clarissa took a seat at the table next to Mia.

The girl smiled through a mouthful of bread and ham.

"I want to stay and help," Clarissa said. "For a while, at least."

"I've got a team en route. Old friends and the kind of guys who can take out three times as many men. We'll have enough help."

"I want to watch over the girl. You've got enough on your hands protecting Dottie and making sure no more harm comes to Erin. Allow me to watch over Mia."

Leon set his fork down. He stretched his fingers out, wiggled them. "How can I trust you?"

"You trusted Jack."

"And that turned out to be a mistake. Erin got shot and the girl's traumatized now. Not to mention a man's dead."

"If they hadn't been with Spiers, they might all be dead. You might be dead. Those men were coming one way or another. I don't know how they knew, but they knew."

Leon nodded. "Been wondering that myself. Only answer I can come up with is that man was crooked."

"Then why'd he end up dead?"

"Collateral damage? I dunno, Miss. Perhaps he knew too much, so they killed him. How do I know it wasn't you that called for them?"

"If that's so, why would I kill one of them?"

"To trick us. You wanted to get close. Hell, you can't get any closer than this, now can you?"

Clarissa shook her head. "It's not like that. You know it. Hell, I could say that maybe you had a hand in it. You sent them off, didn't you?"

Leon slapped the table and rose and kicked his chair into the wall. He hovered over Clarissa. "Don't you ever question my loyalty to this family!"

She stood and went toe to toe, eye to eye, with the man. "Then don't you question mine. I owe Jack my life. I'd do anything to protect those he cares for."

Neither backed down. Their stares remained locked in combat. The anger in Leon's eyes subsided. He reached back and found his chair and reset it.

"I'm sorry. It's just… Erin getting shot. I…"

Clarissa saw the look in his eyes and knew that while Leon's loyalty was to the family, his heart was dedicated to Erin.

"Say no more," she said. "You watch over her. I'll take care of Mia and Hannah. Your team can watch over the house and Dottie and provide whatever other support is needed."

Leon nodded. Said nothing.

"Here's that coffee." Hannah set the mug down in front of Clarissa, smiled and then looked away.

Poor kid, Clarissa thought. *Caught up in this mess.*

Then she heard a scream from the other room. It sounded like Erin. A crash followed.

"Leon," Dottie called. "Come quickly."

Clarissa and Leon raced to the room. Erin lay on the floor. The bandage that wrapped her leg had turned crimson. Blood ran down her leg, pooled on the floor.

"Something's wrong," Erin said through her cries.

Leon said, "Help me, Clarissa. We've got to get her to the hospital."

"We can't risk it. It won't be safe there," Dottie said.

"If we don't, she'll die," Clarissa said.

Dottie glared at her and said nothing.

Leon said, "I'll split my team between here and there. Call in more. Whatever. But there's no way I'm letting her bleed out on the floor. So get the hell out of our way, Dottie."

Dottie backed up to the wall. Hannah pulled Mia close to her, wrapped an arm over the girl's chest.

And together, Clarissa and Leon carried Erin to the car and raced toward the hospital.

CHAPTER 46

Jack placed one hand on the Prime Minister's back and the other on Sasha's. He urged them toward the door. Bear scooped up Mandy and headed that way, too. Jon and Jack were the last to exit. Outside, Jack noticed that the woman who ran the shop had fallen to the ground. Blood trickled from a gash on her forehead and she lay on her stomach, unconscious. He picked her up and placed her in a fireman's carry.

The reporters and their cameramen had fled the area. The only thing standing between the group and the Prime Minister's car was rubble. They ran, disregarding their safety at times.

The first explosion occurred as Jack stepped over the weighed down tape. The street shook beneath his feet. The concussive blast wave nearly caused him to topple over. The roar of the explosion left his ears ringing. The others had crouched, covered their heads. A few moments later, after the shock had passed, they resumed their escape.

Jon opened the driver's door of Alex's Rolls and started the engine. Bear put Mandy in the back seat, waited for Sasha to get in, then he followed.

Alex slipped in the backseat from the other side. He grabbed the open door and pulled himself up. "Jack, come on."

Jack spotted an ambulance and yelled for the medics. Two rushed toward him. They took the woman from his arms and carried her toward a gurney. Jack saw them lift it into the ambulance and shut the doors. He then ran to the Rolls, opened the passenger door and jumped in.

"Go," Alex shouted from the back seat.

Jon put the car in reverse and backed out. He whipped the wheel around. The rear of the vehicle nearly crashed into a news truck. He raced to the end of the street. The road had been blocked off, so there was no traffic to contend with. That luck was about to end. The streets of London were packed most hours of the day, and this hour was no exception. And they had no police escort. Jon pulled out his phone and called for one. With the number of cops that had been assigned to protect the attack site, Jack figured it wouldn't take long for a few cars to come to their aide.

Behind them, another explosion ripped through the street. Jack turned his head and saw a fireball rise into the sky. It turned red to orange to black. Panicked people ran along the sidewalks. Horns blared on the main street. People got out of their cars, shielded their eyes, looked toward the explosion.

He presumed they feared it was another terrorist attack.

"Alex, you need to get someone on the phone so that the truth gets out there before the stories start up and take hold. We don't need the city in a panic over another attack."

Alex nodded and told Sasha to make the call. The woman pulled out her cell. She and Jon tried to talk above each other, and it didn't take long for their voices to rise to shouts. Mandy covered both ears with her hands. Bear pulled her close. Sasha and Jon ended their conversations and the car fell silent.

"They really keep the road noise out in these," Bear said.

Alex let out a single laugh, then the serious look returned to his face.

"Where to?" Jon said.

"Let's go back to Number 10," Alex said. "You good with that Agent Kirby?"

Sasha nodded. "Fine, sir."

"What about us?" Jack said.

"You're coming too."

The police escort arrived a couple minutes later. The cars with their sirens and strobe lights separated the traffic like an adder slithering through a crowd. When they arrived at the Prime Minister's residence, a security team stood outside. They lined up in two rows, faced each other. The team created a human wall that cut through the walkway.

Jon exited the car first. He rushed to Alex's door. The two men hurried to the front entrance. The rest followed. Jack went last. He looked past the security team, studied the faces in the crowd. His eyes quickly dismissed the homogeneous blend. He searched for the person that stood out. Then it occurred to him that if this was an inside job, it might be someone who does blend in with the rest that he had to be worried about.

"Jack, get in here," Sasha said.

He hurried to the door, stepped inside.

"Follow me," she said.

Sasha led him up a flight of stairs, down a hall, and up another flight of stairs. They came to a room with a long rectangular wooden table. Lines and nicks in the rich wood told Jack that many a tense moment had been spent in the room.

Bear sat alone at the far end of the table.

"Where's Mandy?" Jack said.

"They brought her downstairs," Bear said.

"There's a bug out room down there," Sasha said. "Safest place for her."

"We should get Mia and Erin here, then."

Sasha looked at him, said nothing.

"I'll explain when we're all in here together."

She nodded. "Go ahead and take a seat." She started toward the door.

"Where are you going?"

"I need to make some calls."

"You're not bailing on us, are you?"

"You're tasked with protecting the Prime Minister, as am I, Jack. We're working together. Don't worry. I'll be back in a minute."

Sasha left Jack and Bear to themselves. The men sat across from each other. Neither spoke for a few minutes. Jack looked around the room. In the corner he saw a wet bar. He rose and walked over to it. Found an opened bottle of Glenfiddich single malt whiskey. He picked up the bottle with his left hand, grabbed two glasses with his right, went back to the table. He set a glass in front of Bear and placed the bottle in the middle of the table.

Bear lifted an eyebrow. "That's the good stuff."

"Over two thousand dollars a bottle."

Bear grabbed it, filled his glass. He picked it up and admired the liquor in the light. "What do you think, maybe four hundred dollars' worth right there?"

"Probably."

"I'd say I've earned it so far today."

Jack filled his glass. Took a drink. "Me too." After a few more sips, he pulled out his cell phone and placed a call to Mason. The phone rang half a dozen times and went to a generic voice mail. He hung up without leaving a message.

"Who's that?" Bear said.

"Name's Mason Sutton."

Bear nodded, said nothing.

"He tailed me a couple days ago. Stopped me from doing something stupid. I hope he's on my side, but I'm not sure."

"Why?"

"Just something about him. Kinda like those feelings that you get. If it were just him and me, I don't know that I'd sleep with both eyes closed."

Bear nodded. "I got your back now. It's all good."

Sasha, Jon and Alex entered the room. They sat at the table. Sasha dropped a stack of folders in front of her.

"Enjoying your drink?" Jon said.

Bear tipped his glass, said, "You bet."

"Why don't you pass the bottle down this way," Alex said.

Jack rose and carried it down to the other end of the table. Alex reached out and took a pull straight from the bottle.

"I needed that," he said after a loud exhale.

"So what's the news?" Jack said.

"Why do you think there's news?" Jon said.

"Because all three of you came in here at the same time and she's carrying folders. No one carries around folders for fun. Gotta be something going on?"

Alex said, "Jon, why don't you have a drink and relax a bit?"

"Because the whole country is in upheaval and we've basically got our pants down around our ankles with nothing but our hands to support our balls."

"Right," Sasha said. "Well, my balls are fine, so I'm going to move on now and talk about what we do know."

Bear looked at Jack and grinned. Sasha turned out to be like them. Hell, she had to be to have risen through the ranks in a male dominated profession. Jack figured Dottie had been a lot like the woman when she was younger.

Sasha stood, opened the folder and began placing four by six inch pictures on the table. Jack moved to her side of the table to get a better view.

"What are these?" he said.

"These are the men that we got positive identification on from the restaurant's security feed. They had cameras in both the front and the back."

Jack thought about the exterior of the restaurant. He did not recall seeing the cameras. "They hid them well."

She nodded, pulled out another stack of photos. She laid them on the table, said, "And these men they caught on camera the day you arrived. That Bentley is registered to Thornton Walloway, now deceased."

Jack pointed at one of the pictures. "I recognize that guy. Name's Owen. And that one there, Owen killed him."

"That explains that, then."

"What?"

"Why we didn't see that man in the footage day of the bombing."

"That guy looks familiar," Jack said. He pointed to the picture of a man in his early forties. The guy had sandy blond hair, cut close, and striking blue eyes. He didn't immediately place him.

Sasha looked up at Jon.

Jack noticed the glance. "What?"

"His name is Joe Godfrey."

"OK." Jack paused. He recalled the guy who dropped his Fiat in the woods. Thought back to his conversation with Mason inside the guy's house.

Joe's gone and betrayed me.

"Mason's partner," Jack said.

Sasha nodded. "This proves nothing. We've got nothing that places Sutton at these events."

"It explains how they knew where to find me. Mason told his partner."

"But you don't know the intent. Could have been partners sharing information, like they do."

"It also proves that you've got a problem inside MI5. It might even extend into your building."

Sasha turned and walked over to the bar. She opened a drawer, returned with a piece of chalk. She drew two circles on the table. They overlapped in the middle.

"What's this?" Alex said.

Sasha said nothing. She began sorting through the pictures, placing each into one of the circles. The pictures on the left were all middle-eastern looking men. On the right, Caucasian. In the middle, the overlap, she placed four pictures.

"Yazan Abdul-Matin Hadad, Nazim Sab Guirguis, Owen Flynn, and Joe Godfrey. Anyone want to take a guess what these four men have in common?"

"They were at the hotel Jack's first day in town and when the explosions went off," Bear said.

Sasha nodded. "Gold star. And what does this mean?"

"MI5, Thornton Walloway, and Naseer Shehata were all working together," Jack said. "And they all want the Prime Minister, and me, dead."

CHAPTER 47

Naseer lay with his hand behind his head. He liked how the firm mattress kept his back rigid. The swirling pattern in the plaster on the ceiling mesmerized him. He let the air slowly expand and contract in his lungs. His mind drifted and took him away to Tenerife. He enjoyed vacationing there. It was a place where no one knew him, no one judged him. He enjoyed the peace and tranquility and anonymity the island afforded him.

And now he wondered if he'd ever see that paradise again.

Plans had been executed. They'd been in motion for months. Years, in fact, on some levels. There would be many that would try to pin the events of the past day on him. They hadn't seen anything yet, though. While they wasted their time at that hotel and now worrying about the Prime Minister, Naseer's men were setting up for the event of several lifetimes. A massive coordinated attack that would leave the infrastructure of London in shambles.

His cell phone vibrated against his thigh. He reached into his pocket, pulled out the phone, looked at the display. No number was listed. He answered anyway.

"Who is this and why are you calling me?"

There was a moment of silence. Then a man said, "Naseer?"

"Who is this?"

"I can't say."

"Then I'm hanging up."

"No. You need to shut up and listen to me."

"Who do you think you are to talk to me—"

"I'm high up enough that I can have you ended. You got that? So shut your mouth and listen to what I have to say."

Naseer said nothing. He lifted up, crossed his legs at the ankles.

"At this time you are aware of the plans we have for the elimination project. You've pledged your support to us, and in turn we've done the same for you. There's a change of direction. Your men need to carry out the elimination and it needs to go down in the next forty-eight hours."

"Why forty-eight hours?" Naseer said.

"You know why."

Naseer thought about it. The Prime Minister was to host the President of the United States in three days. Security would be extra tight. The window would be closed. The deal would be made. The deal was bad news for all of them.

"This is suicide," Naseer said.

The man said nothing.

"Don't you see that? My men aren't prepared for this. Hell, they won't even be able to get close enough to pull something like this off."

"Then I guess they need to figure out a way to do it from afar."

"This is bull. My men are not some replaceable cog in a wheel. They have value to me."

"As do mine to me. If one of my guys goes down doing this, well that's a story that is going to destroy the foundation of Great Britain. I can't let that happen. I also can't let the Prime Minister go through with what he is planning. Neither can you. When he goes down, Snelling replaces him. You want her in the position, trust me Naseer. She'll do whatever we tell her."

"Is she involved in this?"

"She knows nothing."

"You said her name, why not your own?"

The man said nothing.

"Right, well, I don't think we can make this work. I can give you maybe two guys, but only to assist. You need to provide me with someone to help."

"Then go ahead and hang up right now and forget about any further assistance from me. Your men will be scooped up and detained and tortured and then given over to the CIA and anyone else who wants them. We'll keep you though. You can count on that. You'll spend the rest of your days buried so deep down in the ground not even the tiniest sliver of sunlight will find its way to your hairy dark ass."

Naseer said nothing.

"So that's your answer?"

"I need to think about it."

"You don't have much time."

Naseer placed the phone on speaker and dropped it between his legs. He grabbed the back of his head, pulled at his hair.

Damn those bastards, he thought. He had more money than any of them. He could recruit a trained mercenary for every agent they had. He had over a thousand men waiting for him to call upon them. Men who would die for him if he asked them to. Who was this man to tell Naseer that he had to sacrifice his men for someone else's cause? He didn't need their help. He didn't need anyone's help. Thornton Walloway found that out the hard way. He demanded too much and ended up with a bullet in his brain. Now this man, whoever he was, would find it out too.

"Do you have an answer?" the man said.

"Yeah. Go to hell."

"Very well, then. I'll meet you there."

CHAPTER 48

Gloria brought the chef's knife down onto the cutting board, blade first. It sliced through the wheat bread and meat. She took the two triangles and put them on a plate, brought it to Mason. He thanked her, returned to the documents that had been faxed to him earlier that morning.

"I want to leave," she said.

"Well, you can't," he said.

"Dammit, I'm tired of being here with you."

He smiled, looked over his shoulder at her. "You're loving this and you know it."

"Go to hell. You know I can't stand you."

"At least not for longer than an hour or two." He winked.

"I only enjoy ten of those minutes, if I'm lucky. The rest is cuddle time so you don't come crawling after me."

Mason laughed. He set down the papers and picked up the sandwich, took a bite. The time he'd spent stuck with Gloria hadn't been that bad. They'd talked more than they had since they split up. Hell, more than they had during the last few years of their marriage. He remembered the things he loved most about her. The way her hair smelled. How her soft snores eased him to sleep. The distinct way the right side of her mouth curled right before she smiled.

"What?" she said.

"What?" he said.

"Why are you staring and grinning at me?"

He shrugged.

"No, it ain't happening. Not tonight. Not under these circumstances."

He dropped the sandwich and rose, walked toward her. She backed up, never taking her eyes off of his. She ran into the counter. He approached, placed his hands on her waist, kissed her neck, her mouth. His right hand glided up her side, then back down, past her hips, under her buttocks, down to mid-thigh. He lifted her leg. They pushed into one another. Fast, hot breath intermingled.

"You sure about that?" he said.

"About what?"

"Not tonight."

"Yes. It's still daytime. You'll be too tired for tonight."

They kissed. Off went his shirt. Hers followed. Their hands re-explored one another's bodies.

Mason's phone rang. A series of notes played in a fashion that most would find appealing. Not Mason though. The ringtone was dedicated to his boss.

"Dammit," he said, pulling away from Gloria.

"What? Don't go. I'm sure it can wait."

"It's Mills, Gloria. He won't wait. I don't answer, he'll send someone here."

She placed her palms on the counter behind her and hoisted herself up.

Mason admired her tight abdomen as he backed up toward the couch. He turned, found his phone, answered.

"Yeah, boss?"

"We've found him," Cameron Mills said.

"Who?" Mason feared that a team had picked up Noble.

"That bastard, Naseer. That's who."

"Where?"

"All that's coming to you. You're leading a raid tonight. We're going to take him down."

"How many men?"

"Small team."

"Joe?"

"No one's heard from him. Was hoping you had."

"Not yet."

"I'll reach out, see if I can find him."

"OK, sir. Anything else?"

Mills had nothing else for him, so Mason hung up and dropped the phone on the sofa. Gloria came toward him, but he held out his hands and moved her aside. He rushed upstairs to his office. He made sure the fax was on and the line clear. Then he pulled out a second cell phone from his pocket. He placed a call. Jack Noble answered on the fourth ring.

"We've got him."

"Who?"

"Naseer."

"In custody?"

"No, we know where he is though. I'm leading a raid tonight. I want you there."

"Hold on a minute."

It sounded like Jack's phone was set down on a table, then covered with the man's palm. All Mason could hear were muffled voices. A minute later, Jack got on the line.

"OK, I'm in, but only if I can bring a couple people."

"I've got no problem with that."

"Where are we going?"

"Waiting to find out."

"Gloria still with you?"

"Yeah. You said not to let her leave. I haven't yet."

"Hold on." Jack came back on the line a moment later. "Come to Number 10. Bring Gloria with you."

"Are you with the Prime Minister?"

"Something like that."

"How did that happen?"

"I'll explain later. Get moving. We need you here two seconds ago."

Mason hung up and trotted down the stairs. "Gloria, get your bag. We're leaving."

"Where are we going?"

Mason hit the bottom step, jumped toward the door. He looked over his shoulder and saw Gloria standing in the kitchen, half-dressed.

"Do we have to go now?" she said, her hands on her hips.

"Get your shirt on, Gloria. We're going to Number 10."

"What did you do?"

"What? Nothing."

"Then why are we going to see the Prime Minister?"

"You know I can't tell you that."

"Then why do I have to go?"

"Because."

"Because why?"

"Because they said you did."

Mason waited for her to dress, then he took her hand and led her outside. They walked a half block to his car. He opened the door, waited for her to get in. The door slammed shut with a solid thud.

"They could have sent a Rolls for us," she said when he got in the car.

Mason laughed. "Nothing's ever good enough."

"That's not true. I just think things can be better sometimes."

Mason glanced at her, smiled, said, "I think you're right, Gloria."

CHAPTER 49

"CAN WE TRUST HIM?" ALEX SAID. "I WANT YOUR GUT FEELING, Jack."

Jack leaned back in his chair, looked up at the ceiling. At this point, Mason was an enigma. Jack's instincts fought over the question. "I can't say that we shouldn't."

"But you can't say that we can," Jon said.

"That's right," Jack said.

"Let's wait till he gets here, then question him a bit," Jon said.

Everyone agreed. Whether Mason had told Jack the truth, or was trying to set him up, they'd determine shortly. Before then, he wanted to arrange for Erin and Mia to be transported to the Prime Minister's house. They'd be safest in the bunker with Mandy. Even if someone tried to blow the place up, the reinforced room thirty feet underground could withstand the impact and Jack assumed it had an escape route.

So he got up and left the room and made the call to Dottie.

"Jack, how is it going there?"

"Things are moving in the right direction, I think. We've got some leads and will be following up on them soon. Look, I've asked and Alex has agreed that Erin and Mia should come here. There's a safe room. They'll be protected there. Some of his guys will stay to protect the girls no matter where we go."

A moment of silence, then Dottie said, "Erin's been taken to the hospital, Jack."

"What? I thought she was OK? What happened?"

"Her leg."

"What's wrong with it?"

"She started bleeding. Collapsed to the floor."

"Is she OK?"

"I haven't heard from Leon yet, and I don't want to speculate."

She didn't need to. Jack knew the location of the wound and realized there must have been damage to the femoral artery. The doctor had missed it or perhaps caused it. A tiny perforation at first. Over time, pressure had built, the lining had ripped.

"Which hospital?" Jack said.

"I'm not sure where they went."

"Which one is closest?"

"They wouldn't have gone there. Leon would never..."

Jack waited, but she did not finish the sentence. He didn't have time to pull the answer out of her. "Find out and let me know. In the meantime, we need to get Mia and Hannah here."

"OK. Do you need me to arrange that?"

"It'd help. I doubt I can get them to spare a guy to drive out there. In fact, you might want to bring them yourself. You can wait here, too. No sense in you putting yourself in further danger. The guys that took care of Thornton might want to hurt you as well."

Dottie paused. "The thought had crossed my mind."

Jack wondered if the target was in fact Dottie. Perhaps these guys were not after him. What if they were using him to get to her?

"Maybe you shouldn't come here," he said.

"Why not?"

"It's probably better you and I aren't in the same place. All I can think is that they are using one of us to get to the other. I'm starting to think that you might be their main objective."

"Or both of us to get to the Prime Minister."

"Do you know anything you shouldn't?"

"Of course. It came with the territory in my old job."

"Not that. You know what I mean. Were you involved in any of your husband's dealings?"

"No, Jack. Never."

Jack didn't expect her to tell him if she had been. Not yet, at least. "OK, Dottie. Get the girls here. We'll work on getting you a team for protection."

"I'll be fine when Leon gets back."

Jack ignored her last statement. He wasn't about to argue. They'd send someone and that was that.

He returned to the room. Jon and Sasha were talking about possible attacks and their reactions. Alex seemed to listen intently to their conversation. Jack went to the other end of the table, settled across from Bear.

"They coming?"

"Dottie's sending them."

"So this Mia, she's really your kid?"

"No denying it, Bear. When you see her, you'll know."

"How're you feeling about this?"

"It's settling in. Kind of weird, to tell you the truth. You go through your whole life, and at the end of the day, you're responsible only for yourself. I mean, there's more than just me, of course. But to a man, I'm it."

Bear nodded. "Understood."

"And now that's changed. In the back of my head, I keep thinking, is Mia OK? Will she be safe through all of this? Will they get her just to get to me? Just by sharing my DNA, she's in danger. That's a hell of a weight."

"It's how I feel about Mandy, Jack. I won't let anything happen to that girl."

"You feel good with her here?"

Bear shrugged. "There's better places we could be. But I wouldn't be here and have her down there if I didn't think she was safe. We'd bail. And I mean that with no offense to you, but my life is changing, Jack."

Jack felt a pang of guilt. "I know. You shouldn't be here. Again, I've put you in a difficult situation. I'm done after this, Bear. We'll take a few train rides and clean out some bank accounts when this is all over. Split it up evenly and go on our own ways. It's time for you to release yourself from this feeling of responsibility you have toward me."

Bear smiled. "Gosh, sounds like we're divorcing."

Jack laughed. "Had to happen sooner or later. You've lost that girlish figure I fell for so many years ago."

Bear cackled and almost fell out of his chair.

"Glad to see you two can laugh it up down there while this nation is enduring a crisis."

Jack turned his head and saw Jon standing, his face red, fists clenched.

"Lighten up, Jon. We're in a holding pattern right now. Once Mason gets here, or we get more news, we'll be ready."

Jon stormed out of the room, slammed his palm against the wall on the way out.

Alex rose. "Don't mind him. He gets a little high strung at times."

Jack knew the feeling. He'd been there before. But it was him that had been targeted, not Jon. And it had been Alex that received the death threat. Jon took that personally and Jack understood why.

They relaxed a while longer. The conversations were concise and polite. Sasha joined Jack and Bear while Alex left to discuss the events with members of his cabinet.

"How long have you been close with them?" Jack asked.

"Couple years," Sasha said. "Jon noticed me first, introduced me to Alex. We traded information as we saw fit. I helped them more than they helped me, and now they're paying me back, so to speak. In another ten years, I'll be a serious candidate for Director."

"Is that what you want to do?" Jack said.

"I want to be the best," she said.

"That's not what I asked."

"I want what any good agent wants, to do the best I can, to protect and serve my country. If that means leading the organization, then I'd be honored. This, of course, could be a major road block. If it doesn't go well, it could not only affect my career, but theirs as well."

"Well, death has a way of doing that," Bear said bluntly. "I'd imagine it'd be hard to get re-elected from the grave."

She smiled. "That's not the only possible outcome. Have you thought that maybe all this is a ruse? Just a diversionary tactic intended to get us looking in the wrong place?"

Jack nodded. "The thought's crossed my mind. Guess we'll know more after Mason gets here. If his intel checks out, and we can take down Naseer, maybe this will all be over."

"Or maybe it'll just be starting."

The three were silent for a few minutes as they contemplated this.

"What do we gotta do to get some food?" Bear said. "It's been a long day, and I'm starving."

Sasha rose, went to the bar and picked up the phone. She returned a minute later. "They'll have something up shortly."

But the food never arrived. Jon and Alex did though, and they had Mason with them.

"Let's go," Jon said.

"We got food coming," Bear said.

"No time," Jon said.

"What's going on?" Jack said.

"We'll talk in the car."

CHAPTER 50

THEY HURRIED DOWN THE STAIRS, A HALL, ANOTHER SET OF stairs. Instead of using the front door, they moved to the rear of the house and went down another level and entered a lit tunnel. LED lights cast a bluish hue over them. The passage extended a few hundred yards. They stopped in front of a reinforced door. Alex pulled out a key, stuck it in the top lock. Jon put one in the bottom lock and turned both. The door opened. A gust of air blew past, carried the smell of old oil and gasoline.

"How many tunnels are there under this place?" Jack said.

"Off the record, four that I can tell you about," Alex said.

"Where do they go?" Bear said.

"That I can't tell you."

Jon stopped in front of a panel on the wall. Next to the panel was a keypad. He curled his fingers and punched in at least eight numbers. A hiss and click followed. He pulled the panel open, retrieved two sets of keys. He handed one set to Sasha and kept the other to himself. He pressed the key fob and a black van honked and flashed its lights.

"That's our ride?" Bear said.

"Armor plated, bullet proof glass, equipped with a tactical defense system and enough weapons in back to arm two dozen men," Jon said.

"I was just going to say it's my kinda van," Bear said. "But that other stuff's cool."

Jack shot Bear a look.

Bear hiked his shoulders an inch and held out his hands. "What?"

"Cut the guy some slack. He's wound a bit tight. That's going to come in handy later as long as you don't piss him off so bad he leaves us on the side of the road."

"Yeah, whatever. I'm riding in back."

They piled into the van. Jon drove, Alex took a seat next to him. Bear and Jack settled in the back. Sasha and Mason in the middle.

Jon navigated the van through a network of tunnels. The dash had an LCD screen built in. The van came to a stop and Jon pushed a button below the screen. The LCD came to life and they saw what looked to be a small parking garage. Jon and Alex nodded to one another, then Jon pushed another button. The wall in front of them rose, and the image from the screen appeared in front of the van. The van pulled through the opening. The wall dropped into place behind them.

When they emerged from the garage, Jack wasn't sure where they were. He had little interest in finding out. He wanted to hear what Mason had to say and he wondered what the man had told Jon and Alex already.

"So let's get down to business," Jack said. "What did you tell them that you didn't tell me, Mason?"

Jack felt as if someone was watching him. He looked up and met Jon's stare in the rear view mirror.

"I got a directive from my boss that we're to capture Naseer. The order came down from above him. They want him alive."

"That it? Anything else? Did you figure out any of the other players from that night?"

"I've got the address. He's holing up north with a few of his trusted guys. And no, still no clue who that man was."

"I'd presume the men with him now are the same from the warehouse," Jack said.

Sasha flashed him a look.

"One would assume," Mason said. "Anyhow, I've got a team that is going to meet us there. Still working on reaching my partner."

Jack looked at Sasha. She gave a slight shake of her head.

Don't say a damn word. Understood.

They drove in relative silence for another half hour. They left the city and the suburbs behind. Freshly born leaves, light and bright green, adorned the trees. The sunlight peeked through. Jack felt the van slow. He turned his head forward and saw a break in the tree line.

The van headed off road and down a path. They bounced and rocked at a slow speed until the road was no longer in sight. Jon shifted out of gear, pulled the emergency brake, got out, came around to the passenger side and opened the door.

"Get out." Jon aimed a pistol at Mason.

"What's this about?" Mason said.

"Go," Sasha said. She put her hand in the middle of his back and pushed.

Mason slid out of his seat and hopped to the ground. Sasha and Jack followed.

Jon aimed his pistol at Mason's head. "Tell us everything."

"Jon, what are you doing?" Jack said.

"I swear, I'll put one in your brain if you don't talk," Jon said.

"What is going on?" Mason said. "Jack? What's this about?"

Jack had no idea. Added to that, he was still unarmed. Sasha had her hand on her weapon, but had not yet drawn it.

"Last chance, Mason," Jon said.

Sasha stepped in front of Jon's gun. "You can't do this. There's nothing to back this up."

"Bloody hell there's not."

Sasha said, "We've been on him for the last twelve months. There's nothing. He's clean."

"What do you mean, you've been on me? You've been watching me?" Mason said.

"He probably knows about Joe," Jon said.

"He's not responsible for what his partner's done. We've got no proof he's involved in any way."

"I'll get my proof." Jon pushed her aside and placed the barrel of his gun to Mason's forehead.

Jack felt that he should stop the man, but he didn't. He had lingering doubts about Mason, and this was sure to clear it up. As long as Jon didn't actually pull the trigger.

"What did Joe do?" Mason asked.

No one spoke. Mason looked at them all in turn. His gaze remained on Jack. He didn't look frightened. He looked confused. And the puzzled look on his face deepened.

"Someone want to tell me what my partner did? I don't have a damn clue what's going on here. I thought we were all good guys here going to get the bad guy."

Jon lifted his gun and took a step back. He looked toward Sasha and shrugged.

"Mason," she said. "Joe was at the hotel the day Jack arrived in London. He was also there the days the bombs went off."

"What? No, he's been on a fishing trip. It's what he does with his time off."

Sasha said, "I've been in his home. He doesn't even have a fishing pole. How well do you really know him?"

Mason said nothing. As Jack recalled Mason's files tucked away in the man's desk, he realized that life had begun kicking the guy in the balls two years ago and had rarely let up. All the signs of a corrupt partner might have been there, but he would have missed them. Jack figured that by the look on the guy's face, he saw them now.

Jon looked toward the front of the van and nodded. Alex stepped out. He approached Mason, said, "I'm sorry about that. We had to be sure."

Mason nodded, looked away. Jack saw the anger on the man's face. He didn't blame the guy for being pissed off. Here you had a man who'd not only dedicated his life to his country, he put it on the line every day to protect those who couldn't. And now he had to suffer the indignity of being accused of being a traitor. Someone who worked with terrorists. Jack figured they were lucky Mason didn't pull his weapon and take one of them out.

"So what now?" Jack said.

"We go to the house," Alex said.

"We?" Jack said.

"That's right."

"No, you need to head back to someplace where you'll be safe."

"I can't think of any place safer than around this group of misfits. Right, Jon?"

Jon said, "You know I'm doing this under protest." He walked off toward the front of the van.

"He's not happy about this, but dammit, I'm tired of sitting around and signing papers and watching the news and listening to my cabinet bicker. I'm a soldier, Jack. I need to be in the middle of the action. This guy threatened my city, my country, my life. I want to see him humbled, on the ground, crying. I want to press the muzzle of my rifle to his forehead and watch him beg me for mercy."

The look in Alex's eye told Jack that no one would be able to get him to change his mind. Jack had seen that look dozens of times in the past. It'd had been a look that had crossed his own face, usually right before some of the biggest triumphs, and mistakes, he'd ever had.

"We should get going," Sasha said. "We've got no idea what we're heading into and it'd be good to scout the surrounding area in the daylight."

So Jack got back in the van and parked himself next to Bear. Mason and Sasha sat in the middle. Alex yelled for Jon to join them, and he did. Mason still looked pissed, stayed that way for the next half hour. He'd brought Naseer's head to them on a plate, and his thanks was a gun aimed point blank at his face in the middle of the woods.

Bear and Jack made small talk. They had a lot to catch up on still. Both of their lives had been a whirlwind since the day Jack found Mandy lost in the city.

Two hours later, Sasha turned in her seat and told them that they were close.

"These people that live here have no idea the demon that lurks in the dark, do they?" Jack said.

She shook her head. "I've been sent some satellite imagery, looks like the property is pretty isolated. There's a stretch of woods behind the house that extends fully along the property line and is a half-mile deep. We'll likely approach from there while we have men stationed at points along the road, as well as across from the front of the property."

"How many inside?"

She looked at Mason. "Five? Six?"

Mason nodded. "We believe at least four, up to six."

"So we should plan for eight," Jack said.

They both nodded.

"How big is your team?" Jack said.

"Eight men," Mason said. "These guys aren't desk jockeys. So combined with us, it should be plenty."

They drove for a while longer. They all paid attention to the intersections. Jon turned down several roads, located ones that ran into dead ends. They began to map out possible escape routes.

Jon pointed to a store ahead on the left. "I'm going to pull in there. We'll grab some food and water."

The van bounced across the uneven parking lot, eased into a spot. Alex leaned his seat back, covered the side of his face. Probably best that he not be spotted out here. If the media showed up, Naseer would split.

Jack scanned the lot and the store. A man approached the door from the other side of the slightly tinted glass.

"Get out of here," he said.

"What?" Jon asked.

"Now."

"Why?"

"Put the van in reverse and get moving."

"Jack, what is it?" Sasha said.

Jack pointed at the man exiting the store.

"That's Owen! Go! Now!"

CHAPTER 51

JON THREW THE VAN INTO REVERSE, HIT THE ACCELERATOR, and whipped the steering wheel to the right. Gravel pelted the undercarriage. Dust kicked up and created a haze around the car. Rubber and pavement fought one another. The van flew back, jerked to a stop, then whipped forward. They exited the parking lot and turned onto the road without slowing. Jack was sure they were riding on two wheels for a few seconds.

"Well, that didn't look suspicious," Bear said.

Jack had a laugh, then shook his head. They were too close to Naseer's hideout and the moment of attack for jokes. At least, he had to make it look that way.

Jon drove on and made a series of turns and then pulled off the road into a clearing between two groups of trees. They remained seated in silence for a few moments. Ragged breathing filled the void.

Sasha pulled out her phone and placed a call. She asked for ongoing satellite surveillance. She wanted to know whether or not their arrival had been tipped to Naseer and his men after Jon's driving escape clinic. Sasha's contact told her that there was no new activity at the house and they'd continue to monitor.

"We've got a couple hours till dark," Jon said. "I'd suggest we lay low here."

And so they did. One hundred and twenty minutes passed without a word spoken. Bear slept. Jack dozed on and off. He didn't pay much attention to the others. When the time came, Jon started the van and slipped it into gear and they drove off to meet Mason's tactical team.

They exchanged information with the eight agents. The team had brought several maps of the area. They all confirmed assignments and details, and then they split up.

Mason had one final thing to say before he left with his team. "Naseer must be taken alive."

An hour later, Jack and Bear and Sasha trekked through the dark woods behind the house. Two members of Mason's team were a hundred yards or so to their left. Alex and Jon were a hundred or so to the right.

Jack saw the signature of white bursts lights through the trees. He lifted his night vision goggles, confirmed it.

"We should get low," he said. "They might have thermals aimed out here."

If they did, it wouldn't matter whether they were standing straight up or laying on the ground. The group of them would give off a giant heat signature.

"We should split up," Sasha said.

"No," Jack said.

"Why not? We're easy targets all together."

"And easy targets split up, if someone comes at us from behind for a close range kill."

They lowered to the ground when the edge of the woods came into view. They halted there. Jack and Bear set up their M4 rifles. They split coverage at the back door. Bear had the right, Jack the left. Next to him, Sasha monitored the surrounding area.

Masons' voice piped in through Jack's earwig. "We're preparing to surround the house. So far, we have confirmation of Naseer, Samir, and Yafi inside. No sign of anyone else. Checkpoints, do you have anything to report?"

Two voices spoke one after another indicating that they had seen nothing.

Jon said, "In position."

Sasha said, "We're in position."

"OK. Moving in."

Jack might as well have been in a vacuum. That's how the silence that followed caused him to feel.

His mind drifted. He wondered about their safety in the woods, and when they had to cross the field to the house. Had someone ever rigged it with traps or explosives? Sasha told him they had checked for deed information on the house and found nothing. They had no idea who owned it. How could people that high up in the government not be able to locate this kind of information? Perhaps it was a generational ownership thing. Something that didn't exist in the U.S.

An icy chill trickled down his spine. What if this was a set up? What if his indecisiveness on Mason came back to bite them all here and now?

A flash of light appeared at the back of the house. Jack inched closer to the M4's scope. He peered through, saw that the back door had been opened. Two men stepped out. The frame of the first matched Naseer, but there was not enough light for Jack to verify facial features. The second man lifted his hand, a smaller burst of light flashed between the two. This was followed by two smaller dots that became bright when the men brought their hands to their faces. A few moments later, Jack smelled cigarette smoke.

Could there be a worse possible moment for him to be reminded that he'd recently quit?

Next to him, Sasha eased herself to the ground. She kept a pair of ATN Night Scout night vision binoculars pressed to her face. Her head turned on a swivel, scanned one end of the field to the other.

"Empty," she whispered.

Jack lifted his head an inch or two, then settled. He eased his eye to the scope. Steady hands drew aim on Naseer. Sure, they were to take him alive, but things rarely go according to plan. If it came down to it, he would not hesitate to pull the trigger and end the man's life.

He felt Sasha shift and brush against his side. Instantly, his head rose and he began scanning the area around them.

Sasha cursed under her breath.

"What?" Bear said.

"Two men, roving patrol, off to the east."

Jack looked to his left, saw two shadowy figures fifty yards in front of them. He pulled his night vision monocular down. The men looked like pros. They were armed with sub-machine guns. Jack and Bear and Sasha waited in silence. No one moved. The men continued past them.

"Call it in," Jack said.

Sasha whispered over the radio. "We've got a patrol unit in the field between us and the house. They're armed to the teeth and heading your way, Jon. If there's one, there could be more."

"We're sending two guys your way," Mason said. "Sit tight. Do not engage these men. We'll neutralize them."

The radio went silent, so did the woods. The men on the porch went back inside the house.

"You know any attempt to neutralize these men is going to result in gunfire," Jack said.

"Yep," Bear said.

"And that is going to make a surprise raid on the house a little less effective."

"Unless they are planning to do both at once."

"Without telling us?" Sasha said.

"Or they're coming after us," Bear said.

"Or the Prime Minister," Jack said.

"I'll go." Bear rose and then disappeared into the darkness.

"How's he so quiet?" Sasha said.

"I'll never figure it out," Jack said.

"What's he going to do?"

"Warn them. Let them know something doesn't add up." Jack glanced at her. "You any good with that rifle?"

"I've managed to hit a target or two over the years."

"All right, get ready. I'm not sure what, but something is going down soon."

And it did. Less than three minutes later, the first shots were fired. They came from the right. The patrol team had been neutralized. But the gunfire didn't end there. As Jack had expected, Mason led the raid on the house at the same time. Several shots erupted from across the field. Dark windows burst like fireworks and faded back to black. Shouts rode the wind. Men barked orders.

Then it was over.

Mason spoke over the radio. "All teams except checkpoint come to the house. Move with extreme caution. Mind the fields for any patrols."

Jack and Sasha rose and took a line that angled to the right. Their path would intersect with Bear, Jon and Alex. Jack refused to enter the house without knowing that the men were unharmed.

Jack kept his focus on the house. Sasha watched the field surrounding them. Halfway between the woods and the house, they met up with the other men.

"Everyone's OK here," Alex said.

"Not liking how this went down," Bear said.

Jack agreed.

"That team was closed," Bear said. "They stopped in front of us. That's where they were killed."

"Did it look like they had spotted you?" Jack said.

Bear shrugged. "It happened fast. Couldn't tell."

"Where are the guys that took them out?" Sasha said.

"Still back there, watching the woods until we get clear," Jon said.

Jack said, "So best we can figure, Mason and six of his guys are inside that house right now along with however many of Naseer's men survived the attack."

"Sounds right," Sasha said.

The group approached the house with caution and apprehension. Jack and Bear led the way, with Sasha and Alex in the middle and Jon at the rear.

All the lights had been switched on inside. A flood light warmed up and cast a large cone of bright white light over the back of the property. They altered their path to avoid the light in case someone was watching. Jack did not care for how nonchalant Mason and his men were being. Did they have additional intelligence they were not sharing? Had someone been in place long before they arrived and knew head counts, the layout of the scene, and what had been happening inside?

Bear held up his right hand, balled it into a fist, came to a stop. Jack froze in place.

"What is it?" Sasha said in a low, husky voice.

Neither man spoke. She didn't ask again.

Bear extended his thumb and started jabbing it over his shoulder. He took a few steps back, stopped again. Jack looked at Sasha and gestured toward the woods.

"What is going on?" Alex said.

"Something isn't right," Bear said.

"Did you see something?" Alex said.

"Just a hunch," Bear said.

"Oh, come off it," Jon said. "I'm not waiting out here on a hunch when we've got half a dozen trained agents inside there."

Jon started toward the house.

"Jon, come back here," Alex said.

The man didn't listen. He continued toward the house, deviated in his path to go around the front.

Jack released the tension in his body and tried to attune himself to whatever it was that set Bear's instincts into overdrive. The voices of men shouting from inside the house cut into the silence of the night. He heard at least one man moaning in pain? One of Mason's guys? A terrorist? Had to be one of Naseer's guys. If Mason had a man down, he'd have been shouting for an ambulance.

A burst of static interrupted Jack's concentration. Mason's voice blared through the earwig.

"Everyone get out of the house. Get clear. Go, get out now!"

Whether they had time to react or not wasn't clear. Jack didn't. As Mason finished his last sentence, the house erupted into a fireball.

CHAPTER 52

THE BLAST WAVE KNOCKED JACK BACKWARD. HE MANAGED TO turn mid-air and land on his stomach. His oxygen deprived lungs screamed in pain. They hurt twice as bad when he finally managed to force air into them. To his right, Sasha lay unconscious. He dragged himself to her side, reached over and felt for a pulse. She groaned at his touch. Her head rolled toward him and she opened her eyes.

"Are you OK?" he said.

She licked her lips and softly said, "Yeah."

He forced himself to his knees and hovered over her. His hands acted on instinct and performed a quick assessment. Nothing broken, no major cuts. She had a slight gash on the side of her head, but it didn't appear to be deep. He turned toward the Prime Minister.

Alex bolted upright with his hands planted in the ground behind him. He had a cut that traveled halfway across his forehead. Blood coated half his face. Bear knelt at the man's side, prepared an improvised bandage to place on Alex's head.

"Are you OK?" Jack said.

"Is she all right?" Alex said without taking his eyes off the smoldering house.

"She acknowledged me. Nothing broken. I'm giving her a few to see if she comes to anymore."

The orange blaze cast unnatural light and shadows over and around them.

"Are you OK?" Jack said again.

"I'm OK," Alex said.

Sasha rolled over to her side. She managed to get to her knees, then reached to Jack for assistance. He pulled her up, steadied her. She stood for a moment, then stumbled into him, and they stood for a moment in a tight embrace. The heat from the fire was intense. Sweat trickled down his face, came to a rest and pooled with hers at the spot where their cheeks melted together.

The fire crackled. Wood groaned as it bowed and snapped like matchsticks.

"Let's get to the front," Alex said.

Sasha pulled back. Jack slipped an arm under hers and around her back. She leaned toward him for support. They followed Bear and Alex, at first away from the house, then toward the street. Jack glanced back. The fire rose maybe fifty feet into the air at times.

Mason stood in the middle of the street, stared at the blaze. His blank expression told Jack the man was in shock. Or a great actor.

"Where's Jon?" Alex said.

"Don't see him," Sasha said.

Jack scanned the area. Didn't see any sign of the man. With everything that had occurred, it would be a blow to Alex to lose his closest confidant and best friend.

They stood in the middle of the street, each staring off in a different direction. Alex called for Jon several times. The fire responded with hisses and crackles.

"There he is." Bear pointed to the other side of the street. Jon had been lying in the ditch and had just stood. Either he had the wherewithal to dive into it when the explosion happened, or he had been thrown there.

Alex took off toward Jon.

Jack, Bear and Sasha went to Mason, pulled him away from the house. From what Jack could tell, there were no other survivors.

"What happened in there?" Jack said.

Mason shook his head, said nothing. Jack wondered if the man could think through the shock.

"Did you see anything, Mason?" he said.

"I…" The man paused. "Need some water."

Sasha slung her pack around and pulled out a bottle of water, handed it over.

Mason took a long drink, then emptied the remaining contents over the top of his head. He dropped the bottle and stared at it while it rolled toward the ditch.

"Mason," Jack said.

Mason looked up, nodded. "We stormed the house. I located Naseer, fired a warning shot. That was the first shot as far as I know. I had heard from the team in the field a moment before, and they were ready to take out the PAT."

Jack nodded, said nothing.

"After I fired, all hell broke loose. Naseer ducked into a room. Yafi and Samir fled to the back of the house. We pursued. Two targets were eliminated, and Naseer was alive, as requested."

"Then what happened?"

"I began preparations to transport Naseer, and then, I don't know."

"What do you mean, you don't know?"

Mason looked down, closed his eyes. His hands balled into fists and shook in front of him. He turned in a half-circle. "I turned around, and he was standing there." Mason's right arm lifted and he extended his index finger.

"Naseer?" Jack said.

"Yeah."

"Was he armed?"

"Kind of."

"How is someone kind of armed?"

"No gun. Explosives strapped to his body."

"Why would a billionaire blow himself up?" Sasha said.

Mason shrugged. "I don't know if that was his intention. I think maybe he was trying to leave. He said something to that effect."

"What did he say?"

"He said that he wasn't afraid to use the device. He was prepared to die. He wanted to know who the leader was and then he was going to take them with him. Otherwise, he threatened to use the device."

"And he followed through with the threat," Jack said.

"No, he didn't."

"Then what happened?"

"My guy shot him."

"Who?" Sasha said.

Mason cocked his head, said, "Naseer."

"Which guy shot Naseer?" Jack said.

"Oh, Kemp. Ben Kemp."

Jack looked at Sasha. She nodded, understanding Jack wanted to know if they'd been watching Kemp.

"Did he kill him?" Jack said.

"In the end, yeah."

"Meaning?"

"It was a bad shot. Fatal, but not instant. He rushed it. Naseer fell back. He looked down, saw the severity of the injury. He closed his eyes and then started, I don't know, chanting or something. I couldn't understand what the heck he said. That's when I came on the radio and started yelling for people to get out. Then Naseer, he opened his eyes and locked on to me. He grinned. He held out his hand, lifted his thumb over what I guess was the device trigger. I didn't stick around long enough to see him set it off. I was maybe ten feet outside the house when it happened. The blast knocked me into the air. I remember flying and then crashing. I came to on the street there."

Mason lifted his arm. The flesh had been torn from his right forearm and hand. Jack glanced down and noticed the man's pants were shredded below the knee. He nodded toward Bear, and the big man guided Mason across the road.

Jack and Sasha walked down the street, away from the house, into the dark.

"What do you make of that?" Jack said.

Sasha rubbed the side of her head, blinked hard. She reached out and grabbed Jack's forearm. Her touch felt cool.

"You OK?" he said.

She nodded. "Yeah, just a little dizzy now and then."

"We've got to get you checked out. You might have a concussion."

She smiled slightly. "I'm sure I have a concussion, and I'm not getting checked out, not after all this. There's no time."

Jack said nothing.

"What do I make of it?" she said. "We have a directive to take Naseer alive, but he comes out in a jacket made of explosives with a threat to blow the place up if they don't let him go. I'm thinking that Mason's goal would have been to stall, buy some time by talking to Naseer. Worst case, go with him and let us do what we do best. We had the road blocked on either end, he wouldn't get far. But then Naseer gets shot, fatal but not immediate. And then the house explodes."

Jack nodded, said nothing.

"I don't like it, Jack. Not one damn bit."

Jack looked past her, toward the man. Mason stared at the blaze. His face lacked expression. Did that indicate guilt or shock?

He said, "You think Mason shot him then detonated the device?"

She said, "I'm not saying he didn't. And it's not our place to find out. Despite what Jon did on the way out here, we have people dedicated to questioning our agents. Jon shouldn't have stopped in the woods and questioned him. Especially not at gunpoint. That was unscripted. You know that right?"

"I could tell."

She shook her head. "I could have slapped him for that. It's just like him, getting hot-headed and doing something stupid. Maybe if he hadn't done that, we wouldn't be standing out here while six of our men roast in there."

"Again, assuming that Mason had something to do with this, and that it was Jon's actions that drove him to it."

"Jack, can you honestly say that he didn't have anything to do with this?"

"No, I can't. But I'm not ready to tie him to the stake just yet."

He heard the faint sound of sirens. They grew louder. Blue lights bounced off the trees. The fire engine stopped in front of the house and five men went to work unwinding the giant fire hose. Jack left Sasha to deal with the police car that arrived a few moments later.

Jack found Bear, and together they found Jon and Alex.

"Naseer and at least two of his men are dead," Jack said.

Alex nodded, said nothing.

"And six of Mason's agents."

"How is he?" Alex asked.

"Shock for sure. Guilt, possibly."

"Guilt?" Jon said. "You think he had something to do with this?"

"That's what we've got to figure out."

Jon shook his head. He looked toward the house, then the fire engine. "I'm going to have that cop take me to the van. Anyone want to tag along?"

No one responded.

"Very well." Jon left and went to where Sasha and the police officer were standing. He and the cop got into the cruiser and drove off. Strobe lights faded behind the curtain of smoke.

Jack watched the firefighters battle the blaze. Orange flames retreated and left charred remains in their wake. Some house, some human. Plumes of white smoke rose into the sky as section after section of the fire died.

He noticed Alex pull his cell phone out. The screen lit up and Alex dragged his finger across the display, then placed the phone to his ear. The man nodded several times and said nothing. Jack thought some of the color drained from Alex's face.

"What is it?" Jack said after Alex tucked the phone away.

"He said it's not over."

"Who?"

"We took out the wrong guy."

"Naseer?"

Alex looked at Jack, shook his head. "And he said, I'm next."

CHAPTER 53

Jack placed his hand in between the Prime Minister's shoulders and shoved him toward the fire engine. He pulled the door open and said, "Get in there."

"What are you doing?" Alex said.

"We don't know who's on our side and who isn't. You got that? There could have been more than one."

"What? One what?"

Jack slammed the door shut. He held his Beretta in his right hand. The weapon brushed against his thigh, reassured him. The surrounding darkness didn't.

Bear and Sasha jogged toward him. They looked concerned and confused.

"What's going on?" Sasha said.

"He got another threat. They told him it's not over, we got the wrong guy, and he's next."

Sasha looked all around. "Where's Jon with the van?"

Jack and Bear looked at one another. Bear's mouth hung open an inch.

"You don't think?" Jack said.

Bear shook his head, said nothing.

"He was right there the whole time. Right under our damn noses. Now he's got a head start."

"Jon?" Sasha said. "There's no way. Look, I know he's a bit rough around the edges, but his top priority is keeping Alex safe."

"Then why isn't he here now?"

"None of us are thinking straight."

Jack shook his head. "You stay here, Sasha. Keep him inside the truck."

"Where are you going?"

"Not far."

Jack and Bear headed toward the rear of the fire engine, split up. Jack walked to where Mason stood. The guy had a blue blanket draped over his shoulders and wrapped around his body. Mason's gaze followed Jack as he approached.

"Tell me the truth, now," Jack said.

Mason said nothing.

"If you had something to do with this, you're better off letting me know than having them extract it from you."

A smile formed on Mason's lips. The dying fire reflected in his eyes, cast shadows across his face.

"Dammit Mason, talk to me."

"I left six of my men to burn, Jack. And why? Because I couldn't pull a damn trigger? I was too afraid he was going to push a button and blow us all to hell."

"You were following orders, that's all, Mason."

"Orders? What orders said kill half a dozen men?"

"You were told to bring him in alive. He changed the plans, and you had to improvise."

"I froze, Jack. That's what I did."

Jack said nothing. What could he say?

"And now you want to know what I had to do with it. Nothing, that's what. If I did, I would have taken him out clean and let those men live."

Jack felt the pain of the man's words, but he knew that if Mason were involved, all evidence of it was destroyed. No better way to do that than blowing up the house that held the truth.

But Jack could not deny Mason's apparent mental state. His words sounded true, not a fabrication.

Mason turned his head. Jack looked back to see what the man had noticed. Headlights approached. As they neared the house, the van came into view.

"Wait here," Jack said. He stepped into the middle of the road. It forced Jon to stop beside the fire engine.

Jon jumped out of the van, looked around, and then ran up to Jack. "What's going on? Where's Alex?"

Jack stepped sideways in a half-circle. Jon followed, turned his back to the truck.

"Who'd you call while you were gone?"

"Call? What the bloody hell are you talking about?"

"You made a call. Who was it?"

"I'm not telling you a damn thing. Where's Alex?"

Jon started to turn. He buckled forward when Bear hit him from behind. The men crashed to the ground. Bear wove his arms between Jon's, yanked him up.

"What are you doing?" Jon kicked and thrashed, but could not break free from Bear's grasp.

Jack stepped forward. The men were face to face. Inches separated them.

"Who did you call?" Jack said.

"What the bloody hell are you talking about?" Jon said.

"Dammit Jon, you left and less than ten minutes later Alex got another threat. None of us called in to report this. It had to be you. So tell me, who did you call?"

Jon thrashed side to side in an effort to free himself. Every movement he made resulted in Bear tightening his grip.

"Get him off of me," Jon said.

"Not till you tell me who you called."

"Nobody, OK. Take my damn phone out of my pocket and you'll see I didn't call anyone."

Jack nodded at Bear. The big man released Jon, who pulled out his phone and handed it to Jack. A few flicks of Jack's finger confirmed that no call had been placed.

"He could have erased it," Bear said.

By this point, Sasha had joined them. "Let me see it."

Jack handed her the phone. She tapped on the screen a few times and activated the speaker. The phone rang and a moment later a man answered.

The guy said, "What are you guys doing out there?"

They all turned toward the fire engine and saw Alex looking at them through the side window. He had his cell pressed to the side of his head.

"What was the time stamp on the last call between them?" Bear said.

"Hours ago," Sasha said. "Unless he's hiding another phone, it wasn't him."

Jon turned his pockets inside out. "Search me. Search the damn van. I'm telling you for the last damn time, I didn't call anyone."

About that time, Mason walked over. He stared through them, past them. The expression on his face was null and void. "Couldn't help but overhearing your conversation. I called and reported this to Mills a few minutes after the fire truck arrived."

"Who is Mills?" Jack said.

"His boss," Sasha said.

CHAPTER 54

THE FOUR OF THEM STOOD IN SILENCE FOR A BEAT. THEY looked from one another until all stares fell upon Mason. The moment seemed to snap the man back into reality. His blank expression turned to fear, then anger.

"Wait a minute," Jack said. "Mills is your boss? Mills would have been the one who issued the no kill order then. Right?"

Mason nodded. "It came through him, at least. Could have been from his boss, though. Maybe even another on his level. Maybe outside the organization."

"That would be us," Jon said. "Or them." He pointed toward Sasha.

Jack made eye contact with Sasha. "This whole time you've been watching Mason and his partner, did you ever hone in on Mills?"

She looked at Mason, then back at Jack. "I can't discuss that with him around."

Jack grabbed her hand and pulled her away. They walked until they were beyond the bright pool of light cast by the fire.

"This good enough?" he said.

She looked back, took a deep breath. "We've had Mills under surveillance for over twelve months. He's clean, Jack. I've got nothing to support any notion that he was working with Naseer."

"But you can't say that for sure, can you?"

"Yes, I can."

"Can you say with certainty that Mills isn't the one that's making threats on Alex's life?"

She said nothing.

"Can you?"

She remained still for a moment, then shook her head. "That doesn't mean we can go in and detain him."

"Like hell you can't," Jack said. "So this is what we know. Mason called Mills and told his boss what'd happened here. We've got a gap of what, twenty minutes? Maybe thirty since then? How far could the info have traveled during that time? How high up the chain? And how far up were you looking?"

She said nothing, crossed her arms.

"Look, either Mills called Alex just now, or someone he was in contact with did. We need to find out who he's talked to, and we need to know now. Can your people do that or am I wasting my time?"

She stared at Jack for a few seconds, then pulled out her phone. "Carrie, listen to me. I need you to get the records of every call Cameron Mills placed and received starting three days ago. Yes, all of them. Home, office, cell, tin cans. I don't care from what, I want to know where to. Call me back." She hung up, glanced at Jack, placed a second call. "Send a team to detain Cameron Mills. No, don't bring him in. Keep him wherever he is. Yeah, even if he's on the toilet. Don't be a jackass. Detain him in his house if he's there. Call me when you've got a location, and then again when you've got him."

She hung up and forced a smile at Jack. Despite the gesture, she did not look pleased at being told to do her job by him. "Mills isn't going anywhere."

"OK. We are. Let's get out of here before someone realizes that's the Prime Minister in the fire truck."

So Jack put his hand on her shoulder and led her to the van. He nodded toward Bear, who opened the door to the truck's cab and helped Alex down. Then Bear, Alex and Jon got inside the van, joined by Jack and Sasha. Ragged breathing led to steamed windows. Jon fired up the engine, hit the accelerator. Windows went down and cool air wrapped in smoke whipped around inside.

They were halfway down the street when Jack yelled, "Stop!"

Jon slammed on the brakes. The van veered toward the ditch, stopped when the front tire hit the grass.

"What is it?" Jon said.

"Mason didn't get in," Jack said.

Jon put the van in reverse and traveled backward almost as fast as he had forward. He went easier on the brakes this time and they came to stop next to where Mason was standing. The man got inside without a word and without making eye contact with any of them. Sasha slid over rather than making Mason climb over her.

Jack took one last look at the house. The firefighters had the blaze under control and confined to one small portion of the home. The charred remains rose into the night like a slumbering dinosaur skeleton. He thought about the men who perished inside and he wondered if Naseer had men in there who had managed to escape. Owen, for instance. They'd seen him earlier at the store, but there had been no evidence that he had been inside the house. Mason had told him they only found Naseer and two of his men. Where had Owen gone? Was the guy on the run with Mason's partner?

Mason yawned, stretched his arms. He turned in his seat and leaned against the van's sliding door. He looked toward Jack. The two men stared at each other for a moment.

"What?" Mason said.

"Nothing," Jack said.

He had questions for the guy, but not now. He let his gaze drift and settle on Sasha. Their gazes lingered on one another for an uncomfortable moment. Then the woman had the same idea as Mason. She shifted in her seat and leaned back against the window and let her eyes slowly shut.

"Don't close your eyes," Jack said.

"Why?" she said.

"Your concussion."

"But I'm sleepy."

"Exactly."

"Just five minutes, Dad."

Jack shook his head, tapped Bear on the knee. "Flick her any time she closes her eyes for more than five seconds."

They remained quiet for a few minutes. The sound of the tires gliding along the asphalt was like a 747's turbine.

Bear leaned forward and said, "Can you check and make sure Mandy's doing all right?"

"Gloria too," Mason added.

Jack lifted an eyebrow. Had the forced time together helped the couple settle a few issues? Mason dismissed him with a flick of his hand.

From the front of the van, Alex placed a call to his staff and verified that Mandy and Gloria were safe and doing well. Jack wondered about Mia and Erin. He'd heard nothing of Erin's condition since he last spoke with Dottie. Now that the raid was finished, his thoughts centered on the women and Mia. He cycled through his phone and found Leon's number. He sent a text asking about Erin's condition.

A two word response followed.

Doing OK.

That would have to do, Jack figured. He'd go visit her the first chance he got. Knowing that Erin had pulled through eased his mind. He leaned back, let his head fall to the side. The image of the burning house seemed etched into his mind's eye. He replaced the flames with the faces that surrounded him, and the faces of those he wished surrounded him. A couple of the faces remained the same. Then, after several moments of focusing on Erin and Mia, a new face appeared. With hair as rich and red as the flames that engulfed the house, and eyes as deep as the emerald sea, Clarissa smiled and reached out for him. And in her imagined embrace, Jack drifted off to sleep.

CHAPTER 55

HANNAH TOOK OFF HER THIN BLUE JACKET AND PLACED IT over Mia. The girl had laid down a few hours earlier, her body stretched across three chairs. The cool temperature and relaxing ambient lighting made the small room more conducive to sleeping than the main waiting room. It also helped that they were alone. At the same time, that fact made Hannah more than a little uneasy.

A group of men had shown up at Dottie's an hour after Leon and Clarissa had left with Erin. They had come inside and set up in various rooms in the house, and said nothing. Dottie had spoken with one man at length, and he escorted Hannah and Mia to the hospital. And then he left.

They had been kept in the dark about Erin's condition since their arrival. Clarissa had spoken briefly with them, but Leon had yet to be seen. To make matters worse, they wouldn't allow Mia to see her mother. This frightened Hannah, and she had begun to expect the worst. She put on a brave face for Mia, but with the little girl asleep, she no longer had to.

So she rose and went to the window that overlooked the city. Tears distorted the view. Lights burst into a kaleidoscope of colors. She choked back a sob, wrapped her arms across her chest and hugged tight. Tears slid down her cheeks. They were as much a result of the moment as a reaction to the cumulative events.

What would happen to Mia, she wondered, if Erin didn't make it?

Surely, the child could not live with Dottie. Not now, not with everything Erin had discovered about the woman. The truth had come out about Jack being the father, but she considered him to be in no position to raise a child. She doubted he could take care of himself, let alone a kid, if forced into a regular lifestyle. She didn't know him all that well, but it was obvious the guy wasn't cut out for the nine to five.

Hannah lifted her head and adjusted her gaze toward the horizon. The first traces of the sunrise appeared in the distance. Dark blue faded to pale. She glanced at her watch. Five-fifteen a.m. Would they hear something soon?

She turned and walked toward Mia. The girl had pulled herself into a ball and now occupied the better part of two seats. Hannah settled near Mia's head. She stroked the girl's hair, letting the ends pass through the folds of her fingers and cascade down around Mia's head.

"Mummy," Mia whispered.

"Shh, get your rest, sweetie."

Mia pushed herself up, looked at Hannah, smiled. She scooted closer, then laid her head down on Hannah's lap. The girl fell asleep a few moments later.

Hannah eased back in her chair. Her gaze settled on the eastern skyline. It grew lighter and lighter. Pale blue had been replaced with tinges of pink and orange. The city, as she could see it, looked fresh and new.

This will be a great day, she thought.

The feeling in her stomach told her that was wishful thinking.

She turned her head to the left. A man stood in the hallway. He stared at them through the window. Hannah flinched at the sight of the guy. He stood tall, over six foot. Even in the dim light, his blue eyes stood out. He kept his hands in the pockets of his khaki pants. His gaze switched between her and Mia.

Hannah sat up straight, pulled Mia closer. She had no escape route should the guy come inside the room. One door that led to the hall. One window that led to a ten meter drop. She glanced toward the door, saw no way of locking it from the inside. She looked back toward the man. He remained in place, his gaze fixed on her.

The urge to cry had come over her again. She fought it back. Her mind raced to place the man. Had he been at the house? Perhaps he'd been sent to watch over them. Wasn't that the point of Leon's team, anyway? To keep her and Mia safe?

The guy's head jerked to the right, then snapped back into place. He pulled out his right hand, tapped on the glass, then pointed at Hannah. He mouthed something, but she couldn't make out what he said. Should she get up? Go to the door? Scream?

She hugged Mia tighter. By this point, the girl had awoken and taken note of the man.

"Who's that?"

"I don't know, baby."

"What's he want?"

Hannah didn't answer.

The guy looked to his right again, then turned to his left and walked away. He dragged the tips of his fingers along the glass as he went.

Hannah took a deep breath. Her shaky exhale did not go unnoticed by Mia.

"What's wrong? Who was that man?"

She let go of Mia and rose. "I don't know." She pressed her face against the window and looked down the hall in the direction the guy had gone. Fluorescent light fixtures lined the ceiling. Their yellow-white glow reflected off of the linoleum floor. The man was not out there, though. Had he ducked into another room? Made it to the end and already rounded the corner? Would he come back?

She decided they had to leave the room and find someplace where others would see if something happened to them.

"Mia, I think we should go."

Mia said nothing. The girl's breathing had become loud and fast.

Hannah took a step to the left and placed her hand on the door handle. It turned on its own.

CHAPTER 56

THE DOOR DIDN'T IMMEDIATELY OPEN. IT FELT STUCK, OR blocked perhaps. Clarissa pushed her shoulder into it once, twice. Finally, on the third attempt, she managed to get it open and wedge her left leg inside.

"Go away," Hannah said.

"It's Clarissa," she said.

The door jerked open and Hannah threw her arms around Clarissa's neck. The woman began sobbing. Her tears coated Clarissa's cheek.

"Are you OK?" Clarissa said.

Hannah didn't reply. She continued to cry.

Clarissa hugged her tight and repositioned so she could see the entire room. She smiled at Mia, who looked as frightened as Hannah sounded.

"Did you recognize that man?" Clarissa said.

"No," Hannah said in between ragged breaths.

"I was coming down to check on you two and saw him standing at the window. He didn't look like he belonged. I yelled at him, asked who he was. He didn't say anything. I started running, that's when he took off. He turned the corner before I got to the door."

"So he's not one of Leon's guys?"

"Him? No."

"What did he want with us?"

"I don't know."

"What if he comes back?"

"Don't worry. I'm not leaving you two."

The words seemed to settle Hannah. After all, she'd seen what Clarissa was capable of.

"How's my mummy?" Mia asked.

Clarissa moved Hannah to the side and went to the girl. She seated herself next to Mia. Took the child's hand in hers.

"Is she OK?" Mia asked.

"Your mom is a fighter," Clarissa said. "She's very tough. The doctor in that small village made a little mistake." She held her thumb and forefinger close together to emphasize the point. "But these doctors here, they took care of it. She had a quick surgery to repair her leg. She got through it fine and has been resting ever since. She should be able to leave in a day or two."

"So she's OK?" Mia said.

"She's OK," Clarissa said.

Hannah collapsed into the seat next to Mia and brought both hands to her face. Clarissa realized the woman had never been through anything like the past few days.

"When can I see her?" Mia said.

"As soon as she wakes up. You'll get to visit with her for a bit, then I'm taking you two away for a while."

"I don't want to go anywhere. I want to stay with my mum."

Clarissa stroked the child's hair. "You will. She's going to join us soon, along with Leon. We'll be safe and we'll wait this craziness out. Once everything is back to normal, you'll go home with your mom."

Mia eased into her seat, closed her eyes. Hannah did the same.

Clarissa watched the hall for a while. No one passed by. She shifted her gaze to the window and watched the sun rise and the sky fade from blue to pink to red to faint orange. Would this day be better than the past few? She knew she had to check in with Sinclair soon. She planned to tell him everything that had occurred. He'd find out eventually, so there was no point in hiding any of it. It'd be better that he heard it from her. Nothing that had happened could be pinned on her, either. If her cover had been blown, so be it. He could fire her for all she cared.

She wasn't sure how long she had been asleep when the door opened. Before she opened her eyes, she had her pistol in hand and aimed at the man who stood in the open doorway.

"Relax," he said.

She blinked a few times and then smiled at Leon. "Sorry. There had been a man watching the room when I arrived."

"A man? What did he look like?"

"Kinda tall. Blond hair, blue eyes. Maybe in his forties."

Leon shrugged. "That's probably ten percent of London."

"At least."

"He never came back?"

"Not that I know of."

"Erin's up and would like to see Mia."

Clarissa reached over and shook the girl by the shoulder. Mia sat up, smiled at Leon. Hannah woke, too. They all rose and left the room. Leon led them through the maze of halls, into an elevator, through another maze of halls. Ten minutes later, they stood outside of Erin's room.

"Just one at a time," Leon said.

Mia stepped into the room. The little girl cried and was comforted by her mother.

Clarissa moved away from the doorway. She leaned against the wall, pulled out her cell phone. She stared at the screen, as if she expected someone to call at that moment. No one did. It wouldn't be long, though. She was sure of that.

Mia came out of the room. Tear tracks stained her cheeks, but the smile plastered across her face told a different story. She reached out and hugged Hannah, who then went in to visit with Erin.

Clarissa went to Mia and took the girl's hand in hers. They waited in silence with Leon a few feet away.

Hannah stepped into the hallway and said, "She'd like to see you."

"Me?" Clarissa walked past Hannah and into the room.

Erin righted herself in the hospital bed. She nodded, smiled and patted the mattress. Clarissa went to her, leaned with her hip against the bed.

"You'll take good care of my baby, won't you?"

"The best care," Clarissa said.

"I trust you, Clarissa. And I'm sorry about the things I said about Jack. I didn't mean to offend you."

Clarissa shook her head. "No offense taken. In the end, I believe you're right. I think that's the reason I ran from him."

Erin reached out and placed her hand on Clarissa's. "You shouldn't."

"Shouldn't what?"

"Run."

"Too late."

"It's only too late when it's too late. And it's not for you two. Not yet. He's close by. When all this is over, you need to go to him. He's ready now, I can see that. He wasn't when the two of us were together. Too many demons to expel, I suppose. I can tell that he wants something, someone. A new life. He didn't want that when I was around. You, Clarissa, are the game changer. I'm certain of that. Promise me that you won't run again. I care for Jack, but there is nothing for me and him. There can be for you and him, though."

Clarissa smiled. The woman had read her thoughts and feelings and made sense of them and reported them back to Clarissa in a way that clarified them for her. Erin was right. Clarissa wanted to be with Jack. She was ready. Jack was ready. Together, they could start the life she dreamed they could have together.

"I should get moving," Clarissa said as she rose and turned toward the doorway.

"Clarissa," Erin said.

She turned, said nothing.

"Take care of my baby."

Clarissa nodded, then left the room.

Leon handed her a piece of paper. "Don't open it until you get to the bus station. If something happens, or if someone appears, tear it up, get rid of it. Understand?"

"OK." Clarissa tucked the paper into her pocket without looking at it.

"Everything you need is written there. The bus to take, the stop you'll get off at, and directions from there."

"OK, I got it." She pushed past him and took Mia's hand.

"I'll be along as soon as they discharge Erin," he said. "Hopefully today, but maybe tomorrow. We'll likely be without Dottie for a few days. I don't know yet. But once we're all together, we'll start the next leg of the journey."

"To where?"

Leon shook his head. "Not yet."

They exchanged phone numbers and said goodbye. Leon lifted Mia and hugged her. Then he sent the girl and Hannah down the hall to wait.

"Take this," he said as he handed Clarissa a small backpack.

The bag was heavy, yet not bulky. "What is it?"

"My spare Browning. You need it more than I do right now. It's a great backup piece, or if worst comes to worst, Hannah can use it."

"Think she knows what to do with it?"

"She grew up in the woods with a crazy survivalist for a father. She knows."

Clarissa slung the bag over her shoulder, then reached out and hugged Leon. She kissed his cheek. The stubble on his face bit into her lips like tiny shards of glass.

"Go on, get out of here," he said. "We'll see each other no later than tomorrow night."

Clarissa turned and caught up to Mia and Hannah. She continued on with caution, investigated every hall they passed, looked into every room with an uncovered window. The man hadn't returned, but that didn't mean he'd left. For all she knew, he could be close by watching, waiting.

They exited the hospital. The morning air was warm and fragranced with exhaust. She knew where they had to go, but had no idea how to get there.

"Where to?" Hannah asked. Perhaps she sensed Clarissa's indecisiveness.

"Bus station."

"I'm hungry," Mia said.

"I'm sure there'll be something to eat there," Clarissa said.

"But I want to eat now," Mia said.

Hannah knelt down. "Mia, we have to get going now. There's no time to stop. OK? We'll eat as soon as we can."

The girl nodded and reached for Hannah's hand.

"Follow me," Hannah said. "I know how to get there."

So they started toward the bus station. Clarissa searched for a taxi, didn't see one. She didn't know the city bus routes in this part of London. Even if she did, it would take longer to use public transportation than to walk.

When the car screeched to a stop twenty feet in front of them, Clarissa's first reaction was to turn and run. The second car that stopped behind them negated that thought.

Ahead, a man stepped out of the gray sedan. He was tall, blond, in his forties.

"That's him," Hannah said.

Clarissa slid the bag off her shoulder, unzipped it, reached inside with her left hand. She wrapped her palm around the handle of the Browning and let the bag fall to the ground. She then reached her right hand around her back and under her shirt and pulled her Sig from its holster. She committed the position of the man in front of her to memory. Then she glanced over her shoulder. No one had stepped out of the second car, but they watched her. She noticed a black van that approached at too fast a speed. Tires squealed as the vehicle decelerated. Clarissa looked forward, saw the blond man retreat a few steps. She whipped her head around and saw the black van careen into the second car. The impact drove the parked car toward the women.

Hannah grabbed Mia and dove toward the street. The woman managed to turn mid-air and land on her back with Mia pulled tight to her chest.

Clarissa had no choice but to dive in the other direction, toward the building. The tan car hit the curb and rose a few feet into the air. It headed straight for her. The front wheels hit the sidewalk, bounced up, forward. The man behind the wheel had wide eyes, an open mouth. He clutched the steering wheel, leaned over it. The wheels touched down again. Clarissa scooted backward into the wall. She managed to hop to her feet while in a crouched position. The car was close to the point of impact, an impact that would possibly end Clarissa's life, or likely result in a severed spine.

She lunged to her left with no regard to how she would land. The car crashed into the side of the building. She felt pain radiate through her body. From where, though? It covered every inch of her being. She forced herself to look up, expected to see her leg pinned between the car and the wall. It wasn't though. She'd avoided being hit by a few feet. She pulled herself up. The man in the driver's seat was draped over the steering wheel, half inside, half outside the car. Jagged shards of glass had shredded his flesh.

"Clarissa," Hannah screamed.

Clarissa forced herself all the way up. She scanned the street and sidewalk. The crowd that had formed made it impossible to see much at all. Hannah screamed again. Mia did, too. Clarissa balled her hands into fists. She realized that they were empty. She scanned the ground around her. Couldn't find the Sig, located the Browning. She scooped it up. Her right forearm screamed in pain when she gripped the pistol.

The sliding door of the van started to open. Clarissa moved forward, away from the van. She still was unable to locate Hannah and Mia. She climbed up on the tan car's trunk. From there, she had enough of a view to see everything that was happening on the street. People continued to make their way to the crash site. Police sirens whined in the distance. The car must have been a few minutes away still. She couldn't find it.

She heard more screams. Saw the blond man moving against the flow of onlookers. He had Mia on his right hip. His right hand was wrapped around Hannah's hair and he dragged her toward the car. No one stopped to help or interfere. A second man emerged from the vehicle. She knew him, had seen him before. Maybe at Naseer's house, she thought. He took Mia and put her in the backseat. Then the guy pulled out a gun and aimed it at the girl. He said something indecipherable over the hum of the crowd.

Clarissa shifted the Browning to her left arm, raised it toward the men. She yelled, "Let her go."

The man looked toward her, whipped his arm around and fired. The shot went wide of Clarissa. She heard a woman cry out in pain and then a body hit the ground. The man fired again. Clarissa jumped from the trunk. Pain shot through her knee. She planted her right hand on the ground, but was unable to use it to help her up. She managed to get to her knees, then her feet. She aimed her gun in the direction of the car. The crowd in front of her parted. The blond man stood outside the driver's door. He pulled it open.

"Bastard," Clarissa yelled.

The man looked at her, cross at first, then he smiled. She pulled the trigger. The bullet hit the door next to the man. He shook his head. She took a second, inhaled, steadied her left arm, took aim. An arm crashed down over hers. She fired into the street. Bits of hardened asphalt shot up like molten lava. The blond man smiled again before disappearing into the car. Tail lights lit up then faded. The car pulled away from the curb.

"Come on," a man said from behind her as he pulled her to her feet. His hand squeezed her forearm and she yelled out in pain.

"Let me go," she said, driving her heel into the guy's foot.

He dragged her away, spun her, carried her to the black van. She fought, kicked, thrashed. It didn't matter. She couldn't break free. He tossed her into the van, then got inside. She backed into the corner. Her heart sank when she saw Randy shaking his head at her.

Randy was there to clean up the messes they made.

She had made a massive mess. Sinclair had found out. He'd send Randy to deal with it.

"Screw you," she said.

He smiled, nodded toward the front of the van. The man behind the wheel turned around and stared at her.

"Sinclair," she said.

"It's time for you to go."

PART 5
EPISODE 15

CHAPTER 57

Hannah wrapped her right arm around Mia and pulled her close. Through tear filled eyes, she stared at the man behind the wheel. He glanced up at the rear view and met her stare.

"What do you want with us?" she said through clenched teeth.

Neither man said anything.

"Why don't you let us go?"

Again, no answer.

"You bastards. There's gonna be a whole team of men so far up your asses you'll wish you were dead. And they're gonna accommodate that wish. That's what they do. Your lives are as worthless as that dog crap you just drove through."

"Oh, shut up," the man driving the car said.

"Tell me where you're—"

"I said shut up." He nodded at the other guy, who turned in his seat and aimed his pistol at Hannah.

She pushed Mia away and leaned forward. "Do it, then. Or aren't you man enough?"

The guy smiled. "Don't tempt me."

"You aren't gonna do a damn thing. Aim that gun somewhere else."

The guy shrugged and shifted in his seat. Perhaps he assumed she'd given up. He couldn't be more wrong.

"What are you doing?" the man driving said.

"I'm not going to shoot them and you know it," the guy said. "You know our orders."

Hannah leaned back, turned and stared out the window. Buildings passed by in a blur. Just like the endless trees back home, the city was its own kind of wilderness. The car turned several times and she had lost sight of where they were. Next to her, Mia alternated between sniffles and sobs. Hannah pulled her close again.

They remained silent for the remainder of the trip. The further they got from the city, the more Hannah feared that either she or Mia, or perhaps both of them, would not be alive in a day's time. Although, would the men have taken them in broad daylight, on a crowded street, if their intention was to kill? If only she could gauge what it was they wanted.

She didn't want to think about it any longer. She wished she had stayed home instead of returning to England. In light of everything that had happened, dealing with her father for a few months would have been a breeze compared to the past couple days.

Mia pressed closer. Hannah felt the girl's breath, hot on her hand. She knew at that moment that she was where she was supposed to be. Who would protect the girl if not her?

The car turned onto a residential street in what might have once been a nice neighborhood. They passed several rows of homes, old and dilapidated and in disrepair. They made a left, then another left onto an alley that ran between two streets. The man driving stopped behind a home. The other guy got out, unlocked and opened a gate. They passed through, and the man closed the gate then walked ahead of the car and opened the garage door. They pulled inside and stopped. The driver stepped out. The sunlight faded as the door was once again shut. The driver opened Hannah's door.

"Get out," he said.

Hannah eased her legs out, used the door to pull herself up in front of the guy.

"Back up," he said.

She turned ninety degrees and took a step back. The guy stepped around the door, reached in and pulled Mia out. He set the girl down. She quickly found Hannah and wriggled in behind her.

"What now?" Hannah said.

The men exchanged glances. The younger guy pointed toward a door.

"In there," he said.

"You first," she said.

He pointed his gun at her. "You don't give the orders here."

She thought about taking it a step further, forcing the men to make her move. Then she felt Mia's grip on her hand. The soft touch encouraged her to cooperate. The moment would come when one of the men would slip up, she figured. They underestimated her. A big mistake. It was only a matter of time before she would claim vengeance.

She passed the man and opened the door. The room was dark and musty. Dim light filtered through the painted glass. A half-inch of dust coated everything. It didn't appear that anyone lived in the house. She reached out and felt along the wall. She flipped the light switch, but nothing happened.

"No power here," the guy said. "Move inside."

Hannah pulled Mia along with her as she entered the house through the kitchen. A pile of dishes lingered in the sink. She didn't get close enough to see if they were dirty or clean, but if the smell was to be an indication, they hadn't been washed previously.

"Keep moving," the guy said.

She felt the tip of his pistol in the middle of her back. She pushed Mia forward and continued through the kitchen into an empty room.

"Up the stairs."

They turned and headed up a flight, round a corner, up another flight.

"Down the hall. Last room on the right."

She followed the directions, came to a closed door. She reached out and turned the handle. A burst of stale air escaped the room. Inside, there were two beds with no sheets and a rug in between them. The room was empty otherwise. The window on the wall was covered with dark drapes pulled tight. Not a single sliver of light penetrated through.

"Go in."

She ushered Mia through the doorway and toward one of the beds. The girl settled down on the edge of the bed. Hannah took the other.

The guy followed them in. "There's a battery operated light in the corner. Don't dare open the drapes. We've got someone across the street watching. So help me God, if you do, I'll beat you."

Hannah said nothing. Mia sniffled.

"We'll be up in a little bit with food and to let you use the restroom. Don't even think about trying to open the door. It'll be locked, anyway."

"How long are you going to keep us here?"

"Until they tell me to move you."

"Who?"

The guy did not respond. He wagged his right index finger, took a step back, pulled the door closed. Hannah heard the lock turn into place. She resisted the urge to check the door knob. Mia didn't, though. The girl got up and raced toward the door. She grabbed the handle and turned and pulled.

There was a banging from the other side. "I said don't touch the damn door."

Mia jumped back and started to cry. Hannah reached out for her, pulled her onto the bed and held her tight.

"We'll be out of here soon, sweetie. Don't you worry. We'll be home soon."

CHAPTER 58

"SO WHAT HAVE YOU BEEN DOING?" SINCLAIR SAID.

Clarissa looked at the floor, said nothing.

"You don't know how to respond anymore?" he said.

"I can get it out of her," Randy said.

"Shut up, Randy," Sinclair said.

Clarissa thought through a half-dozen scenarios intended to get her out of the van and away from the men. None logically ended with the result she hoped for. For now, her best bet was to remain silent, still, and see what Sinclair wanted with her. Would he slip up? Say something to give her a clue? Not likely, she thought.

"You know I have ways of making you talk, Clarissa. Think back to the first time we met."

She didn't have to think hard. The encounter had become ingrained deep in her psyche. There wasn't a week that passed where she didn't awake in a cold sweat thinking about Sinclair's needle.

"It doesn't have to come to that, child. I just have a few questions for you. But, as always, it is up to you how we proceed."

Clarissa thought it over for a moment. She knew, no matter what, Sinclair would get the truth from her. He'd get it through any means necessary, if need be. She had prepared herself for this moment long ago.

She figured this conversation would occur over the phone, which would have made her less afraid of the possible results.

"Well?"

"What do you want to know?"

"How did you get here?"

"How did you find me here?"

He grinned, traced his mustache with his thumb and forefinger. "You first."

She glanced from Sinclair to Randy, who looked on, bemused. Her stomach knotted at the possible reasons he was with them.

"Spiers met me on the train. I spotted him early on. He approached and identified himself. It became clear that I had little choice but to remain with him."

"He's a good agent," Sinclair said.

"Yeah, well, anyway he got a call. Told me plans had been changed. We weren't in Paris for long before we took another train to Brussels. There we met two women and a kid and escorted them to a small village. Spiers was to watch over them."

"Who gave him this job?"

Clarissa shrugged, said nothing.

Sinclair studied her for a moment. He didn't need a needle to determine whether or not she was telling the truth. She knew he saw through her lie.

"Go on," he said.

"We went to this old house outside an old village. The next morning, I went into town for some milk, coffee, you know, stuff for breakfast. A car stopped in front of the store, then disappeared."

"What kind of car?"

"Mercedes or BMW, I guess. You know I don't care about cars. It was sleek and sliver and had dark tinted windows. It was foggy out, misty. I couldn't see the house until I was close. I saw that same car there, in the driveway. I approached through a field. One of the men came outside. I waited, then attacked and took him out."

"Took him out?"

She looked away. "Temporarily, I suppose. He was gone when I went back outside."

"What happened when you went inside?"

"I found Spiers dead. Don't think he even had a chance to defend himself. Then I killed the second man."

"Do you know who these men were?"

She shook her head.

"Could you identify them if you saw a picture?"

"Maybe. I don't know. It's all a blur. The guy outside, I never saw his face without blood all over it. The guy inside, I only saw him for a moment. Erin was shot—"

"Who?"

"Erin, one of the women, she was shot. We tended to her and got her out of there. At that point, I didn't know whether or not the guy would come back in or what was going on."

Sinclair nodded. He looked away and eased back in his seat. Randy continued to stare at her. She averted her eyes toward the solid side panel to her left.

"So why didn't you call me?" Sinclair said. He remained seated forward.

"I was scared," she said.

"Scared of what?"

"Your reaction."

"How did you expect me to react?"

"I figured you'd be angry."

"Why would I have been angry?"

"Because I wasn't in Paris. I'd left, possibly blowing everything we'd been working toward. It could have ruined the in we'd built with Naseer and his men. So many people have put in so many hours to get us this far. I'd hate to be the one to destroy that."

Sinclair nodded, said nothing.

"I knew I had to tell you, but I wanted to figure out if things were still OK with Naseer first."

"Well that won't be much of a problem since he's dead."

"What? When did that happen?"

"Last night. But he had a contingency plan and he still has men he trusted who can run the operation. And yes, you are going to figure out whether or not we still have our connections with his group. And if we don't, you'll be the one paying the price. You'll be going in unsupported."

Clarissa said nothing. His words had been intended to threaten or scare her. They didn't. She had been prepared to walk into the lion's den, alone and unarmed. The fact that Naseer was no longer there might make it easier. Or harder, depending on who stepped up and took over.

"One last thing," Sinclair said.

Clarissa looked up.

"Why did you continue to help those women? Even today, you were with them. Why?"

Something about the way he looked at her told her that he knew. Maybe it was the twitching of his fingers or the intense burning in his good eye. Regardless, she decided to come clean.

"Jack," she said.

"Noble?"

"Yeah."

"Go on."

"He was the one that wanted them protected. He called Spiers."

"Because he knew you were with them?"

She shook her head. "He doesn't know that I'm in London. I haven't reached out to him. I played dumb with Spiers. Jack knows nothing about me being here."

"I wonder how he and Spiers knew each other."

"We all know each other," Randy said. "You're just never invited to the convention."

Sinclair shook his head. "Yes, well, we'll determine whether or not he knows you are here at a later date." He put the van into gear and pulled away from the curb.

"Where are we going?" she said.

"Away," he said.

"But the girls," she said.

"What about them?"

"I've got to help them. Didn't you see those men kidnap them?"

"One of those men was a British Intelligence agent. I've got every reason to believe they thought you were going to harm the two girls and that's why they took them."

"That's a load and you know it."

Sinclair said nothing.

They drove until they reached the M11. They merged onto the highway and headed north.

CHAPTER 59

JACK DOUBLE PARKED THE AUDI AT THE BACK OF THE emergency room parking lot and ran toward the entrance. Halfway between the car and hospital the thought occurred that he might have left the door open. He felt the keys strike his leg with every step he took, so no one could steal the vehicle, easily at least.

Bear had remained with Alex and Jon. He'd said he wanted to spend a little time with Mandy to make sure she was OK. The kid hated being cooped up for more than an hour or two. Jack imagined she'd had a tough time being underground in a box for so long.

Sasha had left Number 10 before Jack had. She had to go to the office and wanted to stop by the hospital and check on Mason. The same hospital Jack was about to enter. But that wasn't the reason Jack was here. Erin had been taken to the same hospital the day before. She'd been rushed into emergency surgery to repair her torn femoral artery.

Jack walked past the double sliding doors that led to the emergency room and instead used the main hospital entrance. He hadn't bothered to wash up or change his clothes from the night before. He'd gotten used to the smell by the time they reached the outskirts of London. His dirty appearance drew several stares from patients, visitors and staff. The woman at the information desk was no exception. She avoided making eye contact and spoke to him with disdain in her voice as she told him Erin's room number and gave him directions.

He thanked her and moved quickly through the halls. When he reached Erin's room, he found the door open. He took a step inside and rapped his knuckles against the door. Leon, who had been asleep in the chair next to the bed, jolted up. The guy's hand slipped inside his coat, eased out when he realized it was Jack in the room.

Erin turned her head from right to left and smiled. The tension Jack felt in his neck and shoulders lifted.

"Hi, Jack," she said.

He crossed the room, leaned over and kissed her cheek. "You OK?"

She nodded. "Going to be fine."

Leon rose. "I'll be out in the hall." He bumped into Jack's shoulder as he passed. The space between the bed and wall was tight, but not that tight.

"What is it with him?" Jack said.

She shrugged. "No clue. Grumpy, I guess."

"Where's Mia?"

"She's with Hannah."

"Where are they?"

"They left a while ago."

"Erin, where did they go?"

"I shouldn't tell you this." She bit her lip, reached for his face. "Then again, maybe I should."

Jack intercepted her hand and placed it on the bed, resting his on top. "What?"

"They're with an old friend of yours."

"The only old friend I have in London is with the Prime Minister right now."

"Clarissa."

"What do you mean, Clarissa?"

"She's here. She's watching the girls. Taking them someplace safe."

Jack glanced over his shoulder. Leon stood in the doorway. The man nodded. "Someplace safe."

"How did this happen?" Jack said.

"She was with the man you called to help us in Paris," Erin said.

"Spiers? How did she end up with him?"

Erin shrugged.

Jack remained quiet for a moment. He processed the new information and let it settle. The pieces began to fall into place. He knew the connection between Clarissa and Spiers intersected through Sinclair. That must've been the reason she left.

"OK," he said. "We can deal with this soon enough."

"Don't be a fool, Jack."

"What's that mean?"

Behind him, he heard Leon answer his phone and step into the hall.

"It means that you and this woman are meant to be together. Don't be a selfish jackass and drive her away."

"You don't understand. That's not how..."

"That's not how what?" she said. "I know you better than you think. Seven years hasn't changed you all that much, you know."

"There's more important things than my love life at play here, Erin. The Prime Minister has been threatened. We thought we eliminated the threat, but it's ongoing."

Her face became worried. "Do you think they are still after us?"

"I don't know if the two are related. It seems that way. Yet, there's a link missing. Every person I suspect turns out to be clean. What the hell is the connection between me, you, and the Prime Minister?"

"You're the spy, not me."

"Thanks for the observation."

Leon entered the room, the color drained from his face.

"Leon," Erin said. "What is it?"

He opened his mouth, but no words came out.

Jack turned and walked up to him. "What's going on?"

He looked from Erin to Jack. "Come to the hall."

Jack followed him out of the room. The lights in the hall shone brighter and he squinted to adjust to the brightness. Three nurses, one who looked fresh out of nursing school, passed. They all stared at Jack's dirt covered clothes. He heard one make a comment, but dismissed it after *did you see*.

Leon interlaced his fingers behind his head and forced out several quick, deep breaths.

"Leon, what's going on?"

"The girls," he said.

"What about them?"

"They've been abducted."

"All three?"

"There's only two."

"The woman you sent with them."

He shook his head. "They don't know what happened to Clarissa. Something about a car crash, bullets flying."

Jack's vision darkened around the edges, his head spun. His lungs felt like they had collapsed. He couldn't force a breath into them. He reached for the wall, fell against it.

"Jack?"

Leon's words sounded like they came deep inside a canyon, over a mile away. He heard his name over and over, more and more diminished each time. He'd experienced this in the past, but it had been a few years at least since the last episode. Jack felt himself collide with the wall, then the floor. The world around him went black.

A burst of ammonia roused Jack from his unconscious state. The three nurses hovered over him. The young one looked scared.

"Are you all right, sir?" one of the older ones said.

"Fine." He struggled to find his balance and rose. He reached out and used the wall to steady himself. "What happened?"

"You passed out. Have you been feeling well?" the nurse said.

"I'm OK. Go on."

Leon stepped back, looked Jack up and down. A certain amount of fear hid behind the man's eyes.

"That's never happened," Jack said.

Leon shook his head in short, smooth bursts. "No worries. It was nearly my reaction as well. Look, Jack, whatever you need, I'll help."

They both brushed the incident aside. Jack nodded. "We've got to tell her."

"I know."

Together, they reentered the room. Erin sat upright in the bed, tears streamed down her cheeks. She shook her head when they approached.

"No," she said.

"I'm sorry," Jack said.

"We'll do everything we can to find them," Leon said.

Jack hugged Erin for several seconds, then pulled away. "I'm going to find whoever did this, and I'm going to kill them. Erin, I won't rest until these people are dead."

"Just find my baby, Jack." She took a deep breath and wiped the tears from her eyes. "Find our baby."

CHAPTER 60

"I WILL," JACK SAID AS HE LEANED OVER AND KISSED ERIN ON the forehead. He gave her one last look, pushed off the bed and headed for the door.

"Jack," Leon said.

Jack pushed past the man, said nothing. Leon followed him into the hall, called for him twice. Jack kept going. He navigated the maze of hallways and exited through the ER waiting room. Through it all, he ignored the stares from people offended by his dirty clothes, and the harsh words of those telling him he didn't belong in a certain part of the hospital.

Single, focused thought and action.

To hell with them and anyone else who managed to get in his way.

The ambulance lane was packed four deep. Medics unloaded gurneys with people who looked like they had been lucky to survive a major accident. For a second he wondered if there had been another attack. He figured the hospital would have been buzzing if that were the case.

He walked between the front and back of the first two ambulances and then jogged across the traffic lane between the parking lot and hospital. A white mini-van stopped and waited until he passed. The parking lot was full. Fuller than it had been when he arrived. He reached into his pocket and pulled out the key fob and pressed the panic button. A horn went off in three second intervals. He saw the silver Audi and its flashing lights.

The driver's door was closed. An electric car no bigger than a refrigerator had wedged itself between the Audi and a car next to it.

Jack slid into the driver's seat. He had to adjust himself to being on the right hand side of the car. Every time he drove in London it played with his brain. He'd narrowly avoided a few accidents due to habit taking over. He didn't avoid hitting the electric car when he backed out.

Oh well.

Being a motorcade vehicle, the Audi was equipped with strobes and a siren in addition to its advanced GPS navigation features. As he pulled out of the parking spot and neared the exit, he switched all three on. The drive, which could have taken upwards of an hour in London's parking lot they called roads, took Jack fifteen minutes. The GPS unit led him to the parking garage that adjoined the underground room that connected to the labyrinth of tunnels beneath and around Number 10.

He parked and stepped out of the car. Gas fumes surrounded him. The only door in the room opened following a series of clicks. Multiple locks, various types. Jon entered the room.

"How's your lady friend?" Jon asked.

"She's going to be fine."

Jack walked past Jon without looking at him and took the tunnel in the only direction it led.

Jon caught up and placed a hand on Jack's shoulder. "But?"

Jack jerked to the side to free himself from the man's grasp. His opposite arm brushed against the tunnel wall. Condensation coated his hand.

"There's more trouble." Jack said.

"What happened?" Jon said.

Jack cast a glance behind, verified no one else was inside the tunnel. He decided it was time to test Jon. He twisted to his left, drove his right fist into Jon's solar plexus. The guy let out a wheezing gasp. Jack grabbed the man by his throat, refused to let him bow over and relax his diaphragm. He hoisted Jon up and slid his back against the domed wall, head to the ceiling so he was forced to look down at Jack.

"What?" Jon tried to say. It came out hollow.

"Why'd you do it?"

The man said nothing. It wasn't that he had nothing to offer. He couldn't speak. His face turned deep red. Veins poked out on his forehead, like serpents riding the surface of a blood red sea. Jon's eyes started to bulge and roll back. Jack let go. The man fell to the floor, knees, forearms, then face. His body formed a huddled mass. He rolled to his side. A loud gasp escaped his mouth when he finally managed to force air into his lungs.

"That's enough," Jack said. He reached down, grabbed Jon by the collar and yanked him back up. He pushed the guy into the wall, pinned him there, but did not choke him this time.

Jon panted, caught his breath. "What are you doing?"

"You tell me."

"I have no idea what you're talking about."

"No idea, huh? Ask me why I don't believe you."

Jon said nothing. He closed his eyes and swallowed hard.

"Ask me!" Jack yelled. He pulled out his Beretta, jammed it under Jon's chin.

"Ask me," Jack said again.

"Why?"

"Tell me why you did it."

"Did what?"

"The girls. Why'd you have them kidnapped? What kind of game are you playing here?"

Jon went slack. Every tensed muscle in the guy's body seemed to relax. Or maybe he entered some kind of forced paralysis. The guy leaned his head back against the wall, his shoulders drooped. He looked down his nose and leveled his gaze with Jack's.

"Tell me," Jack said.

"Jack, I didn't do anything. My sole responsibility is to Alex. That's it. I'm one hundred percent legit. I'll give you anything you need to find them. I'll scour the damn city with you. You have to believe me. I didn't have anything to do with it."

Jack lowered his hands and took a step back. Jon didn't move. Jack holstered his weapon and kept his gaze fixed on Jon.

"I don't know if I believe you."

Jon extended his hand, sideways, fingers spread.

Jack didn't accept it.

"I've been there before, Jack. Everyone is an enemy until proven otherwise."

Words that Jack lived by. And Jon still hadn't proved himself, one way or another. On one hand, he'd been distant and snapped at them. On the other, the guy had managed to pass every challenge they'd put him through.

"Let's go," Jack said.

Jon led and Jack followed through the maze of tunnels. He kept one eye on Jon, one eye ahead. He kept track of each turn in the event he walked into a setup. When they reached the main tunnel that led to the house, he relaxed. They reached the end, climbed a set of stairs and continued past the first level of the house. Two more flights with a hall in between deposited them into the meeting room with the old long wood table and the bar with the two thousand dollar bottles of whiskey. Jack forced himself not to take a line that led to the first opened bottle he spotted.

Bear was the first to greet Jack when he entered. The big man rose and took a few steps forward.

"We just got word," Bear said.

Jack said nothing. Alex approached and grabbed him by the shoulders and moved his head in front of Jack's until they made eye contact.

"I pledge to you every man I have."

"You need them," Jack said.

"So do you."

"This is a tactic. We all know it. They're trying to divide us, get us away from you, Alex."

"Won't work," Alex said. "I'm going to be by your side, and I'm going to put a bullet into the head of whoever took your little girl."

"Appreciate it," Jack said. "Where's Mason? Still at the hospital?"

"No," Alex said. "Sasha picked him up and dropped him off here. He's down with Gloria."

"Think he'll be any use to us anymore?"

"Not sure. He's still pretty shaken up about all of this. Might be better to keep him in the bunker room."

"We might need him. I'd presume he knows more about his partner Godfrey than anyone else."

"If that were true, then he'd have known that the guy was corrupt," Jon said.

"Point taken," Jack said. "I'd still like to talk to him."

Jon's cell rang. He excused himself and stepped out of the room to take the call.

"I'll phone down and have Mason sent up," Alex said.

Jack took a seat next to Bear, who had poured two fingers of whiskey into a glass. Jack took the glass and drained it in one pull. He hoped the alcohol would settle his nerves. Doubted it would, though. He'd reached the point of no return.

Alex set the phone down. "He'll be up in a few. Go easy on him, Jack."

Jack nodded. He didn't think treating Mason the way he had treated Jon in the tunnel would exact any results other than damaging the guy further.

Jon rushed back into the room. He placed both hands on the table, leaned over, could hardly breathe.

"What is it?" Alex said.

"They've located Godfrey," Jon said.

CHAPTER 61

THE NEWS CAME AS A SHOCK TO THEM, BUT THEIR DISBELIEF soon turned to excitement. As best any of them could tell, a huge piece of the puzzle lay with Godfrey. They had to act on any tip that placed them within the vicinity of the man. For all Jack knew, taking him down could put an end to the whole ordeal.

A tense moment passed as each man looked at another.

"Where is he?" Bear said.

"Other side of town," Jon said. "Someone reported a suspicious car that pulled in behind an abandoned house. They got the plates. The car's registered to Joseph Godfrey. Our Joseph Godfrey."

"And the house?" Jack said.

"That's the kicker. The house is owned by Joe Godfrey and Ben Kemp. That second name sound familiar to you?"

"Yeah," Jack said. "Mason said he pulled the trigger on Naseer."

Jon nodded. "Seals the deal."

"That doesn't make sense," Jack said.

"How's that?"

"If we believe that Godfrey worked with Naseer, why would he own a house with the guy who killed Naseer?"

"We need Mason up here, now," Jon said.

"He's on the way," Alex said.

"Maybe this didn't go down the way Mason told us," Jack said.

"Jack, what are you thinking?" Alex said.

Jack took a moment. He stared at the checkerboard inlay in the center of the table. He set his glass down and stood. "I'm wondering if maybe Kemp had started attacking his own men. He was going to be a pretend hostage to get Naseer out of the house. Naseer alone, forget it, he'd be shot dead with or without those explosives. But take one of Mason's men, the guy might have a change of heart. Once Naseer and Kemp were clear of the house, their escape would have been easy. Heavily wooded area. Nothing but small towns nearby. Local police forces couldn't be much more than a couple cops one at a time. So you've got at least the two of them, maybe more. Hell, there could have been others waiting nearby to pick them up."

Jon said, "They might have known. I think they did know about the raid ahead of time. Things just got out of control."

Jack nodded as he paced the area between the wall and the table. "That might explain why we saw Owen in that store, but never at the house. Kemp and Owen are close. One might have introduced the other to Naseer. I saw Owen kill Thornton. He did it in Naseer's presence. Hell, he did it for Naseer."

"How would Mason have known?" Bear said.

"Because I saw Kemp shoot two of my guys in the back of their heads."

They all turned toward the door and saw Mason standing there. He looked twenty times worse than he had that morning. The bruises on his face had darkened. His eyes were swollen and purple. His knuckles were the size and color of plums. His arms were wrapped in gauze, and bandages lined his forehead.

"I saw him shoot my men, and then I shot him, and that bastard Naseer. That's when things went downhill. I realized the explosives were going to detonate. It wasn't instant, you see. I had time to think. That's the only reason I yelled on the radio beforehand. It was for effect, mostly. My guys were all dead or had no chance of getting out of the house. Between Kemp and Naseer's guys, they'd executed almost all of them. Naseer had two men in the house. Both had managed to get out. I thought that maybe this would all go away with Naseer dead. If he was behind the attacks and the threats, it'd end with his death. So I barked the orders to get out and managed to clear the doorway just in time. In all honesty, it wouldn't have bothered me if I'd blown up."

"Why didn't you say anything?" Alex said.

Mason leaned to the side and rested his head on the wall. "I didn't want to sully the reputation of my men. If the truth about Kemp came out, then the integrity of all those who perished would come into question. They don't deserve that. Their families don't deserve that."

No one said anything for a moment. Stares were shared from across the table. Everyone sat in a state of disbelief.

"What was Kemp's relationship with Godfrey?" Jack said.

"They were friends. Better than he and I, that's for sure. They used to do stuff together outside the job. I always figured if something happened to me, they'd find a way to bump Kemp up so the two of them could be partners."

"You ever hear anything about them owning a house together?" Jack said.

Mason shook his head. "Why?"

"We've got a lead on a man entering an abandoned house. House is owned by Kemp and Godfrey. Description of the man matches Godfrey."

"There's more," Jon said.

"What is it?" Jack said.

"A second man."

"Description?"

"No match."

Godfrey, plus one. Who could it be, Jack wondered. "We've got to get to that house."

"One more thing," Jon said while staring down at a pencil he rolled from one hand to the other.

"What else?" Jack said.

Jon looked up, took a moment, then said, "The caller said he saw a woman and a young girl in the backseat of the car."

Jack watched as each man's expression changed. Either everyone shared a bad batch of coffee, or they all came to the same realization at that moment. One MI5 agent, perhaps two, possibly more, had Mia and

Hannah in their possession. It made no sense. Some would say it was a downright illogical conclusion just based on who they had been talking about.

It tied Alex and Jack even tighter together in the web of deception. Someone, the same someone at that, wanted both of them dead.

"Let's get to that house," Alex said.

"We're sending a team to surround the neighborhood now," Jon said.

"Keep them at a distance," Jack said. "We don't need these guys to realize they've been surrounded. That could be disastrous for those girls."

"They're worth more to them alive," Alex said.

"When it comes to me, yeah," Jack said. "Not to you, though."

"I give you my word no harm will come to them if it's up to me," Alex said.

"What haven't you told me?"

"I'm not following."

"Where's the connection? I can't find it. Mia and Hannah are connected to me, not you. The only connection we share right now is someone wants both of us dead."

Alex shook his head. "Does it matter, Jack? We're in this together now."

Jack nodded.

"Any ideas?" Alex said.

"We both pissed off the same person."

"I piss off lots of people, Jack. It comes with the job. Who have you upset?"

"Got an hour or two?"

Alex nodded, smiled.

"What about Sasha?" Jack said.

"We're wasting time," Jon said.

Alex rose and started toward the door. "You're right. We'll meet up with her later. Let's go."

CHAPTER 62

A CLOUD OF DUST RUSHED IN FROM UNDER THE DOOR AND plumed into the air. Hannah stiffened in preparation of someone entering the room. What now? The door flung open. Mia jolted up, broke free from Hannah's grasp. Hannah adjusted her position and clasped her hands together and pulled the girl back into her chest. The light that flooded in silhouetted the man in the doorway. Without seeing his features, she could tell he was the older guy. Tall with short blond hair. Even if she hadn't been able to see him, she would have known. He stunk like rotten trash.

"Get up," he said.

"Why?" Hannah said.

"Because I said so."

"No, we're staying right here."

"No you're not. You're coming with me."

"Where are you taking us?"

"Someplace else."

"What are you going to do to us?"

The guy said nothing.

"Answer me."

He crossed the room, grabbed Hannah by the hair and dragged her out of bed. "You shut up and do what I tell you."

She screamed and kicked and punched. One shot managed to connect with his midsection. Pain radiated through her wrist and arm. She howled. He laughed and dropped her on the floor.

"If you're not in that hallway in thirty seconds I'll put a bullet in your brain. If you don't believe me, then believe this. It's not you they care about. Only the little girl."

The guy left the room and Hannah curled up into a ball. Her tears slid across her face and pooled on the dusty floor. She felt Mia's small hand on her shoulder. The girl grabbed a fistful of Hannah's shirt and began pulling.

Hannah's right arm felt like lead and hurt like hell, so she pushed off the floor with her left, then used the mattress to help her stand.

"Let's go, Mia," she said.

Mia stayed close to her as they exited the room. The guy stood in the hall on the other side of the stairs. Beams of light came in through dirty windows. They cast shadows across his face, distorting his smile and making him look like an evil comic book character.

"After you," he said.

Hannah ushered Mia in front of her, then she descended the stairs. She proceeded with caution, as the stairs were rickety, and she had to use her left hand to stabilize her right arm, which she feared to be broken. Without the benefit of the rail, she worried that she'd slip off a broken step and collapse on top of Mia. Step by step they traveled until they reached the bottom of the stairs. From there they made their way into the kitchen. The other man rested at the small table in the corner. He had a large radio on the table and fidgeted with the dial. Based on the chatter that came through the device, Hannah figured it was a police scanner.

"Keep moving," the older guy said.

They passed through the kitchen. The guy at the table didn't bother to look up. Hannah could have burned holes into him with her stare. She stopped in front of a door that led to the garage.

"Open it," the guy said.

She did, and then she took the three steps down into the garage. Confined gasoline vapors choked the air out of her. When she swallowed, the taste burned itself into her mouth and throat where cottonmouth had moments ago prevailed.

She let go of her broken arm and grabbed Mia's hand. She led the child to the car and pulled open the back passenger side door.

"No," the guy said.

She turned. "No what?"

He held two black sacks in his hands. Tossed them to her.

"One on the girl's head. The other on yours."

Hannah let the bags bounce off of her. She stood defiant, glared at the man.

"You want the other arm to match? How about a leg?" He smiled, looked at Mia. "How about hers?"

"Enough," Hannah said. She did as told. She maintained eye contact with the guy up till the moment she slipped the bag over her head. In the darkness, she guided Mia to the open door.

"Stop," the guy said.

"What?" Hannah said, frustrated.

She heard the trunk pop open.

"You're not riding in the back seat."

Mia began to cry. Hannah had to force herself not to join the little girl. She felt a large hand in the middle of her back. She reached out and swatted side to side with her left arm, attempting to drive the man away from Mia. In her futility, she hit Mia in the head. Hannah grasped Mia's shirt. The little girl called out. Not from the hit, or from being held. The guy had pulled her away.

"Up you go," the guy said.

Hannah's hand slipped free of the child's shirt. A moment later, the guy's hand wrapped around the back of her head and forced her forward.

"Easy goes it, lady," he said. "Wouldn't want you to bump your head."

Hannah gave in and let him guide her into the trunk. Her knees bumped against the car's frame. Her right arm hit the carpeted trunk first. She groaned, but refused to yell out in pain. When the lid slammed shut, she found herself in an uncontrollable panic. She struggled to breathe. Her heart raced well over one hundred beats per minute. She kicked at the trunk lid, the back seat.

Please get me out of here!

"It's going to be OK, Hannah."

At once, Mia's quiet voice soothed and settled her. For all the thoughts Hannah had that she had to be the one to remain strong and protect Mia, it was the girl who'd calmed her.

The car began to back up. Mia scooted closer. Hannah wrapped her arm around the girl. Every time the vehicle started and stopped, they rolled together. Being confined and behind a double wall of darkness, she lost track of time. The drive could have taken five minutes, or it could have been an hour. She had no idea. The car came to a stop. She waited. The breeze that blew into the trunk when the lid finally lifted coated her sweat soaked body and drove a chill through her. She clutched Mia tight as someone, the man she assumed, tried to pull the little girl away.

"Come off it," he said. "Let her go."

She refused to release Mia. A fist to her stomach was her punishment. Or reward, she thought, for being the protector. The shock of the blow was worse than the actual shot she took. Still, it had been enough to loosen her grip on Mia. The girl's screams were muffled by the bag on her head and likely the hand that covered her mouth.

Footsteps and voices faded, then returned. Hannah had managed to get upright and had the bag halfway up her face.

"Out you go," the guy said.

Hannah felt a hand on her upper arm. The guy yanked her up. Her head banged into the trunk lid. A dull pain spread across the back of her skull. She wanted to reach behind and check for blood, but he jerked her around so quickly she didn't have the chance. The guy pulled her forward, then let go. She fell face first. It felt like a hundred tiny rocks dug into her cheeks, lips, nose and forehead. Not concrete, gravel.

"Get the bloody hell up," the guy said as he pushed her forward with the heel of his shoe.

She instinctively placed her right hand on the ground in front of her. Her arm buckled, pain radiated through her wrist. Any remaining doubt that her arm was fine disappeared at that moment.

He grabbed a handful of her shirt, and pulled her up, and led her forward. "Three steps up."

"Where are we?" she said.

"Shut up."

She knew they couldn't be someplace populated. Not with the way he treated her. The woods, perhaps? Her body lunged forward and she fell once again. This time, a soft surface broke her fall. It felt like a tightly knit rug. Smelled like the ground. A mat you place at the front door, she figured. The air no longer felt light and airy. It was still, oppressive, warm. Not quite as bad as the trunk, though. They were inside.

"About ten paces forward, then sit down."

Hannah got to her knees, then her feet, then she shuffled forward with her good arm extended in front of her. Her left shin bumped into the edge of a chair or sofa. She ignored the pain and turned and took a seat. A small hand grabbed her thigh. Hannah let out a sigh and reached out for Mia. The girl responded to her touch with a soft cry.

"You can take those hoods off now," the guy said.

Hannah wondered where they were. What would this place look like? Surely it had to be in the middle of the woods, worn down. She expected it to be messy and old. Cobwebs in the corners, dirt on the floor. That would match the welcome mat.

She tugged at the hood until it pulled up over her nose. One final pull released her from the veil of darkness. Her eyes adjusted to the bright light. It didn't take her long to realize she knew exactly where they were.

CHAPTER 63

JACK LEANED WITH HIS BACK AGAINST THE SPLINTERED wooden fence. Bear crouched next to him. The big man had to get lower, being four inches taller. The earwigs they wore remained silent. They waited for Jon to give the go ahead. Jon and Alex were at the front of the house. An argument had ensued over what and how much of a part Alex would take in the raid. No amount of persuading convinced the Prime Minister to back down. He wanted to be there for Jack.

Sasha had arrived at Number 10 moments before they left. They'd convinced her to remain behind. Under normal circumstances, she'd have been an asset to the operation. She still didn't seem right after the blow she took to the head the previous night, though.

"I've got your back."

Jack looked to his left, at Bear, and nodded. "I know, big man. You always have."

"If something happens in there, I want you to know that Mia will always be looked after."

"Same for Mandy. But nothing's gonna happen, Bear. We watch out for each other in there like we always have and we'll get through this just fine."

A break in the clouds sent bright rays of sunshine in their direction. Jack glanced up, over the top of the fence across the alley. Faces pressed against windows, eyes watched them. He gestured for the people in the windows to move away. The last thing they needed was for Kemp and Godfrey to be tipped off by the prying eyes of neighbors.

Jon's voice came through the earwig. "OK, backup teams are in place and we've got four more guys at the entrance. We are good to go. Jack, you and Bear move now. Call out when you're inside and then we'll enter."

"Ten-four, we're moving," Jack said.

He and Bear slipped through the gate after Bear cut the lock. They stayed low and moved quickly toward the house. It would have been better to perform the raid in the dark, but that was a luxury they couldn't afford. Not with so much at stake.

They hit the back door hard and went in yelling. Jack clicked his mic on for a moment. It was enough notice for Jon and Alex to enter.

The rear entrance led into an area between the kitchen and an empty room. A man took a seat at an old table against the wall. The guy looked up, shocked, unmoving for a moment. Then the man rose, kicked the table away. The table flipped forward. The radio that had been perched on it crashed to the floor and broke into a hundred parts. The man reached for the pistol at his side.

Jack recognized the man. He couldn't forget that face. It was the guy in the warehouse who'd killed Thornton and his partner. The man was unmistakably Owen.

Jack aimed, but not fast enough. Owen had outdrawn him. He grimaced, but didn't flinch. He had to get a shot off. Before he could, Bear pulled his trigger, hit the guy dead center. Owen stumbled backward, crashed into the door at the far end of the kitchen. He slid to the floor, leaving a red trail in his wake.

Bear walked up to the guy, nudged him with the tip of his boot. Owen didn't move. That didn't stop Bear from firing one more shot into the guy's head.

At the same time Jack and Bear had encountered Owen, Jon and Alex and their team had raced upstairs. Their footsteps shook the ceiling. Bits of plaster fell and collided with the floor, sending up plumes of white powder.

Jon was the first one down. "It's empty."

"Are we sure they were here?" Bear said.

Jon nodded. "Two beds, unmade, one more than the other. Couple spots of blood on the floor, on the sheets. Pretty fresh. I'd say under an hour."

"The girls were moved," Jack said. He pointed at the dead man in the kitchen. "Owen was waiting for Godfrey to return or to be given his next location."

"Maybe," Jon said. "Maybe Owen was hiding out here. In light of everything that happened, he had to be scared. Who would look for him here?" Jon tipped over the bulk of the shattered radio. "That's a police scanner. Maybe they figured someone would show up here. That could explain why Owen waited around."

"Perhaps," Jack said. "How long do you think he and Godfrey were working together?"

Jon shrugged. "No idea how it even happened. Owen's a career criminal. Was one of Thornton Walloway's top guys. Worked his way up over the past five years or so. As you said, he popped Walloway, so he must have had something going with Naseer for a while now. Maybe Sasha or Mason can shed some light on that. I'd imagine that'd be how he and Godfrey hooked up."

Jack walked into the empty room, crouched and studied the footprints on the floor. "Tiny feet. Mia was in here."

No one said anything.

"So what then? You think maybe they're acting alone?"

Jon shrugged, offered no reply.

"What does this have to do with me and my daughter? What do they want with me?"

"I don't know, Jack," Jon said. "Wish I did."

"You men, out," Alex said to the group of agents that hovered near the front door.

The agents cleared the room, leaving Jack, Bear, Jon and Alex alone with Owen's corpse. Jack's phone rang. He pulled it out, looked at the display.

"It's Dottie," he said.

"Put her on speaker," Alex said. "She might have heard something."

“Hello, Jack.” Dottie’s voice sounded different than normal. Deeper, unemotional, no inflection.

“Have you heard anything, Dottie?”

“About?”

“The girls.”

A pause stretched for several seconds. “I know where they are, Jack.”

“Where?”

“Mia’s right here with me. She’s safe, for now. That will all depend on you, shortly.”

“Dottie, you’re making no sense. You found her? They released her?”

“Not exactly, Jack. I have her.”

Jack said nothing. The reality of the situation had begun to settle in. All heads leaned forward. All stares were on him. The men waited, mouths open, for her next words.

“Are you with Alex?” Dottie said.

Jack looked at the Prime Minister, who nodded.

“Yeah, he’s with me.”

“Who else?”

“No one. The rest are attending to the dead body.”

“Who’s dead?”

“Owen.”

“Oh well, just a cog in the machine.” She paused to clear her throat. “Now Jack, I want you to say hello to your precious little daughter.” Her voice faded. “Mia, say hello to Jack. He’s your dad after all.”

Mia into the phone. “Jack, I’m scared. Please help me. Get me out of here. Aunt Dottie’s gone…” The little girl’s voice trailed off.

“That’s enough of that, dear,” Dottie said.

“What have you done?” Jack said.

Dottie took a deep breath, exhaled into her phone’s speaker. It sounded like a gust of wind through a leafy tree.

“What do you want?” Jack said.

“Oh, it’s pretty simple, Jack. I want you to kill the Prime Minister.”

Jack fought for a response. Couldn’t find one. Jon reached for his gun, pulled it from its holster, aimed it in Jack’s direction. The guy looked confused, scared. Alex took a step toward Jon, reached over and pushed Jon's arm down.

Not yet, Alex mouthed.

"Jack?" Dottie said. "I haven't heard a gunshot yet. Perhaps I haven't made myself clear."

Mia's screams burst through the speaker. "Don't shoot me."

Alex took off his jacket, dropped it to the floor. He unbuttoned his shirt and slid it off his right shoulder.

Jack hit the mute button on the phone. "What do you think you're doing?"

"Shoot me, Jack."

"Have you lost your mind?" Jon said.

"Do it," Alex said. "In the shoulder. I've got a plan, but we don't have time to discuss it. You've got to do this now. Then I want you to start firing afterward, Jon. Into the ceiling, not at Jack."

"Do I have your attention!" Dottie yelled.

Jack unmuted the phone. "You're a sick woman."

"And you're about to become a dead man. You and the Prime Minister." She laughed. "That is, unless you want young Mia to suffer a painful death."

Mia's cries slipped through the speaker.

"I've got people all over this city," Dottie said. "Don't even try to fake this. Your Mia will pay with her precious young life."

Jack looked at Jon, then Alex. Both men nodded. Jon took a step back. Alex took a step to the side.

"Go to hell, Dottie."

Jack raised his Beretta, aimed at Alex's shoulder and pulled the trigger.

Alex's screams blended with the ringing in Jack's ears. Men burst into the house through the front door. Jon and Alex held out their hands to stop the men from doing anything. Then Jon shot four times into the ceiling. Chunks of plaster crashed to the floor. Alex's blood mixed with some of the white residue.

Dottie laughed. "Yes, Jack, yes. Enjoy your trip to hell."

"I'll be waiting there for you." Jack cut the phone off.

Bear had lunged in front of Jack, placing himself in front of men with itchy trigger fingers.

"Phone's off," Jack said.

Jon said, "Stand down. This was planned."

Alex wriggled in pain along the floor.

"Are you OK?" Jon asked.

"No," Alex said. "I've been bloody shot."

"We need an ambulance here now," Jon said.

"And the news," Jack said.

"What?"

"She said she had people everywhere, watching. Well, what better way to tell her this went down than to show me being escorted out by the cops, and Alex with a bunch of damn tubes sticking out of his body while he's covered with a blood soaked sheet."

"That's a damn good idea," Alex said through his clenched teeth.

Bear knelt next to Alex. He steadied the Prime Minister and applied pressure to the wound. "Take it easy."

"Have you ever had a GSW to the shoulder?" Alex said.

Bear pulled his shirt collar to the side and showed off an impressive scar. "As a matter of fact, yes I have. And Jack was there for that one, too."

"I must be bad luck," Jack said.

Bear and Jon laughed. He felt the Prime Minister would have, had he not been the recipient of the bullet.

A couple minutes later strobing lights bounced off the walls.

"Ambulance is out front," Jon said. "And it looks like the news isn't that far behind. There's a helicopter incoming."

The medics entered the house. Already serious, their expressions changed to panic when they saw who their patient was. Jon did his best to ease them.

"It's not a fatal wound. But I need you to make it look that way."

"What?" a medic said.

"Tape everything you can to his face, chest, wherever. Douse the sheets with his blood. This needs to look bad."

The woman, her nameplate said Nikki, went to work without questioning him further.

The agents in the room escorted Jack outside. The helicopter hovered overhead. News vans lurched to a stop in front of the house. Cameras were pointed in his direction.

"Jesus, that's the Prime Minister," someone shouted. "He's been shot."

The media bought it. Now they had to hope that Dottie would too.

CHAPTER 64

"LOOKY THERE," RANDY SAID. "AIN'T THAT YOUR BOYFRIEND?"

Clarissa shifted her gaze from the dirt and grime covered window and the distorted view of the street to the television. The image on the screen showed Jack being led from a house that looked as worn down as the one they occupied. A banner scrolled along the bottom of the screen. It said, *Prime Minister Shot*.

Could Jack have done that?

"This makes no sense." Sinclair rose and pulled his phone from his pocket. He left the room.

"Always knew Noble was a piece of dog doo," Randy said from his seat beside her.

Clarissa glanced over her shoulder and waited for Sinclair to step outside. Randy leaned forward, closer to the TV, as if he was inspecting the Prime Minister's injuries himself. She brought both of her hands up and lunged forward. Her arms wrapped around the side of his head. Her fingernails met in the middle of his face. She raked her hands in an outward motion, across his eyes and cheeks and ears.

Randy threw himself forward, onto his knees and into the wall. He pulled up on the TV cart. The television toppled over, barely missing his head and coming down on his shoulder.

Clarissa kicked him in the kidney, followed it up with an elbow to the back of his neck. He fell against the wall, turned. Blood from his eyebrows and forehead cascaded down his cheeks in thin crimson lines. He wiped his face with the back of his left sleeve. In his right hand, he held a pistol. Clarissa drove her foot into his stomach. He bowed forward. She grabbed the back of his head, struck him three times in the face with her knee. She let go and watched him fall to the floor, unconscious. His gun fell beside him. She scooped it up and moved toward the front door.

Sinclair stepped inside, his phone in one hand, pistol in the other. Both were down by his waist. The phone pointed toward the floor. The pistol toward her.

"What are you doing, Clarissa?" he said.

She took a step back, nodded toward Randy.

"What did he do to you?" Sinclair said.

"Nothing," she said. "Preemptive strike."

"What do you plan to do now?"

"Help Jack."

"I can't let you do that."

"Why not?"

"I can't tell you."

She noticed that he cast a quick glance over her shoulder. A third man entered the room. She had not been aware of the guy. Clarissa moved too late. Thick arms wrapped around her, met in the middle, interlocked hands pressed into her chest. She kicked and thrashed to the side, threw a reverse head butt that missed. Each movement resulted in the grip around her growing tighter.

Randy pushed himself up off the floor and charged. "I'm gonna kill you."

"Enough, Randy," Sinclair said. "You more than likely deserved what she did to you."

Randy stopped five feet away from her. He looked like a deranged bull, bloodied and battered and ready to tear off the matador's head.

"Go get my bag," Sinclair said.

Randy walked up to Clarissa, spit at her feet, then continued past.

"Don't dare do that again," Sinclair said. He turned his attention back to Clarissa. "Just relax, child. You need to calm down."

She choked back her tears. “I need to help Jack.”

“The best thing you can do is stay out of his way.”

“I have something that can help him.”

“Nothing can help him now, I’m afraid.”

Clarissa didn’t believe that. She couldn’t believe that.

Randy entered the room and handed Sinclair his bag. The same worn bag he’d carried when she first met him over six months ago. Clarissa wondered how the guy had managed to get it through customs. She realized he hadn’t had to deal with customs. Not the way they traveled. He could have left from Langley and landed on base in England. They all had luggage with false bottoms and hidden compartments. Even if they were stopped, no one would ever find what they had.

“Don’t,” she pleaded.

“It’s for your own good,” he said.

“Please, Sinclair,” she said. “Just let me go.”

Sinclair approached her. He adjusted the needle in his hand.

Tears streamed down her cheeks. Rage more than anything else. Through blurred vision, she watched as drip after drip of the evil liquid fell from the tip of the long needle. Sinclair reached out, grabbed her jaw, plunged the needle into her neck.

Clarissa whipped her head side to side the moment he let go. She kicked, thrashed, and screamed. She thought she did, at least.

The room shrunk, dimmed, hazed over.

Slowly, quietly, calmly, she fell asleep.

CHAPTER 65

From the back of the car, Dottie watched the images of the agents escorting Jack out of the house. The gurney carrying Alex toward the ambulance followed. The bloodstained sheets, tubes in his mouth and into his lungs, and the speed at which they traveled told her that Jack had done as she requested. Not perfectly, but good enough. The problem was that Jack had always been better than good enough. At the same time, good enough meant that she could find someone to finish the job. They didn't have to be as good as Jack Noble.

Only good enough.

"You think he can do this?" she said to Godfrey.

"Yes, ma'am," Godfrey said.

The guy with the red beard turned in the seat. "Ma'am, I'm more than capable of—"

"Shut up," she said. "I wasn't talking to you. I was talking to Godfrey."

The relationship was an old one. Twenty years ago, when Dottie was rising in the ranks, Godfrey had just come on board. They'd worked together, remained close. He'd done everything she'd asked up to this point. She knew he'd do one last task for her. And if he failed, it wouldn't matter. There was no way they'd be able to locate her after today.

But she couldn't risk his life yet, and that's why they brought this man along to take care of the prime minister.

She had hoped to be able to make the final call to Jack after they'd left England. Perhaps from the stern of the boat as it coasted through the Celtic Sea. But when she realized Jack and Alex had located the house where Mia and Hannah were being kept, she had to act quickly.

"Where are you taking us?" Hannah said.

Dottie looked back at the young woman, smiled. "Someplace safe, dear."

And she meant it. She'd keep Hannah safe as long as the woman did what she was told, when she was told. She had no reason to harm her. She also had no reason to keep her around for much longer. The moment she stepped out of line, that would be it.

Hannah comforted Mia. That had been the worst part for Dottie. She hated to threaten her great-niece's life. But bargaining chips were called so for a reason. When it came down to it, Dottie's life was most important. If people she cared about had to fall along the way, so be it.

The car came to a stop. Godfrey opened his door and stepped out. He met the other man at the front of the car and shook his hand.

"Good luck," Dottie muttered.

Godfrey reentered the car, put it into gear and pulled away from the curb, leaving the man behind.

"What's he going to do?" Hannah said.

Dottie didn't respond.

Betrayed didn't begin to describe the way Hannah felt. Dottie had been like a grandmother to her. Kind and warm, Dottie had invited the young woman into her home and made her a part of the family. The past two years would have never led Hannah to believe that the woman could be so cold and cruel. Dottie had threatened to kill Mia. When Hannah spoke up, Dottie slapped her across the face. Three times. With a book.

Now, it hurt when she opened her mouth and when she turned her head.

Mia leaned into her. The child's fingers intermingled with hers and squeezed tightly. Poor thing, she thought. To have to suffer through this ordeal. Hannah held out hope that Dottie would drop them off on a corner. She wanted to plead for that very thing, but feared retribution.

She turned her head and watched the buildings pass. They drove west, away from the city. She had no idea where they were going. Dottie hadn't mentioned it to the man who had gotten out a few minutes prior, or to the guy driving. She suspected that was because the guy who left them was not going to rejoin the group. What did he plan to do? Could anything be worse than forcing Jack to shoot the Prime Minister?

Her eyes began to water. She choked back a sob and waited as long as she could before sniffling. Dottie turned her head, looked Hannah up and down, then shifted her gaze forward. The same images replayed on the small screen in front of the woman. Jack being led from the house, the Prime Minister being taken out of the house on a gurney, and the ambulance heading toward a hospital.

That's why the man had gotten out. She saw that now. As best as Hannah could remember, there was a hospital located two blocks from that corner.

The tears fell across her cheeks. A man was about to die. Not just any man, either. The Prime Minister. She had advanced knowledge of it, and there was nothing she could do about it.

Please God, she thought. *Wake me from this nightmare.*

CHAPTER 66

THE AGENTS TOOK JACK UNDERGROUND. THERE HE SWITCHED cars and reunited with Jon and Bear and Sasha. There was no holding her back now. They headed toward the hospital.

"Any reports?" Jack said.

"He's doing fine," Jon said. "You're a good shot."

"I don't see how they're ever going to let me back in this country after shooting the Prime Minister."

Jon nodded. "Yeah, I wouldn't count on it."

Sasha leaned over and in front of Bear, who inconveniently sat in the middle between her and Jack. "At least he has the power to pardon you. You might make it out all right after all."

The driver flipped on the sirens and the strobe lights and the thick London traffic split in two. Occasionally the driver had to weave to the left or the right, even slammed on the brakes twice. Other than that, they raced down the streets. He estimated they were doing over sixty in spots where cars normally crawled along like turtles.

Twenty minutes later they entered the hospital parking lot. The front entrance was jam-packed with news trucks that had their booms and antennas extended into the sky. Reporters and cameramen hovered outside the front door. Police created a barricade. A disaster, really. Those who needed help from the hospital would have trouble on this day.

So the driver continued around to the side where four police officers waited for them. One came up to the passenger side of the SUV, the side that faced the hospital. He opened the front and rear doors. The man extended his hand for Sasha. She angled her body to avoid him.

The cop stepped back when Bear stuck his leg out.

"What, no hand for me?"

The cop looked unsure of what to do next. Bear's laughter sent him back toward the unassuming hospital door propped open an inch.

"Follow me," the cop said as he stepped inside. He led them through empty passages. The guy's partner picked up the rear.

Jack figured the halls were empty on purpose. He'd inconvenienced not only the sick who needed the hospital today, but also the staff. Nothing new, in a way. He'd become used to being a nuisance.

They reached a hallway where four agents Jack recognized from Number 10 stood. This had to be where Alex was being kept.

"Right in there," the guard said, his finger extended.

Jon entered the room first, then Sasha. When Jack entered, Alex greeted him with a nod and slight smile.

"How's it feel?" Jack said.

"Pretty bad," Alex said. "But, they've numbed it up and given me some pain killers. Nothing too strong, though, so don't ask for any. This isn't over." Alex paused and waited until everyone smiled or laughed at his joke. "Fortunately, I'm left handed, so my shot won't be affected."

"You're not involved in this anymore," Jon said.

"Like hell I'm not."

"Alex, listen to him," Sasha said.

"I want to face her and ask her why. Why did she want to kill me? Why did she threaten this man's child in an effort to have me dead? Surely there had to be better ways than this."

No one said anything.

"What's the plan now?" Jack said.

"We've got bait in another hall," Jon said.

"Meaning?"

"A man, brain dead after an accident. He's bloated and unrecognizable and on life support. He's got hair like Alex's though, so—"

"He's being passed off as the Prime Minister, near death," Jack said.

Jon nodded. "We figure she'll send someone to take care of him."

"Who's watching?" Bear said.

"Plenty of people," Sasha said. "A whole damn team is set up near the room."

"We should get Alex out of here then," Jack said.

"No," Alex said. "Not yet. I want to question whoever is sent."

"Those pain killers are going to your head," Jon said.

Alex smiled. Upon further inspection, Jack would agree with Jon's statement.

"Surely Dottie would expect that you'd be heavily guarded," Jack said.

"I think she's lost it, Jack," Jon said. "She's acting completely irrational. How did she plan to ever get away with this? It's impossible."

Jack wondered if she did plan to get away with it. Any of it. The whole thing, he realized, had been a setup, right from the very beginning. She hadn't brought him here to kill Thornton. She already had that planned. She brought him here so he could die. Why?

"Unless she has a plant," Jack said.

They all turned toward the door at the sound of echoing gun fire. The radios lit up with calls of *shots fired*. Three men rushed into the room. Could any of them be trusted? Jack didn't think so and apparently Jon didn't either.

"Everyone out," Jon said. He drew his gun and stood in front of Alex. His own men were a risk at this point.

The men backed up, guns aimed at the floor. They stared at Jack and Bear.

"Not them," Jon said. "You three, out. Now."

The men cast confused glances toward the Prime Minister as they left the room. It went against everything they had been trained to do, leaving him alone during a time of crisis. A time when the man's life was on the line. He'd survived one attack today. How many more would there be?

Jon pulled out his phone and began placing calls. He reached a man named Wells, put him on speaker phone.

"What do you have down there, Wells?" Jon said.

"We don't know who it is, sir. Big guy, red beard. He bypassed the initial security and made it into the room."

The sound of five people drawing their breath in filled the room.

"How did that happen?" Jon said. "The one person we were sure wouldn't show up did, and we missed it?"

"We're trying to figure that out, sir."

Jack noticed that Jon's face had turned bright red. The veins on his neck stood out. They pulsed so quickly that Jack figured the guy's heart was pumping over one-hundred beats a minute.

"Don't worry about that now," Jon said. "What happened?"

"I heard the machinery power down, looked in, saw him in there. He held a pillow to the guy's head. We took him out right there."

"Christ. Is he dead?"

"Yes, sir."

Jon looked up. "Dammit, we needed him."

"Sorry, sir."

"It's all right, Wells. You did what you had to do." Jon hung up and looked at Alex. "Satisfied?"

"What if there's more?"

"All the more reason to get you the hell out of here, Alex."

This time, Alex did not protest.

"I need to check on Erin before we leave," Jack said.

"Already did," Jon said. "She was taken away earlier."

"She was cleared to leave already?"

Jon shook his head. "Didn't say that."

Jack ran a hand through his hair, grabbed the back of his head. "I don't believe this. This whole time, they were both right there, right under my nose."

No one said anything for a moment. Jack felt the weight of their stares upon him. He turned in a half-circle, made eye contact with each. He stopped when he reached Bear.

"Who?" Bear said.

"Dottie and Leon. They were in this together."

"You sure about that?" Bear said.

"Yes... No. I need to see Leon."

"We'll find them," Jon said.

"How?" Jack said.

"We've got all the man power and brain power in Great Britain available to us. There's no way they can get away."

"I managed to get in," Jack said.

"Not without us knowing," Jon said.

Bear's phone rang. He answered, then said, "Hold on." Then he looked at Jack and said, "It's for you."

Jack took the phone. "Yeah?"

"It's Clarissa," she said.

He said nothing.

"I know it's not a good time, but, I think I can help you."

"How so?"

"Jesus, I don't have long, Jack. Look, I had the girls with me when they were taken. Leon gave me a piece of paper. He said directions to where he wanted me to take Mia and Hannah were written on that paper."

"Where?"

She read off the information on the page. Jack repeated the address.

"That's an hour away, at most," Jon said.

"Dottie's probably almost there," Jack said.

"If she's going there," Sasha said.

"She is," Jack said.

"We need to get going," Jon said.

"Clarissa, where are you?"

"I can't say, Jack."

"Why not?"

The line went dead.

"Clarissa?" He waited a moment, then handed the phone to Bear. "Can we trace that call?"

"No number," Bear said.

"We'll help you find her when this is over," Jon said.

"OK. Let's go put an end to this."

CHAPTER 67

THE FIVE OF THEM WALKED DOWN A FLIGHT OF STAIRS, through a hall, then down two more flights of stairs. One level below the ground floor of Number 10, they entered the network of tunnels. Two more agents met them there. Jon refused to allow Alex to travel without them there to protect him. They walked as a group, then split up after fifty yards or so.

Jon, Alex and two agents took the east fork. Jack, Sasha and Bear went west.

Sasha led the way. She knew the codes. She had the keys. Jack and Bear followed close behind. They entered the same garage he had parked the Audi in earlier. It was the only vehicle in the room.

"Get in, guys," she said.

Bear took the back seat. An odd choice, given his size. But he liked to kick one leg up when he had a rear seat available to himself. Jack headed around the trunk to the passenger side. He opened the door, but did not get in. Sasha unlocked and opened a locker. He watched on as she removed several weapons.

"Want help?" he said.

"No," she said. "Get in."

He continued to watch her load three M4s, three MP7s, and six pistols into the trunk. She made one last trip for extra magazines for the MP7s.

"Expecting to face an army?" Jack said.

"I thought I said get in," she said.

Jack raised his hands in surrender, then lowered himself into the passenger seat. The car had a citric smell that he hadn't noticed earlier.

"You smell that, Bear?"

Bear lowered his chin to his chest and his nose to his armpit. "It's not me."

This elicited a chuckle and head shake from Jack. "Never mind."

Sasha pulled the driver's door open and stuck her head in. "Just one more thing."

Jack watched her walk back to the locker, close it, then open another. He couldn't see what she pulled from it, or put in it.

She came back to the car and said, "Either of you unarmed?"

Neither Jack nor Bear spoke up.

"OK, good." She slipped behind the wheel and fired up the V-8 engine. A button press, then the wall lifted and she pulled through into the empty level of the parking garage. Jack wondered what they did when the garage was full. Perhaps they had a system to prevent that from happening. Maybe someone went up there and put up a sign to barricade the bottom level.

A few minutes later they were on the city streets of London, a good half-mile from Number 10. They used the siren and the strobes to get them through the city and to the M25. The motorway was only half-congested. In most cities, that meant bumper to bumper, but in London there was plenty of room in between cars if you had a motorbike. Also, the shoulder made a great way to do eighty when everyone else alternated from brake, gas, brake. From the M25, they exited and merged onto the M3, which took them west and away from the city.

Sasha cut the siren and switched on the radio. It had been previously tuned to a Jazz station.

"This OK?" she asked.

Bear shrugged. "I can live with it."

Jack nodded. "I love it."

"Really? That surprises me."

Jack shrugged, turned toward his window, then back at her. He opened his mouth to give her a hard time.

She glanced over and offered him a half-smile. "Me, too."

"I didn't always," Jack said. "My dad forced us to listen to it when I was a kid."

"Us?"

"My brother and I."

"What's his name?"

"My dad?"

"Your brother."

"Sean."

"And I bet your dad's name was John, wasn't it? And you were named after him, so that's why they called you Jack. But, John and Sean? Sean's the Irish form of John. Did your parents want you two to have the same name?"

"Cute, isn't it?" Bear said.

Jack glanced over his shoulder and shook his head at Bear. Then he switched his gaze to Sasha and said, "My dad's not John and neither am I. Jack isn't a nickname for anything. It's just my name. Always been that way. Says so on my birth certificate."

"Who's older?"

"Him."

"By how much?"

"Two and some change."

"Years?"

"Would've been a medical marvel if otherwise."

She rolled her eyes. "Do you get along?"

"We did."

"Now?"

"We talk."

"How often?"

"Occasionally."

"Do the conversations go like this?"

"More or less."

"So, back to jazz." She turned the volume up a notch.

"Grew up on it. Miles Davis, Stan Kenton, Ralph Sutton, Tristano, Stan Getz."

"All the big names of the fifties and sixties then."

Jack nodded.

"Do you listen to anything new?"

He shrugged. "Whatever's on or whoever's on stage."

"Always better live," she said.

"Yes, it is," Bear said.

"Goddamn right," Jack said.

He eased back and listened to the angst ridden tones of Miles Davis and his trumpet. Coltrane complimented with his tenor sax. Smoother than butter. Finer than silk. Jack wished he could fast forward to midnight right about now. The music, created during a time of unrest and filled with an undying passion, still evoked long buried feelings and memories within Jack. Fortunately, he'd become more than capable of brushing them aside when necessary. And most times, it was necessary.

They exited onto the M27 in Eastleigh. A few miles later the motorway ended and they drove along a dual carriage way that Jack didn't bother to get the number of. There was no point. He wouldn't have to navigate back unless something bad happened. And if something bad did happen, he knew it would involve him anyway.

A jazz-filled half hour passed. Traffic continued to thin until they were basically alone on the road. They reached their turn, made a left onto a narrow one lane that could accommodate two cars traveling in the opposite direction so long as one pulled into the grass to let the other pass. Jack looked back and saw that Jon and Alex were close behind.

And the two agents.

Seven people, which Jack figured was about four too many.

Up ahead, warning lights blinked at a railroad crossing. They had a full view of the oncoming train. Probably three hundred cars long and moving slow, like a caterpillar stuffed fat and ready to hibernate.

"Speed up," Jack said.

"What?" Sasha said.

"You heard me."

She glanced over at him. Had both hands on the wheel. Her knuckles were white. "Why?"

"We need to get a few minutes ahead."

"Have you gone mad?"

"Do it, Sasha."

She shook her head, pressed the accelerator. The car picked up speed, but due to the curve in the road and the curve in the track, he couldn't work out the angles in his head. Would they beat the train? If the train reached first, they might have been traveling too fast to stop in time.

"I don't like this, Jack," she said.

He studied the distance again. The train had the edge. "Faster, Sasha."

Her foot went down, the car went faster. Jack felt his seat inch back, looked over his shoulder, saw Bear's large hand next to his head. The big man leaned forward in between Jack and Sasha. If adrenaline had a defined look, it was the one plastered on Bear's face.

"You might want to strap in," Jack said as he lifted his seat belt around his abdomen to show it off to Bear.

"It ain't gonna make a difference if we hit that train," Bear said.

"Point taken." Jack reached for his seatbelt release.

"Don't you dare," Sasha said. She'd also had the foresight to buckle her seatbelt.

The car went faster.

The train plowed forward.

The tracks approached.

The road straightened.

It would be close.

Too close?

Jack wasn't sure.

He looked to his left. In the side mirror he saw that Jon and Alex had fallen far behind. Headlights flashed, then remained on. High beams followed. Sasha's phone began to ring. Had to be them.

"Don't answer," Jack said.

"Like I'm taking my flipping hands off the flipping wheel."

Jack grinned. If ever there was a time to curse, that would have been it. He didn't figure her to be so proper. He glanced at her. A sheet of sweat covered her forehead. Her eyes were narrow and focused. Jaws locked, small muscles rippled. Her hands were wrapped around the wheel, knuckles white.

Gun to his head, he'd admit she looked attractive.

The car went faster.

The train plowed forward.

The tracks were a hundred feet or so ahead.

Who would get there first?

CHAPTER 68

THE TRAIN'S CONDUCTOR STOOD WIDE-EYED. HIS MOUTH HUNG open like he he'd become locked in a perpetual scream. Of course, nothing could be heard over the roar of the train, not even the warning bells anymore. It sounded like an F5, as best Jack could guess. He'd only ever encountered an F3.

The Audi crashed through the thin guard rail painted red and white. They hit the asphalt hump that housed the tracks doing over one hundred miles per hour. He could no longer see the conductor. Probably better that way. The guy might be having a heart attack, and the last thing Jack needed today was added guilt.

He looked to his left as the car launched a foot or so off the ground. He'd passed the train, but Bear and the rest of the Audi hadn't yet. Death would still be the result as the impact would spin the vehicle around sending him and Sasha face first into the solid steel engine. And if that didn't kill them, surely the force of Bear crashing into them would.

Sasha screamed. So did Bear. Jack clenched his jaw for a tense few seconds. Then he yelled. The sound inside the car matched that of the first couple of seconds after the lead car on a roller coaster crept over the edge of the first big drop. The feeling, not so much.

The Audi hit the ground, dipped and bounced and grated and skid. Sasha powered on the brakes. They slipped and spun and screeched along the road, through the grass, coming to a stop facing the opposite direction, looking right at the train.

The glove box in front of Jack opened when they hit the ground. An air freshener landed in his lap. It had a picture of two oranges on the front. That explained the smell in the car. Must have been faint enough that only he had smelled it.

The train lumbered on, three hundred cars or so to go. It'd take at least fifteen minutes, maybe more. That, Jack figured, was all they needed.

"OK, want to tell me what all that was about?" Sasha said.

"First turn the car around and get moving."

She threw it into reverse, plowed backward, not seeming to care that the car went off road. Not like it would do any more damage than jumping the tracks had done.

"I still don't trust Jon," Jack said.

"Jon? He's clean. You can trust me on that."

"I trust you. I don't trust him. And I don't want us to be in a situation where we have Leon and Dottie in custody, and then have Jon turn on us. I don't think a single one of us wants to be responsible for Alex being murdered."

"Sure about that?" Bear said. "You shot him once already."

"And if it means saving my daughter's life, I'd do it again. So how about we not let it come down to that? We've got the drop on Leon and Dottie. Let's keep it that way."

"What if Jon called ahead?" Bear said.

"He hasn't," Sasha said.

"How do you know?" Bear said.

Sasha shook her head, said nothing.

"What?" Jack said.

She still said nothing.

"Tell us."

"You're not that far off, Jack."

"Say what?"

"We've been watching him for some time. The suspicion is there."

"And you just gave me crap over implicating him in this."

She glanced at him, then back at the road.

Silence resumed for the next twenty minutes. Jack figured by this point Jon and Alex were moving again. Either the train had passed, or they'd backtracked and found another route. If his hunch had been wrong, and he hoped it had, they'd just have to deal with being ditched.

The surrounding area started to show signs of life. Generously spaced cottages lined the road. Views of the coast on the south side filled in the gaps between homes.

"How much further?" Bear said.

Jack glanced at the GPS. "We're close. Sasha, I want you to get us a street inland. We can approach the house on foot."

"Should we pass by first?"

"I wouldn't chance it."

So Sasha turned at the next street and ignored the GPS as it pestered her to turn left. When they were even with the location, she stopped the car. All three got out. The trunk popped open. Jack grabbed a spare Sig P226 and strapped an HK MP7 across his chest. The M4 would be a bit much, so he left it in the trunk and encouraged Bear to do the same. He hoped the area was as deserted as it looked. Even if someone phoned the police, it'd take at least ten minutes for a car to arrive. The ordeal should be finished by then.

They passed through someone's yard and stepped into a narrow wooded area. Dead leaves crunched under their feet as they moved closer to the house. Two playful squirrels scurried up a tree. As they neared the last row of trees, the house came into full view.

A car Jack didn't recognize sat in the driveway with its trunk and rear doors open. No signs of life were present otherwise.

"Think that's it?" Bear said.

"That's the address she gave us," Sasha said.

A car passed by. A child in the backseat made brief eye contact with Jack. He watched the car as it raced down the street. The brake lights he anticipated never flashed.

The front door of the house across the street opened. A screen door squeaked on rusted hinges. An older woman stepped into view.

"Dottie," Jack said.

"Really?" Bear said.

"That's her."

"She got old."

Jack said nothing. He watched not only the woman as she approached the car, but the house behind her. No one else emerged. No faces concealed themselves behind darkened windows. That he could see, at least.

Dottie's hands were empty. She leaned into the backseat, pulled out a bag and tossed it to the ground. Then she walked to the rear of the car, turned her back to them and leaned into the trunk. She pulled out another bag, tossed it next to the other one. She was unloading the car. Either they were going to wait it out at the house, or they had other plans made for their escape.

"Let's go," Sasha said.

Before Jack could tell her to wait, the woman took off running.

"Wait," Bear said.

"Come on," Jack said.

They crossed the street after Sasha. Jack prepared himself to take a bullet. They were sitting ducks. This was not the approach he had anticipated.

Dottie rose up, looked over her shoulder. She leaned back in the trunk and emerged again, this time with a rifle. She fired blind. The recoil nearly knocked her into the trunk. The shot echoed in the woods behind them. The bullet had hit none of them.

Jack drew his pistol to fire, but Sasha already had. Dottie jerked back to the left, then fell forward to her knees. She then eased over and rested against the car's rear bumper.

Jack had a dozen things he wanted to say to the woman. Questions he had to ask. But he didn't. He kept going right past her and said, "Keep an eye on her."

CHAPTER 69

"WHERE THE HELL ARE YOU GOING?" BEAR SAID.

Jack didn't answer him.

"What's he doing?"

"I don't know," Sasha said.

Bear glanced around at the neighboring houses. No doors had opened. Nobody hung out on their front porch watching what happened. There were no sirens approaching. The place must've been abandoned. A neighborhood full of summer vacation houses, he figured. Maybe during the off season it was the type of neighborhood that was busy on the weekends, deserted during the week. Didn't matter. He wasn't going to complain about the lack of attention.

Sasha bounced from one foot to the other. She, too, scanned the area. Although her focus seemed to be centered more on the house in front of them than those that surrounded them.

"Help me move her," Bear said.

Dottie remained barely conscious. Blood flowed from her wound and stained her clothes crimson. Bear doubted she would last long enough for an ambulance to arrive.

Sasha positioned herself near the woman's feet. She refused to holster her weapon. Instead, she threaded her left arm around Dottie's ankles and hoisted the woman's legs into the air. Together, she and Bear moved

Dottie from behind the vehicle to the side of the house. A couple tall hedges blocked them from the street.

Bear set her on the ground and assessed her condition. He confirmed what he thought earlier. Dottie had little time left. Pulse weak and thready. Respirations short, labored and infrequent. Her eyes focused beyond anything that existed. She was slipping into that uncertainty that is death.

"She doesn't have much longer," Bear said. "Go find Jack and make sure he's OK."

There was no answer.

"Sasha?" Bear looked over his shoulder, rose, turned, didn't see her.

The wind came in off the coast and rattled the leaves of the hedges.

"Sasha?" he repeated.

Again, no answer.

"Dammit." He looked down at Dottie. He'd spent time around the woman in the past. Not as much as Jack, so the bond wasn't as strong. To him, she was a woman dying. Nothing more, nothing less. He wrestled with what to do next. Despite what she'd done, did she deserve to die alone?

It didn't matter. She had to. He had others to attend to.

Bear eased around the hedges and scanned the area in front of the house. Deserted. He hunched over, a move that did little to conceal him, and ran to the front door. There, he stopped, pressed against the wall, closed his eyes and listened. The wind whipped around the house, coating him with fresh salt air. The sweat on his forehead cooled. His lips dried. He licked them, tasted the salt. He heard a soft cry from beyond the front door. Mia? Had to be.

He reached over with his left hand, found the door handle. It turned without resistance. With a slight motion, he pushed the door open. Then he spun quickly, 9mm leading the way. A quick scan of the room revealed it was empty. Bear eased forward, following the sounds of the little girl crying. The room he stood in opened up to a dining room and kitchen. On the right side, in the middle, loomed a dark hallway. From the hall was where the crying originated.

Bear holstered the pistol and took hold of the MP7 on his chest. He switched the safety off, adjusted from single shot to three-round bursts. No need to be deadly accurate. Just had to hit it somewhere in the ballpark.

He angled toward the wall, pressed back against it, stopped right before the hallway opening. From there, he had a view of the entire kitchen. Aside from the closed pantry, he verified the room was as empty as the first one.

Another cry floated by.

He took a deep breath and spun around, leading with the sub-machine gun. The empty hall beckoned him to proceed forward. And he did. Bear pressed his left shoulder against the wall and walked toward the end of the hall, toe to heel. He kept his eyes focused ahead, where there were two doors, one on either side. At any moment he expected one of them to open up.

The sound of Mia's cries grew louder. Indecipherable whispering followed. He stopped, hunched over, narrowed his eyes. He took a step. A floorboard popped. The crying stopped. So did the whispering. He heard footsteps move toward the door softly and slowly.

His instincts told him to fire. Logic overruled. At the very least, Mia was in that room. Her mother and the other woman might be too. Who else? He had no idea. The only way to find out? Open the door.

And so he did.

The doorknob turned to the right with no resistance. He pushed the door forward, took a step back. The barrel of the MP7 moved with his eyes. Mia and her mother huddled in the far corner of the room. The other woman stood holding a lamp like a baseball bat.

"Who are you?" she said.

"That's Bear, Hannah," Erin said.

"Are you alone in here?" Bear said.

They both nodded. Mia still hadn't looked up at him. She kept her face buried in her mother's chest.

"Who the hell are you?"

The voice didn't come from inside the room.

Bear stepped back and turned and saw a tall blond man at the other end of the hallway. He hurried to wrap his hands around the weapon strapped to his chest.

Apparently, Bear's presence had startled the man at the other end of the hall, too. He had to reach around his back for his pistol. Neither man had the advantage. Three quick bursts erupted from Bear's weapon. The man produced his firearm, which appeared to be an HK45 Tactical pistol, and fired at the same time.

Searing pain spread through Bear's abdomen and around his side and back. It centered on the right side. He didn't look down. Looking down would make it real, and as it was, he felt he could continue moving. He blinked away the flood of tears in his eyes. The other guy's right arm hung at his side, useless, shattered and splintered at the wrist. Bear hadn't hit in the right ballpark it seemed. His shot had traveled into the stands. He fought the pain, aimed again, pulled the trigger. The weapon had jammed.

The guy looked from his hand to Bear. Disbelief spread across the man's face. Bear charged toward him. He didn't want the man coming closer to the room with the women in there. The guy bent over, wrapped his left arm behind his leg, returned upright wielding a knife with a six inch blade.

Bear tried to lift the sub-machine gun and strap over his head. Pain prevented him from doing so. He yanked hard, snapped the strap. With the MP7 is his left hand, he deflected the knife blade. He didn't stop moving forward. The guy swung again, wide and wild. Bear whipped the gun to the left, caught the guy just above his left wrist. The bone snapped. The knife fell to the floor. Bear drove his knee upward. The pain in his side nearly became too much for him to handle. The knee connected with the man's groin. The guy fell forward. Bear grabbed the back of the guy's head, pulled it back. Then Bear drove his head forward and down into the bridge of the man's nose. The skin on the guy's forehead split in two. Bear shoved the guy backward. The man fell to the floor.

Bear moved forward until he stood over the man. He reached behind his back and retrieved the Sig P226. He wished he'd have thought of it a few seconds earlier. He wiped the blood off his hands and gripped the pistol. The pain spread through his hip and up into his chest. He aimed, took a breath.

"No, don't," the girl said from behind.

Bear looked over his shoulder. Mia stood in the hallway, tears streaming down her cheeks.

"Please, don't kill him."

Bear's vision began to darken. He saw Mia, but also Mandy. Both girls standing there, tears in their eyes, begging him to spare the man. He fell to one knee, onto his butt, then to his side. He blinked hard, saw the guy on the floor next to him. The man's head dropped to the side and they stared at each other.

The other woman appeared a moment later. He remembered her name was Hannah. She took the Sig from his hand, stepped back and aimed it at the other guy.

"I'm from West Virginia, creep. One move and I'll make your face look like your right arm."

Bear smiled, then closed his eyes.

CHAPTER 70

JACK STOOD ON THE PACKED SAND CLOSE TO WHERE THE SMALL waves gently lapped onto shore. A dozen yards away Leon stepped out of the small boat he had just run ashore. Leon looked toward Jack and nodded. Both men remained motionless for a few seconds. On the beach, in front of the boat were several bags. Some filled with clothes, Jack presumed. Others, perhaps, with cash. He glanced out, across the sea, and saw the large boat that Leon had been ferrying the items to.

"Where're you headed?"

"Away."

"Why?"

Leon said nothing.

"Must be running from something."

Leon shook his head. "I don't run from anything or anyone. Unlike you."

The shot was not lost on Jack. He ignored it, though. "Why'd you do this?"

"Do what?"

"Get involved with this scheme Dottie was involved in."

Leon took a few steps forward.

Jack aimed his pistol at the man. "That's close enough."

"You screwed her life up, Jack."

"How so?"

"That crap you pulled in Monte Carlo with Thornton."

"He had it coming."

"Not saying I disagree."

"So how did that mess up her life?"

"She didn't run from Thornton because of that, Jack. He kicked her out. It cost him over a million in legal fees and bribes. He blamed it on you, and in turn, her. That house, it's not hers. It's mine. A family home. She didn't have any money to speak of. Her retirement was screwed. See, she thought she had it made with Thornton. Sure, she had to take her lumps now and then, but to Dottie, those lumps came with the territory no matter what she did. How else would she have risen through the intelligence ranks like she did?"

"So this whole thing was a setup then. She didn't bring me here to kill Thornton, did she?"

Leon shook his head.

"Thornton's death was already in the works. She brought me here to kill me."

Leon nodded. "I was supposed to take care of you that first day. You got the drop on me, though. I didn't want to hand you that Browning. If I didn't, you would have killed me. I could see that. I had no choice. Adapt and overcome, right, mate?" He paused, looked toward the house, then back at Jack with a pained expression. "Remember that cook in the restaurant?"

"The red bearded one? The guy we saw on TV who'd been giving us the tough guy look in the kitchen?"

"That's the one, and that was no look, Jack. He's my step-brother. He was going to help me take care of you. I figured you'd be a corpse in the bathroom and he was going to come in after the first shot."

"What about the guy that took me to the warehouse?"

"One of mine."

"Why?"

"We figured that you'd be spotted in there and Naseer would do what Naseer does. Apparently, you're better at hiding than figuring things out."

"Mason?"

Leon shook his head. "He's legit. His partner not so much, though."

"I figured that out."

"Too late, though, right?"

Jack said nothing. Neither did Leon.

"The bombing at the hotel?" Jack said.

"Two purposes, really. To scare you and to eliminate some possible witnesses."

"You two were behind it?"

Leon shrugged.

"What connection did Dottie have with Naseer?" Jack said.

"Coincidental, really."

"Why have me kill the Prime Minister?"

"Two birds, one stone."

"Meaning?"

Leon glanced out toward the sea. He inhaled deeply. He swung his head back around, glanced at the ground, then back up toward Jack. "Get rid of you and him without having to be directly involved."

"She was involved. She was on the phone."

"Prove it." Leon held out his arms.

"I get that she wanted me dead. But why him? What did he do to her?"

"He led the inquisition that got her removed from her position."

Jack searched his memory, but had no recollection of this.

Leon must have noticed the confused expression on Jack's face. "A few years back there had been a cover up of something that happened. Dottie gave an order to do something that shouldn't have been done. Parkin was a fresh face on the political scene at that time, and he had some knowledge of this action. He'd been involved. Me too. He wanted to make a name for himself, so he used his inside knowledge and took her down. She lost her job, her pension and all retirement money. After that she took up with Thornton."

"So she blames him for ruining her life and me for making it even worse."

"Basically."

"Why tell me all this?"

"To clear my conscience and let you know how this happened. She'd changed a lot over the last few years, Jack. She wasn't the same woman you knew."

Jack nodded, said nothing.

"All right, Jack. I'm done playing with you. You've obviously got Dottie, so let me be. I did what I was told. I'm a soldier one hundred percent, through and through. I followed orders." He took a step back. "Let me get on my boat and go. I've shoveled so much garbage in my life, it's time for me to retire."

"You and me both."

Leon turned around and stepped into the boat.

"I can't let you leave," Jack said as he extended his arm and aimed at Leon.

Leon looked over his shoulder.

"Jack!" Sasha called from behind.

Jack glanced to the side. In his peripheral vision he saw Leon turn. Jack whipped his head back around. Leon lifted the pistol into the air that he must've had concealed. Jack did the same. The second that passed stretched into minutes in his head. He couldn't fire too soon. The bullet would miss and it'd spell death for him. He couldn't wait too long, either. Leon was trained, skilled, and would get his aimed shot off quickly.

Then the explosive roar of a shot ripped through the air. Jack pulled back in anticipation. Seagulls rose from their perches on the sea. Jack waited for the pain to spread. But no bullet penetrated his flesh. He refocused and watched as Leon's body jerked forward, bowed backward. A mist of pink rose into the air above the guy's head. Jack stared on with an open mouth as Leon's body turned slightly to the side. He saw the bullet hole in the guy's head. Then Leon fell over the side of his boat into the shallow water.

Jack looked to his right. Bear stood atop a small sand dune with the MP7 clutched tight in both hands. Blood covered the big man's stomach, torso and upper legs.

Small waves lapped over Leon's body. The pull of the sea began turning him over and over. Jack and Sasha dragged the corpse out of the water and dropped him on the sand. Jack then turned his attention to Bear.

"Jesus, Bear. Are you OK?"

"Just a flesh wound."

"You sure? Looks nasty."

"I'm all right, Jack. Ambulance'll be here soon and they'll get me checked out."

Jack and Sasha each took a side and wrapped an arm around Bear's back. They started toward the house. Jack looked over his shoulder. The small boat had slipped into the sea and drifted away.

"What about Dottie?" Jack said.

"Dead," Bear said. "Godfrey's detained inside, although he might bleed out and join Dottie soon."

"Let him," Sasha said.

"Mia? Was she in there?"

"And Erin and Hannah. They're all OK. Shaken up, but OK." Bear's knees gave out, he nearly dragged the other two to the ground.

Jack and Sasha stabilized the big man. They heard a car pull into the drive. Four doors opened and closed. Alex and Jon began shouting for them.

"Back here," Sasha called.

Sirens approached. Cops, maybe. Ambulance, hopefully.

Alex and Jon repeatedly asked questions.

Jack, Bear and Sasha repeatedly ignored them.

Jack entered the house and located the two women and Mia, huddled together by the front door. They came to him, Mia leading the way. He lifted her in the air, wrapped his arms around her and pulled her close. Erin and Hannah joined them in a tight embrace, filled with tears.

CHAPTER 71

THE VAN DROPPED CLARISSA OFF AT THE EDGE OF THE suburban nightmare and the asphalt jungle. She walked down familiar streets toward Naseer's mansion. She wondered if she should think of it in those terms any longer. Who would be in charge now with Naseer dead? The organization had contingency plans, she knew that, but she didn't know the content of the plans. Naseer's death would be nothing more than a speed bump in their journey.

Her organization had a contingency plan as well. And whether or not it went into effect depended heavily on what happened after she entered the home.

The cool evening air found its way inside her coat wrapped around her body. The sun set behind her. Its final rays warmed her neck and the back of her head. The two sensations left her feeling as though she floated down the street. As she continued further into the neighborhood, she saw the last of the local children leave their posts outside and head in for their dinner or their baths or perhaps their favorite TV program. Maybe all three. She had trouble remembering what it was like to be a child.

Clarissa kept walking.

Her cell phone buzzed through her coat lining against her stomach. She reached into her pocket and pulled it out. She didn't recognize the number on the display. It didn't matter, though. Only a couple people had the number, and only one would be calling it. And she couldn't talk to Jack. Not tonight. Maybe not ever again. She tossed the phone onto the street and stepped on it, grinding her heel to ensure its destruction.

The palatial estate rose up as she reached the crest of the hill. She could see over the concrete fence that surrounded the property. The front lights were on. Several cars were parked at the far end of the driveway, near the house. They wasted no time getting back to business.

What was that business? Did it have anything to do with her disappearance?

She still had nothing concrete on what Naseer's plans had been. And now she wondered if the organization would be more aggressive with him out of the picture. Naseer was native to Great Britain and at times Clarissa figured that might have worked against him. He would have denied it, but the truth lie in his actions.

She reached the gate and pressed the buzzer. A camera rotated and pointed at her. A golf cart approached. The man that appeared at the gate knew her, and she knew him. He let her through, but did not offer her a ride. She watched as he hopped into his golf cart, turned around and headed back down the driveway. It didn't bother her. The possibility that she only had a few hours left to live was very real. And if that was to be the case, she wanted to enjoy her last few minutes outside.

She kept walking. The cherry trees that lined the driveway no longer had their blossoms. She spotted one or two trapped between blades of grass or pressed into the concrete below her feet. Other than that, they were gone. Carried away by the same gusts of wind she might have later felt pass through her body while in Belgium. And with the blooms went the sweet fragranced air. Only a faded memory now.

Funny how quickly that happens.

The man in the golf cart waited by the front door. It made no sense how he left her behind only to now stand obviously annoyed by how long it took her to reach the house.

She approached him and nodded.

"Samir will see you," he said as he opened the door and allowed her inside.

"Where?"

"The office."

"Naseer's office?"

"Samir's office."

She understood. Naseer was gone, and Samir had taken over. At times, she felt a connection with the man and felt by his actions and words that he had a soft soul. She'd also seen him angry, and that side of him appeared to be ten times worse than anything she'd seen from Naseer. Day and night, north and south, ying and yang, whatever one wanted to call it. The guy was polar opposites of himself, sometimes in the same conversation.

She feared that would spell bad things for the world.

Clarissa kept walking. She made her way past the foyer, through the hallway. Cameras turned from their positions on the ceiling. Every movement she made was under scrutiny. When she reached the office door, she stopped, took a breath, then knocked. She heard the clicks of the automatic locks. She opened the door and stepped into the office.

"Hello, Samir," she said. "So glad to see you were unharmed in that—"

"Sit down, shut up."

She walked across the room and placed a hand on the chair. She would have felt much better with the heft of a pistol pressing against her lower back. Unfortunately, she was unarmed. Sinclair insisted.

"Why weren't you in Paris?"

Clarissa had prepared herself for this question. But in her head, it had been Naseer asking her. After she heard of his death, she had no idea who would be the one to question her. She never expected the face across from her to be present. And this time, she could not judge his mood.

"Well?"

"I was in Paris, Samir. Right up until I got word of what had happened."

His eyes narrowed. "How'd you find out?"

"I saw it reported."

He nodded. "We had men in Paris at the train station."

"I know."

"You know?"

"I saw them."

"Why didn't you go to them?"

"Because, outside of you and Naseer," she paused, "I don't trust any of these guys."

He smiled. "Smart girl. They say it looked like you were being followed by some agents."

She hadn't been prepared for that. "I was. I gave them the slip too."

"Why would French agents be pursuing you?"

She leaned forward, placed both elbows on the desk and leaned into her palms. "Do I look like a choir girl to you?"

Samir leaned forward. His face stopped a foot or so from hers. "No, you don't."

She smiled, said nothing, hoped the fear was not evident in her eyes.

He eased back in his seat. The harsh look faded, and a smile crossed his face. He tapped a pen on his chin, then bit down on it. "Go get cleaned up. We'll have dinner in an hour."

"I can stay?"

"You can stay. On one condition."

"Name it."

"You'll treat me the way you treated Naseer."

"I'll treat you better."

"Go on, get ready."

"Thank you," she said as she rose and turned for the door. She slipped into the hall and made her way to her room. The cameras remained stationary and did not track her every move.

CHAPTER 72

Jack spent two weeks with Mia and Erin. A vacation of sorts. They toured the countryside. Drank wine. Visited Scotland. Drank wine. Went to Edinburgh, Glasgow, and he even convinced them to visit Loch Ness. It hadn't taken much to convince Mia, but Erin had been a bit of a hard sell. In the end she caved. Perhaps it was the extra three glasses of wine that night.

The trip taught him a lot about himself, allowed him to learn a bit about his daughter, and helped him to realize that he and Erin had no future together, no matter how much he wanted to be around Mia.

They returned to London the night before Jack was to leave for the States.

Jack and Erin stood on her flat's balcony on a cool May evening. The blooms were gone from all the trees that lined the street below.

"I'd like to see her as often as possible."

"I think she'd like that too, Jack. She's warmed up to you. There's some walls to take down yet, but I'll help with that. I think in time she'll abandon the father she thought she had and accept you."

"Seems like she's started to."

"She has."

"Would you mind if she came to the States for a month or so each year?"

"As long as you come here one weekend a month."

"You need a break that often?"

"From reality."

He held out his hand. "Deal."

She smiled, took his hand, looked up at the moon.

"Erin, you don't think there's a chance you and I—"

"Don't be crazy, Jack. We couldn't make it work when we were young and dumb. Why on earth do you think we could now?"

He paused. Followed her gaze and watched thin silver clouds pass over the moon. He thought about saying something along the lines of he'd changed, she'd changed, perhaps they could continue to do so until they were one cohesive unit.

He didn't.

"You know I'm right," she said.

"Yeah, I know." He pulled her close and hugged her. Her soft cheek felt cool against his. He closed his eyes and inhaled her lavender scent. Her lips brushed against his jawline. He opened his eyes. Through the window, he saw Mia sleeping on the couch. In her arms she held the stuffed Nessie he purchased for her in Scotland.

"Maybe you can stay tonight?" she said.

"No, I should go."

She pulled back, nodded, reached for his face.

He turned and left the balcony.

Erin remained outside.

He stopped at the couch, knelt down and kissed Mia's cheek. "I'll be back before you know it, sweet angel." He rose and went to the door. He cast a final look over his shoulder. His eyes may have watered.

The next day he met Bear and Mandy at the bank. He'd arranged for a large portion of their funds to be deposited in a joint account that he planned to sign over to Bear. That'd settle them, mostly. Could you settle a debt with no intrinsic value?

"Sorry you didn't get to do a little more during your time here," Jack said to Mandy.

She shrugged. "It's OK. Number 10 is a pretty cool place when you're not stuck in that basement. And that was pretty neat too."

Bear tousled her hair. “Nothing’s ordinary about her life, Jack.”

“I know. Comes with the territory when someone hangs around with you all the time.” He slid the form in front of Bear. “Now sign.”

“How much is in there?”

“Over eight million.”

“That’s a lot more than half.”

It was closer to eighty percent. The majority of the other twenty was going to Erin in cash and a trust fund for Mia.

“What do I need? I’m going to buy a house on an island and sleep and drink and swim. Maybe not in that order. You’ve got her to look out for and take care of. Food, clothes, lots of clothes.” He smiled at Mandy. “Then college, a big wedding.”

The girl giggled.

“She’s not dating till she’s thirty,” Bear said.

Mandy elbowed him in the hip.

“I can’t take that much, Jack.”

“Forget about it, Bear. I’m good.”

Bear sighed, then signed, and they went inside an office and settled down into uncomfortable chairs opposite a banker. The man across the desk explained each part of the form. Jack tuned him out. It didn’t matter to him anymore.

Fifteen minutes later they stood on the sidewalk.

“Hey, what happened with Mason?” Jack said. “He recover all right?”

Bear nodded. “He did. And get this, he and Gloria are going to remarry.”

“Good for them. Hope it can last.”

Bear shook his head. “Never does.”

“Catch a cab to the airport together?” Jack said.

“Nah,” Bear said.

“Staying here?”

“Paris. Gonna catch that tunnel chunnel thing. Remember, we saw that show on Discovery one time, the Brits and the French digging under the channel.”

Jack smiled, nodded. “I remember. What’s in Paris?”

Bear shrugged. "Figured I'd go check up on Pierre, see how he's doing."

Jack nodded. He knew about Kat, but didn't say anything. For as good of friends and partners as they were, Bear preferred to keep some things to himself. And Jack wouldn't interfere with that.

A black taxi pulled up to the curb. Jack hugged Bear and Mandy, then got in the cab.

He rolled the rear windows down. The air washed over him. A confirmation, or baptism perhaps, of sorts. He'd left so much behind, yet had so much ahead. Nothing was as he thought it'd be. Nor could it ever be as it had been. New friends, old friends, all left behind. The adventure lay ahead.

Heathrow teemed with life, as it always did. He purchased the first ticket available to the U.S. He didn't care where. He'd circle the globe in reverse and go to L.A. if that's all they had. That turned out to be unnecessary, though. The ticketing agent put him on a flight to Atlanta, due to board in two hours.

So he made his way through the airport. Security posed no problems. He found his terminal, then his gate, and he took a seat near the broad window that looked out over the runway. Today, the view allowed him to watch the planes as they landed. Always a sight he enjoyed. If he closed his eyes, he could tune into the anticipation of all those on board.

If he had been looking the other way, he would have noticed the four armed officers headed toward him. As it was, he didn't.

"Jack Noble," one said.

He looked over his shoulder.

"That's him," another said.

"Get up," the first one said.

Jack lifted his arms above his shoulders and rose. Whatever this was, it had to be a mix up. Not that he had anything to worry about. He was clean, both in person and in any database.

"Come with us."

"And if I don't?"

"Don't make us force you."

"You couldn't. Relax, fellas." He smiled at the lone female officer.

Brown hair, pulled back. Mid-twenties. Attractive. The uniform fit her well. The guys, not so much. "And lady. I'll go with you."

They surrounded him, front, sides and back, and led him to a small windowless room at the end of the terminal. The female officer remained in the room with him.

"Just so you know," she said. "I'm not afraid to shoot you. That's why they left me in here. Less inquisition if I pull my gun than if they do."

Jack nodded. "No trouble from me. Although I would like to know why I'm in here."

She shook her head.

"You don't know, or you won't tell me?"

"Yes." She arched an eyebrow, looked over his head and smiled.

Five minutes passed, then ten. Finally, about thirty minutes later, the door opened. Jack looked up, prepared to raise hell with whoever entered. He realized that wouldn't be necessary.

"Hello, Jack."

"Sasha? What are you doing here?"

"He brought me."

"Greetings," Jon said.

"I'm gonna miss my flight because of you two. You know that, right?"

"We know," Jon said. "Not to worry. The Prime Minister will take care of you." He nodded at the attractive officer and she left the room.

"So what gives?" Jack said.

Jon and Sasha looked at each other, smiled. They turned to Jack, forced serious looks upon their faces.

Jon said, "You know, Jack. You're too young to retire to the islands."

"I think that's a personal choice that every man should be free to make."

"You'll be bored."

"I'll be drunk."

"You'll be alone."

"With thousands of new tourist women flocking to the place every week."

"No action or excitement."

"I'll get up, watch the sunrise, drive to the other side of the island to watch it set. Who says that isn't exciting?"

Jon laughed. "Let's cut to the chase."

"Please do."

Sasha said, "Jack, we have a proposal for you."

Jack Noble's story continues in *Never Go Home*. Read on for a sneak peek, or purchase your copy today!

Join the LT Ryan reader family & receive a free copy of the Jack Noble story, *The Recruit*. Scan the QR code below to get started:

NEVER GO HOME CHAPTER 1

THE WOMAN EMERGED FROM A pack of pedestrians. They parted as she passed. They stared at her in awe. I imagined them asking each other, “Who is that woman?” She drew attention in part because of her beauty. In part due to her confidence.

Surrounding her were six men.

Dressed in black.

All armed.

Not a sight you see every day on the outskirts of London.

Yet people didn’t notice them. She made them look invisible.

I presumed the men had training on a level close to my own.

The woman and the men continued their approach down the street. Her black hair was parted down the middle. It splashed across her shoulders. The breeze lifted it at the edges and it danced in the wind.

They stopped in front of Cataldi’s. The restaurant had a wood burning stove. The cooks had started it a few minutes ago. The exhaust fan spit flavored smoke into the sky. It passed by me. My stomach ached with anticipation. As much for the meal as for the job.

The woman and her bodyguards continued on. They’d stopped in front of the restaurant the previous three days. They never went in. Three doors down sat the cafe. If the woman were as much a creature of habit as I thought, and counted on, they’d go in there again this morning.

The roof offered a view of the entire street. The downside to that was that I could be seen from the street from both directions. With the woman and her security team close by, I retreated. No big deal. Their plans weren't secret.

I touched the button on the device connected to my ear. Steady static ensued. "I've got visual confirmation. Heading inside now." I tapped the button again. The static faded away.

Noise crawled along the building's two hundred year old facade. The chatter of those passing, a moped racing by, the steady thud of the bodyguards' hard-soled shoes, and the woman's stilettos attacking the sidewalk.

They stood out from the rest.

Staying low, I crossed the rooftop, coming to a stop in front of the building access. Nothing in the surrounding environment had changed. I pulled the door open, kicked the prop out of the way and hit the stairs, taking them two at a time.

The lobby door crashed open. Heavy steps hit the stairs. The person ran up. Their heavy breaths indicated that they had been running even before they entered the building.

I froze in place, pulled my Beretta and leaned back against someone's door.

A mother scolded her child. The little kid raced through the apartment behind me. A door slammed. The mother let out a frustrated sound.

The footsteps kept coming toward me. Had they spotted me? I moved away from the wall and toward the stairs. The person stopped. I held my breath. They let out theirs. Then they took a deep breath and exhaled again.

"Good run," they said, followed by a door opening and closing.

Shaking my head, I reflected on how close I'd come to killing an innocent bystander. No time to dwell. I continued my descent.

Sasha's voice filled my ear. "She's in front of the cafe, Jack."

I didn't stop to reply. Five steps separated me from the lobby. I'd see for myself in a few moments.

Black and white checkered tile led to the front of the room where double doors swayed back and forth a few inches. I ran up to them, stopped, scanned the street in front of me. I couldn't see her. The two men positioned behind her were too tall and too wide.

Where'd they find these guys? The pro wrestling circuit? They sure as hell weren't former Special Forces.

I drove my shoulder into the door, pushed it open and stepped onto the sidewalk. Down here, the smell of the grill was stronger. It combined with that of the pastry shop next door. It was almost enough to throw me off.

I turned left and started walking, using the windows next to me to watch the scene on the other side of the street. One of her security detail studied me. He was mammoth in size. He stayed outside along with another big guy, while the other four accompanied the woman into the cafe.

"They're heading inside, Jack."

I reached up and activated the speaker. "Are we set up?"

"We never got inside."

"Say again?"

"They had two waiting."

"So she's got eight bodyguards today?"

"The threat was high. You knew this. You said you were prepared for it."

Three elderly women approached. I said nothing with them in earshot. One of the women smiled at me. Bright red lipstick coated her lips, as well as skin above and below. Even her teeth were shades of red. I smiled back and nodded at her.

"Jack? Do you want me to call everyone back and abort?"

I looked over my shoulder. The woman was no longer in sight. Two men stood in the doorway. The elderly women crossed the street. One of them skipped a step. Must be one good cup of coffee inside.

The older women approached the two behemoths standing guard. The guards demanded that the ladies open up their purses so they could search them. They tossed items on the ground. One of the women protested loudly. The guy said something to the effect of, "Don't like it? Get lost."

"Jack?" she yelled.

"Call them off," I said.

"You're giving up?"

"They weren't doing this yesterday."

"What?"

"I'll see you in an hour."

"Jack, what are you going to do?"

I pulled the device off my ear, tossed it into the trash, continued on another half block. I reached behind my back and drew my Beretta. It went into the trash, too. I stepped off the curb, paused for a white Fiat that honked at me as it passed, then crossed the street. A group of teenagers told me to go back to America. I ignored them.

Ahead, the last of the elderly women stepped inside the cafe. The guard closest to me turned his head in my direction. He watched as I approached.

I stopped in front of the cafe. Placed my foot on the first step.

The guy stuck his thick hand out. He wagged his finger in front of me. When he spoke, his accent was Irish, thick, like he was from Cork. "I saw you exit the apartment building and head up the street."

I nodded. "Had a coffee date with a woman. She called it off. Kind of happy, actually. This place has the best brew in town. First time I've seen security here, though. What's going on? Did the Queen stop by today?"

The men glanced at each other. They looked like two defensive linemen about to converge on the quarterback at the same time.

"Come up here," the guy on the right said. He was local.

I stepped up, held my arms out to the side.

"Turn around," Cork said.

I faced the apartment building. A kid walking by looked up at me. I stuck my tongue out at him and crossed my eyes. He smiled. The guy behind me patted me down, stuck his hands in my pocket, and cupped me somewhere he shouldn't have. I rose up on my tiptoes.

"You gonna buy me a pastry now?" I said.

"Shut up," Cork said.

"Go on in," the other said.

Neither held the door for me. I felt cheated after how close we'd become.

I used the hard toe of my right shoe against the door's kick plate and nudged it open. The aroma of dark roast met me. My mouth watered. It was necessary to stay focused, so I scanned the room, breaking it down into quadrants.

The woman sat in the corner, surrounded by guys smaller than the two at the front door. These were the pros. The other two were meatheads whose only purpose was to scare the store's patrons. I kept my eyes moving. Didn't want to linger on her too long. Or on the men.

There were three people behind the counter. The day before there had only been two, and those two weren't present today. I figure most people would assume that the biggest one would be the plant, if there was one. Not me. And not the skinny guy with red hair and acne either. I pegged it as the cute girl with the dimples. She smiled and winked and put my mind at ease.

Not an easy thing to do.

I ordered a Cafe Americano and took a seat at a table fifteen feet away from the woman.

Her name was Marcia Stanton. The name meant nothing to me. I'd been told Marcia was an up and comer in politics. She had gained relevance by attacking and bringing down some powerful people. A grassroots movement built, and next thing she knew, people encouraged her to run for office.

At first, she declined. The offers didn't stop. So when a heavy hitter stepped in and told her she owed it to her country, she agreed.

And that opened a Pandora's Box of hell for her. Death threats came. Bodyguards were hired. Three attempts on her life had resulted in the hiring of three more bodyguards to replace her core four.

All of that led to me being seated in that cafe, mid-morning, hungry, tired, unarmed and uncaffeinated. At least one condition was close to being remedied.

"Sir?"

I glanced up at the cute girl with the dimples. She threw a pale elbow on the counter and held out my mug with the other hand. I rose, stole a glance at Marcia and her bodyguards, and walked to the counter. The girl watched me the whole way. One hand wrapped around the mug. The other dropped a tip on the glass top.

"Cream or sugar?" she asked.

I shook my head. "Black is fine. The rest of the stuff gets in the way."

She shrugged. "Anything else?"

Behind her, the big guy glared at me. I noticed a swastika tattooed on his wrist. We engaged in a stare-off. He looked away first.

"Sir?" the girl said.

"I'm fine," I said.

She turned around, rolling her eyes. I was just another schmuck to her, and that was OK. I returned to the same table, sat in a different seat. This one allowed me to see the counter and Marcia's booth. The downside to that was that the table created an obstacle that I had to go around in order to do my job.

One of the bodyguards rose. He headed toward the hallway that led to the restrooms.

Hand Tattoo passed through a beaded curtain. I figured he went into the kitchen. Dimples glanced around the cafe. Her gaze came to a stop on Marcia's table. A minute later, the girl joined the guy in back, leaving the skinny red-head all alone.

I stood, walked to the counter and leaned against it.

Skinny Red said, "Help you?"

"I'm good," I said.

Skinny Red seemed too calm, relaxed, confident. If there was a plant, it had to be him.

The front door opened. A man stepped inside. A sheet of sweat coated his forehead. His breathing was erratic. His eyes shifted side to side. They never settled on anything. He looked at me, Skinny Red, the beaded curtain, and at Marcia. And when he saw her, he bent over and reached for his ankle.

NEVER GO HOME CHAPTER 2

ONE HAND REACHED TO MY ear, and the other around my back. Neither found what they were looking for. I'd thrown away the ear piece and pistol a few minutes ago. I hoped to recover them soon. Making it out alive became priority number one. There was no backup now. I had no idea who was and wasn't trustworthy in the cafe.

The nervous man caught the attention of Marcia's table. One of her men rose. He strolled over to the guy. This left Marcia with two bodyguards. One next to her, and one across the table.

The guy who'd stood up now blocked the path of the nervous man, who was bent over with two fingers in his sock. The man lifted his head three inches. His gaze followed along. His eyes angled inward. They focused on the barrel of the pistol aimed at his forehead. The expression on his face took a few moments to change.

"Don't move." The bodyguard's accent wasn't easy to place. South Africa, maybe? Perhaps New Zealand. I get those mixed up quite often.

The nervous man let out a sound I'd once heard a dying squirrel make. A couple seconds later, drips of water hit the floor. It wasn't water though. A puddle formed at his feet.

"Disgusting," the bodyguard said. He jabbed the end of his pistol into the nervous guy's chest.

Around the cafe, patrons stared in horror at the scene unfolding. It seemed everyone was enthralled by the event. All except for one of the elderly women. She bit into her pastry and refused to put it down.

I remained still, watched the scene play out.

"Get up, slowly," the bodyguard said.

The nervous man shook. He came up halfway, convulsed, then straightened his body. The front of his shorts were wet. His *weapon* shook in his hand. The bodyguard swatted at it. Two five-pound notes drifted to the floor.

The bodyguard looked over his shoulder. He laughed, and said, "You believe this?"

The other two members of Marcia's security detail laughed. One held up his hands and shrugged.

I heard footsteps behind me. The fourth bodyguard, presumably, returning from the bathroom.

I was wrong.

Dimple's perfume hit me before she passed on my left. Hand Tattoo's body odor eradicated her sweet smell. He had a gun dangling from his right hand. He lifted his arm and aimed at the bodyguard who stood in the middle of the cafe.

The bodyguard's training forced him into action. Already armed with an M40, he spun. He drove his shoulder into the nervous guy's chest. The man flew backward, sprawled out, skidded to the door. Hand Tattoo fired first. He caught the bodyguard in the gut. A crimson bloom formed near the man's navel. He fell backward, landed on the nervous guy's legs. Feeble attempts to lift his sidearm failed.

I heard another shot, glanced toward Marcia's table. One of her men lay face down on top of it. Unfocused eyes stared toward the display cabinet. Above them, blood flowed from a hole in his forehead. The bullet he took ended his life.

I grabbed a mug off the counter. It felt thick, heavy. I whipped my arm around and slammed the mug into the back of Hand Tattoo's head. His scalp split in two. The coffee cup shattered. The only thing left in my hand was the handle. Hand Tattoo fell to his knees. I struck him twice with each fist. He fell forward, unconscious.

The men out front tried to get back inside. One drove his shoulder into the front door. It dinged as it opened. It didn't get far, though. The nervous man and the bodyguard who took the gut shot blocked the door's arc, preventing it from opening all the way. That didn't stop the two men outside from driving it open repeatedly. The nervous man took the brunt of the door's steel frame. He screamed with every thrust.

I looked away after his arm broke. There were more pressing issues to deal with at that time.

With Hand Tattoo out of my way, I had a good view of Dimples. She fired a second shot. The live guard at the table covered Marcia Stanton. The bullet entered through his lower back. Dimples fired again. It hit the wall. A plaster cloud loomed in the air. Dimples cursed.

I glanced over the counter and located Skinny Red. He lay on the floor, hands over his head. I felt disappointed in being wrong about the guy.

Dimples retracted then extended her arm. The trigger clicked. The bullet didn't fire. She turned the gun sideways. Her head lowered an inch. She shook the weapon and tried again. Nothing happened. The pistol had jammed.

Already moving forward, I reached inside my pocket and pulled out a pen. Dimples looked over her shoulder. Her eyes grew wide. Her right shoulder ducked. She turned on the ball of her left foot. Four feet separated me and my pen from her and her gun.

She reached out and screamed and squeezed the trigger.

I cocked my left arm back, and twisted and jumped.

Her pistol roared. The muzzle flash was bright and instantaneous. The bullet sliced past me and smashed into the plaster wall. A chunk fell to the floor.

She looked pissed. Her mouth contorted. She turned and reset her aim.

I swung my left arm and drove the pen into the side of her neck. I wasn't going for her jugular, or even a kill shot. The pen did damage in a different way. My only job was to insert the tip. The fluid inside the hollow body did the rest. I watched and waited. She brought her hand up to her neck, wrapped it around the pen. Her twisted expression told me that the fluid coursed through her system.

Quickly.

Dimples dropped to one knee. She fell sideways against the display case. Her lips smeared against the glass as she slid down it on her way to the floor.

"What just happened?" Marcia Stanton said.

I pushed myself off the floor, got to one knee, and said, "You're OK now. It's safe."

The front door burst open. The two men came in shouting.

"Just stay there," Marcia told them.

Like well-trained dogs, they remained in place.

With one foot off the ground, a pen in one hand, and Dimple's Glock in the other, I rose. The adrenaline letdown had begun, and delayed my reaction to the footsteps behind me.

Marcia's hands went out and she shook her head side to side. I think she might have said, "No, no, no," but I can't be sure.

Something smashed against the back of my head. I fell forward, catching the side of my face against Marcia's table, inches from the dead bodyguard's blood. Might have slid into it. Maybe not. Hard to tell, because that was about the time that I blacked out.

ALSO BY L.T. RYAN

Find All of L.T. Ryan's Books Today!

The Jack Noble Series

The Recruit (free)

The First Deception (Prequel 1)

Noble Beginnings

A Deadly Distance

Ripple Effect (Bear Logan)

Thin Line

Noble Intentions

When Dead in Greece

Noble Retribution

Noble Betrayal

Never Go Home

Beyond Betrayal (Clarissa Abbot)

Noble Judgment

Never Cry Mercy

Deadline

End Game

Noble Ultimatum

Noble Legend (2022)

Bear Logan Series

Ripple Effect

Blowback

Take Down

Deep State

Bear & Mandy Logan Series

Close to Home

Under the Surface

The Last Stop

Over the Edge (Coming Soon)

Rachel Hatch Series

Drift

Downburst

Fever Burn

Smoke Signal

Firewalk

Whitewater

Aftershock

Whirlwind

Tsunami (2022)

Mitch Tanner Series

The Depth of Darkness

Into The Darkness

Deliver Us From Darkness

Cassie Quinn Series

Path of Bones

Whisper of Bones

Symphony of Bones

Etched in Shadow

Concealed in Shadow (2022)

Blake Brier Series

Unmasked

Unleashed

Uncharted

Drawpoint

Contrail

Detachment

Clear (Coming Soon)

Dalton Savage Series

Savage Grounds

Scorched Earth

Cold Sky (Coming Soon)

Maddie Castle Series

The Handler

Tracking Justice (Coming Soon)

Affliction Z Series

Affliction Z: Patient Zero

Affliction Z: Abandoned Hope

Affliction Z: Descended in Blood

Affliction Z : Fractured Part 1

Affliction Z: Fractured Part 2 (Fall 2021)

ABOUT THE AUTHOR

L.T. Ryan is a *USA Today* and international bestselling author. The new age of publishing offered L.T. the opportunity to blend his passions for creating, marketing, and technology to reach audiences with his popular Jack Noble series.

Living in central Virginia with his wife, the youngest of his three daughters, and their three dogs, L.T. enjoys staring out his window at the trees and mountains while he should be writing, as well as reading, hiking, running, and playing with gadgets. See what he's up to at http://ltryan.com.

Social Medial Links:

- Facebook (L.T. Ryan): https://www.facebook.com/LTRyanAuthor

- Facebook (Jack Noble Page): https://www.facebook.com/JackNobleBooks/

- Twitter: https://twitter.com/LTRyanWrites

- Goodreads: http://www.goodreads.com/author/show/6151659.L_T_Ryan

Printed in the USA
CPSIA information can be obtained
at www.ICGtesting.com
CBHW071203290524
9246CB00017B/1405